"I'D LIKE TO GET TO KNOW YOU BETTER."

Alejandro's eyes flashed with dark fire as he spoke.

Jennifer caught her breath helplessly. "We have so little in common—"

"People don't need a lot in common to be friends," he cut in swiftly. "Or lovers." His last words were a whisper, buried in the golden mane of her hair.

She closed her eyes against his tender, sensual assault, reveling in the heady rush of feelings he awoke in her. She couldn't give in to him—yet she longed to! His lips traced the contours of her neck, and suddenly hungry for his caress, she melted against him.

But the expected kisses didn't come. When Jennifer looked up, the passion in his eyes was gone. It had been replaced by a calculating look that chilled her with its underlying message....

EMILY MESTA
is also the author of
SUPERROMANCE #34

FUGITIVE HEART

Even for an archaeologist, a job working
on shipboard in the sun-dazzled Caribbean
didn't come along every day. Nor did a
chance to be surrounded by attractive
bronze-skinned men.

But Sydne didn't trust men, any of them—
especially not her virile new boss, Brian
Stevens. From the moment she met the
masterful tanned giant, he proved himself
adept at penetrating her every defense. His
subtle gibes set her temper blazing, and his
dizzying kisses invaded her senses.

He aroused her in other ways, too—to
fevered heights known only to a woman
in love....

EMILY MESTA

FORBIDDEN DESTINY

A SUPERROMANCE FROM
WORLDWIDE

TORONTO · NEW YORK · LOS ANGELES · LONDON

My special thanks to Alba Rivero for
sharing with me her knowledge of her
country and its wonderful people.

———————◆———————

Published July 1983

First printing May 1983

ISBN 0-373-70073-3

Printed in Canada

CHAPTER ONE

THE SCREECHING HALT of the taxi was the fitting finale to the harrowing ride through the congested streets of Bogotá. The driver stopped the meter and turned to his silent passenger. "Here ju are, *sumerced*," he said in his own brand of English. "De Avianca Building."

The local obsequious term of *sumerced* was totally lost on Jennifer Blake. She swallowed the lump that had developed in her throat with the first of many near misses along the way and relaxed her fingernails, which had been digging into the seat of the late-model Chrysler. Although the driving habits in certain foreign countries had always made her a little nervous, in the past she had been able to maintain a certain measure of equanimity. But not anymore. The memory of the accident was still too recent, too painfully fresh in her mind. An accident that, ironically, had occurred on the roads of her own country.

Her hand was still trembling a little when she reached inside her purse for her wallet. "*Cuánto*—how much do I owe you?" she asked the waiting driver.

"Sixty pesos, *sumerced*."

Jennifer counted the bills and handed them to the driver. "Thank you. Keep the change."

The generous tip brought a pleased, *"A usted, señorita,"* from the man before she opened the door and got out.

As the yellow-and-black taxi pulled away from the curb, several smartly dressed passersby were forced to go around the young blond woman who stood on the sidewalk. For a long moment she looked up at the tower of concrete and steel that, rising amid colonial-style buildings, was a proud exponent of modern Colombian architecture. But Jennifer wasn't admiring its lines, nor was she impressed by the fact that the building was the tallest in the country. Instead she was wondering if Alejandro Adler, the man who was the reason for her long trip from Los Angeles, was at that moment looking out of one of those windows and could see her.

But what difference would that make, she asked herself. Even if he were standing next to her, he wouldn't know who she was or why she had come.

You can still turn around and go home, a little voice said, and for a fraction of a moment Jennifer hesitated. Then, with an inward shrug, she decided not to give herself time to lose her nerve.

There was no hesitation in her step as she climbed the few steps to the entrance of the building, not sparing a glance at the magnificent display of emerald and gold jewelry in the windows of the Joyeria Bauer.

A nice-looking young man, in a brown suit and sporting a dark luxuriant mustache, reached the heavy glass door at the same time. Courteously he opened it for her and was rewarded by the swift smile she gave him as she went in.

With steady precision Jennifer's high heels clicked across the ample expanse of polished marble floor in the lobby. She didn't let herself be diverted by the paintings on the walls, by the lines of customers forming at the Avianca ticket counters to her left or at the post office to her right. She stopped only at the information booth, to ask directions from the man in a blue uniform trimmed with gold braid.

"Adler Exports?" the man repeated. At her nod, he said, "Thirty-fifth floor, *señorita.*"

He gave the information courteously, but without the smile that would come so easily to his American counterpart. This cool, rather aloof politeness was something Jennifer had been encountering since her arrival in Colombia that very morning.

"Thank you." She turned away, and with the assurance of a woman who knows where she's going and is confident of her purpose, she headed for the elevators.

The young man who had held the door open for her was still there, waiting for the elevator that had just arrived to discharge its passengers. Once it was empty, he stood politely aside and then followed her inside.

Conscious of the sudden acceleration of her heart-beat, Jennifer watched with wariness as the light on the floor indicator leaped quickly from one number to the next. As they got closer to the thirty-fifth floor, she was again assaulted by doubts. What if Alejandro Adler refused to see her? After all, busy executives did not usually concern themselves with the hiring of underlings.

Trying to ease her worries about the coming confrontation, Jennifer switched her attention to the people who came and went each time the elevator doors swooshed open. The young man with the mustache was still with her. She noticed that the glances he discreetly cast in her direction every now and then contained a certain amount of admiration, and this indication of interest served to fortify her confidence.

It wasn't that Jennifer was vain about her looks. She knew she was reasonably attractive, and she seldom thought about the fact. But at this particular moment she was grateful nature had been generous to her. As unfair as it was, she knew that men were often more favorably inclined toward women they found attractive. Alejandro Adler was not a man who played fair, and with Tommy's life hanging in the balance, she had no qualms about making the most of every advantage at her disposal to gain her ends.

When the doors finally opened on the thirty-fifth floor, she returned the young man's tentative smile before stepping out. The name Adler Exports was written in gold letters on the double doors facing her. She opened them immediately, not giving herself a chance to back out.

The receptionist was a young woman, whose dark hair was pulled back to display a pair of exquisite emerald-and-diamond earrings. Her beautiful face was so expertly made up—and devoid of expression—that it made Jennifer think of a mannequin.

"May I help you?" she inquired in English.

Jennifer was not surprised that she had been recognized immediately as a foreigner. After all, the combination of ash blond, almost silvery hair and green eyes such as hers could not be very common in Colombia.

"I would like to see Mr. Adler, please. My name is Dawn Maitland." She had given her false name without hesitation.

"Have you an appointment, Miss Maitland?" the receptionist inquired rather indifferently.

"No, I haven't," Jennifer replied, without showing her disquiet. "I arrived from the United States only this morning, and it's very important that I see him."

"I'm sorry, but Mr. Adler does not receive anyone without an appointment." The receptionist paused briefly before asking, "Would you like to speak to his executive assistant?"

Jennifer was familiar enough with office procedures to know that the secretary, rather than the receptionist, was the main obstacle to surmount at this point. At once she replied, "Yes, please. I'd like to see her, if I may."

"Certainly." There was another flash of emeralds and diamonds as the young woman reached for the phone; they came from the cocktail ring on her finger.

Her Spanish was clear enough for Jennifer to understand. After she had hung up, the young woman said, "Mrs. Vargas will be with you in a moment, Miss Maitland. Won't you have a seat?" She gestured toward the leather sofas grouped in one corner of the plush reception area.

"Thank you."

Only minutes after she had sat down an elegant mature woman emerged from the inner office. She paused briefly to speak to the receptionist before advancing toward Jennifer, who stood up to meet her. In spite of her diminutive stature, the woman managed to convey a very imposing, dignified presence.

"Miss Maitland, I'm Mrs. Vargas, Mr. Adler's executive assistant," she identified herself. Again the politeness without the smile. "I understand you wish to see Mr. Adler. Perhaps I can help you."

"I appreciate your seeing me, Mrs. Vargas," Jennifer replied, "but I'm afraid that what I have to discuss with Mr. Adler is of a personal nature and highly confidential."

"Mr. Adler is a very busy man, Miss Maitland." The woman's dark eyes had turned very cold. "Unless you explain with more clarity the reason for your visit, I'm afraid your seeing him is out of the question."

Mrs. Vargas was proving to be a formidable stumbling block. This was no time to plead, Jennifer recognized; and affecting a haughtiness totally foreign to her nature, she said, "I assure you that Mr. Adler will receive me if you just let him know I'm waiting, Mrs. Vargas. Please be kind enough to do so."

Apparently the woman had not expected such a drastic change in Jennifer's attitude, for she hesitated momentarily. "Very well," she said at last. "If you will excuse me, I'll see what Mr. Adler has to say."

Still finding it hard to believe the partial success of

her audacity, Jennifer had to steel herself to keep from collapsing with relief after Mrs. Vargas left her. She hoped no one could see how badly she was trembling. But she had good reason to be: the next few minutes would determine the success or failure of her mission—a mission of life or death.

To hide her apprehension, she reached for one of the magazines someone had carefully arranged on the gleaming glass top of a low coffee table and started leafing through it. As she had intended, her outward appearance was one of cool composure.

"Miss Maitland?"

It took a moment for Jennifer to realize that the secretary had returned and was now addressing her. It was little things such as this—answering to her new name—that she would have to watch. One mistake could give her away and ruin all her carefully laid plans. Yes, she'd definitely have to be more alert in the future.

"Yes?" she looked up from the magazine.

"Mr. Adler will see you now."

Even though she had fervently hoped for it, Jennifer could hardly believe her success. Her gamble had paid off!

Playing for time to allow the rate of her pulse to slow down a little, she calmly returned the magazine to the table. Next she collected her purse and the large manila envelope she had left on a nearby chair, and hoping she didn't look as edgy as she felt, followed the secretary along the thickly carpeted corridor. It led to the inner sanctum of the head of the largest export company in Bogotá.

Pausing before a heavy walnut door at the end of the hallway, the secretary opened it and gave a cold nod as she stepped aside. Jennifer took a deep breath, squared her shoulders and, fixing a smile on her face, marched into a spacious and elegant office.

The muted drapes were open, allowing sunlight to stream through windows that covered one entire wall and commanded a magnificent view of the city and mountains beyond. Dark wood paneled the other walls. A far corner by the window had been set aside for informal conferences.

But Jennifer's attention was not on the decor; it was immediately concentered on the man who stood up as she entered. Towering well over six feet, Alejandro Adler was much taller than she had expected. She felt a little intimidated by the fact; at the same time she was reluctantly attracted by the face so familiar to her from the photographs she had pored over while formulating her plans. Perhaps under ordinary circumstances, when the sharp aristocratic features were more relaxed than they were at this moment, his face would be compelling if not handsome; right now, she read a thrilling kind of danger in the slate-blue eyes that examined her appearance as she advanced toward him. She noted firm determination on his slightly squarish jaw. There was only a hint of waviness in the thick dark hair, meticulously styled at a conservative length, as conservative as the white shirt that enhanced his tanned complexion and the dark vested business suit he wore.

Had she not been so alert for his every reaction, the telltale widening of his pupils might have gone unnoticed by Jennifer. Aware of the little shiver that went through her own system, she was suddenly glad she was wearing the apple-green suit that went so well with the emerald of her eyes.

"Mr. Adler." Extending her hand, she offered him her most charming smile. "How nice of you to receive me."

"Miss Maitland."

A little shock went through her as her hand was swallowed up by the firm clasp of his. Absently she noticed that his long lean fingers were strong and square at the ends. Perhaps that was an omen of how easy it would be for a man like Alejandro Adler to crush her if he only suspected the real purpose of her visit. Jennifer became aware of the million butterflies that had suddenly begun fluttering in her stomach, and she was assaulted by the urge to turn and run. But this was no time to back out.

"Won't you have a seat, Miss Maitland," Alejandro invited, gesturing toward the chairs facing his desk.

"Thank you."

Making a conscious effort not to betray her uneasiness by sitting on its edge, Jennifer sank well back into one of the two elegant armchairs of soft burgundy leather.

Instead of going back to his executive swivel chair, Alejandro perched his large frame on the edge of the massive desk. Having to look up at him from the depths of her seat made Jennifer ill at ease. The fluttering in her stomach became a surge of fear as she realized it had been a calculated move on his part.

She had already known he was a very dangerous man, but the ease with which he could put an opponent at a disadvantage served to drive the point more sharply home.

Jennifer struggled to hide her inner tension as Alejandro Adler reached across his desk for a beautifully lacquered Oriental box. With deliberation he opened it, peering down in her face as he offered her a cigarette.

Wishing she had not given up smoking, Jennifer declined the offer. Not that she missed the addiction; but a cigarette would have given her something to do with her hands. As it was, she folded them primly in her lap.

"Mind if I do?" he asked politely.

"No, of course not."

She tried to gather her courage while he lit his cigarette with a gold lighter no thicker than her little finger. Expelling a jet of blue smoke, he returned the lighter to his breast pocket.

"Well, Miss Maitland? Perhaps you'll be kind enough to explain the nature of this personal and confidential matter you have to discuss with me so urgently."

His English was flawless, and it would have been easy for Jennifer to be taken in by the deceptive softness of his rich, deeply masculine voice, made even more attractive by the slight lilt of a foreign accent.

But she had come this far. It was now or never. "I understand that you're planning to expand your export line to the United States, Mr. Adler," she began smoothly.

"That is correct," he nodded slightly.

"Up until now your firm has been dealing exclusively with coffee and industrial products," she continued, "but consumer products are an entirely different matter. I'm sure you're well aware of how rapidly trends change in that market, and how costly the wrong selection could be to your business." Doggedly, she went on, "As a purchasing consultant I can help you not only select items that will have wide appeal to the American public but also I can help you in the merchandising phase as well."

Hoping he could not see the slight tremor of her hand, she proffered the large manila envelope. It contained the false credentials that had taken her three long months to compile to her satisfaction—three more months that Tommy had to spend behind bars because of this man.

He was regarding her with a mixture of annoyance and of something else she could not define, so she hurried to say, "If you will be kind enough to examine my credentials, I'm sure you will agree that your company can greatly benefit from my services, Mr. Adler. They could make the difference between success and failure."

A strange look appeared briefly in those eyes of steel. Then, instead of accepting the envelope, Alejandro rose abruptly to his feet. "I am a very busy man, Miss Maitland," he said testily. "We do have a personnel department. I suggest you file an application with them. Now, if you will excuse me, I have another appointment."

Even though Jennifer had been prepared for this

reception the moment she presented him with the true nature of her visit, her heart constricted painfully. She had fervently hoped she would not have to resort to other tactics to achieve her purpose. Faced with that very situation, however, she didn't hesitate to forge ahead on a more dangerous course.

Ignoring his dismissal, she let her skirt ride a little higher up her thighs as she crossed her long slender legs. With a low-lidded glance she tugged demurely at the skirt, which still left a good amount of leg showing. Overused as it was, her action immediately produced the desired result: to call Alejandro Adler's attention to what she knew were one of her best features.

"I'm well aware of the existence of your personnel department, Mr. Adler," she laughed, a small seductive quaver in her voice. "Just as aware that leaving an application with them would be a complete waste of time, something I can hardly afford after coming all the way from the United States. But neither can you afford to pass up what I can do for your business. Hiring me is a decision only you can make, and that's the reason why I insisted on seeing you in person."

Watching the slate-blue eyes for his reactions, Jennifer thought she detected a glint of amusement, a glint he was quick to mask. The fact that he didn't throw her out on her ear, however, was proof enough that her persistence stood at least a slight chance of being rewarded.

With quiet deliberation the executive moved around his desk. Folding his lean frame in the swivel chair, he reached for a gold digital clock and turned it around to face her. "Very well, Miss Maitland," he said challengingly. "I have a meeting to attend in five minutes. That's all the time you have to convince me of how indispensable you are to my business." With that he leaned back and, forming a steeple with his fingers, prepared to listen.

The time he had allowed her was less than half of what she needed for the speech she had prepared. Jennifer managed to provide him with the most salient points in recorded time, rattling off memorized statistics and stressing the constantly changing trends of the American market. She accompanied her words with well-rehearsed glances and body language that, she was aware, were not lost on him in spite of the indifference he affected.

"Thank you, Miss Maitland," Alejandro said at the end of the five minutes. "I will study your qualifications in more detail as soon as I can. If you will leave your telephone number with my assistant, you'll be informed of my decision." With that he stood up, putting an end to the interview.

Jennifer stood up as well and in vain searched his impassive features for a sign of encouragement. "And may I ask when that will be, Mr. Adler?"

"Soon," he replied blandly. "Very soon."

I've lost, Jennifer thought desperately. In one last reckless attempt to salvage her plans she put a sexy undertone in her voice as she offered him her hand again and said, "I'm staying at the Tequendama Hotel. Please don't keep me waiting *too* long."

JENNIFER HAD TO THANK the drivers of Bogotá for keeping her from sinking into a deep depression as soon as she left the Avianca Building. Bullfighting, she knew, was one of the greatest passions of the Colombians, and apparently the act of sitting behind a steering wheel released their secret fantasies of the arena. Rather than brave matadors, however, many drivers seemed to become raging bulls, charging every obstacle in their path including pedestrians. It took all of her attention to venture the city streets and remain unscathed. Jennifer smiled wryly at the thought as she crossed the busy *Carrera Séptima* and entered a lovely park area. Parque de la Independencia, a sign read. There was a sizable crowd of university students gathered here, enjoying the sunshine.

While sitting in the shadow of a white marble statue—Estatua de la Rebeca were the words carved into the base—she went over the interview in her mind, trying to find a thread of hope as to its outcome. What would she do if she had failed, she wondered. How could she ever be able to prove Tommy's innocence to the authorities? Prove that Alejandro Adler, a man of great wealth and impeccable reputation, was the one who belonged in that prison?

The fact that she suddenly felt a little light-headed did not alarm her. In addition to the stress of meeting Alejandro Adler, she had arrived in Bogotá only that morning, after all. It would take some time for her system to adapt itself to the unaccustomed altitude of over 8,600 feet. . . .

Perhaps she would have handled the interview much better if she had waited at least a day before going to see him, Jennifer lamented—if she had allowed herself some time to rest. Now it was too late. She had been too anxious to get her project under way, for every day she wasted was another day Tommy was deprived of his freedom. Had she, in her anxiety to succeed, been too forward and made Alejandro suspicious?

These and other questions crowded her mind, until she was gradually diverted from her reflections by the uneasy feeling of being watched. When she looked around distractedly for the source of her discomfiture she spotted a man a short distance away. He was staring at her.

The man saw that she had noticed him, and almost at once he began advancing toward her. Jennifer got nervously to her feet, but when she tried to speak she couldn't find her voice. Suddenly the park started spinning around her.

"You okay, *señorita*? I help you." Putting his words into action, the man took her by the arm and helped her back to the park bench.

Jennifer offered no resistance. Even in her distraught state she couldn't have mistaken the concern in the stranger's polite generous offer.

"Thank you," she managed to get out as she collapsed on the park bench, trying to catch her breath. A few seconds later everything started going slowly back to normal.

"You feel okay now, *señorita*?" the man inquired in a hopeful tone.

"Yes, thank you." She felt a little guilty for having been so suspicious of him and explained weakly, "I suppose it was the altitude. I'm all right now."

"Ah, *sí.*" Nodding emphatically, the man grinned, revealing a gap left by a missing front tooth. "The city in high mountain. Makes you dizzy."

"Mmm, yes," she nodded. "Thank you for your help. You've been very kind."

A flicker of her apprehension returned when the man began looking warily about him. "Want to buy emerald?" he asked furtively. "I sell to you cheap."

With the flood of relief that washed over her came the insane desire to laugh. Good Lord, she was becoming paranoid!

Even to Jennifer's untrained eye the emeralds the man took out of his pocket seemed unimpressive, and his furtive manner made her wonder about the legality of a transaction. All she needed now was to be arrested for buying illegal gems she didn't want! But even though he did look a little sinister, the man had been kind. She noticed then the state of his clothes—clean but threadbare—and didn't have the heart to refuse spending a few pesos for the smallest stone. Still, she could ill afford such gestures; the money she was carrying in her purse represented all that was left of her savings, and she had to watch her expenditures very carefully.

She had felt it would be to her advantage to present a sophisticated affluent front to Alejandro Adler if and when he tried to reach her. And since for that reason a cheaper hotel was out of the question, she would have to conserve her resources by spending as little as possible on food.

The thought reminded her that it had been more than seven hours since her last meal, and that perhaps her light-headed feeling had more to do with an empty stomach than with the altitude. Determined to remedy the situation, Jennifer decided to look for a restaurant that would offer a good meal for a reasonable price.

She soon found what she was looking for, a cross between a tea salon and a modest restaurant. Following the advice of a waitress in a crisp white uniform she ordered a frothy hot chocolate drink, and with it something called *almojábanas*—delicious soft rolls loaded with cheese. They had the consistency of doughnuts, Jennifer found, except they weren't sweet. She also discovered that, although Colombia exported its best coffee, it retained for domestic consumption its best chocolate.

The last rays of the setting sun had turned the sky to a deep rose color by the time Jennifer left the restaurant. Joining the wave of Colombians rushing home after the day's work she headed for the Hotel Tequendama.

When she reached her room, however, she found that in spite of her exhaustion she was too keyed up to be able to sleep. The memory of Tommy's face, as she had last seen it during her visit to his island prison, was indelibly etched in her mind. How different he had looked from the brother with whom she had grown up, with whom she had shared so much!

Physically they were such opposites that people had found it difficult to believe they were brother and sister, let alone twins. Tommy had their father's dark hair, brown eyes and strong build, while she had inherited the ash blond hair and Nordic looks of their mother. Jennifer had her mother's deceptively frail build as well—deceptive because both slender figures, which could look appetizingly feminine in frilly gowns and spiky high heels, had been finely tuned by years of hiking, swimming and skiing.

Fostered by their active parents, the love both Jennifer and Tommy shared for the outdoors had taken prominence in their choice of careers. It had been the nature of the assignments they had accepted after obtaining their degrees as soil scientists that had separated them for the first time in their lives. For several years now they had seen each other only between assignments.

Six months ago Tommy had been hired as a consultant by Alejandro Adler and had gone to Colombia. He was to determine how to get the best use of the Adler's extensive landholdings, land which had been in Alejandro's family since the time of the conquistadores. That was all Jennifer had learned from the only letter she'd received from her brother while she was performing a similar service in a remote area of Brazil; so remote in fact, that it had taken almost three months for the missive to reach her.

She had accepted the Brazilian assignment—which no one else in her office had wanted—mostly to get away from the well-intentioned friends who had kept trying to fix her up with men. They didn't seem to understand that none of those men could make her forget the one who was to have been her husband. Jim had become a statistic on the list of traffic fatalities a week before their wedding day, and at barely twenty-five Jennifer had become a widow without first having been a wife. Tommy had been the only one who had understood her need to purge the deep feelings of guilt that plagued her. Guilt for having survived without a scratch the same accident that ended Jim's life.

During this, the darkest period in Jennifer's life, the Brazilian assignment had been the purgatory she had so ardently sought. It had allowed her to find a measure of inner peace in the hard work she had to face—not only in the normal performance of her duties and in the lack of creature comforts, but also in surmounting the deep-rooted prejudices she encountered among those she was trying to help.

The situation was far from being a new one for her. Even in the States, where women had achieved a considerable amount of recognition in many professions that until recent years had been the dominion of men, many a rancher or farmer had watched her with amusement while she went about collecting her samples. Then, when all her hard work was completed, they refused to accept her advice about which crops would grow best in certain areas or how to improve their soil. Their fragile male egos would not accept that a ''pretty little thing like her'' could possibly know more than they did about their business.

Why did some men have to be so narrow-minded, Jennifer asked herself with exasperation every time she was faced with that situation. And it wouldn't surprise her if Alejandro Adler was counted among their ranks....

Her thoughts drifted once again to the enigmatic Colombian. Analyzing their earlier exchange once more, Jennifer refused to admit she had found him attractive. Instead she concentrated on her impression that, although she couldn't put her finger on anything definite, the executive had not been as indifferent to her as he had appeared on the surface. It had been more than the admiration she had seen reflected so briefly in those slate-blue eyes. . . .

Until today, Alejandro Adler had been a two-dimensional face she had studied from the photographs she had started collecting so painstakingly after visiting Tommy in La Gorgona, his island prison off the Pacific Coast of Colombia. A prison that would rob so many years of his life unless she could prove his innocence.

A shiver of dread went through Jennifer's body at the thought of failure. For a man like her brother, who felt even the walls of an office as a confinement, a prison sentence carried with it a slow painful death. But he had been tried and convicted, based on evidence given by Alejandro Adler. And the memory of his haunted look had been with her every minute of every day. . . .

Despairing of sleep, Jennifer got up and padded on bare feet to the dresser. Pulling open a drawer, she took out a briefcase and carried it back to the bed. Inside was all the information she had collected on her enemy, and she took out a photograph and held it in her hand.

She had thought that by now she knew every line, every contour of his face as well as she did her own.

Yet meeting Alejandro Adler in the flesh had still taken her by surprise. For the first time Jennifer was aware of the sensuality of the full-lipped mouth that smiled from the clipping; of the difference it made to know the color of those eyes that looked directly at the camera as if they had nothing sinister to hide.

One of the photographs showed him in a polo outfit, holding the reins of a pony. It had been taken after a match at the Jockey Club, and Jennifer could see the exhilaration of victory still written on his elegant features. Absently she wondered how that face would look in defeat, after she had helped put him where he belonged. Somehow the thought did not comfort her as she had expected it would, and in frustration she put back in her briefcase all the pictures she had scattered on the bed. Only one was left, face down and she didn't have to turn it over to know which one it was.

Her hand was trembling a little as she picked it up, and her eyes filled helplessly with tears. In it a little girl looked lovingly at the man who had become Jennifer's enemy. It was his daughter, Heidi.

The pain in her heart was sharp, and Jennifer shut her eyes tightly so that she wouldn't have to see that young trusting face any more. The little girl would be paying a high price for Tommy's freedom, she knew, but she couldn't let that stop her from seeking justice for her brother.

Without hesitation, Jennifer shoved the picture inside the briefcase with all the rest and snapped it shut. She couldn't allow herself to feel sorry for the girl. There were innocent victims in every war, and

Alejandro Adler had framed an innocent man to save himself. Jennifer realized how careful she had to be with such a dangerous man. From the very first moment he had been wary of her, she imagined, but why? Was it possible he suspected a connection between herself and Tommy?

No, Jennifer admonished herself, he couldn't have.

JENNIFER WAS RELUCTANT to leave her hotel room the next morning in case he got in touch. She had little rest during the night and was now famished, however. Resisting the temptation to call room service because of the cost, she finally ventured out to the same restaurant where she had eaten at the previous day. There she was disappointed to find that breakfast consisted of *changua*, an egg poached in some watery milk and flavored with onion and coriander. She found herself unable to eat it.

"I should have called room service," she muttered, pushing the plate aside. Having learned that she would have to wait until lunchtime for a more substantial meal, she went to the bakery at the front of the store and bought a delicious-looking pastry, which she savored with a cup of aromatic coffee.

When she had finished eating she wandered out onto the sidewalks of Bogotá. *City of Eternal Spring* was what they called it, she knew. It was so high up in the mountains that even on approach for landing she had had the impression that the aircraft was going to crash against the mountain range in the middle of nowhere. And then, all of a sudden, the surprising vision of a city had risen from a great plateau, surrounded by the mauve and gray peaks of the Andes. The sight had exhilarated Jennifer.

With nothing to do and little money to spend, she took the rest of the morning to visit the bustling noisy city. A few of Bogotá's many churches, with their deep rose decorations, their magnificent gold altars, their artistic and historic treasures occupied her until noon. At that point she decided to go back to the hotel, for she was anxious to see if Alejandro Adler had left any messages.

She was glad for the underground pedestrian tunnel that connected her hotel to the last church she had visited. It enabled her to avoid the heavy traffic on the busy street. She was halfway through the tunnel, however, when a boy on the run forcibly shoved her aside. At the same time he wrenched her purse from her hand.

Jennifer was momentarily stunned, but she quickly regained her faculties. "Help!" she cried, clinging to the wall to keep from falling. "Thief!"

Her cries attracted a good deal of attention. A number of people gathered around her, but all they accomplished was to block her view of the agile lad who was running away with all the money she had left in the world.

When she realized no one was doing anything to help her, Jennifer pushed her way through the crowd, just in time to see her thief disappear at the end of the tunnel. She started after him, but her shoes were not meant for sprinting; one of the high heels broke and she twisted her ankle.

She was out of breath when she had finally and painfully hobbled the distance to the mouth of the tunnel. As she feared, she found no trace of the thief or of her purse when she got there. Resisting the temptation to break into tears, she leaned wearily against the wall, trying to steady herself.

This couldn't really be happening, she prayed. But it was: one solitary act on the part of a stranger had caused her situation to suddenly become desperate. She was all alone and penniless in a strange city where she knew not a soul; dependent on a phone call that might never come. And she couldn't even appeal to the U.S. embassy because she had entered Colombia with a passport bearing the name of a dead woman. She had broken the laws of both countries, and now she had no one to turn to. Even if she could reach someone back home to wire her funds, she would have to present identification papers that would show she had entered the country illegally.

What was she going to do?

CHAPTER TWO

THERE WERE NO MESSAGES for her when she returned to the hotel. With the new turn of events she simply couldn't sit around waiting for the phone to ring, so as soon as she got to her room Jennifer kicked her shoes off, went to the phone, and dialed Adler Exports.

"Mr. Adler, please. This is Miss Maitland."

"I'm sorry, Miss Maitland," a composed voice answered coolly. "Mr. Adler is in conference. Would you care to leave a message?"

Jennifer, who had recognized the voice of Mrs. Vargas, replied, "Will you please let him know that I called?" She added the number of her hotel room and hung up with a weary sigh.

What a fool she had been, she ruefully reflected. How had she ever imagined she would be able to get away with such an insane scheme! Well, she could always march into the American Embassy, but after she had admitted what she had done, she would surely be deported to the United States. Perhaps the courts might be lenient with her, but even so that meant she would never be able to return to Colombia. Tommy would languish in prison without hope of help from anyone. No, as long as there was the slightest chance of being hired by Alejandro Adler, she would not give up hope!

And so, for the next twenty-four hours, Jennifer remained in her room, waiting for the phone to ring and trying to save her strength for the moment when—and if—she would meet with Alejandro Adler. Fighting the dizziness that was the companion of hunger, she succeeded in keeping herself from picking up the phone and ordering a meal from room service. But why not, she asked herself when she was finally at the end of her rope. Taking a cool practical look at her situation, she realized that she was already in trouble because she couldn't pay for the hotel room. Starving herself in the process wasn't going to gain her any sympathy from the hotel management.

Once she had rationalized her decision Jennifer picked up the phone and dialed room service. This was not the time to experiment with the exotic foods of the *cocina criolla* listed on the menu. She decided instead to stick to the familiar, and ordered a tossed green salad, a filet mignon medium rare, baked potato with both butter and sour cream and asparagus with hollandaise sauce. As an afterthought she added the avocado vichyssoise, and for dessert an orange torte.

The prospect of the juicy steak with all the trimmings that would arrive was enough of an incentive to revive her sagging spirits. Throwing a short bed jacket over her pink satin nightgown she went to the bathroom, splashed cold water over her face, and briskly brushed her hair to make herself at least presentable for the waiter when he came.

She had barely finished her quick *toilette* when she heard someone at the door and ran to answer. But it wasn't the waiter with her meal. The tall virile man standing there, was the last person she wanted to see, looking the way she was. It was Alejandro Adler.

Unable in her weakened condition to withstand the shock, Jennifer cried out as the room began spinning all about her.

"Miss Maitland!" Alejandro exclaimed in alarm, catching her in his arms as she started to fall. With a minimum of effort he carried her to the bed.

Jennifer was only dimly aware of his warm fingers as they felt her neck for her pulse, his palm as it rested briefly on her forehead. Then he was gone, and she heard the sound of his voice speaking to someone in rapid Spanish. All she could understand of the conversation was the word "doctor."

"I don't need a doctor," she protested feebly, trying to sit up.

"I'll be the judge of that," Alejandro replied as he hung up the phone. It was at that precise moment that the waiter knocked on the door, which had been left open. The man wheeled in the cart carrying her dinner and handed the check to Alejandro, whose face registered his surprise as he read it through. "This must be a mistake," he told the waiter. "You'd better take it away."

By now partially recovered from her shock, Jennifer bolted upright on the bed. "No, please!" she cried. "Don't take it away!"

Looking from one to the other, the waiter hesitated for an instant, until Alejandro put an end to the tableau by signing the check. He returned it to the waiter with a generous tip saying, "It's all right. Leave it."

He waited until the door had closed again before he turned to her sternly. "You little fool! Haven't you any sense at all?"

"But I'm hungry!" Jennifer protested indignantly.

He heaved a sigh of exasperation, but at the sight of her trembling lower lip adopted a more tolerant expression. "Look, Miss Maitland," he said calmly. "Eating a heavy meal like this before your body has become accustomed to the altitude will make you very ill. I don't want you fainting on me again."

"If I fainted, it was because I'm starved! I haven't had anything to eat for almost two days!" she snapped. Silence stretched between them for a moment, then she went on, "I'm sorry. I didn't mean to yell at you." Her voice was contrite. At this point she had no choice but to explain her situation. "It's just that I...I was robbed. All my money is gone, even my passport. Everything!"

"Were you carrying all your cash in your purse?"

Because she had felt uneasy about using false identity papers, Jennifer had converted all her traveler's checks to Colombian currency. "Yes," she nodded.

Wryly he shook his head and asked, "When did it happen?"

"Early yesterday afternoon."

"So you locked yourself in this room waiting for

me to call you with a job offer, is that it?'' Again
Alejandro shook his head. After a few seconds he
said, ''All right, Miss Maitland, you'd better eat your
dinner before it gets cold.''

He helped her get up from the bed, and after in-
stalling her in a chair, rolled the cart toward her so
that she could enjoy her meal. Then he went to the
telephone and canceled his earlier request for a doctor.

When the delicious aroma of the food wafted toward her, Jennifer had to restrain herself from wolf-
ing down her food. The vichyssoise, made of buttery
avocados from the lowlands and the small white
potatoes for which the Colombian highlands were
famous, was creamy and delicious. Much to Jennifer's chagrin, however, she found that her appetite
was gone before she had finished the bowl. She
pushed the cart aside in frustration. All this marvelous food would now go to waste.

''Were you?'' she asked, as if their conversation
had just ended. At his quizzical look, she added,
''Were you going to hire me?''

''Well, that presents us with a little problem,
doesn't it? I cannot legally hire you without papers or
a work permit.'' He let a few seconds of silence go by
before adding, ''Tell me something, Miss Maitland.
Is there any reason why you didn't go to the American Embassy for help, or did the idea simply escape
you?''

Oh, what a fool he must think her, Jennifer
thought with no little vexation. She couldn't really
blame him. ''Of course I thought about it,'' she

replied dryly. "I wasn't feeling well, that's all. I was planning to go tomorrow."

"Tomorrow is Saturday and the embassy will be closed," he reminded her.

"Then I'll just have to wait until Monday, won't I?" she replied acidly. Then, realizing there was nothing to gain and much to lose by antagonizing him, she tried to make amends. "I'm sorry. I'm not usually this disagreeable."

Alejandro accepted her apology with a philosophical shrug. Jennifer chewed her lower lip as she watched him light a cigarette.

"I'll tell you what," he said at last. "Any arrangement between us will have to be off the record. I'll hire you as a visiting purchasing consultant. But in order to avoid legal entanglements, your salary will have to be paid in the United States, transferred from my bank account into yours. That way no one will be the wiser."

Here was a man who knew how to find a loophole when he wanted to, Jennifer thought as she listened to his proposition. But she had no right to resent his manipulations, she reminded herself.

"In the meantime, you'll be provided with an expense account and living quarters for the length of your stay in Colombia," Alejandro went on. "Don't worry about your hotel bill. I'll take care of it, and tomorrow my car will collect you to take you to my home."

She looked up sharply. "Your home?"

"Well, not exactly," he replied almost blandly. "There's a small cottage on the grounds, which my late wife used as a studio for her painting. It's been empty for quite some time and it'll need some work, but I'm sure you'll be comfortable there.''

The offer, far more generous than she had expected, made her instantly suspicious of his motives—and his intentions. She couldn't help asking, "Why are you going to so much trouble for me, Mr. Adler?"

The corner of his mouth twitched in mild amusement as he took a few bills out of his wallet and laid them on the dresser. "Let's just say that...the arguments you presented were very convincing, Miss Maitland."

Jennifer wasn't sure how to interpret his reply. Did he expect her to repay him with sexual favors? After the performance she had put on during the interview, she couldn't really blame him.

But a man as attractive as Alejandro Adler—she had to concede that he *was* incredibly attractive—had no need to resort to such extremes to gain the favors of a woman. And she couldn't overlook the fact that in being so close to him at home as well as at work, she had been provided with an enviable opportunity to watch every move he made. If worse came to worst, though, how far was she willing to go to gain her brother's freedom?

THE QUESTION WAS STILL UNANSWERED in her mind when Alejandro came to collect her the next day. He had abandoned his conservative business suit in favor of casual brown slacks and a beige sports jacket worn over a cream-colored silk shirt. He seemed far more approachable than he had appeared to her during their first two encounters, Jennifer decided as she got in next to him in the back seat of the chauffeur-driven Mercedes sedan. The change was not solely to the casual clothes he wore. His attitude toward her, as well, was no longer entirely businesslike. It was nothing Jennifer could really put her finger on, since there had been no lack of courtesy or undue familiarity on his part. But something intangible had definitely changed in their relationship, and she wasn't sure she felt comfortable about it. Perhaps what made her so uneasy was that fate, in the form of a young purse snatcher, had made her so totally dependent on this successful, powerful man.

As the Mercedes purred along the city streets, Jennifer couldn't help being aware of the way Alejandro's brown slacks stretched over his strong muscular thighs. For some reason a passage from *Lady Chatterley's Lover* came to her mind. She had read the book years before, but suddenly she recalled Lady Chatterly's discovery of the sensuality of men's thighs, a discovery she had made after her own sexuality was awakened by her lover, the gamekeeper Mellors. By any standards Alejandro's thighs were sensuous, Jennifer thought distractedly. As were his hands, which were resting on them. His long masculine fingers were bereft of rings of any kind, she noted, wondering how long after the death of his wife he had taken off his wedding band.

But why was she entertaining such personal thoughts about a man whom she could only think of as an enemy, she asked herself abruptly. *Because I am so keenly aware of him in a sexual sense,* she had to admit, realizing that many of the physical symptoms she had attributed to nerves during their first meeting had more to do with her instinctive response to that rare aura of masculinity, that untamed sensuality she could feel radiating from Alejandro Adler. It was nothing he said or did; it simply was there. The conservative, elegant clothes he wore were nothing more than a veneer of civilization. Beneath them existed a primitive male who, she sensed, had the power to make her aware of her own femininity as no other man had ever done before.

To avoid this perturbing train of thought, Jennifer looked out of the window and tried to keep her attention on the mass of humanity moving along the sidewalks. There were all kinds of people—most of them fashionably dressed, but others who were probably from the country.

By now the car was barely moving in the congested traffic.

"Is it always like this?" she asked.

"Most of the time," Alejandro replied. "This is Carrera Séptima, the main street of the city." He was silent for a few seconds and then observed, "I wonder how many of those people know they are walking over a hundred tons of gold."

She turned to look at him quizzically, but her eyes were instantly drawn to his sensual mouth. "Gold?" she echoed absently.

"In the underground vaults. That building over there—" he leaned toward her to point toward a building on her side "—is the Banco de la Republica.

You could say it's the Colombian equivalent to your Fort Knox.''

His clean male scent as he came so near affected the rate of her pulse, and she turned away to hide her confusion.

"Now, if you look at that terrace over there," he added, pointing at the same building, "you might see black smoke coming out the top. Then you will know that they're burning money—millions and millions of bills.''

Jennifer looked up, but all she was aware of at the moment was his nearness, and that a shortness of breath had been added to her other physical symptoms. "Why do they burn money?" she asked huskily, and her eyes met his only briefly before they dropped in confusion.

"Old bills out of circulation," he replied. Calling her attention to another point of interest, he added, "You might be able to get a better view of it from your office window, but look over there. That's the Parque Santander. Now there's quite a place. Always something going on.''

Jennifer felt the need to keep the conversation going. "What kind of things?" she asked, looking at the green oasis that appeared so unexpectedly in the middle of the congested thoroughfare.

"Mmm, a little bit of everything." He shrugged his broad shoulders. "Sellers of birds, flowers, books, food. Prophets of doom and entertainers.''

He paused, but in her confusion all she could think to say was, "Entertainers?''

A little smiled flickered on his face as he replied,

"Acrobats, mostly. All in all, just simple ordinary people trying to make a living the best they can. But also loan sharks, and pickpockets who can strip you naked with such skill that you don't even notice until you feel the draft."

The way he said it invited her laughter, and she was almost grateful to him for keeping her from making a fool of herself.

"I already learned about your pickpockets. the hard way," she added wryly, clutching the new purse she had just bought in a shop near the hotel.

"I'm sure you'll be able to get a new passport next week," Alejandro assured her. "And as far as money is concerned, I'll see that you get an advance for your expenses. Not that you'll need much unless you plan to go on a shopping spree. All your basic needs should be provided for. The cottage will afford as much privacy as you desire, and as for meals—well, the choice is yours. You may join us or not, this evening being the exception." At her quizzical look, he added, "My mother would like you to join us for dinner, to meet the family."

"Will your daughter be there?" Too late Jennifer could hear the alarm in her own voice.

He arched a brow. "Do you know about my daughter?" Without giving her a chance to answer he added dryly, "Yes, Heidi will be there."

He fell silent, and after a minute Jennifer cast a wary glance at him. The stern lines that had returned to his face made her uneasy. Had she given herself away? Had she made Alejandro aware that she knew more about his personal life than she was supposed to? For a moment he had made her forget that she was playing a very dangerous role. She would definitely have to be more careful in the future.

Still worried about her blunder, Jennifer tried to derive some comfort from the knowledge that other people would be at his home. Surely he wouldn't try anything if his mother and his daughter were nearby. If indeed that were true. Or was he only giving her a false sense of security, she wondered, feeling her alarm increase.

She still couldn't get over the feeling that Alejandro Adler had been suspicious of her from the very beginning. So why the sudden change? Or was it really a change? And was he really taking her to his estate?

Suddenly, the danger of her position was driven sharply home to Jennifer: the man who had framed her brother on a drug charge was now in total possession of her person. Good Lord, what a fool she had been to put herself so completely in his power! So afraid had she been of letting anyone talk her out of her plans to save Tommy—or of having them find out she had obtained a false passport— that Jennifer had not told a soul where she was going. All her friends had believed the story she'd given, that she was returning to complete her assignment in Brazil. If she were to disappear from the face of the earth, no one would ever think of connecting such an occurrence to Alejandro Adler. There wasn't even a record of her entering the country!

I must tell someone where I am and what I'm do-

ing, she told herself silently, praying that she would get a chance to do so.

Except there was no one she could trust.

The Mercedes had left the heavy city traffic behind and was now traveling on a less frequented road, heading toward the mountains. Where was Alejandro taking her? Perhaps she would never get a chance to—

Stop it, Jennifer commanded herself sternly. If she went on like this, she would end up by becoming hysterical and *that* would be the end of her for sure. There was nothing she could do at this time except keep her head and hope for the best, wait and see what happened. Perhaps Alejandro was telling the truth, and she was seeing ghosts where there were none. *Just wait and see*, she kept repeating to herself over and over, *You'll find out soon enough*.

In spite of her efforts, Jennifer was unable to still her restless mind. If Alejandro's motives had been legitimate, a simple phone call summoning her back to his office would have been sufficient. Instead, he had appeared at her hotel room without even letting her know in advance that he was coming. Before she had told him about her stolen purse had he intended to hire her? Or had he come with other ideas in mind?

Perhaps he intended nothing more sinister than having an affair with her, Jennifer reflected, trying to give herself courage. She felt she could handle that. Then she began to have doubts again. Keeping a man like Alejandro Adler at bay most certainly wouldn't be easy. Somehow she knew he wouldn't use force; instead he would use other more subtle means to get what he wanted from her.

Jennifer didn't consider herself a prude, although she recognized that perhaps she was a little old-fashioned about sex. Her own experience was limited to her relationship with Jim, the man she had loved and trusted enough to want to spend her life with. After losing him she had been grateful for all that they had shared for at least a little while. It had been a tender kind of passion. They had been friends first and foremost, and their physical relationship was comfortable, loving, relaxed.

But she wasn't friends with Alejandro Adler. What did she know of him other than that he had sent an innocent man to prison for a crime he hadn't committed? And yet there was something inside her that against all reason drew her to him. It wasn't love, it couldn't be! What was happening to her? Perhaps more than her life was in danger. . . .

It was a lovely day, nearly cloudless, and had she been less worried Jennifer would have been curious to explore the picturesque business center they were driving past. Probably at one time a small village of its own, it had now been swallowed by the expanding metropolis. A vast jumble of goods and produce was on display—pots and pans, local handicrafts, neat pyramids of oranges, limes, tomatoes and other vegetables and fruit. The handsome Indian women milling among the stalls wore long full skirts and colorful embroidered shawls, and they had black derbies perched jauntily atop their plaited tresses.

Jennifer didn't have to wait much longer to dis-

cover where Alejandro was taking her. Neither the
electrified fence nor the guard at the gate did anything to ally her fears, however. Even though she said
nothing Alejandro must have been aware of her reaction, because he explained, "All this protection is
necessary in a place as isolated as this *quinta*."

He didn't have to say more for Jennifer to understand. The number of kidnappings had risen sharply
in recent years. It was not a problem unique to
Colombia, but an insidious disease that was spreading throughout the entire world. It was obvious that
Alejandro Adler was not a man to take chances
where the safety of his family was concerned.

Jennifer wondered how it would feel to live under
constant guard. Alejandro himself seemed able to
bear that particular cross remarkably well. But when
the Mercedes sedan entered the estate it became apparent to Jennifer why life in this remote *quinta*
could hardly be considered a hardship.

The dwelling itself was set back at least half a mile
from the entrance. To reach it they had to travel
through an extensive park of carefully manicured
lawns dotted with venerable trees. Jennifer momentarily forgot her anxiety when she finally caught a
glimpse of the house. Although of modern construc-
tion, it followed the traditional colonial Spanish
style, gleaming white in the sun, with sienna-colored
tiles on the roof. The immense front door had elaborate brass hinges, and a flowering bougainvillea crept
up the sides of the porch.

The car did not stop in front; instead, it followed
the paved driveway around the house. Only then did

Jennifer realize that this was not just an ordinary home, but a mansion of generous dimensions provided with all the amenities of luxury—a large swimming pool, a tennis court, a riding ring.

"I'll take you to the cottage so you can get settled in," Alejandro told her. "We have some houseguests for the weekend whom you'll be meeting at dinner this evening."

A servant was waiting at the cottage when the car pulled up to it. The young woman, who had light brown skin, a vivid face with handsome Indian features, and plaited glossy black hair, had apparently just finished preparing the place. Alejandro introduced her as Magdalena.

Pronouncing *Maitland* was an impossibility for the woman. When she addressed Jennifer as Señorita Don, Alejandro offered, "If you don't mind, it might be easier to use the Spanish version of your name, Alba."

"Alba," Jennifer repeated. "Yes, I like that. It sounds very romantic."

"Then Alba it is." He smiled, and for the first time Jennifer caught a glimpse of his white, even teeth.

He does have a beautiful smile, she decided, a little flustered by her own reaction to it.

When her two suitcases had been brought in by the chauffeur, Alejandro said, "Magdalena will show you around. Don't hesitate to ask for anything you need. She doesn't speak English, but I hope you can manage."

"I'm sure we'll be fine," Jennifer assured him. "I

can speak a little Spanish, and I suppose we can use sign language for the rest.''

''Good,'' he nodded. ''Feel free to use any of the facilities on the grounds. Do you play tennis?''

''I do swat a ball around occasionally, but I'm no champ,'' Jennifer admitted.

''Well, you won't have to worry about that.'' He smiled again. ''You'll find that none of us would qualify for any tournaments.'' As he turned away he said, ''I'll call for you at eight. See you then.''

After Alejandro had left, Jennifer followed Magdalena around her new domain. The living room was quite spacious. Its large windows and the skylight in the beamed ceiling made it perfect as an artist's studio. It was tastefully decorated, with modern furniture arranged in front of a carved stone fireplace.

The furniture in the bedroom was French provincial in style and upholstered in rose damask. The cottage was self-contained, with a full bathroom and a small kitchenette. The pantry was stocked with canned goods, and the refrigerator held perishables such as eggs, milk and fruit juices. Jennifer would be able to cook her own meals on the two-burner hot plate if she wanted to.

Perhaps Magdalena didn't understand Jennifer's attempts to tell her that she would unpack her own things. In any case the Colombian woman continued with the task and wouldn't leave until Jennifer, mostly to get rid of her, conveyed by a mixture of broken Spanish and a great deal of gesturing that she was tired and wanted to take a nap.

''*Ah, sí,* Señorita Alba,'' Magdalena smiled. ''*La*

siesta.'' She turned down the bed and drew the curtains shut to darken the room before she finally left, taking with her the dress she would press for Jennifer to wear to dinner that evening. When at last she was left alone, Jennifer had to admit to herself how easily one could become spoiled by such solicitude.

Having a nap had only been an excuse. She was too restless to sleep, and after hiding her briefcase in one of the dresser drawers, she went out for a walk. The grounds seemed to be deserted, at that hour of the afternoon, anyway. Jennifer was just wondering if everybody else was napping when the sound of hoofbeats caught her attention. Turning around and shielding her eyes with her hand, she watched the approaching rider.

She didn't have to wait long before recognizing Alejandro's daughter, Heidi. The little girl was riding a handsome gray pony with a flowing white mane—riding quite competently, Jennifer thought. She was rather small for her age, and perhaps a little thin. But she did seem perfectly at ease on the animal, pulling at the reins when she had come near.

"Hi," Jennifer greeted. "You must be Heidi. I'm Jen—Alba, a friend of your father's."

Heidi's eyes dropped shyly as she stroked her pony's neck and said, "Hello."

"That's a nice horse you have there," Jennifer said in an attempt at friendliness. She wondered if the girl spoke English or if she should try speaking in Spanish. "What do you call him?"

"Niebla," Heidi replied. "It means fog."

So she did speak English after all. "You ride very

well," Jennifer went on with a smile. "Did your father teach you?"

The child's chestnut braids were long enough to swing from side to side when she shook her head. "Renato did," she said.

Whoever that was, Jennifer said to herself. And why was she trying to be friendly to this little girl? It was wrong of her to do so when she was planning to unmask her father. She should keep way from Heidi, the farther, the better.

But there was something...something vulnerable about the child that Jennifer couldn't resist. Perhaps it was loneliness; a feeling that could be immediately recognized by someone who knew the meaning of the word. As she did. *But I must stay away,* Jennifer admonished herself. Aloud she asked, "Does Renato let you go riding by yourself?"

"Only if I don't go too far. Daddy said I couldn't, you see. But I won't fall. I'm a good rider."

Jennifer heard the unmistakable touch of pride in the little girl's voice. It was the challenge in her soft brown eyes that made her realize that this time she had disobeyed her father's orders.

"Yes, I'm sure you are," Jennifer replied. "But even experienced riders can suffer a spill every now and then." Suddenly she wanted to put an end to this meeting, and glancing at her wristwatch, she added, "Well, I think I'd better go back and start getting ready for dinner. I don't want to keep anyone waiting. I'll see you later, Heidi."

Without replying, Heidi touched her heels to her horse and rode away.

Jennifer sighed. She really couldn't afford to get emotionally attached to Alejandro Adler's child!

Magdalena had obviously returned to the cottage during her absence, for her long white dress with its metallic gold-rimmed ruffles was hanging in her room. With plenty of time before Alejandro came to pick her up, Jennifer turned on the taps of the pink marble bathtub and added a capful of scented bubble bath. She pinned up her hair while the tub filled.

Immersed in the fragrant warmth a moment later, Jennifer willed her body to relax, but her mind would not be still. Her task was difficult enough without adding other emotional burdens to it. She had to think of Tommy, her handsome laughing brother, who was now paying for a crime that Alejandro Adler himself was probably guilty of. Perhaps she had made a mistake in accepting this arrangement, which would bring her in contact with those closest to her enemy. She didn't want to know his daughter, his mother as individuals who would suffer when she destroyed that mask of respectability Alejandro wore. It was bad enough to be aware of their existence. But to get to know them, to sit at their table and pretend friendship while all the time she was planning Alejandro's destruction was more than Jennifer could bear.

And then there was Alejandro himself. She had been with him for only a short time, yet he had already almost made her forget he was her enemy. What if her brother had been mistaken and someone else, not Alejandro, had planted the evidence against him?

"Now I'm trying to believe in his innocence," Jennifer muttered in disgust. Just because she was attracted to the man didn't make him less guilty.

She had always tried to be honest with herself, and she could not deny that she felt a response for Alejandro Adler that she had never felt for any other man. The fact disturbed her deeply. Why did a man forbidden to her have to be the one who had awakened these emotions? She sank down farther in the tub and let the warm water swirl around her.

CHAPTER THREE

GOLD ON WHITE was a combination highly flattering to Jennifer's delicate blond beauty. In spite of her cool outward appearance she was still deeply disturbed when Alejandro, looking more handsome than ever in a white dinner jacket, arrived promptly at eight.

"Is everything all right?" he inquired. She had remained quiet as they walked side by side toward the main house. "Is the cottage to your satisfaction?"

"Oh, yes, it's lovely, thank you," she replied as airily as she could manage. "I was just wondering about what your mother must think of my being here. I hope I'm not imposing too much."

"Of course not," he assured her. "And if you're wondering whether I mentioned our arrangement to her, you don't have to. All she needs to know is that you'll be working with me for a while."

Jennifer meant it when she said, "You've been very kind."

"Bringing you here wasn't entirely selfless on my part," he told her.

Abruptly, Jennifer stopped walking. Alejandro did, too, and when she looked up at him she felt a flicker of fear. His words had caused some very disturbing emotions to churn up within her. She gave a little shiver when his eyes fastened on her mouth, and she found herself wishing he would kiss her and hold her in his arms.

Alejandro made no move to kiss her or even touch her. Instead he turned away and resumed walking. Struggling to regain her emotional balance, Jennifer followed, catching up with him when they reached the front door.

"This way," he told her as they stepped into the spacious vestibule, and he was careful not to touch her as they crossed the expanse of polished tiles.

Inside, the house followed the traditional Spanish style. It was built around a beautiful courtyard filled with trees and flowers, and a singing fountain stood in the center. Alejandro escorted Jennifer through the passageway, broken by doors and windows, that went around the courtyard and led to the inner rooms.

A small group of people was already gathered in one of the rooms, which was furnished with a mixture of colonial French and Spanish antiques. The delicate hues of a beautiful rug served to bring the decor of the entire room together in a harmonious blend.

The only stranger in the group, Jennifer became the center of attention as the two of them entered. Alejandro introduced her first to his mother.

Mariana Navarro de Adler was of medium height and every inch an aristocrat. Her dark hair was sprinkled with just a touch of gray, and her eyes were so dark and unfathomable that Jennifer could not read in them whether or not she was welcome.

"I'm very pleased to meet you, Mrs. Adler," she said.

"Miss Maitland." The Colombian woman's voice was as cool as her handshake. The lack of warmth in her manner made Jennifer wonder if the aristocratic lady was naturally cold, or if her aloofness was simply her way of stating that she wasn't too thrilled with her guest's presence. Still a little shaken from her earlier conversation with Alejandro, Jennifer imagined that the woman suspected her relationship with Alejandro was more intimate than he had claimed.

The only other man there besides Alejandro wore a dark suit and the collar of a priest. He was introduced as Monsignor Navarro, Mariana's brother. Even though his fair complexion was unlined, the silver strands appearing at his temples made Jennifer estimate his age at somewhere in the late forties to early fifties. It became obvious to her that Alejandro's height must have been inherited from his father, since the monsignor was only slightly taller than his sister. As with Señora de Adler, an innate elegance was very much apparent.

Elvira Guzman, the next woman Jennifer met, was related to Alejandro's mother in some distant way that wasn't very clear to her. A little younger than Mariana perhaps, she was neither as beautiful nor as imposing. Her daughter, Ofelia, was a lovely girl, however. In her late teens or early twenties, she had long brown hair, thickly lashed soft brown eyes and a sweet face. Her manner was reserved, almost shy.

All the ladies wore elegant evening gowns and discreet but expensive gold-and-emerald jewelry. Even Heidi, who had looked like a tomboy that afternoon, had been transformed with ribbons and lace into a pretty young lady, who curtsied when she was at last introduced. The girl seemed a little relieved when Jennifer refrained from mentioning their earlier encounter.

When she had finally met everyone present, Alejandro said, "We're having *aguardiente* cocktails, but I can get you a glass of wine if you prefer."

Jennifer was strictly a social drinker. When she was by herself, she found it hard to enjoy the same concoctions that tasted so good to her at a party or when she went out to dinner at a good restaurant. "The cocktail is fine," she replied.

"An *aguardiente* cocktail coming right up," Alejandro said with a half smile.

Hoping she hadn't made a mistake in not sticking to what was familiar, Jennifer watched him pour a whitish liquid from a mixer into a delicate long-stemmed glass of baccarat crystal. When he handed the drink to her she tasted it tentatively. It was very mild and had the distinct flavors of coconut and anise.

"Is this your first visit to Colombia, Miss Maitland?" Monsignor Navarro inquired pleasantly.

"Yes, monsignor," Jennifer replied and felt obliged to add, "from the little I've seen so far it's a very beautiful country."

"We think so," he nodded with natural pride. "I hope you will take time to explore some of it before you return to the United States."

"There'll be plenty of opportunity for that, uncle,"

Alejandro put in. "Miss Maitland will be doing quite a bit of traveling in the course of her business."

"Is that so?" the clergyman commented politely.

"Yes," Alejandro nodded, taking over from Jennifer, who until that moment hadn't known anything about his plans for her. "She's here to help me in the selection of consumer goods to export to her own country."

"And what, may I ask, will you be looking for in particular, Miss Maitland?" Señora de Adler inquired.

"Articles typical to Colombia that I believe will have the widest appeal to the American public," Jennifer answered. Regaining a little of her confidence, she rattled off what she knew to be the most popular products in addition to coffee and emeralds: "Leather goods, pottery, woolen knits, Indian jewelry. Things like that."

"Indian jewelry, hmm?" The monsignor arched an aristocratic brow.

"Yes," Jennifer nodded. "It's very popular in the States."

"Well, I suppose the jewelry the Indians are selling nowadays is inexpensive enough to find a wide market. Nothing like what they used to make," he scoffed mildly. At Jennifer's puzzled look, he added, "The Chibchas and Taironas, to name two of the tribes, were master goldsmiths long before the Europeans reached our shores. Have you had a chance to visit the Museo del Oro as yet?"

"No, not yet." She shook her head, aware that he was referring to the fabulous gold museum of

Bogotá, where a collection of more than 27,000 objects handcrafted by the Indians were on display. "I wanted to see the exhibit when it came to Los Angeles, but I never did get the chance. From what I heard, it was magnificent."

"That was only a small portion of the collection," the monsignor replied with a deprecating shrug. "Besides, one of the main pieces, the Muiscan barge of El Dorado, was a replica. The original never left Bogotá."

"Oh, I didn't know," Jennifer replied. "Why was that?"

"Because it is too valuable, not only from a monetary standpoint but for its historic significance as well." The monsignor paused briefly before asking, "Are you familiar with the legend of El Dorado?"

"The cities of gold?" Jennifer said diffidently. "Yes, of course I've heard about them."

"That's what the Spaniards believed when they came to Colombia," the priest grinned, warming up to the subject. "But each time they asked the Indians about them, they were told to go farther. They never found the cities of gold, because they didn't exist. El Dorado was not a place. It was a man."

By now Jennifer's curiosity was aroused and she echoed, "A man?"

"There were many legends on the subject," the monsignor nodded. "One of them was that the Indians honored a golden god that had come from the heavens and had fallen into a lake high in the Andes. It may have been a meteorite, who knows?" he shrugged. "But whatever it was, they believed it was a god, and their *caciques*, or chiefs, took part in very elaborate ceremonies where they were stripped naked and their bodies covered with gold dust. Then they boarded a barge with four high priests and an offering of gold and emeralds.''

"And they threw the treasures in the lake?'' Jennifer interjected, imagining the ritual. At the clergyman's nod, she shook her head. "Amazing.''

"Yes, but even more amazing is that from such a ceremony a legend like that could be created. And the question is, was it a legend or history?'' Dramatically he paused. "It was said that one such barge was found in the nineteenth century, but was sold to Germany and later disappeared during the Second World war. Until a second one was found, and that was only as recently as 1970, mind you, there was nothing to confirm the legend.''

"But what of the lake itself?'' Jennifer wanted to know. "Was it ever discovered?''

"Many people believe it to be Lake Guatavitá, and the fact that the barge was found not too far from there suggests that it may be true. From the sixteenth century until it was declared an archaeological park, the lake had been searched and dragged many times. Much gold had been recovered from it. Needless to say, what the Spaniards discovered was melted down and converted into ingots that were sent to Spain.'' He added wryly, "I am sorry to say that we Colombians were not much wiser. For a long time after gaining our independence we continued to destroy many treasures for their gold value. I shudder every time I think of it. You will see what I mean when you visit the museum.

The realism, the simplicity and beauty of those objects make them absolutely irreplaceable.''

"Shall we go into the dining room?" Señora de Adler interposed. "Dinner is served."

Jennifer put down her empty glass and followed the others into the adjoining room. It was of ample proportions, and gold and silver serving ware gleamed from atop a massive carved sideboard. The table was set with porcelain from Limoges, baccarat crystal and silver; the centerpiece was an elaborate arrangement of orchids and other local flowers. The napery was exquisitely embroidered linen.

Jennifer was seated between the hostess, who was at the head of the table, and her brother, while Alejandro, at the foot, was flanked by Ofelia and her mother. Heidi sat opposite Jennifer.

"Did you say you live in Los Angeles, Miss Maitland?" Señora de Adler inquired politely.

"I only go there on occasion," Jennifer replied, dreading the inquisition she felt coming from the older woman. "Actually, I live in Newport Beach."

"Newport?" Mariana echoed. "We have friends there. Are you acquainted with the Harringtons?"

Trying not to shift uncomfortably in her seat, Jennifer shook her head. "No, I'm afraid I don't know them."

"Alex went to school with their youngest son and spent a marvelous summer with them," the woman continued. "Didn't you, Alex?"

"That was in Rhode Island, mother," Alejandro replied. "Miss Maitland lives in Newport Beach, California."

"Oh! Is there a Newport in California?" Señora de Adler looked at her guest uncertainly. "I'm afraid I've never heard of it."

Jennifer gave her a tentative smile. "It's not surprising. The most famous spot in the area is Disneyland, but that's in Anaheim, which is only a few miles away from us."

"Disneyland!" The exclamation had come from Heidi, who had been very quiet so far. Now her eyes were as wide as saucers and she inquired avidly, "Have you ever seen Mickey Mouse?"

Her intensity brought amused chuckles from the adults, but Jennifer answered seriously, "Oh, yes, many times. Also Donald Duck, Goofy, Snow White and a few of the dwarfs."

Heidi regarded Jennifer in awe, and it was Ofelia who queried, "Is it really as wonderful a place as we've been led to believe, or is it just another amusement park?"

"Oh, it's definitely special," Jennifer replied. She paused for a moment to gather her thoughts. "You could call it a feeling, a mood, if you like. Do you know the story of Alice in Wonderland?" At Ofelia's nod, she went on, "I suppose each person may feel differently about it, but for me it's like when Alice followed the rabbit into the hollow tree. No matter how many times I've been to Disneyland, each time is a new experience. It's as if I had suddenly entered a world of fantasy, a fairy tale come to life. Regardless of how young or old you are, it's just wonderful. I don't think there's another place quite like it in the world."

The silence that followed her words made Jennifer look diffidently from one face to another. "Of course, there's also Disney World in Florida," she added lamely. Everyone continued watching her, and the speculative look she read in Alejandro's eyes made Jennifer wonder if she had made a fool of herself. To hide her uneasiness she turned her attention to the soup before her. "This is delicious," she said to change the subject.

At her observation, everyone seemed to remember the food. "It's called *sancocho*," Ofelia volunteered, sketching in the main ingredients.

The dish reminded Jennifer of the French *pot-au-feu*, or the Spanish *cocido*. Chicken, pork, and salted beef had been simmered with a variety of vegetables in a savory broth. It was the broth that was served as the first course. Then came the meats, sliced on a platter, and the vegetables—potatoes, yams, onions, squash, plantains. There were others that were new to Jennifer, but not knowing how her hostess would like being questioned about them, she simply enjoyed her food and the excellent haute sauterne with which the servant kept refilling her glass.

Reluctant to become the center of attention again, Jennifer made few contributions to the ensuing conversation. She had always been a good listener, and she was content to let the others discuss current events.

When the dessert was brought in, it was the monsignor who exclaimed, "Ah, *batido de curuba*! You remembered, Mariana."

"How could I forget your favorite?" There was

none of the coldness Señora de Adler had exhibited thus far in the affectionate smile she gave her younger brother.

Jennifer dipped her spoon into the flamingo-colored mousse. "Mmm, this is marvelous," she agreed. "What is it?"

"I knew you would like it," the monsignor grinned. "*Curuba* is the fruit of a vine unique to this region, and Mariana's cook prepares the best *batido* in all Colombia." Lowering his voice as if to reveal a secret, he went on, "Actually, it's the reason I visit my sister so often."

"And you think I don't know it?" Señora de Adler quipped in return. Their easy bantering gave Jennifer a glimpse of the deep affection existing between brother and sister.

"A splendid meal, Mariana," the monsignor said at last, smiling with satisfaction. "As usual."

"Yes, it really was," Jennifer echoed, "And such a lovely table. I've never seen more beautiful linen."

"Ah, this is one of the items you may want to consider for export, Miss Maitland," the priest replied. "The sisters in Villa de Leyva, a small town in Boyacá, earn their living by making and selling them."

"That sounds like a good idea," Jennifer replied. "Their work is the loveliest I've ever seen."

"Even if you don't come to an agreement with the good sisters, you should go there," he said. "The town itself is worth the trip. It has been maintained almost as it was centuries ago and is probably the most beautiful colonial town in existence."

"Ofelia is also very skillful with the needle," Señora de Adler told Jennifer. "You should see all the beautiful things she has embroidered for her trousseau."

"I'd love to," Jennifer answered politely.

"Yes, Ofelia is a very gifted young lady," Mariana went on. "But not only that. Unlike many girls today, she has not forgotten that the main role of a woman is in the home, as a wife and a mother. And such a lovely girl, don't you think?"

If there had been any doubt before, the message was now clear: Señora de Adler expected Ofelia to marry her son. Glancing down the table, Jennifer was glad that the older woman's words could not be heard by the two people in question. Ofelia seemed like a sweet young woman and Jennifer was confident that all Mariana said about her was true. The obvious praises of a hopeful mother-in-law could only serve to embarrass her, however.

"Yes, she's very lovely," Jennifer admitted, aware of a gnawing feeling in her heart. Suddenly she wanted to get away from this room, from this woman who had recognized her as a threat to her son, a threat of a different kind than the one that had brought her here. It took a considerable amount of willpower for her to sit through the *sobremesa*, the traditional after meal coffee hour. The family remained at the table conversing, while the men enjoyed tiny cups of strong, black Colombian coffee and the women herbal teas. To Jennifer the evening seemed to last forever and ever.

It was well past midnight, and at least two hours

after Heidi had been sent to bed, when much to her relief the long evening ended. After a general discussion of the activities planned for the next day, she said good-night to her hostess and the other guests.

Was Alejandro aware that his mother wanted him to marry Ofelia, she wondered as he escorted her back to the cottage. And, most of all, was it what he wanted? These and other thoughts were going through Jennifer's mind when she realized he had spoken to her.

"I'm sorry, I didn't hear what you said."

"You were miles away," Alejandro observed. "Did you enjoy the evening? You've hardly said a word for the last hour."

"I'm just a little tired," Jennifer excused herself. "I suppose I'm not used to dining this late. But, yes, I did enjoy the evening. Thank you."

They continued to walk in silence for a few more minutes, and they had almost reached the cottage when she gathered enough nerve to add, "Your cousin, Ofelia, seems very nice. I'd like to get to know her better."

She saw the corners of Alejandro's mouth curl as if he had been amused by her remark. "I'm afraid the two of you have very little in common," he said as they paused at the cottage door.

"Oh, I don't know. People don't really have to think alike to be friends," Jennifer retorted mildly.

"Or lovers."

Alejandro had spoken the words so softly that Jennifer wasn't sure she had heard him right. But when her gaze flew to his face she knew that her ears had not deceived her. Through half-parted lips she drew in her breath, and her heartbeat quickened as she read in his eyes that he was going to kiss her.

She could have turned away, slipped into the house, and in all probability Alejandro would have left her alone. The thought of doing so passed through her mind, but only fleetingly. She lacked the will to move. Instead she let Alejandro draw her pliant body into his arms.

Cupping her head in one hand, he let his eyes move slowly over her features until they fastened on her tremulous lips. Feeling the warm flush of sensual stirrings, Jennifer closed her eyes as his lips traced featherlike caresses on her cheeks. He teased her mouth with his own, briefly, tantalizingly, then moved away again. Leaning down, he kissed the curve of her neck, the pulse of her throat, prolonging the moment of fulfillment until she found herself wanting the taste of his kisses with every fiber of her being.

Jennifer's arms went around his waist, and with wanton excitement she pressed her body to his. One of his hands moved sensuously along her spine, while the other stroked her neck, her slender shoulders before it slipped under her blouse to cup her breast. Pushing aside the wisp of lace to expose her hardened nipple, his questing fingers fondled the sensitive tip until the heat that had been steadily growing inside her flared and spread through her body like fire. He was driving her wild with his caresses, yet giving her nothing to mitigate her desire. "Oh, Alex!" Jennifer breathed raggedly as she clung to him, wanting and waiting to quench her desire for the taste of him. She didn't notice that she had used his family's pet name for him. That this was the first time she hadn't addressed him as Mr. Adler.

"You're so beautiful," Alejandro whispered huskily. Still holding her close, he stroked her cheek gently, sensuously. "So very beautiful that a man might sell his soul to the devil just to hold you like this."

She waited for his kiss, and when it didn't come, she opened her eyes. To her utter surprise she found that passion no longer burned in his own; it had been replaced by something else—a calculating look that Jennifer was unable to understand. She bit her lower lip to stop the cry that threatened to escape. Just at that moment he released her and took one step back. "Good night, Alba," was all he said.

Trembling with need, her mind still refusing to believe what had just happened, Jennifer watched him turn and walk away. She stood there for an endless moment, barely able to keep from calling after him. Then she turned around, blindly managing to open the door and rush inside the cottage.

She went straight to the bedroom, where she stood before the mirror, pressing the icy palms of her hands against her burning cheeks and staring hard at her reflection as if it were that of a stranger. A convulsive tremor went through her as she again felt the warmth of Alejandro's hands on her body. Oh, God, how could she have let something like that happen? She had almost begged for his kiss, she had wanted him so. Without love, she had responded to his caresses, and in the heat of passion she had been willing to give herself to him. How she had wanted him!

JENNIFER WAS STILL tossing and turning in her bed hours later, unable to get those moments in Alejandro's arms out of her fevered mind.

"Damn him!" she muttered for the millionth time that night. He must have purposely aroused her to passion. Had it been just to prove his supreme male dominance? Whatever the reason, Jennifer couldn't forget or forgive; that made two scores she had to settle with him. At the moment she hated him more than ever, she told herself, more than she had ever dreamed she could hate another human being. But most of all she felt betrayed by her own body, which still clamored for the man.

"Damn him!"

She tried to think of something else, but in her mind's eye Tommy's face, tormented, haunted as she had last seen it, was supplanted by Alejandro's compelling and proud one.

Too restless to remain in bed any longer, she threw the covers aside at last and got up. But even the walls of the cottage seemed to close in on her. What she needed was space, and the healing solace of nature. Without bothering to throw a robe over the ice-blue satin nightgown she had worn to bed, she went out into the moonlit garden.

The soft chirping of crickets was the only sound to disturb the pervasive quiet as Jennifer strolled barefooted on the damp grass among the willows. From this vantage point, high up the mountain, she could see the lights of the city blinking in the distance.

As she prowled through the grounds she had no idea of the picture she made in her gown that reflected the moonlight, with her long silver hair undulating down her back. All she knew was that both her body and soul were in torment. And when she came upon the darkened pool and watched the steam rising from the water as it mingled with the cool night air, in her mind it became a source of purification where she would find peace. As if hypnotized, she slipped the straps of her gown off her shoulders and let it fall to the ground. Then she poised on the edge of the pool for a moment before she plunged in.

A strong swimmer, Jennifer stayed underwater for almost the length of the pool, emerging only to fill her lungs with air. Then she dove under again and swam back, eventually doing laps across the pool in long strokes that became more leisured as she grew tired. Fighting the thoughts that kept tumbling through her mind, she finally turned on her back and looked up at the full moon. Through the ages the moon had witnessed many deeds and rituals of the human race. What would it think of her now, she wondered.

The scent of flowers made her moonlit pool a magical place. The tension slowly flowed from her body as she floated in the warm liquid. Finally she felt at peace, and she swam almost soundlessly toward the edge.

Water streaming down her naked body made it glisten in the moonlight as she climbed the steps of the ladder. As the night air caressed her she was suddenly chilled, and wished she'd brought a towel. But nothing could dispel the deep relief and contentment that she felt as she strolled toward her abandoned gown. Before she could reach it, however, the tip of a cigarette glowing in the dark drew her attention. She looked up in alarm to see a tall, familiar figure silhouetted against the night. Suddenly frozen, she watched as the figure turned and dissolved in the shadows.

All at once she was cold, cold to the very marrow of her bones. Picking up the gown, she ran back to the cottage and hurried inside, locking the door behind her. She took a hot shower and towel dried her hair, then lay in bed thinking about Alejandro's behavior. What could he possibly have been doing at the pool at such an hour of the morning?

The obvious answer made her smile suddenly to herself. But of course. He hadn't been able to sleep, either. And in that case it wasn't unreasonable to assume that he had been more affected by their earlier episode than he'd wanted to admit.

Alejandro found her beautiful; he had told her so. Would he really be tempted to sell his soul to the devil for her, she wondered. But he wouldn't have to. The devil had already taken possession of it the day Alejandro framed an innocent man to save himself.

IT WAS LATE the next morning when Jennifer finally awoke. Grateful that she didn't have to go to the main house until the afternoon, she opted for fixing her own breakfast rather than sharing another meal with the Adler family.

After slipping on a pair of jeans and a white knit top, Jennifer briskly brushed her hair, gathered it in a knot and pinned it on top of her head. Then, barefooted, she padded into the small pantry where she searched through the cupboards until she found a bowl and a frying pan.

Since there was no bacon to be had, some scrambled eggs would do nicely, she decided as she broke the shells and dropped their contents into the bowl. Before she began beating them with a fork, she put a dab of butter in the frying pan, which she set on the electric hot plate.

The sudden burst of optimism she had experienced before going to sleep had completely vanished. No matter how much she may have affected Alejandro, the fact still remained that she herself was very much affected by him. The thought was a daunting one. What she should do—if she had any brains at all—was pack her bags and return to California without wasting another minute. Perhaps it wasn't too late to do what she should have done in the first place: hire a detective, a professional who would be able to expose Alejandro's illegal activities better than she could.

But then the whole argument she was having with herself was purely academic; she had no money, no papers, and the only reason she had not been arrested so far was because she had reached this working arrangement with Alejandro.

The butter was beginning to sizzle in the pan. Jennifer poured in the egg mixture and began stirring with the fork until it was cooked through the way she liked it, soft and creamy. Tommy liked his eggs very dry. She hated them that way, and the two of them had argued about it constantly....

Poor Tommy, Jennifer mused. *How can I be so callous as to worry about my own feelings when I'm in the midst of all this splendor and he's behind bars?*

No, she admonished herself, she shouldn't be so selfish. Even if she came out of the adventure with a few scars, it would all be worth it as long as her brother was vindicated.

After sliding the scrambled eggs onto a plate, Jennifer poured herself a glass of milk and sat down at the small dinette table. She was about to dig into her food when she heard someone knocking at the door. *Please don't let it be Alex,* she prayed as she got up to answer.

"Hi." Heidi was standing at the door, looking up at her with a tentative smile on her elfin face.

Trying to hide her dismay, Jennifer answered, "Hello, Heidi."

The girl held up the covered plate that she carried in her hands. "I brought you some tamales for breakfast, Miss Maitland."

"That's very nice of you. Thank you." Jennifer accepted the offering, hoping the girl would go away. But when the child stood there, obviously waiting for an invitation, she was unable to resist her impish charm in spite of her earlier resolution. "Won't you come in? I'm just having breakfast. Care to join me?"

"No, thank you, Miss Maitland." Leaving the door open, Heidi followed as Jennifer returned to the table. "I ate mine after we came back from church."

Church, Jennifer thought. The last time she'd been in church was at Jim's funeral service.

Trying to keep her mind away from that particular subject, she put the plate on the table and lifted the napkin. "Tamales, hmm?" Quizzically, she looked at the small bundles of tightly wrapped, waxy green banana leaves. They were completely different in appearance from the Mexican tamales so familiar to most Californians. A little bemused, she looked up again. "But for breakfast?"

"We always have them after church on Sundays," Heidi replied eagerly. "Everybody does. Tamales and chocolate."

Jennifer unwrapped one of the fragrant little parcels and cut a piece of the yellow dough center with her fork. Tentatively she tasted it. Olives, raisins, and bits of chicken and pork had been mixed together with ground corn, seasoned with garlic, and then wrapped and cooked in banana leaves. "Mmm, this is good."

"Daddy said you might not like them," Heidi confessed, grinning at the fact that she'd outguessed her father. "He said that you probably were used to Mexican ones."

Jennifer couldn't stop herself from asking, "And does he know you brought me these?"

She had her reply when Heidi became so engrossed in looking around the kitchen that she ignored the question. The evening before the girl had seemed almost relieved when Jennifer hadn't mentioned their earlier meeting. It was obvious she had been told not to come near Alejandro's guest. For what reason?

Out of respect for her privacy, or because Alejandro had other plans for her?

He wouldn't dream of keeping her as his mistress, not on the grounds of his estate, with his mother and his daughter in such proximity. Her only evening with the Adlers had been enough for Jennifer to know that these were not the kind of people who would create—or tolerate—such an unsavory situation.

Heidi was still looking a little uncomfortable, and to relieve the tension Jennifer commented, "You speak English very well. Did you learn it in school?"

The girl nodded.

"Perhaps I should be ashamed of myself," Jennifer shook her own head wryly. "After all the years I studied Spanish, I scarcely remember more than a few words of it. Will you help me practice, Heidi?"

Heidi bobbed her head again emphatically. "Daddy says you have to practice all the time so that you don't forget. That's why I have to speak German when we go visit my cousins."

Germans cousins, Jennifer repeated inwardly. Of course, Adler was a German name; it meant eagle. And that branch of the family must be where Alejandro had got his blue eyes and his height.

The real reason for Heidi's visit became apparent when she asked, "Is it true that you have been to Disneyland many times, Miss Maitland?"

"Mmm?" It took a moment for Jennifer to pull her attention back to her young guest. "Oh, sure, many times. As a matter of fact, my parents used to take me and my brother every year until we were teenagers.'' Realizing too late that she had given away a certain piece of information that she didn't want anyone in Colombia to know, she went on hurriedly, "Oh, how I loved watching the parades they have on New Year's day! The marching bands, all the cartoon characters who come to you and shake your hand.... You can have your picture taken with them, you know. It's a lot of fun.''

Resting her elbows on the table, Heidi cradled her chin in her hands and listened intently as Jennifer went on to tell her about the different attractions offered by the most famous amusement park in the world.

"I guess my favorite is It's a Small World," she reflected at last. "They have thousands of dolls in native costumes from all over the world, all singing the same song in their different languages. And it's such a happy song that no matter what mood you're in when you enter the pavillion, you always come out smiling. There's only one problem, though," she added. "That song keeps playing over and over in your mind for hours.''

When she spoke of the Haunted Mansion, Heidi interrupted, "Are they real ghosts?''

"Oh, of course not," Jennifer laughed. "But it's very spooky going through that dark tunnel and hearing all those creaking noises and chains rattling, I can tell you. Every time I go through it, I get goose bumps all over.''

"And your brother," Heidi gurgled with laughter, "did he get goose bumps, too?''

So she had not missed that bit of information after

all. Jennifer shook her head, knowing that children often heard more than adults wanted them to. "Yes, he did," she had to admit. Not wishing to attract the girl's curiosity any further, however, she went on, "But you know there are no real ghosts, don't you?"

Heidi nodded and was thoughtful for a moment before she asked, "Where do people go when they die, Miss Maitland?"

The totally unexpected question caught Jennifer by surprise. "Well, they say that if one has been good, one goes to Heaven," she hedged.

"*Abuela*, that's grandmother in Spanish, says my mama is there now," the child said quietly. "With the angels."

"I'm sure she is," Jennifer replied gently. She looked away, wondering how to tactfully change the subject. Her eye caught an unexpected movement, and she drew in her breath sharply.

Heidi in turn straightened up and turned abruptly to face the door. Her own eyes widened in surprise at the sight of her father standing there. The strange expression written on his face told them both that he had heard at least the last part of their conversation.

"Your grandmother is looking for you, *mi hija*," he told his daughter shortly.

Heidi edged away from the table and made her way to the door. The stiffness of her back was a clear sign of apprehension.

When Alejandro started to follow his daughter, Jennifer called, "Just a minute, Mr. Adler."

He turned and waited for her to speak.

"Heidi just brought me some breakfast," she said

defensively when she knew the little girl was out of earshot.

"She's been warned to leave you alone."

"What are you afraid of?" Jennifer threw at him angrily. "That I might contaminate her?"

He heaved a sigh of impatience. "Look, Heidi is a very willful child. She needs to be disciplined."

"A child needs to be loved, too, you know."

"There is no love in permissiveness, Miss Maitland. Only indifference."

Jennifer had to bite her lower lip to keep from retorting. She knew that Alejandro's argument was irrefutable, yet she was feeling dreadful as she watched him disappear through the door.

The man was implacable even with those he loved, she reflected with apprehension. How would he act toward his enemies—such as herself?

CHAPTER FOUR

EVEN AN AFTERNOON FULL OF SUNSHINE failed to improve Jennifer's disposition after her disagreement with Alejandro. The only reason she joined the others at the tennis court was that she didn't want him to think she was afraid of facing him after all that had transpired between them.

After the lovely gowns the women had been wearing the previous evening, she wasn't surprised to find them now in elegant sports clothes. Elvira Guzman wore a soft classic shirt made of tan silk and hand painted with a floral design, while Señora de Adler's petite trim figure looked very chic in a fluid long-sleeved dress with an intriguing wine-colored paisley print on a gray background. A matching scarf was tied dashingly around her shoulders. But it was Ofelia's smart tennis outfit that made Jennifer feel rather self-conscious about the plain sports attire she had on—all she had that was remotely suitable since she hadn't come to Colombia prepared to take part in this type of social event. She didn't realize that the cut of her yellow satin athletic shorts attractively molded her softly rounded hips and buttocks and displayed her long slender legs, or how the matching yellow tank top hugged her high youthful breasts. Instead she decided to pay a visit to some of the fashionable shops of Bogotá as soon as she could cash her expense check.

Clothes had never been very high on Jennifer's list of priorities. She paid extra for the privilege of living near the ocean—that was worth every penny. The maintenance of a car, a necessity rather than a luxury, was another one of her major expenditures from a paycheck that could only stretch so far. Living in Southern California, where the dress code was so relaxed that it was practically nonexistent, she suited her wardrobe to her simple life-style and the nature of her job. But one thing Jennifer had discovered in the short time she'd spent in Colombia was that the people of Bogotá were extremely fashion conscious. If she was going to be mingling with the elite—which seemed likely if she continued to be a guest in Alejandro's house—she might as well dress the part.

She couldn't help stealing a glance at her host's own tennis clothes. The white shorts he was wearing not only confirmed her earlier assessment of his strong muscular legs and thighs, their fit also allowed her a delightful view of the narrow hips and very sexy masculine contours his suits had been concealing until then. Seeing him for the first time without a jacket, Jennifer reluctantly had to admire his shoulders, so broad and powerful. And his sinewy arms, covered with a fine veil of hair as dark as that which she glimpsed curling on his chest, reminded her of the moments when those arms had been around her.

Playing doubles, with Monsignor Navarro as her partner, and Alejandro and Ofelia as their opponents, didn't help her equilibrium. Just watching Alejandro move on the other side of the net caused Jennifer to feel the same sensual stirrings she had experienced before, and this made her miss several shots that ordinarily she would have returned without much trouble.

What bothered her more than anything was that her instincts could refuse to accept the dictates of her reason. How could she feel such a strong physical attraction for a man she knew was guilty of such terrible deeds? Whom, by all rights, she should despise?

It had been easy for her to hate him before coming to Colombia and seeing him in the flesh. But now, no matter how many times she reminded herself of what he'd done, it was becoming more and more difficult for her to see him as the monster she had expected.

Perhaps she was too naive for this cloak-and-dagger business—certainly she was if she could be so easily taken by the handsome appearance of such a villain. And this was not a staged drama; real lives were involved, and among them, her own.

Ofelia proved to be a fair player, but Alejandro was better than he had claimed to be. For that reason, and given her present state of mind, Jennifer was relieved when the set was over. The final score came to six-love in favor of their opponents.

"I'm sorry," she said, feeling the need to apologize to the monsigner as they went over to the net to shake hands with the winners. "I'm afraid my game was really off today."

"Ah, don't worry about it, my dear," the clergy-

man replied cheerfully. "We all have our bad days."
Despite his valiant efforts on the courts, he seemed to
take their resounding defeat in stride.

Yes, but this one is worse than most, Jennifer said
inwardly as she approached the net, where Alejandro
and Ofelia were waiting. She wanted to leave abruptly rather than feign good sportsmanship. It wasn't
that she minded losing; in reality, she couldn't care
less about that. But she strongly resented the arm
that Alejandro had so casually looped around
Ofelia's shoulders, and the way the young Colombian woman was smiling up at him.

Distractedly she heard someone say, "Congratulations." The monsignor was shaking hands with Alex,
and with a smile that was more of a grimace Jennifer
had to accept Ofelia's own handshake. Only last
night she had felt a certain sympathy for the girl, and
now she was almost hating her. Hating her for all the
things she had in common with Alejandro, for the
ease with which she stood so close to the man Jennifer herself wanted.

She caught her breath as she realized what she had
admitted to herself. And it was true—she wanted
Alex.

Having recognized her feelings for what they were,
Jennifer was suddenly afraid to touch him. Her hand
was actually trembling when he took it in his own—
the very hand that had so intimately caressed her.
The weakness she abruptly felt in her legs had absolutely nothing to do with the physical workout
she'd just had.

"Come on, I'll buy you a drink," he was saying

with a grin. "You look like you could use one."

He didn't let go of her hand, and she followed him off the court to the table from which the older women had watched the game, protected from the sun by a colorful striped umbrella. The four players dropped wearily onto chairs around the table and welcomed the tall frosty glasses of sangría that a servant brought to them.

Commenting on the set they had just finished, Alex and the monsignor lit cigarettes and stretched back in their chairs. Jennifer, meanwhile, sipped her drink in silence. She was in no mood for small talk, and after all that had happened between them, she didn't know how to act around Alejandro.

And she was sitting next to him! She tried to keep her eyes away from his hands, which she so vividly remembered the feel of. How could she pretend last night hadn't happened when she could think of nothing else? It was becoming an obsession. Her mind kept playing the same scene over and over, and she was powerless to stop thinking that if only he had kissed her, she would have at least resolved some unsatisfied question within her. As it was, he had left her to wonder and want.

He was cruel, she told herself, and she was crazy to want him. Why, of all the men in the world, did she have to desire him? Because there was no other word for what she felt for him. . . .

She was startled by the deep voice that said close to her ear, "Don't be such a sore loser."

Turning her head, she found Alejandro's face was only inches away. So out of touch had she been with her surroundings for a moment, she hadn't realized the two of them had been left alone.

"I'm not a sore loser," she laughed—a nervous laugh.

"Then you're giving a pretty good imitation, Miss Maitland." Irony or humor—Jennifer wasn't quite sure which—curled the corners of Alejandro's mouth when he asked, "Or is something else bothering you?"

He knows. Jennifer's annoyance was mainly directed at herself for being so transparent. *He knows how I feel, and he's laughing at me.* "Yes, something *is* bothering me," she replied dryly. Trying to save face, she asked, "What did you do to Heidi?"

He smiled and took a sip of his wine before replying, "Oh, I beat her within an inch of her life and threw her in a dungeon. You may never see her again."

She gave him a puzzled look, then exclaimed, "Oh, be serious!"

"But I am serious," Alejandro protested with a poker face, yet his eyes were laughing. "That's what you expected, wasn't it?"

Whatever Jennifer was going to say completely slipped her mind when his gaze dropped to her mouth and remained there as if he was fascinated. His eyes finally released her lips, only to wander slowly, sensually over her face—with such intensity that it momentarily stopped her breath. When they moved again—to the curve of her neck, to the pulse that was beating wildly at the base of her throat, to the swell of her bosom—Jennifer could feel his touch just as vividly as if it were physical.

With a strange sense of unreality, she felt everything around them dim and recede into the background, then quickly vanish as Alejandro made love to her with his eyes in a way Jennifer would have never believed possible. It was a giddy sensation to be touched like this, to be aware of the response of every nerve in her body to the caresses that only existed in their minds. Her taut nipples strained against the thin fabric of her tank top; it was this visual proof of her response to his open sensuality that made Jennifer's cheeks blaze, made her fight to recover control of her emotions.

She wanted to run away, but she didn't even have the strength to stand up, so rubbery were her legs at that moment. She was half dismayed, half relieved when she heard the others returning.

Ofelia was the first to join them. "Ready for another set?" Her question was addressed to Alejandro.

He turned to Jennifer, who shook her head and forced herself to answer, "I think I've caused enough damage for one day, thank you." She was surprised that her voice sounded almost normal.

Alejandro swung his gaze back to Ofelia and also shook his head. "Then I guess I'll sit this one out, too, cousin."

With a *moue* of disappointment Ofelia turned to the monsignor, who had sat down on the chair next to Jennifer. "Uncle?"

As he started to get up, Señora de Adler placed a discreetly restraining hand on her brother's arm.

"Oh, do go on, Alex," she said. "Give your uncle a chance to rest." She smiled and signaled to the servant to refill his glass of sangría.

This smooth maneuvering left Alejandro with little choice but to follow Ofelia back to the court.

Jennifer would have sighed in relief had she not been so tense in Mariana's company. She knew that sooner or later Alejandro's mother was going to give her another warning, however veiled, to keep away from her son. Perhaps the others had not taken notice of what had transpired between herself and Alex, but Jennifer was convinced that very little escaped Señora de Adler. She was wondering how to excuse herself gracefully when her hostess's voice broke into her thoughts.

"More sangría, Miss Maitland?"

When Jennifer looked up, she could read neither friendliness nor hostility in the unfathomable dark eyes. Unnerved, she stammered, "Y–yes, yes, thank you."

Señora de Adler was quiet while the servant refilled Jennifer's glass. Afterward, a tight smile accompanied her discerning gaze as she said, "You were right in declining that last game of tennis, Miss Maitland. You do look a little flushed. Are you feeling well, or is the altitude bothering you?"

Without thinking, Jennifer blurted out, "Oh, I'm all right, thank you." As soon as the words were out of her mouth she could have kicked herself. The woman had given her the perfect excuse to go back to the cottage, and she had missed her chance. What was worse, the monsignor had moved to a lounge chair under a tree, and was engrossed in a conversation with Elvira Guzman. That left her alone with Señora de Adler.

"Still, you must take care," Señora de Adler said. "The food, the water, everything here is different from what you are accustomed to."

Her tone was polite, concerned, but Jennifer was acutely aware of the underlying message.

For the next few minutes they sat in silence watching the players on the court. Then her companion observed casually, "Ofelia plays very well, don't you think, Miss Maitland?"

"Yes, she does," Jennifer admitted.

"She's a very accomplished young woman in every respect," the Colombian woman nodded with a complacent smile. "I think my son is fortunate."

This time, Jennifer could not pretend ignorance. "But is it a good idea for relatives to marry each other?" she asked, trying to mask her vexation.

Señora de Adler gave a little laugh, only there was no trace of amusement in her dark eyes, which did not waver even for an instant. It was Jennifer who had to look away. "They are only distantly related, Miss Maitland." After a brief but thoughtful pause, she added, "Perhaps it may be difficult for you to understand how important it is for a family like ours to marry into another with the right background, what we call *abolengo*. It's not simply a matter of wealth, it's the right combination of breeding and family tradition. That is why it sometimes becomes necessary to look among the members of our own extended families."

At Jennifer's silence, she continued, "The...situation does not develop often enough for it to become a problem, I assure you." She shrugged casually. "Both of my children found suitable partners elsewhere, and Alex's first marriage is another good example. We have no ties to his wife's family other than a long-standing friendship." She paused briefly before she went on, "We were all very happy about their union, and we felt her loss deeply, but it is time for Alex to marry again. He must have a son, and I can't think of anyone more suitable than Ofelia to give it to him."

With every passing second, Jennifer was becoming more and more uncomfortable. The conversation only served to confirm that Señora de Adler's dislike for her stemmed from the older woman's suspicions of a romantic entanglement between her and Alejandro. Momentarily irritated by the assumption, Jennifer almost blurted out that there was no possible danger that she'd try to snatch her precious son. She kept quiet instead. In a way, Mariana's instincts about her were right. Hadn't she traveled thousands of miles with the purpose of "snatching" Alex? Only not for the reasons his mother had in mind.

Her irritation was immediately tempered by pity for the woman. If things turned out in Jennifer's favor, she would manage to clear her brother. Señora de Adler would receive a terrible blow when that name she was so proud of was dragged through the mud.

"I didn't know you had other children," Jennifer commented, trying to veer the topic of conversation away from Alejandro.

"My daughter, Nancy, lives in Cali," Mariana replied, more amicably this time.

This abrupt change in attitude told Jennifer that Señora de Adler's reticence toward her was due only to her fears—fears that she would try to come between Ofelia and her son. Again, she felt sorry for the woman. "Is Nancy older or younger than Alex?" she asked.

"Younger by eight years," Mariana replied. "She and Carlos will be celebrating their tenth anniversary in the fall."

That meant Nancy had been eighteen at the time of her marriage, Jennifer calculated rapidly. At that same age, she had been planning a career rather than a wedding....

"I must admit I thought she was a little too young for marriage," the *señora* interrupted her thoughts. "She had planned to go to university and study medicine, but when she and Carlos met, all her career plans were put aside."

"And she never went back to school?" Jennifer inquired.

"No, she didn't. But I guess it's just as well. Carlos would not take kindly to her practicing a profession, especially with the children still so young."

"How old are the children now?"

"Carlitos is eight. Susana barely six."

She said no more, but she didn't have to. Jennifer could see that where children were concerned, the haughty grande dame became as doting a grandmother as any other woman would.

Jennifer felt herself reluctantly warming toward

Alejandro's mother. With a sinking feeling, she sat there listening to the older woman speak of her daughter and her grandchildren, while all the time she was wishing she could escape her own troubled conscience.

But it was not to be. That same guilt—guilt for the pain and suffering she was about to bring upon the heads of innocent people—kept her awake that night, until the small hours of the morning. She fell into an uneasy slumber then, full of restless dreams that made her toss and turn. Finally she cried out in her sleep, and woke up sitting in the middle of the bed and looking around her in confusion. In her befuddled state, it took her a moment to become aware of her surroundings.

In the pale gray light of dawn, the armoire loomed like a silent shadow in a corner of the room. She had left the window partly open before going to bed, and now she shivered in her white satin nightgown, which, damp with perspiration, clung to her body.

With a sigh she lay back on the pillows and pulled the covers up to her chin. Staring at the ceiling, she tried to decipher her dreams, but she had difficulty remembering them clearly. More vivid than anything else in her mind were the sounds she had heard in her dreams. They seemed to evoke that day when she had gone to La Gorgona to visit Tommy. She remembered how the idea of an island prison had frightened her. Where had they sent her brother? To a hell on earth, like the nefarious Devil's Island?

It had turned out that the prison was less gruesome than she had imagined. The inmates had to do work, of course, but there were parks and swimming pools, and other recreational activities for them.

At first glance, from the ship that had taken her there, the island had seemed like a tropical para- dise—except for the oppressive humidity. Jennifer's spirits had lifted a little as she crossed the entryway with two of the nuns who worked on the island. Sure- ly nothing very sinister could be happening to the prisoners if sisters were there. Even today she remem- bered that a sign at the gate had read, Work + Good Conduct = Freedom.

But once she'd heard the sound made by the steel door as it clanked shut behind her, Jennifer would never forget it. It had such finality to it that even though she was there as a visitor, she'd felt a panic, the need to run, to escape, even if it meant risking her life.

She had seen the same kind of desperation in the faces of the men trapped there, and she had to re- mind herself that not all of them were innocent like her brother. There were murderers and rapists, and others who killed not with weapons, but with drugs that could destroy lives just as effectively. She couldn't let her momentary pity make her forget their victims.

In spite of the natural beauty of the island, there had been signs everywhere to remind her of its real purpose: the wire fences, the watchtowers from where rifle-bearing guards could cover every corner of the yard. And there had been other even more sobering signs: crosses marking the graves of those who had tried to flee from that unwanted paradise. It had been the sight of those graves that had made Jennifer embark on this adventure. She knew Tommy well enough to know that he would rather die trying to escape than die a little each day while serving his long sentence. And for a crime he had not committed, which made it even worse. Sooner or later he would make a break for freedom.

He didn't belong in prison at all, Jennifer had wanted to shout at the world. She'd even tried to talk to the authorities, only no one believed her. The evidence against her brother had been far too damaging. Evidence provided by the man whose name she remembered crying out in her sleep. . . .

How convinced she had been of Alejandro's guilt, Jennifer reflected, stirring restlessly in her bed. That was before she knew him, before she'd been touched by him. Now she no longer knew how to judge him—with her heart, or with her head. Each one told her a different story. . . .

It didn't make sense for Alejandro to be involved in the traffic of narcotics. He certainly didn't need the money. Even if the business he had inherited from his father was not as profitable as she imagined, the estate he would one day receive from the Navarro family was even greater. So why would he bother with drugs? Why would he do something as terrible as that?

Maybe, it was power he was after, she thought ironically. She wouldn't be surprised; he seemed to know where people were most vulnerable. He had already extended his power over *her*—in a way she hadn't at all expected. . . .

FOR HER FIRST DAY on the job, Jennifer selected a suit of mauve linen. The simplicity of the cut made it elegant—tailored skirt and blazer that she wore over a blouse of slightly darker color. A bow tied loosely at the deep V neck added a soft touch of feminity.

Jennifer was so nervous that morning that she couldn't even eat breakfast. Her stomach was tied up in knots of tension at the thought of the challenge ahead of her. Still, she was glad the weekend was finally over. Since she had to spend time with Alejandro, she preferred to do it under professional circumstances. This was much safer from an emotional point of view; because at the rate she was going it wouldn't be too long before she wound up in Alex's bed. And she had no intention of doing that.

It was easy to make resolutions, but harder to keep them. Even though Alejandro had reverted to the conservative suit and white shirt that seemed to be the uniform of the businessmen of Bogotá, he was still vitally attractive. Sitting next to him in the back seat of the chauffeur-driven limousine, Jennifer had a hard time resisting the aura of virility that he radiated so unconsciously.

Alex seemed to invade all her senses. His recent shave had left his cheeks so smooth looking that Jennifer, who had never been an especially forward woman, had to keep herself from touching him. And the faint scent of his after-shave haunted her all the way into Bogotá.

Two Avianca stewardesses wearing *ruanas*, the native ponchos of Colombia, over their smart navy uniforms were leaving the building when the car pulled in front.

Inside, lines of customers had already formed at the airline ticket counters and at the post office. People were everywhere, coming and going across the lobby intent on their business. Jennifer and Alejandro went straight to the elevators and silently rode to the thirty-fifth floor.

The pretty young receptionist looked up from her work alertly the moment they stepped through the front door. Jennifer noticed immediately that it was not the same young woman who had been on duty during her previous visit to the office.

"Buenos días, Señor Adler," she said in greeting. The glance she sent in Jennifer's direction was full of interest. Alejandro answered pleasantly but continued on to his office without breaking his stride.

Mrs. Vargas got up from her desk as they came in, and again Jennifer was struck by the imposing presence of such a petite woman. This time she noticed that the fluorescent lights gave a blue cast to the woman's carefully coiffed black hair. Her good-morning was in English for Jennifer's benefit, but there was no smile accompanying it. The woman occupying a second desk continued typing, without looking up.

"Will you be so kind as have someone show Miss Maitland around the office and introduce her to the employees, Mrs. Vargas," Alejandro asked, after performing an introduction that was only a formality, since both women had met before. "Is her office ready?"

"Yes, Mr. Adler."

"Good," he nodded. "What's on my schedule this morning? Am I free for lunch?"

"You have a meeting at ten with Mr. Mendoza, and another at eleven with the salesman from Medellín," his executive assistant replied. "And there's a message from Mrs. Roman on your desk."

Alejandro nodded again. "Please make a reservation at the Vatel for Miss Maitland and me." He turned to Jennifer. "Is twelve-thirty all right with you?"

After she had nodded in silent assent, he added, "Please don't hesitate to let Mrs. Vargas know if there's anything you need."

"I won't," Jennifer replied. "Thank you."

"Come into my office when you've finished with Miss Maitland," Alex told his assistant. "I want to give some dictation." With that, he left them.

After the door had closed behind him, Mrs. Vargas turned around. "This way, Miss Maitland," she said.

Jennifer followed her out of the executive area and along a carpeted hallway that led to many smaller offices. The one they entered was far from being as luxurious as Alejandro's, but at least it had a view.

Thank heaven for small favors, she thought. If she was going to have to spend a whole day cooped up in an office, it was nice to have more than four walls to look at.

"If you care to leave your things here, I'll see that you are introduced to the other employees," Mrs. Vargas said.

Jennifer did as the older woman suggested, then followed her out into the hallway again. They went straight to the office next door. A young woman approximately the same age as Jennifer sat behind a desk leafing through a magazine, which she immediately put aside when it drew a disapproving glance from the formidable lady.

Sara López, Mrs. Vargas explained after she had introduced her, was secretary to Mr. Ricardo Tejeda, the general manager of Adler Exports and Alejandro's right-hand man. He was presently away on business, and Sara had little to do in his absence.

She was delighted at the prospect of having a non-routine task to take on, especially something of a social nature such as showing Jennifer around.

All the employees in the office were at least partially fluent in English, Sara explained. That was to be expected because of the nature of their business. The information relieved at least one of Jennifer's worries, since her Spanish was quite rusty. She hoped it wouldn't be for long. She had a good ear and wasn't afraid of making mistakes, since she knew that was the only way of learning another language. In the time she'd spent in Brazil, she had picked up an amazing amount of Portuguese.

Mrs. Vargas returned to her office, and the two young women were exchanging pleasantries when the door to the office opened and a boy came in, pushing a cart laden with a coffee service.

"This is Ramón," Sara said. "He's one of the most important people in the office, because he brings the coffee."

"Hello, Ramón," Jennifer said, smiling at the boy.

Sara had made the introduction in English, and now she spoke to the boy in Spanish, apparently translating what she had told Jennifer.

Ramón nodded emphatically and grinned at Jennifer. *"Empanada?"* he asked, offering a plate of pastries in the shape of turnovers.

Jennifer realized suddenly that she was quite hungry. After spending the afternoon with Alejandro and his relatives, she had declined their dinner invitation. Instead she had quickly put a light meal together in her cottage kitchen. She hadn't had breakfast that morning, so she was famished by this time. Without hesitating she accepted one of the pastries and tentatively bit into it.

The tasty crust, made out of corn flour, was filled with a savory mixture of ground beef and eggs. Mentally she noted that these little meat turnovers, or *empanadas*, as Ramón had called them, made very satisfactory breakfast food.

Next Ramón poured coffee—the dark brew she knew was called *tinto*—into tiny silver cups, one of which he handed to Jennifer.

Jennifer had already tasted Colombian coffee, and because she thought she was familiar with it, she promptly took a sip. The tiny silver cup was so hot, however, that it burned her lips. She blinked rapidly and her eyes watered.

Sara noticed that something was wrong. "Are you all right?" she asked in concern.

"Y-yes," Jennifer managed at last. "The cup—and the coffee—is very hot."

The Colombian woman immediately rushed to fill a glass from a water pitcher that was on the credenza behind her desk. "Here, drink this," she said.

Jennifer accepted the glass gratefully. The ice water effectively soothed the sting—at least momentarily. She wondered if her lips would blister.

"Those silver coffee cups are elegant but dangerous," Sara pointed out. "The very same thing happened to me the first time I had coffee here."

Their laughter seemed to break the ice between them. All at once the two of them were talking away, about the different coffee-break customs in their respective countries.

Although Sara was fluent in two languages— French and English—in addition to her native Spanish, she had never traveled abroad, she confessed. She had started saving a good portion of her salary to finance a trip to Europe—after her application for employment had been turned down by Avianca Airlines because she wasn't tall enough. Her parents had been relieved; they still thought of her as "their little girl."

Jennifer could believe that the airline hadn't accepted her. Although Sara was a very pretty brunette, whose brown eyes sparkled with life, she was scarcely five feet tall on her high heels. Even though Jennifer was only four inches taller than her new friend, she felt almost like an Amazon standing next to her.

Nor was she surprised to find out that Sara was twenty-one and still living at home. That was the custom in most Latin American countries, she knew.

Children left home only to marry and establish their own families.

Sara spoke of her older brother, Mateo, who was an attorney working for a firm housed in the very building they were in. She obviously wanted Jennifer to meet him and suggested eventually that perhaps all three of them could go out some evening after work.

Jennifer remained noncommittal. She liked Sara instinctively, but she was tired of blind dates being forced upon her and she wasn't ready to accept this brother sight unseen. Still, she decided, it would be nice to have friends outside the Adler circle. Real friends she could relax with.

Their tour of the offices didn't take very long. The other employees Jennifer met were polite but reserved. At least on the surface, there was none of the easy camaraderie that existed in American offices. But then, the influence on the country was more European than American, the relationships more formal.

Later on she would be visiting the warehouses, Jennifer learned. In addition to textiles, the firm's main export was the coffee produced on the Navarro lands and by a few other coffee growers. Ricardo Tejeda, Sara's boss, was in charge of the warehouses.

Jennifer took mental notes of every facet of the operation as Sara explained it. She would have to get to know Mr. Tejeda and gain unrestricted access to the warehouses if she was ever going to discover who was using the Adler shipments to smuggle narcotics....

Not until Jennifer returned to her own office much

latter did she realize that, in her mind, she was already believing in Alejandro's innocence. She couldn't absolve him of suspicion as easily as this, she assured herself quickly. But on the other hand, she would have to keep an open mind if she was going to learn the truth. He was still her prime suspect, true, but there were others who might be responsible instead.

As Alejandro had promised, the window in her office offered a view of the park across the street, except from the thirty-fifth floor all she could see were the tops of the trees. For some reason it became terribly important to Jennifer to remember the name of the park in question, as if in doing so she could postpone all those other distressing thoughts. All too soon, it came to her, however: Parque Santander. She was immediately sorry she had remembered so quickly.

With a sigh, she turned from the window and glanced at the stack of catalogs and magazines someone had left on her desk while she was on the tour with Sara.

At the beginning her main concern had been to land the job. Now that she'd been hired, she had to learn how to perform whatever chores a purchasing consultant was supposed to do.

She glanced at her watch. She still had two more hours to kill before she met with Alejandro again.

CHAPTER FIVE

"MISS MAITLAND?"

Jennifer looked up from the catalog she was leafing through. A young man was standing at the door, and he looked a little uncertain.

"Yes?" she asked kindly.

The fellow gestured with the envelope he carried in his hand. "This is for you," he said.

She motioned him to come in and accepted it with a smile. "Thank you," she said.

Jennifer examined the bulky envelope with curiosity. Her name was written on it in a bold hand unfamiliar to her. She waited until the lad had gone before she ripped it open and almost gasped when she found it was full of Colombian currency. No explanatory note had been included, but she didn't need to be told where the money had come from.

Jennifer counted the bills, which were of different denominations. Even though she wasn't sure what the equivalent amount would be in American dollars, she was certain the sum was considerable. Once again Alejandro Adler had been generous in his dealings with her. Jennifer had expected to be paid by check, having forgotten the difficulties she would have encountered in cashing the draft without proper identification papers. But he had remembered.

This served as another reminder to her that she was going against a very formidable enemy, one who didn't let any details escape him, no matter how insignificant. If there had been any doubt left in her mind, Jennifer knew now that it would not be easy to prove his guilt.

Through the open door of her office she saw the other employees file by toward the lobby. She didn't have to consult her wristwatch to know it was lunchtime.

A few minutes later Sara paused at the door and poked her head in. "How about some lunch?" she called.

"Thanks," Jennifer smiled, "but I've already made other plans. How about tomorrow?"

"Fine," Sara nodded. "I usually go home, but there's a new restaurant nearby that I've been meaning to try. See you later." Sara waved and disappeared, and Jennifer returned her attention to the catalogs.

She didn't have to wait long before Alejandro came to collect her. And as they left the office together, she didn't miss the attention they drew from the few employees they passed.

Alex's chauffeur was waiting, and he opened the car door as they emerged from the building. Jennifer climbed in first, followed by Alejandro. They had hardly exchanged three words since he had come for her, and she waited for him to speak after the car was in motion. His mind seemed to be elsewhere, however.

"Thank you for the advance," she said at last, mostly because she felt uncomfortable with their silence. "Isn't there a receipt or something I should sign?"

In the level glance that he gave her, Jennifer saw that she now had his full attention.

"There's no need," he replied with a shrug of his shoulders. "We have a verbal agreement. I'm sure you'll keep your end of the bargain just as I'll keep mine. By the way," he went on, almost as an afterthought, "if you need any help replacing your papers, you will let me know, won't you? I'll do everything I can to help."

Her heart constricted suddenly and she couldn't help the nervous start she gave. He was looking at her narrowly, and Jennifer felt at once that he was baiting her; that he knew she had no intention of going to the embassy....

"You've done so much already," she replied evasively. "But I'll keep it in mind." With the tip of her tongue she nervously licked her lower lip. Her action drew Alejandro's attention to her mouth. As his eyes remained focused there, her heart began to thud helplessly against her ribs. Luckily, they were arriving at the restaurant. The car wheeled up a circular driveway and came to a halt, effectively distracting them.

El Gran Vatel, located halfway up a hill, offered a marvelous view of the city—a jumble of colonial-style roofs pierced by modern towers of concrete and steel surrounded by mountains. Jennifer could hardly tear her eyes from the fascinating sight to examine the menu. When she finally did so she discovered that, like many of the most exclusive restaurants in Bogotá, it featured Continental cuisine. So far, the meal she'd had with the Adlers had been her only opportunity to sample the native dishes.

"See anything you like?" Alejandro asked after she had been staring at the menu for a while.

Jennifer hesitated. Although not all the items were familiar to her, she was far from being mystified when faced with a menu in French. More than bewilderment over the delicacies listed, her indecision was due to the still unsettled condition of her nerves. Her mind seemed unable to retain anything she was reading.

"Would you like me to order for you?" Alejandro offered at last.

What a ninny he must think her, she thought with not a little amount of annoyance. She'd have to make an effort to stop feeling so gauche. Every time she was alone with Alex, she acted as if she'd never left Newport Beach High School. It was ridiculous. Nothing even remotely similar had ever happened to her with a man before.

Feigning indifference while Alejandro selected from the menu and then proceeded to discuss the wine list with the steward, Jennifer was very much aware of each of his words and gestures. He always appeared so much in control of every situation, such a man of the world, she decided almost enviously.

A dry and clean tasting white burgundy—a product of Meursault, in France, she had heard the wine steward tell Alex—accompanied the delicate salmon mousse, which was topped with thinly sliced cucumbers set in aspic.

"How was your morning?" Alejandro asked as they began to eat. "Did you have a chance to look at the catalogs I sent you?"

"Yes, I did," she replied, and proceeded to chatter about various products that had caught her fancy.

Their empty plates were taken away by a waiter and replaced by the main course. A deliciously fragrant sauce enhanced the pot-roasted leg of lamb, which was served with a tempting array of vegetables. Unobtrusively, their empty glasses were replaced by clean ones and filled with red wine.

"This Bordeaux is one of my favorites," Alejandro said conversationally. "I hope you like it."

Jennifer raised the glass to her lips. He had selected well, she noted without surprise. The wine was dry and hearty.

"It's very good," she had to admit. "Of course, I'm not much of a connoisseur."

"I thought Californians were fond of wine," he said. The corner of his mouth curled in a faint smile.

"Well, it's true Americans are drinking more wine now than ever before," she replied, picking up her fork again. "And in California we're proud of the recognition the quality of our wines is already earning around the world. Still, a glass of white wine every now and then is more my speed."

Their conversation during the entrée was desultory; that of two temporary allies aware that the tenuous truce existing between them was ephemeral and that they had to take pains to avoid provoking each other with a careless remark.

As the meal progressed, however, Jennifer felt her tension begin to lessen. The change was so subtle, so elusive, that when she thought about it later, she didn't know at what point the conversation became easier and she found herself truly enjoying Alejandro's company.

He was well informed and educated, and proved to be a fascinating conversationalist. A man who, secure of his masculinity, had that special gift few men possess—to make a woman more aware of her own femininity, and be glad she was a woman.

In answer to some of her comments, Alejandro spoke of the years he had spent in the United States as a student. The subject arose naturally. For some reason or other, they had found themselves discussing housing, and Jennifer mentioned how much she liked her ocean-front apartment.

Alex asked if she lived in one of those "singles only" apartment complexes, which during his student days had been starting to spring up everywhere.

"No, I suppose I'm not the swinging type," she laughed spontaneously. "I'm afraid television and the movies have created a very distorted image of California living. Some of us lead quite ordinary lives, I assure you. As a matter of fact, the building where I live is not even restricted to adults. There are lots of families—three on my own floor."

"Don't the children disturb you?" he inquired.

"They're well behaved for the most part," Jennifer replied. "Of course, they have the beach to play on, but as far as I know, no one in the building has had a reason to complain about them." When Alejandro made no comment, she asked, "Is that the reason why you wouldn't let Heidi come to the cottage? Because you thought I would object?"

"You seemed upset when you found out she'd be there. I assumed you were concerned about your privacy."

Jennifer colored slightly. It was true she had been upset, but not for the reason he had just given. "Did you—" she began. "I mean, I hope she wasn't punished."

"She disobeyed," he replied, nodding. "And that I can't allow. A few of her privileges were temporarily suspended, but she'll survive."

Jennifer shook her head. "I can't help feeling a bit responsible."

"You're not."

"Perhaps, but still—"

"Look, it wasn't only her going to the cottage," he said quietly. "I also found out she'd been riding outside the area where she is allowed to go on her own."

Jennifer refrained from admitting that she had suspected as much.

"Heidi knows perfectly well what she's allowed to do and what not." Alejandro continued. "It is not an arbitrary rule that I've made, either—her safety may be at stake if she wanders too far. My mother has a tendency to spoil her, and I'm afraid she always takes advantage of her grandmother's visits, to see how much she can get away with."

"Doesn't your mother always live with you and Heidi?" Jennifer asked.

Again Alex shook his head. "Her visits have been longer and more frequent in the last few years," he replied. Jennifer knew he was avoiding any mention of the loss of his wife. "She has her own home right here in the city, but most of her time is divided between my sister, Nancy, and me."

"Yes, she mentioned that your sister lives in Cali. She also told me a little about her and the children." As an afterthought, Jennifer added, "It's a pity she had to give up her schooling after she married."

"She made her own choice," Alejandro shrugged. Casually, he asked, "Have you ever been married?"

"No, I haven't," Jennifer answered promptly. They had finished eating, and she was feeling a little light-headed. She was surprised to see that her wineglass was again empty.

She realized then how easily this man had manipulated her once again. The food, the wine, the view—even that warm appreciative gaze of his was designed to induce a false sense of security and loosen up her tongue. And it had almost worked.

Worriedly chewing her lower lip, Jennifer tried to think back. How much had she given away of what she didn't want Alejandro Adler to know?

But perhaps she was just being paranoid. After all, his question had been a perfectly natural one between two people who were just getting to know one another. Still, she would feel better discussing something less personal than the romantic aspects of their lives. She harbored no illusions. She was no match for

Alejandro when it came to intrigue, and she needed all her wits about her to avoid those traps he was so adept at setting for her.

"Isn't it time to get back to the office?" she inquired after glancing at her watch. It was only then that she realized they had spent more than two hours together.

Alejandro also consulted his watch. "There's plenty of time," he said. He motioned to the waiter anyway, and the check was brought to him as they were finishing their coffee. He signed it, and they left the restaurant escorted by the headwaiter, who was profuse in his encouragement that they come back again to grace the establishment.

"The pace is slower here than it is in the United States," Alejandro told her once they were installed back in his car. "The midday break is long enough to allow employees to go home for lunch if they want to. We don't resume work until 2:30."

"Then that will give me time to do some shopping during lunch hour," Jennifer commented.

"Hardly," Alex replied. "You see, all the shops are closed during that time as well."

"Oh," she said lamely. What on earth was she going to do with all that time on her hands in the middle of the day? The *quinta* was too far from the city to think of commuting.

Once again Alejandro was sensitive to her dilemma. "If you like, you may use my apartment," he suggested.

"Your apartment?" Jennifer echoed, a little appalled not only by the offer, but by the knowledge that he maintained a bachelor apartment in town. She shouldn't have been surprised. After all, he was unentangled—as far as she knew—and far too attractive to be sleeping alone every night.

A name she had overheard that morning and filed away in her memory came back to her then. Mrs. Roman. For some unexplained reason, Jennifer suspected that the woman's involvement with Alejandro didn't have anything to do with business.

The fact that he was discreet enough to keep his liaisons from his mother and daughter confirmed Jennifer's earlier belief. Alex would not try to make her his mistress as long as she was living in the cottage, which he considered an extension of his roof. However, would he still feel bound by his honor if she accepted the use of his bachelor apartment?

"Sometimes I have to stay downtown until late in the evening," he explained. "When that happens during the week, I'd rather sleep at the apartment than drive to the *quinta*. But I rarely use it during the day. You're welcome to go there if you wish."

"That's very kind of you," she replied noncommitally. Perhaps she should have refused, but something—curiosity, or jealousy perhaps—kept her from closing that door entirely.

Alejandro obviously took her response as acceptance. He reached into his pocket and detached a key from the ring. "Here's the key, then," he said, holding it out to her. "The chauffeur will know the address."

Jennifer was too flustered to speak as she accepted the key, but he didn't seem to notice. "By the way," he continued, "I won't be driving home with you tonight. I'm placing a car and a chauffeur at your disposal, so you'll be free to do your shopping at leisure. The downtown stores close at six, so I suggest that you visit Unicentro instead. The shops in that center are open during the evening, and you'll probably find everything you need. Moreover, there's no danger of having your purse snatched again while you're there. Unfortunately, that's a very common problem we have here in Bogotá.

The car, which had pulled onto a side street, parked by a modernistic granite building. Jennifer noticed curiously that it had been built very near an old church. She recognized the church, Iglesia de la Tercera, she had already admired its beautiful altar, executed entirely in gold.

"I thought that, after my uncle told you about the legend of El Dorado, you'd like to visit the Gold Museum," Alejandro explained at the inquiring look she gave him.

He dismissed the car after she had alighted. They were within walking distance of the Avianca Building, which was practically across the street, just past the Parque Santander.

While Alejandro went to the admissions window to purchase tickets, Jennifer glanced at the notices listing the times when the tours, offered both in English and Spanish, were scheduled to depart. The next one was about to begin. A sign indicated that they were now near the administration offices of the museum.

In the middle of the salon, a guide, a very attractive young woman dressed in a blue skirt and blazer and a white blouse, was gathering a group of American tourists.

"We're just in time for the next tour," Jennifer said excitedly as Alejandro approached her with the tickets. "Another five minutes and we would have had a long wait."

He took her by the arm as they joined the group of tourists, and the gesture felt completely natural.

"If I had known we were coming, I would have brought my camera," she whispered, eyeing the paraphernalia many of their tour companions carried with them. However, a few seconds later the entire group was informed that taking pictures of the collection would not be allowed.

"Ladies and gentlemen," the tour guide said, calling the group to order. "Welcome to the Museum of Gold of Colombia."

The museum, the woman went on to explain as they began their ascent of a wide staircase, was under the direction of the Banco de la Republica. The objects they were about to see—over 27,000 of them—were what had survived several centuries of the systematic melting down of artistic treasures for their gold value, first by the Spanish conquerors and later by the Republic itself for the manufacture of coins. Only as recently as 1939 had this practice ceased, and the museum been established for the preservation of those national treasures for their artistic and historical significance more than for their intrinsic value.

The objects bore evidence to the highly developed skills of artisans from many different Indian tribes before the advent of the Europeans, she went on. Some of the pieces had been worn as ornaments, while others had been used in ancient religious ceremonies.

By this time the group had reached the second floor, where they assembled to examine the first display.

The guide explained the significance of the items, which to Jennifer looked like gold-plated brassieres. She was not far off the mark, since that was what they were. Only they weren't gold plated, they were made of solid gold....

She and Alejandro chuckled when they overheard a young member of the group joking about how uncomfortable they must have been to wear. "Not exactly the eighteen-hour bra," was the comment.

In a country where high mountain ranges separated its peoples, different styles of workmanship had developed. In regions where gold was found in abundance, the objects were executed in pure gold. Others, who had to trade for the gold, had compounded the precious metal with a copper alloy called *tumbaga*.

The tour guide pointed out the different styles of workmanship as they examined the display cases along the length of the salon. Delicately filigreed earrings, nose guards of complicated designs, pendants with sculptured faces—each item was a minute marvel of superb workmanship and attention to detail.

Many animals were represented, figures of eagles, snakes, birds—creatures of the land, which had once been offered to the god of the Sacred Lake. At this point, the guide narrated the Legend of El Dorado, which Jennifer had already heard. They ended up at the display case containing the prize possession of the museum—the Muiscan barge. It was the one artifact that had confirmed the famous legend, and so precious was it to Colombians that it had never been allowed outside the country.

After they had admired the barge for a while the guide opened a door at the end of the salon and said, "Ladies and gentlemen, please step this way."

Jennifer, who thought the tour had ended, hesitated at the entrance of the room, which had been left in total darkness.

"Come along," Alejandro encouraged, taking her by the hand. "It's all right."

The voice of the guide, instructing the group to move along and make room for those behind, rose over the sound of footsteps and casual chatter. In addition to the suspense, Jennifer was conscious of the warm arm Alejandro had placed around her waist, of the imprint of his hand, and how their bodies touched. Her right shoulder rested against his chest—she knew it even in the dark because she could feel the steady beating of his heart. She felt the pressure of his hip, the muscles of his thighs and legs against hers as the group crowded forward to hear the guide.

Trying to steady her nerves she took a deep breath, but Alejandro was so close that it only served to make her even more aware of his clean masculine scent.

The rest of the group kept moving in and surrounding them, but Jennifer heard their hushed voices, the nervous coughs and muffled laughter only vaguely. All her senses were concentrated on the strength and warmth of Alejandro's body as he held her against him.

With his hand at her waist, he must have sensed the treacherous signals of her body—the accelerated heartbeat, the tensing of her stomach muscles—because he leaned forward, and his lips touched her ear as he whispered, "Are you afraid of the dark?"

Jennifer closed her eyes for a second. Even the wine she had consumed earlier hadn't made her feel such heady sensations as the warmth of his breath. It played havoc with her responses as it brushed her earlobe and the very sensitive area behind it. He was waiting for her answer. Fortunately, even if she'd been able to give one, the collective gasp that exploded at that moment would have muffled her words. The lights had suddenly been turned on, and as the tourists' eyes grew accustomed to the change, everyone exclaimed aloud at what they saw. They were standing in the middle of a circular vault, and on the walls, from the ceiling, in every direction hundreds, thousands of small gold pieces danced and glittered before their eyes. Earrings, tools, frogs—frogs everywhere; lizards, nose ornaments, necklaces of intricate design. Everyone was completely dazzled and naturally so. It was the most extraordinary collection of golden objects that had ever been assembled in one place.

It was like a dream. The feeling of unreality was so intense, so fantastic, that for a moment no one was able to speak coherently. And then, all at once, everyone seemed to recover and began pointing out different objects with great excitement.

They were allowed several minutes for a closer appreciation of the objects, and then the tour ended and the group was taken to the nearest exit.

Once outside the building, Jennifer walked along in silence for a while. She was in a daze, so wonderful had the display been. Yet their return to the office would mark the end of an afternoon that to her had been a mixture of pleasure and torture.

As they crossed the street, a *mota*—the Colombian counterpart to the American meter maid was called that, Alex explained, because of the motorcycles they rode—was writing out a parking ticket. Jennifer noticed that the pretty young woman had added the feminine touch of a silk scarf to break the severity of her uniform—navy trousers and a vest worn over a white shirt.

Jennifer was glad to have Alejandro at her side as they crossed the Parque Santander. The confusion there was just as he had described it to her. A disgruntled speaker was voicing his discontent with the conservative government to an audience of one, a very old man who, although looking extremely bored, nodded his head every now and then.

A collection of birds for sale were squawking and screaming. Jennifer recognized the colorful parrots and toucans, but others she'd never seen before.

A photographer with an old-fashioned camera, complete with black drape, was taking a picture of a pretty Indian woman who was holding a parrot in her hand. Jennifer had to stifle a giggle. The woman was doing her best to keep still, as the photographer must have instructed, but the mischievous bird was pecking at the brim of the jaunty dark derby she wore over her braids.

"Would you like to have your picture taken?" Alejandro offered.

"With the parrot?" Jennifer laughed.

"How else?" he replied with humor.

"All right," she agreed. "But only if you pose with me."

He shrugged. "It's a deal."

They waited until the photographer had finished with his customer, and then holding the parrot between them, they stood in front of the camera.

"Ouch!" Jennifer winced when the picture was finally taken and they were able to relinquish the bird. The talons of the large creature had dug into her finger as she handed it back to its owner.

Before she could react, Alejandro had taken her hand and was examining the wound. A drop of blood had formed on her finger.

Jennifer's stomach muscles tensed again as he lifted her trembling hand to his mouth. Unable to look away from the hypnotic gray eyes, she could only shiver as he sucked the blood from the tip of her finger. She felt the touch of his tongue on her fingertip, and at the same time, as if suffocating, she drew in her breath.

The photographer was the one to break the spell between them. The man had returned the offending bird to his perch and was now giving Alejandro a claim ticket for the photographs, which he put in his pocket.

"I asked for two copies," he said casually, taking her arm again as they walked away. "One for you and one for me. I assume you would want a keepsake of this afternoon?"

"Yes. . .yes, of course," she managed to get out. As if she needed a souvenir to remember any of it!

Flower sellers called to them as they went on, but nothing else in the park could distract Jennifer from the erratic thoughts that kept going through her mind. Only after they left the elevator on the thirty-fifth floor was she able to thank Alejandro for lunch and for the visit to the Gold Museum. She tried to keep her voice and the expression on her face from revealing the confusion she felt, and after they parted she applied herself diligently to her work for what was left of the afternoon.

If not for the doubt she felt about Alejandro and the need to free her brother, Jennifer would have found her new occupation rather pleasant. It would be like going on a shopping spree—without having to worry about exceeding her budget.

Sara joined her during the afternoon coffee break. "So how was lunch?" she inquired after she had settled in the chair across from Jennifer's desk. "I hear that the big man himself took you out."

Jennifer didn't want any talk about her involvement with Alejandro circulating around the office. "We had business to discuss," she said simply.

She didn't elaborate on the subject, since it would only serve to increase Sara's suspicions in that direction. But there was a lot Sara could tell her, she was sure, about Alejandro, about other people in the office who might have played a part in incriminating her brother.

For once luck was in her favor. Sara was not adverse to sharing a little gossip. Nothing malicious—it wasn't in her nature—but she was very observant and was interested in people.

The new receptionist became their first topic. Nothing of interest there, Sara reported. However her predecessor, Regina Quintana, had been another story. Apparently the girl had left her job because she'd found a generous protector who was willing to keep her in the style she wanted to become accustomed to. There was still quite a bit of speculation going on around the office as to the identity of the generous lover who had freed the beautiful Regina from the bonds of labor.

Jennifer tried to picture the young woman Sara was telling her about. All she could remember was how perfectly made-up her face had been. But since she had been so nervous at the prospect of facing Alejandro with her outrageous proposition, she had failed to pay too much attention to the girl's looks.

Most of the men, except for the very young ones, were married, Sara warned. And had children. She didn't know about the others, but she suspected that her own boss, Ricardo Tejeda, was having an affair. About this she swore Jennifer to secrecy.

Jennifer made a point of dropping Mrs. Roman's name casually during the conversation. The only person by that name Sara knew of was Leticia

Roman. Could it be the same? Jennifer didn't know.

Leticia Roman had been one of the first women in Colombia to take advantage of the recently established divorce law. The daughter of a successful businessman, she had traveled abroad after shedding her unwanted husband, and she had lived there for almost two years before returning to Bogotá and opening a modeling agency.

But even her successful business and her father's money had failed to open the doors of the elite to Leticia Roman—because of her Mestizo blood. In a country where the large majority of the population was of mixed European and Indian or European and African ancestry, Sara explained, members of the minority white class went to great lengths to maintain the purity of their lineage. Family trees dating back to the original conquistadores were jealously kept by modern aristocrats.

Sara's words reminded Jennifer of Señora de Adler's statements the day before—about how she hoped her son would marry Ofelia. . . .

A couple of romances were flourishing among the younger employees of Adler Exports, but to this portion of the conversation Jennifer listened with only one ear.

If she felt any guilt about pumping her new friend for information, she quelled it by telling herself that Sara would volunteer her cooperation if she had known the reason. Of that Jennifer had no doubt, and she was actually tempted to take her new friend into her confidence. She was convinced that Sara would never withhold information that would free an innocent man from jail. And she would also prove a very helpful ally.

But wouldn't she be placing the girl in danger by enlisting her cooperation? Almost regretfully Jennifer decided to wait a little longer. Her investigation was just starting. Only if she ran into a brick wall would she consider placing someone else in jeopardy.

"Are you doing anything after work this evening?" Sara was asking.

"I've got some shopping to do," Jennifer replied. "Alex—er, Mr. Adler—suggested that I go to Unicentro. Why?"

"Mmm, I thought you might like to go out or something."

Jennifer gave her a searching glance. "Did you have anything special in mind?"

Sara laughed in reply. "To tell you the truth, I did," she admitted. "I told my brother about you when I saw him at lunch, and he thinks he's seen you before. Now he's after me to make the introduction."

Jennifer's first thought was to decline. The last thing she wanted at the moment was to be courted by an ardent Latin lover. But she needed friends. She was in too vulnerable a position now, with no one in her corner. Perhaps Sara and her brother—an attorney, at that—were the precise friends she needed.

"I just let him suffer," Sara added. "Just to get even with him."

"Why?" Jennifer asked. "What did he do to you?"

"He has this friend— Oh, he's just dreamy, but he

doesn't know I'm alive.'' Sara heaved a wistful sigh. "At any rate, I've been trying to get Mateo to ask Flavio to join us after work for some time, and he just ignores me. But now that he's the one who wants to meet *you*, he'll have to make a deal with me.''

So that was her game, Jennifer thought with amusement. "All right,'' she said at last. "I suppose I can do my shopping tomorrow just as well.''

"Great!'' Sara said, getting up from her chair. "I'll give Mateo a call and tell him we'll meet them in the lobby at . . . is quarter past six all right with you?''

"Fine,'' Jennifer nodded. "See you then.''

CHAPTER SIX

"MATEO SAID HE'D BE WAITING for us in front of the portrait of La Libertadora," Sara said, pressing the down button for the elevator.

The course on South American history that Jennifer had taken in college had dedicated a generous amount of time to Simón Bolívar, the patriot who had dreamed of a united Latin America. He was often called El Libertador, she knew. However, this was the first time she had ever heard that a woman had a similar title.

"Who was she?" she inquired curiously.

Sara gave her a blank look. "Who was who?"

"La Libertadora," Jennifer replied.

"Oh, her." At that moment the elevator arrived, and they stepped in. She waited until the doors had closed before she went on, "Her name was Manuela Sáenz, but everyone refers to her as Manuelita, or La Libertadora. She was a woman of great courage, one who knew how to go after what she wanted. She not only fought at the side of Simón Bolívar and saved his life twice, but their love affair was perhaps one of the most passionate ones in history." She paused thoughtfully, then said, "I think I have a book somewhere at home based on her life. I'll lend it to you if you want it."

"Oh, I'd definitely love to read about her," Jennifer replied.

The elevator doors opened with a quiet swoosh. They had reached the lobby. Because it was after the usual quitting time, most of the people who worked in the building had already left. They had obviously just missed the rush hour exit, for there were just a few stragglers besides themselves, and they were rushing past toward the main doors.

Jennifer followed Sara toward the far side of the building. Standing before the group of paintings on the wall were two young men. In their late twenties, Jennifer guessed, both were of medium height and had the self-assured, almost elegant look that was the mark of the successful professional.

Sara introduced her brother first. His handsome features, his dark brown hair seemed faintly familiar—as was the luxuriant mustache he sported. Only Jennifer couldn't recall where she had seen him before.

One thing that always made an impression on her was the way a person shook her hand when they first met. As far as she was concerned, a limp handshake, especially from a man, automatically turned her off. On the other hand, a firm handshake created a very favorable impression. Fortunately, it was the later that she received from Mateo López—fortunately because she had hoped to find a new friend in Sara's brother.

Jennifer was reminded that beauty is in the eyes of the beholder when she met Flavio García. Perhaps due to Sara's infatuation with the young man, her description of him had been a little idealized. But he still looked pleasant enough, and his eyes were dark and intense.

As soon as the introductions were over, Sara paired up with Flavio and left Jennifer with her brother as they headed for the nearest *salón de té*—one of the popular tea salons, Sara had explained earlier. Apparently in Bogotá people of all ages liked to gather for a cup of tea, which they consumed with scrumptious European pastries or an early evening repast. In addition to tea and refreshments, the establishments offered the diversions of music and dancing.

"You know," Mateo told Jennifer as they were walking down the street, "when Sara told me about you, I thought she was pulling my leg."

Jennifer was puzzled by his comment. "Why?" she asked.

"Because every day for almost a week, I've been asking her if she had finally found out who you were."

Such an admission coming from someone she had just met took Jennifer by complete surprise.

Noting her reaction, Mateo explained, "I met you last week—but only briefly. And we weren't introduced. You were going into the Avianca Building at the same time I was."

Jennifer's eyes registered her recognition. "Oh, yes, I remember now!" she exclaimed. "We took the elevator together."

"As to that, I have a confession to make," Mateo said a little sheepishly. "While you were asking directions, I let three elevators go by so that I could ride up with you.''

''You didn't!'' Jennifer laughed.

''Not only that,'' Mateo chuckled, ''I went past my floor just to find out where you were going. Silly, wasn't it?''

''No,'' Jennifer shook her head. ''I think that was very sweet. As a matter of fact, now that I remember, *you* made me feel a lot better that day.''

It was Mateo's turn to look a little puzzled. ''And how did I manage to do that?''

''Well, I had...I had a lot on my mind at the moment,'' she began. ''You seemed—oh, I don't know—friendly, I suppose is the word.''

''I was feeling friendly, all right,'' Mateo admitted candidly. ''Well, here we are.''

They had arrived at the tea salon. A waiter escorted them to a table surrounded by such an abundance of hanging and potted plants that the area felt like an indoor garden. Several young couples were already dancing on a minuscule dance floor to the music of a small band.

Even though Jennifer's appetite had been more than satisfied by the generous lunch she had enjoyed with Alejandro, her curiosity made her at least sample one of the marvelous pastries that were served with their tea.

Later, she accepted when Mateo asked her to dance. Their companions were already on the dance floor. From the looks of it, Sara was finding no difficulty in getting the attention of her brother's friend, Jennifer observed.

Mateo was an excellent dancer, and she found him easy to talk to. She was glad she had followed her instincts in accepting Sara's invitation. It had been a long time since she had enjoyed an evening like this one, and when the men began talking about moving on to a restaurant for supper, she was startled to discover that it was nearly ten o'clock.

Before leaving the office, she had called the chauffeur Alejandro had placed at her disposal to let him know that she would not be going back to the *quinta* immediately after work. But she had never intended to stay out so late, especially when she still had such a long drive ahead of her.

She could now see the convenience of the apartment Alejandro maintained in the city for those evenings when he, too, had late engagements—social or otherwise.

The key to that apartment was in her purse. Fleetingly, she entertained the idea of spending the night there.

"I'm sorry, but I really have to go," she said at last, pushing away the temptation to take advantage of Alejandro's offer. Had he meant it only for her daytime use? She had no idea whether or not he would be there tonight. "I hadn't realized it was so late."

"I'll be more than happy to drive you home," Mateo offered immediately.

"Thanks, but I'm afraid it's too far out of your way."

Only then did Jennifer realize that none of her new friends were aware that she was a houseguest of Alejandro Adler's. For some reason she was reluctant to tell them that, or that he had given her the use of a car and chauffeur.

But she had to, in the end, treating it as if the arrangements had been part of her contract from the beginning—which was only partially true.

The look in Mateo's dark eyes was a little pained, as if he didn't entirely believe her story and wasn't quite sure if he had the right to be disappointed.

Impulsively, Jennifer touched his hand. "Please be my friend, Mat." Her voice carried the same pleading note as the look in her eyes. "I do need someone I can trust."

Not until she had spoken those words did she realize that she had already made up her mind to take him into her confidence.

Hours later, safe at home in her cottage, she went to sleep still remembering the warmth of Mateo's hand pressing hers with his answer. Her heart felt lighter because she had found a friend.

WHEN SHE ENTERED HER OFFICE the next morning, Jennifer went straight to the window to pull open the drapes. Stifling a yawn, she stood there for a moment, wistfully admiring the view and wishing she could be out there instead of having to spend the best part of such a beautiful sunny day in this small room. As a soil scientist she spent very little time working indoors, and only when the weather itself kept her there—certainly not on a day like this.

With a weary sigh she turned away from the window. At this moment, she would have gladly traded her elegant outfit, a soft peach-colored light wool dress, for a pair of serviceable jeans; her fragile high-heeled sandals for a pair of sturdy hiking boots. She would go exploring those mountains she could see so clearly this morning, mountains surrounding the fertile plateau where centuries earlier Spanish conquerors had established the city of Santa Fé de Bogotá, capital of the New Granada. The extensive viceroyalty had comprised not only Colombia but also what later became the republics of Venezuela, Ecuador and Panama.

She wondered what it would have been like to live in those days, when men left behind everything that was dear and familiar to sail into the unknown and conquer new lands for king and country. It sounded romantic, but reality had been far different. Jennifer was glad she was a woman of the twentieth century.

She put her purse in one of the desk drawers and, reluctant to commence working, continued to pace restlessly around the office for a minute before she even glanced at the stacks of catalogs and photographs. The pile seemed to have increased in height during her absence, she noted in dismay.

When she finally got to work, she discovered that a calendar of events in Colombia had been included with the new material someone had delivered. A page had been marked for her attention, and when she opened the book, she found a note written in the same bold hand as the envelop she had received.

Alejandro suggested that she attend a leather show to be held at the Conventions and Exposition Center the following week. With cattle so abundant in Colombia, the manufacture of leather goods—

ranging from wallets to furniture—had become an important and prestigious industry, one she could not overlook in her position as a buyer.

"Good, I see that you found my note," Alejandro said as he strolled into her office. "I wanted to make sure you got it before you made any other plans for next week. This event is perhaps the most important of its type in all of Latin America, and buyers from all over the world will be there."

"Good morning," Jennifer said in a tight voice. She was curiously annoyed by the fact that he had sat down in the chair facing her desk without waiting for her invitation. She was perfectly aware that her attitude was silly. This was standard behavior at her office back in the States, where the atmosphere was relaxed and casual, and she had never resented it. Why should she be annoyed now at Alejandro, who owned the firm and had every right to come and go as he pleased?

He must have sensed her mood, for he gave her a level glance as he said dryly, "If keeping late nights make you this grouchy, I suggest you confine them to the weekends, Miss Maitland."

How did he know that she had not returned home until well past midnight, Jennifer wondered. The answer was so obvious that she felt like a perfect fool for not having thought of it before. The chauffeur, of course. His duties must include reporting on her comings and goings. But if Alejandro was keeping her under surveillance, wasn't this one more clue pointing to the fact that he definitely had something to hide? And that he was suspicious of her, had been from the very beginning?

Jennifer's first inclination was to give him a piece of her mind for spying on her, but she stopped herself abruptly. The success or failure of her mission depended to a great extent on the rapport she established with this man. She couldn't let her pride, her outrage at this obvious invasion of her privacy, endanger a relationship that was tenuous enough already. She managed to dampen her temper, therefore, and pretended to be oblivious to any subterfuge on his part.

"Yes, I suppose you're right," she admitted wryly instead. She thought in passing about mentioning her new friends but instinctively decided not to. Instead, she simply said, "I didn't mean to stay out so late, but time just seemed to fly by. I can see now how convenient it is for you to maintain an apartment here in the city."

She waited to see if Alejandro would offer her the use of his apartment at night and wasn't very surprised when he didn't. Her staying there might interfere with his own plans.

She hated to feel so miserable at the prospect of him using the apartment to be with other women. Her response was insane, she knew, and she berated herself for it, but she couldn't seem to help the way she felt any more than she could stop breathing.

Alejandro himself didn't comment further. Getting up from the chair, he said casually, "Well, I just wanted to make sure you didn't make any plans for Friday evening."

Jennifer gave him a quizzical look, but before she could ask why, he added, "There's a party I don't think we should miss, since it'll give you a chance to make some useful contacts.''

Jennifer felt relieved his invitation was for business reasons, but she felt a certain amount of disappointment as well. The ambiguity of her reaction made her feel a little fearful, as if she were standing on the edge of a precipice and about to fall into a void. She tried to cover her disquiet by reaching for a pencil from the caddy on top of her desk. "Very well." She flipped through her calendar, and when she reached the day she was looking for said, "Friday. What time?"

"Cocktails start at seven."

"Fine," she nodded.

As he was leaving, Alejandro paused at the door and said casually, "By the way, you may want to change at my apartment for the party."

Jennifer looked up abruptly, but all she caught was a glimpse of his back as he went out the door.

Once she was alone, Jennifer tried to concentrate on her work and ignore the sinking feeling that she had inside. She failed miserably. She tried to tell herself that she didn't know what was causing it, but she had always been too honest with herself to start lying now.

Could it be possible that she was falling in love with Alejandro Adler? Or was she using the word love for what she felt because she was uncomfortable with the word desire?

There was no question in her mind that she responded to him as she had never responded to another man before. This had been driven home each time he had touched her—if only with his eyes. But love? Could there be love without trust? Could there be love when there was fear?

"Hi!"

Jennifer dragged her attention back to the present to find Sara standing at the door. "Oh, hi," she answered warmly.

"Ramón is bringing coffee. I thought you might want to spend our break together."

Jennifer was grateful for Sara's company. Her debate with herself had given her the beginnings of a headache. "Sure come in."

"I've been waiting for coffee break all morning long," Sara said, heaving a dramatic sigh as she plopped herself down in the chair. "I was all set for another day of peace and tranquility, when Mr. Tejeda decided to come back a day early. With a ton of paperwork, and needless to say, all of it urgent. I thought I'd go mad if I didn't get away from my desk for at least a few minutes."

Jennifer gave her a sympathetic smile. "Did you stay out very late last night?"

"Heavens, no!" Sara replied. "We didn't even go out to dinner. Mateo wanted to take me home right after you left, just as I was making progress with Flavio. I could have wrung his neck."

She illustrated her words with gestures, and her comically sinister grin made Jennifer laugh. "Oh, Sara, I didn't think you were faring so badly earlier in the evening."

This time Sara's grin was one of satisfaction. "No, I wasn't, was I?" She paused briefly, as if enjoying a private joke, then confessed, "He asked me out again. Oh, Alba, he's so nice! If I liked him before just from seeing him, I like him even more now that I had a chance to get to know him a bit. I think I'm in love! And I finally got to meet him, thanks to you!''

Arching her brows, Jennifer pointed a thumb at herself. "Me?" she laughed. "It's very nice of you to give me credit for it, Sara, but Flavio's your brother's friend. I know how brothers are, believe me, and he would have introduced the two of you in due time."

"Don't be so sure," Sara frowned. "He only did it because I used you as a lever. Flavio isn't really Mateo's friend. They just work in the same office. You see, we are conservatives. Flavio and his family are liberals."

For Sara that cryptic explanation seemed sufficient, but Jennifer looked puzzled. "Just because they have different political views doesn't necessarily mean they can't be friends, does it?" she ventured.

"*Alá!*" Sara exclaimed, a little perplexed. "Perhaps in your country belonging to different political parties doesn't interfere with friendships, but believe me, it does here in Colombia. Not only that. I have an aunt who never married because the man she was in love with was a liberal."

"I don't believe it!" Jennifer exclaimed.

"Believe it," Sara nodded. "We don't go to such extremes anymore, but remember, we went to civil war over these differences."

"Civil war?"

At that moment Ramón arrived, momentarily interrupting their conversation. It was not until the boy had left and they had settled back to enjoy the midmorning repast that Sara continued.

"Haven't you ever heard of the *bogotazo*, the rioting here in Bogotá?"

"I'm afraid not," Jennifer shook her head.

"The time of *la violencia* was perhaps the darkest page in our history," Sara said without a trace of the good humor that seemed to be her most engaging characteristic. "You may not know it, but Colombia is one of the oldest republics in Latin America, and sentiments run high when it comes to politics.

"At any rate, I'll try to make a long story short," she continued. "Colombia was a firm supporter of the Allies during the Second World War, to the extent that the properties belonging to any Germans in the country were confiscated. By the way, that included the airline that is now Avianca. There was a lot of discontent after the war. The economic situation was very bad.

"A Liberal who promised reforms—a man named Jorge Eliecer Gaitán—became the hero of the masses. He was shot to death in the streets of Bogotá during the Inter-American Conference of 1948, and that started a series of riots that almost destroyed the city. One of the reasons you don't see as many colonial buildings as you would expect in a city as old as this one is that a lot of them went up in flames during that time.

"But the *bogotazo* was only the beginning of the violence," Sara went on. "The cities were relatively quiet after that, but in the countryside, whole villages started arming themselves and fighting one another. The disagreement got so out of control that it became a cruel savage war. Nobody really knows how many people were tortured and killed during those years. Then what had started for political reasons became private wars. The countryside was in the hands of bandits who ravaged and pillaged at will. No one was safe.

"After years of this terror, a coalition was made between the two parties, and they started taking turns at office. The Conservatives one term, the Liberals the next, and so forth. It may not have solved all our problems, but at least we achieved peace, especially when amnesty was granted to the bandits and they gave up their arms."

At Jennifer's silence, Sara added, "Of course, this is an extremely condensed version of the real story, but even so, you can see now why politics play such an important part in our relationships. To us the words freedom and peace are not hollow or meaningless. We have paid a very high price for them—a price of blood."

There was a pause after Sara finished. Jennifer finally ventured, "But, Sara, if Flavio and his family are of different political views, don't you think it's wiser to stay away from him?"

"*Alá!* Don't be silly," Sara replied airily, becoming her old blithe self again. "I'm not planning to marry the man. Call it a little rehearsal for the real thing," she added mischievously. "I'm just sick and tired of being told by my parents and even by my brother the things I may and may not do. I'm not a child anymore. I'm twenty-one years old! Liberal or not, Flavio is divine, and I intend to have as much fun with him as I possibly can."

"You might be courting disaster," Jennifer warned, feeling a little responsible for the part she had unknowingly played in her friend's schemes. In spite of Sara's age, Jennifer suspected that the girl had a great deal of emotional maturing to do. On the other hand, Sara was probably correct; she had as much right as everyone else to make her own mistakes and learn from them.

"You never told me what you thought of my brother," Sara pointed out.

"I liked him very much," Jennifer replied without hesitation.

"Are you going out with him again?"

"That will depend on if he asks me," she answered.

"Oh, he will," Sara assured her.

By this time they had consumed their *empanadas* and emptied their coffee cups, break was over.

"I've got to run. Mr. Tejeda will have my hide if I don't finish his dictation before lunchtime," Sara said, standing up reluctantly. "You haven't made any other plans, have you?"

"Of course not."

"Good. See you then." She smiled and waved before she disappeared through the door.

Sara's conversation had distracted Jennifer from her earlier thoughts. Refusing to fall back into the same rut, she concentrated instead on what she had just learned about the history of Colombia—a history that so much affected their lives today. Having lived all her life in the tranquility and safety of a small Southern California town, she felt a little frightened at the extreme violence that had shaken this strange land.

It was hard for her to understand that people—ordinary people she'd seen walking down the street—could suddenly become so savage that they could tear each other to pieces without pity. Yet it had happened, time and time again since the beginning of mankind, in almost every part of the world.

Her musings were again interrupted, this time by the telephone. Automatically Jennifer picked up the receiver. "Hello?"

"Alba? This is Mateo. How are you?"

"Mat! This must be telepathy. I was just thinking about you."

"Mmm, that sounds very encouraging."

Jennifer laughed. "Sara was here a few minutes ago. We spent our coffee break together."

"I was wondering if you were free for lunch?"

"I'm having lunch with Sara. Perhaps you'd care to join us."

"Just the two of us is more what I had in mind," Mateo replied. "What about this evening? I was planning to ask you during lunch, but will you have dinner with me?"

Jennifer took a moment to think. She really had to shop for a new dress. Still, she had two more days before the party on Friday, and she wanted to see Mateo without Sara being there.

"All right, Mat, but I must get home early. I didn't get much sleep last night. It's a long drive to the *quinta*."

"We'll make it an early dinner then. I promise you'll be in bed before midnight."

"Where should we meet?"

"I can stop by your office."

For some reason she couldn't fathom, Jennifer was reluctant to let other people in the office know that she was seeing Sara's brother. Other people, she reflected, or one particular person? She tried to make it sound casual when she said, "Oh, don't bother coming up. I'll meet you in the lobby, same as yesterday."

"Then I'll see you later."

"Bye, Mat."

When Jennifer hung up the phone, she found Mrs. Vargas waiting at the door. How long had she been standing there? How much had she heard?

"Mr. Adler would like to see you in his office, if it's convenient, Miss Maitland," she said. "There's someone he would like you to meet."

As she followed Mrs. Vargas to Alejandro's office, Jennifer wondered cynically how long it would be before the woman reported the telephone conversation she had overheard. Was she seeing ghosts where there were none, imagining that she was being watched by all of Alex's employees? Perhaps, but the fact remained that the only way Alejandro could have known about her activities the previous evening was if the chauffeur had reported them. Why then had he warned her so subtly that she was being watched? Had it been a slip on his part?

Hardly, Jennifer reflected. Alex was too shrewd to commit such a simple error. . . .

Mrs. Vargas was motioning her into the office. As Jennifer went in, she returned to her desk.

The two men inside got to their feet at her entrance. The man she didn't know was tall, not quite as tall as Alejandro himself, and his dark hair was beginning to turn to gray. He was slender and quite elegantly dressed; at first glance Jennifer placed his age somewhere between his late forties and early fifties. As she approached him, however, she noticed the network of fine lines that began at the corners of his light brown eyes and ran in ridges down beside his hawkish nose to his thin-lipped mouth. That fact alone made her revise her first impression.

"Miss Maitland, I'd like you to meet Mr. Rıcardo Tejeda," Alejandro said. "He's the general manager of Adler Exports."

Jennifer offered her hand. "How do you do, Mr. Tejeda."

Later she tried to rationalize that the unpleasant feeling she had when Ricardo Tejeda shook her hand was due to her state of mind. She had been suspicious of everything and everybody for so long now. At the moment, she was conscious of a certain wariness she couldn't explain. Had she imagined it, or did she detect a flash of annoyance—or even hostility—in Tejeda's eyes, in spite of the politeness he had shown her?

"Mr. Tejeda has been with the company since my father's time," Alejandro said, and from the tone of his voice Jennifer knew he held the man in great esteem.

After the initial pleasantries were over, Alejandro conducted his two employees to the corner of his office that had been set aside and furnished for informal meetings. A coffee service on a silver tray rested on the low table.

For the next half hour or so Jennifer tried to keep

her mind wholly on the discussion, which focused on her future activities with the company. She had a bit of trouble, though, for during the course of the conversation she learned that Alejandro was planning to accompany her on her first purchasing trip— to Medellín, Colombia's second largest city. This was something she had not envisioned.

"There's no need for you to abandon your other obligations on my account, Mr. Adler," she said. "I'm sure I'll be able to manage, without bothering you."

Because Tejeda was with them, she had made her protest sound as if she were concerned for Alejandro. The amusement she saw reflected in her employer's eyes told her he was perfectly aware of her dismay at the news. "It's no bother, Miss Maitland," he said silkily. "Actually, I'm looking forward to it. It's been a while since I've been away from the office."

The buzz of the intercom interrupted the conference. Alejandro consulted his watch as he got up and went to the desk. He picked up the phone, listened for a moment and answered simply, "Thank you, Mrs. Vargas," before he hung up. Then he turned back to his companions. "Well, if there's nothing else to discuss, I'm afraid you'll both have to excuse me. I have a luncheon engagement in a few minutes."

Jennifer practically sprang to her feet, she was so anxious to get away. Alejandro escorted them to the door. "Perhaps it would be a good idea to show Miss Maitland the warehouses, Ricardo. She may want to make special arrangements for the storage of the merchandise she'll be sending us."

"Yes, of course," the general manager replied. "When would it be convenient for you, Miss Maitland?"

"Er, anytime, I suppose. This afternoon?"

"Well..." Ricardo Tejeda hesitated. "This afternoon is going to be difficult. A shipment of coffee is scheduled to arrive and—"

"There's no rush," Alejandro intervened. "I'm sure Miss Maitland can have your secretary schedule a visit whenever it's convenient for both of you."

The meeting ended and Jennifer returned to her office to wait for Sara, who appeared a few minutes later. "Are you ready?" she asked as she came through the door. "I don't know about you, but I'm famished."

The restaurant she had selected was located in an old colonial-style house with a splashing fountain at the entrance. It was a rather modest operation run by a married couple, and Jennifer was disappointed to discover that the fare was again Continental rather than Colombian.

"I finally met your boss," she confided after they had ordered. "Alex said that he's been in the firm since his father ran it."

"Oh, gosh, yes!" Sara replied. "He's been with the company forever!"

"Do you like working for him?"

Sara shrugged eloquently. "He's all right, I guess." She paused thoughtfully before adding, "The only thing that bothers me about him is that he's so distant and secretive. You know, I've worked for that man for almost two years, and in all this time we haven't had one single solitary conversation that didn't involve the business. I know nothing at all about his personal life, only that he's married—and that was because I once talked to his wife on the phone.''

"You said you suspected he was having an affair,'' Jennifer reminded her. "What makes you think he is?''

Again Sara shrugged. "Nothing definite, but with him it's hard to say. I went into his office once to take him his mail, and he was talking with a woman on the phone.''

"How did you know it wasn't his wife?''

"His whole attitude. Believe me, it was a woman. And when he saw me, he tried to pretend it was a business call.'' She was silent for a moment. "Besides, I know that at least once when he was supposed to be traveling he was right here in Bogotá. Can you believe it? A man his age.''

Jennifer laughed, "He didn't seem that old to me. There's hardly any gray in his hair.''

Sara giggled. "Yes, but do you know that there used to be more when I started working for him than there is now?''

The look Jennifer gave her friend was one of disbelief. Somehow Ricardo Tejeda had not seemed like the type of man to resort to cosmetics. "Are you saying that he colors his hair?''

With a mischievous grin on her face, Sara bobbed her head. "It didn't happen overnight,'' she said, "but very gradually. And he takes more pains with his appearance now than he did before. When you put all those things together, what do you come up with?'' Not waiting for a reply she added, ''An older man involved with a younger woman, right?''

''It's certainly possible,'' Jennifer said. Inwardly she added, and such a man would have to have an additional source of income.

But even if Ricardo Tejeda was involved in the traffic of narcotics, this didn't clear Alejandro of suspicion. She couldn't let her antipathy for one man influence her evaluation. They might both be in it together.

During the rest of lunch, Jennifer had to resist the temptation to confide in her friend. Sara's observations demonstrated that very little escaped her, and she was in a position where she had access to information that was definitely off limits to Jennifer. Both of these qualities would make her an invaluable ally.

Still she hesitated. It wasn't that she didn't trust Sara. In spite of the woman's fondness for gossip— and innocent gossip at that—Jennifer didn't believe she would ever purposely reveal a secret entrusted to her. Playing the spy for a cause as noble as clearing an innocent man's name would certainly appeal to Sara's sense of adventure. But Jennifer wasn't sure that the girl's immaturity wouldn't make her reckless.

Once again she decided to save her confidence for Mateo that evening. Only if he agreed would she involve his sister in her schemes.

The afternoon went on uneventfully. Jennifer would have enjoyed her work had she not been so nervous about her decision to spill her story to Mateo after such a brief acquaintance. Was she making a mistake? She was a highly intuitive person whose first impressions of people seldom steered her wrong. However, at this moment she had to give careful consideration to her motivations. Could the strong positive feelings she had about Mateo be the product of her own need to find some safety in her present situation? How could she still trust her instincts when they had completely failed her where Alejandro was concerned?

In the end, she made up her mind to do what had always worked best for her: to play it by ear.

RELUCTANT FOR HER RELATIONSHIP with the young attorney to raise speculation, Jennifer waited in her office until most of the other employees had gone home. Mateo was already standing in the almost deserted lobby by the time she emerged from the elevators, and they wasted no time in leaving the building by a side exit.

"Do you know that you surprise me each time I see you?" he said once they had been seated in the same tea salon they had gone to the previous evening.

"Surprise you?" Looking up from the menu, Jennifer arched a quizzical brow. "How?"

"Because you are even more beautiful than I remembered you."

The statement was said with such sincerity that Jennifer couldn't help but feel a little flattered. "Now I know why Latin men have such a reputation as lovers," she quipped with a coquetish smile.

"We're not afraid to tell a woman how we feel about her," Mateo said, reaching across the table for her hand.

Jennifer didn't pull away. The contact was warm and pleasant, nothing more, but she still found comfort in the gesture. It was like a measure of normalcy in a world that had suddenly turned topsy-turvy.

Mateo released her hand when the waiter came to take their orders. She had no appetite and simply ordered a cappucino amaretto.

"Let's dance," Mateo invited.

"All right."

They got up and made their way through the tables to the small dance floor where other couples were moving to the slow romantic music the band was playing. She turned to face Mateo, and he took her in his arms.

Four-inch heels increased Jennifer's height so that she was at a comfortable level with Mateo. Consequently, as their bodies came together to follow the music, it was only natural for their cheeks to come in contact as well.

His spicy cologne mingled with the aroma of tobacco to remind her of a very different male scent. The hard muscles she felt moving beneath the fingertips of her left hand made her think of other moments and other arms.

Jennifer found herself wishing she could feel some excitement at being held so close by an attractive man and under such romantic circumstances as the softly lighted dance floor. In her determination to wash away the memories of Alejandro, she pressed herself more closely to Mateo, who immediately responded by holding her tighter.

To her frustration, nothing had changed by the time

the music ended, and she declined a second dance.

Mugs topped with whipped cream had been brought to the table in their absence. After stirring her cup, Jennifer sipped pensively at the delicious creamy concoction of coffee and almond liqueur.

Mateo, who had been gazing at her in silence, finally asked, "What's the matter, Alba? Have I offended you in any way?"

Jennifer shook her head.

"Then what is it? What's wrong?"

"What makes you think there's anything wrong?" she asked.

Mateo gave her a probing look. "Something happened—I don't know what—while we were dancing," he said at last. "One moment I was holding you in my arms, and the next you seemed to be miles away from me."

When the lump that had suddenly developed in her throat kept Jennifer from answering, he added, "Is it Alejandro Adler?"

"Of course not!" she protested swiftly. Perhaps too swiftly, if the disappointed expression on Mateo's face was anything to go by. It was then that Jennifer made up her mind to tell him the truth.

"When I told you yesterday that I needed a friend, I meant it, Mat," she said sincerely. "I have to confide in someone, and I want that someone to be you. Will you give me your word that, even if you disapprove of it, what I'm going to tell you will remain strictly between us?"

Mateo's expression was bemused as he nodded.

Once she had his assent, Jennifer continued. "Yes,

I was thinking of Alex Adler a few minutes ago, but not in the way you think. He was the reason I came to Colombia in the first place, you see. My brother is dying little by little, and all because of him."

Mateo drew his breath in sharply. "What are you saying? How?"

"You're an attorney," Jennifer replied. "Do you recall, about four months ago, that Adler testified at a trial where an American was convicted of smuggling narcotics?"

"Yes, I do," he nodded. "A shipment of pure cocaine was found in several bags of coffee. The whole thing was kept rather quiet, but I learned about it from Sara."

"That man who was sent to prison is my brother, and he was innocent. I came here to prove that he was framed by Alex Adler."

"Oh, my God!" Mateo had turned pale as she spoke. "Have you any idea of what you've gotten yourself into?"

"I know it's dangerous, but—"

"Dangerous!" Mateo exclaimed. "That's an understatement if I ever heard one!"

"My real name is Jennifer, by the way." She added quietly. "Jennifer Blake."

"Wait a minute! Don't say another word." Mateo got up, and after reaching into his pocket for his wallet, he took out a bill and tossed it on the table. "Let's get out of here."

Jennifer obeyed immediately, and they maintained a wary silence until they were out on the street. When she tried to speak again, he silenced her with a gesture. "Not yet."

It wasn't until they had reached the park that he turned to her, and still regarding her in disbelief, said, "Okay, let's consider for a minute that your brother really *is* innocent."

"He is!" Jennifer put in.

Mateo waved his hand to dismiss her words. "Fine, but if he's telling the truth, you may be dealing with much more than you bargained for."

"What do you mean?"

"What I'm trying to say is that the traffic of narcotics has a lot of ramifications, Jennifer. And all of them are very dangerous."

"What kind of ramifications?"

"Mafia for one. Political for another."

"I can understand the Mafia, but why political?"

"I'm not giving away any secrets if I tell you that the people involved in smuggling narcotics out of Colombia are the same ones who are smuggling arms in for the guerrillas. Not only here in this country, but in other parts of Central America as well. I'll give you one guess as to where the guns are coming from." He paused briefly, and at her blank look continued, "It's a matter of public record that Colombia broke diplomatic relations with Cuba because they were supplying weapons to the guerrillas." He shook his head. "It's not just a question of money, Jennifer. It's also a struggle for power."

Jennifer listened in silence. Until that moment, she had had no inkling of the forces she would have to face in trying to gain her brother's freedom. "What am I going to do, Mat?" she asked in dismay.

Mateo took her hand. "You're risking your life with very little chance of success. As much as I hate to say it, the only advice I can give you is to go home, Alba...I mean Jennifer. Forget the whole thing.''

"And what about Tommy, Mat? I can't simply walk away, let him rot in prison. I know that sooner or later he'll try to escape from that island, and I've seen the graves of those who have tried it before." She shuddered. "Besides, my leaving the country is not as easy as you think. I have no papers, and my going to the American Embassy will only succeed in getting me deported. I can't risk that. Not as long as Tommy is here in Colombia.''

"Deported?"

Jennifer nodded, then proceeded to tell her story to Mateo from the start. She couldn't blame him for shaking his head in disbelief every now and then as the story unfolded. Now that she was more aware of the dangerous ramifications, she realized that only insanity—or ignorance of the situation, as in her case—would have made a person undertake such an adventure.

"Can you see now how much I need your help, Mat?" she asked when she had finished her narrative. "No one else knows where I am or what I'm doing. My friends in the States believe that I went back to Brazil. If I were to vanish from the face of the earth, no one would connect my disappearance to Alex Adler.''

"Are you convinced he's involved?"

Jennifer shook her head. "I really don't know," she admitted. "All I have to go by is what Tommy said. Do you think his export business is a front for illegal activities?''

"It's possible, but if you want my opinion, it's also unlikely," Mateo replied. "Drug smuggling, which usually involves tons of marijuana, is mainly done by sea. They ship it out of the peninsula of La Guajira, a remote area inhabited mostly by Indians. It's no longer a secret that the Cuban government makes quite a handsome profit providing smugglers not only with the protection of their gunboats, but also with the use of their ports for repairs and refueling."

"Yes, but what they found inside the bags of coffee was cocaine," Jennifer reminded him. "How do you explain that?"

"The only reason I can answer your question is that, because my sister is employed by Adler, I did a little investigating at the time," Mateo replied. "I remember that the smugglers had had a run-in with our patrol boats and lost a few ships shortly before that happened. Things were quite hot for them for a while. My guess is that the dealers in the States were probably running dry. Since cocaine involves smaller quantities, they resorted to the coffee shipment because they had an urgent delivery to make and no other way of doing so."

"That means they do have a connection for when the need arises," Jennifer pointed out triumphantly. After a thoughtful pause she added, "Sara mentioned that the government confiscated the properties of Germans during the Second World War. I may be grasping at straws, but do you think Alex might be sympathetic with the guerrillas because of that?" Even as she voiced it, the reasoning sounded very thin to her own ears.

"I don't think so," Mateo replied with a shake of his head. When Jennifer looked at him quizzically, he said, "Let me explain. Originally the Adlers came from Austria, not Germany. Oh, there may be some German ancestor in their background, but that's beside the point. Alejandro is third-generation Colombian, not Austrian or Spanish. The Adler fortune, which is considerable, was never touched by the government. And marriage to Mariana Navarro brought important landholdings to Alejandro's father."

"You make the marriage sound like a business merger," Jennifer pointed out.

"It may well have been," Mateo replied. "I understand that the Navarro women always had better heads for business than their men did. It was Señora de Adler's mother who managed to hang on to the land while her husband squandered their fortune, for example. It was probably she who arranged for her son to join the church and for Mariana to marry into the Adler money."

"How do you know so much about them?" Jennifer inquired in amazement.

He shrugged. "When Sara told me about the drugs that had been found, I was concerned that she might be working for some cover-up operation."

"And you were satisfied that it wasn't?"

"Yes," he nodded. "I thought the evidence against your brother was conclusive, and as far as I was concerned, the case was closed. You must be very sure of his innocence to be willing to risk your life in order to prove it."

"I am," Jennifer replied without hesitation. "It

may be hard for you to understand, Mat, but Tommy and I have always been very close. We have a very special relationship. We're twins, you see, and perhaps that's why we know things about each other that other brothers and sisters might not.''

Mateo gave her a level glance. ''Then if your brother is innocent, the matter is far from being closed, isn't it?''

Jennifer gazed back in silence.

''It's obvious, therefore, that the smugglers have someone in the Adler organization working for them,'' he went on thoughtfully. ''The question is who?''

Jennifer took a deep breath. ''Will you help me then?''

Shaking his head wryly, Mateo reached for her hand. ''What else can I do when the two women I care for most are up to their pretty necks in smugglers?''

Impulsively, Jennifer kissed him.

CHAPTER SEVEN

JENNIFER HAD TO STIFLE a nervous giggle as she got out of the car. The uniform worn by the doorman who rushed to open the door for her had more gold braid on it than that of a rear admiral.

She covered the distance to the entrance with quick steps and entered a spacious plush lobby. At the security guard station she stopped for a moment while the man scrutinized his list for her name. When he found it he allowed her to continue on to the elevator.

On the way up to the penthouse apartment, Jennifer kept hoping that she would have time to give it a quick search before Alejandro arrived. Exactly what she expected to find there she didn't know, only she hoped—and dreaded—that she would recognize something that connected him to the smugglers.

The elevator doors opened quietly, and she stepped out into a thickly carpeted hallway. There were only two doors, one at each end of the floor, and she hesitated momentarily, not knowing which direction to turn. The key Alejandro had given her had no number on it, and she felt like a fool for not having asked the guard. Finally she decided to try the door to her right.

Not wishing to go through an embarrassing explanation if she were caught trying to unlock the wrong door, Jennifer rang the doorbell and waited, wondering how in the world she managed to get herself into such situations. When after a few minutes no one had answered the door, she inserted the key in the lock and held her breath while she turned it. Luckily, it worked.

Before closing the door behind her, she reached for the light switch on the wall and flipped it on. The beauty of the room made her draw her breath in sharply, and for a full minute she stood there gawking. The man who inhabited this place must be highly refined.

Unlike the *quinta*, where the ambience was a more traditional one, the apartment was a feast for the senses. Furnished and decorated in serene Oriental splendor, it combined the richness of pecan veneers and gleaming brass with the soft sensual texture of velvet. Everything she saw was meant to please the eye, to invite the touch.

Later Jennifer would realize that the many Oriental pieces on display must be very valuable. At the moment all she could think about was their exquisite beauty, their simplicity.

She almost had to shake herself from her trance when she realized that she was wasting precious moments. Immediately she began looking around, wondering where she should begin her search. The gleaming desk in the study seemed like a logical place.

She was careful not to disturb the order in which she found the papers she quickly riffled through. There was nothing that could be considered of interest, however. Even the balance listed in the checkbook she found in the middle drawer was small enough to indicate that the account was meant only for the maintenance of the apartment.

Fearful of being found there by Alejandro, Jennifer allowed herself only a few more minutes of searching before she finally went into the bedroom. It too was beautifully reminiscent of the Far East.

The dress she had purchased the previous evening, which she had entrusted to the chauffeur earlier, had been carefully laid on the king-size bed. Of red angel crepe, it was the brightest note of color in the room.

The naked branches in an asymmetrical Japanese arrangement made Jennifer pause thoughtfully. Among the colors around her—those of earth and sky and living things—the note of those delicate bare branches almost made her weep. She didn't know why she felt so profoundly moved by them, and she found herself wondering if Alejandro felt the same as she each time he looked at them.

With a shaky sigh Jennifer consulted her wristwatch. It wouldn't be too long before he arrived. Giving up all thought of searching further, she began to undress. She was being fanciful again, she decided as she unbuttoned her blouse—attributing Alejandro with a sensitivity he most likely didn't possess. In all probability the apartment had been professionally decorated, and all he'd had to do with it was to scribble his signature on a check.

Not wanting to run the risk of having Alejandro come into the bedroom unexpectedly, Jennifer locked the door before she finally stripped down to her skin and padded on bare feet to the bathroom. The bathtub was large enough for two, and she couldn't help thinking what a sensual experience it would be to share a bath with Alejandro. Chiding herself for her wayward thoughts, she pinned her hair up, turned on the gleaming taps of the separate shower, and after stepping into the stall closed the glass door behind her.

Letting the warm water ease the tense muscles between her shoulder blades, Jennifer tried to relax as she stood under the spray. The fact that Mateo was now aware of what she was trying to do and had promised his help gave her a tremendous amount of relief. But she would need all her equanimity if she was going to spend an entire evening with Alejandro Adler.

Instead of wrapping up in the enormous bath sheet that she used to dry herself, Jennifer couldn't resist reaching for the robe of thick white terry cloth that she found hanging in the bathroom closet. It was enormous on her, and she giggled as she pushed up the sleeves, trying to find her hands so that she could fasten the belt around her waist.

Going into the dressing area, she modeled the robe in front of the full-length mirror. As she held the collar around her face, she became aware of the scent, so clean and masculine, that clung to the fabric. Her heartbeat quickened in response, and she abruptly gave up her game. It was time to get dressed anyway.

A quick glance around the room told her that she had left her purse, with her makeup in it, somewhere else, and she went in search of it. She found it on one of the velvet sofas, and as she picked it up, the clink of ice on glass made her whirl around with a gasp of surprise. Alejandro was standing behind the gleaming counter of the bar.

"Sorry I startled you," he said blandly. "Can I get you a drink?"

Her first impulse was to dash back into the bedroom. But when she willed her legs to move, they didn't respond. It was happening again, she thought with a great deal of mortification; she was standing there staring back at him while he waited for her answer.

At that point her pride came to her rescue, and tossing her head up, she answered, "Sure, why not. What are you having?"

"Scotch on the rocks."

"Mmm, sounds good. I'll have the same."

She approached the bar while he poured her drink, and perched herself on one of the stools.

"Thanks," she said when he put the glass in front of her. She waited for him to pick up his, and raising her own offered, "Cheers."

Without responding to her toast, he simply touched her glass with his.

While sipping the Scotch, which was definitely mellowed by age, Jennifer thought of the improbability of her situation. Here she was, alone with a man she should hate but instead desired like no one else she'd ever met. Beneath the voluminous robe, which belonged to him, she was stark naked; and she was sharing a drink with him as if it were the most natural thing in the world. The fact that they were in his bachelor apartment might have removed any qualms he had about making love to her while she was a guest in his family home. With a thrilling sense of anticipation, Jennifer wondered if he would try to kiss her.

In immediate response she felt a sudden rush of blood through her body and the tingling sensations that usually followed her ingestion of alcoholic beverages. But since Alejandro had the same heady effect on her, at this moment she wasn't sure which was responsible for her euphoria.

"This is such a beautiful apartment, Alex," she said at last.

"Have you seen all of it?"

"Not really," she shook her head. "Just this area, and the bedroom." She had forgotten that she'd searched the study earlier. "Is it very large?"

"Fairly," he replied, taking a slim gold cigarette case from the breast pocket of his gray suit. "There are only two apartments on this floor."

"I imagined so. When I got out of the elevator I wasn't sure which one to try first. I should have asked the guard before coming up, but I forgot. Imagine how embarrassing it would have been to be caught trying to unlock the wrong door!" she went on, chattering nervously. "I lucked out on the first try, though."

"You didn't need to worry," he replied, lighting up a cigarette. "The other apartment belongs to my sister and her husband. They're not in town now. They only use it during their visits from Cali, which have become very rare."

Jennifer watched him expel a jet of blue smoke and said, "I think I'll have a cigarette, too."

Alejandro opened his cigarette case and offered it to her. "I didn't know you smoked."

"I don't anymore," she replied, accepting a cigarette. "This is just my first slipup from all my good intentions."

Holding the cigarette to her lips she waited for Alejandro to flick his lighter. As she did so she noticed that his hand was rather unsteady. A little puzzled she looked up at his face, but Alejandro had turned toward the window.

"There's a nice view of the city from here," he said, moving toward the window to draw the drapes open.

Jennifer put out her cigarette in an ashtray before she got up from the stool and came to stand next to him by the window. Like Los Angeles, Bogotá looked prettier at night. It became a fairyland, an expanse of glittering lights that stretch toward the horizon like jewels against a tapestry of darkness.

Side by side they stood in silence, looking out at the beautiful sight. As they did so, all Jennifer's earlier disquietude left her. At this moment she felt at complete ease with Alejandro, which for her was a new experience—and a far from unpleasant one at that. Taking her eyes from the view, she glanced at the face of the man beside her. She realized then that he was blind to the splendor before them.

"Alex?" She touched his arm.

His eyes swung suddenly to her face, and she saw him then as she had never seen him before. She was startled to notice the tension around his sensual mouth, the naked pain showing so briefly in his gray eyes that afterward she thought she had imagined the whole thing. Her puzzled gaze followed him as he turned away and went back to the bar, where he re-filled his glass.

Aware of the accelerating beat of her heart, she kept gazing out the window even after she felt him standing next to her again. Then before she knew how it had happened, she was suddenly being crushed in his arms.

Hungry, consuming, his mouth cut off her protest with a kiss that was startling in the force of its passion. Taken by surprise, Jennifer offered no further resistance to his warm invasion of her senses, to his compellingly sensual caress.

This lack of resistance on her part seemed to disarm him completely, and his kiss became gentler then, yet filled with such need, such longing, that if at that moment he had asked for her life, she would have given it gladly. She had waited for this kiss, but the waiting had been well worth it, for she had never experienced anything like it, had never known an embrace that had moved her so deeply, so completely. That Alejandro had been affected in a similar way was made patent by the way his arms trembled as he slowly lowered her onto the velvet sofa.

She needed desperately to touch him. Automatically her hands crept up the front of his shirt, loosened a few buttons and slipped inside, where she reveled in the feel of his heated skin beneath the soft and springy hair curling on his chest. Meanwhile, his feather-light kisses were raining on her cheeks, on her eyes, on her mouth. On the curve of her shoulders, her breasts. Murmuring words in Spanish that she didn't understand, he trailed a fiery path down the slender column of her throat, while his own hands found the part in his voluminous robe and opened it to caress her naked, eager flesh.

Delighting in his warmth, his strength, Jennifer lost all track of time and place. She was soaring through space, floating on air. With wild abandon, her sensitized skin responded to every melting touch of his molding hands. The languor spreading through her made her limbs grow weak. Every pore in her body seemed to have come alive as his mouth captured and teased the rosy crest of a taut nipple, and she was unable to withhold her moans of exquisite pleasure.

"Don't leave me!" she gasped as he drew back. "Alex, don't leave me now!"

"I'm not leaving you," he whispered, caressing her cheek and gently touching his lips to hers. "But I must undress to make love to you, Alba *querida*."

Alba. Hearing the strange name on his lips had the sobering effect of a cold shower. When he returned to her and took her in his arms again, she felt stiff and unresponsive.

Oh, how she longed to hear him speak her own name, her real name! Even as she, despite herself, returned his kisses, her mind still rebelled against the deception, and she was tempted to tell Alejandro the truth right then and there. He had to be innocent of Tommy's charges. How else could she have fallen in love with him? Because it was at that very moment that Jennifer realized she had fallen in love with Alejandro Adler. No matter how hard she had fought her emotions, there was no question left in her mind.

But what if she had made a mistake? What if Alex was really involved with the smugglers? Confusion warred within her. . . .

That something was definitely wrong became apparent to Alejandro, who stopped kissing her and drew back only to find tears trembling in Jennifer's lashes, tears that she had been unable to stop.

"*Mía vida!* Why are you crying? What's the matter?"

"Oh, I'm sorry, Alex!" she wept. "I—I can't! I just can't!"

She was crying in earnest now, and misunderstanding the reason for her tears, he smiled at her and cradled her in his arms. "Hush, love, don't cry. It's all right. You don't have to be afraid. I understand."

"You do?" she hiccuped, regarding him tremulously. How could he? But she wasn't about to argue.

"Of course I do, my darling. I'm only sorry I didn't realize that you. . . ." At her bemused expression, he simply added, "Never mind, it's all right."

By this time Alejandro had covered his nakedness so unobstrusively that Jennifer had not even noticed his subtle gesture. Now she gathered the ends of the robe to cover herself.

It was only then that she remembered she was there in his apartment to change for a party they might already have missed. On the one hand she wanted to stay like this with Alejandro; on the other, she realized that temptation was sure to return, and next time it might overcome their scruples.

"Did we miss the party?" she inquired softly.

"You mean the *other* party?" He gave a soft

chuckle. "Perhaps not. Do you still want to go?"

"Mmm, maybe we should."

He reached out with both hands and seemed to take great pleasure in threading his fingers through her long fragrant tresses. "Do you remember the first night you spent at the *quinta*?"

"Yes." How could she forget?

"I couldn't sleep after I took you back to the cottage." His voice was still husky with emotion. "All I could think of was how much I wanted to kiss you, to make love to you." He paused briefly, continuing to stroke her hair. "I went out for a walk and like a lovesick calf found myself standing outside your cottage. I was still there when you came out, and I followed you to the pool. Do you know what you made me think of then, as you stood there dressed only in moonlight?"

She shook her head.

"A goddess."

"Oh!" she breathed. Did he really see her like that?

"You're so lovely, my dove. I wanted you then just as much as I want you now." He leaned forward to cover her mouth with his own. Jennifer parted her lips to allow him access and was disappointed when, rather than deepen the kiss, he drew away.

"We'd better go to that party," he said, heaving a wistful sigh. "I don't think I'll be able to keep myself from making love to you if we stay here."

"Yes, perhaps we better."

"I'll take a shower while you dress."

"It's a deal."

"Will you do something for me?" he asked.

"Sure, what?"

"Don't do your hair up. I like to see it loose like it is now."

"Very well, sir. Your wish is my command."

The mock curtsy she gave him prompted him to throw back his head with a hearty laugh. "If only I could believe that! I know from experience, Miss Dawn Maitland, that you can be quite a handful when you set your mind to it."

Now more than ever Jennifer hated to hear Alejandro call her by her false name. If she had entertained doubts about his guilt before, this new facet of his personality—the passionate yet tender lover she had discovered in the last hour—had finally convinced her that Tommy's suspicions had to be wrong.

She was about to voice her thoughts when he said, "I'd better get to that shower," and gave her a swift kiss before he turned and hurriedly walked away.

Jennifer let go of a sigh as the bathroom door closed behind him. Then she gathered her makeup, and after adjusting the lighting, proceeded to apply it.

She did it with a light touch. Her fondness for the outdoors had given her complexion a healthy golden glow that only required the finishing touches of a delicate blusher for evening wear. Although long and thick, her lashes were light in color and needed the darkening effect of mascara to make her eyes more dramatic, however. After applying a coat of a rosy lip gloss she bent over and gave vigorous brushing to her hair. This added extra fullness to her naturally heavy mane, and all she had to do when she straightened up again was to add a few finishing touches to her hairstyle.

The dress she had purchased for the occasion was devastatingly feminine. It had long fitted sleeves, and the uneven petal hem of the flowing skirt was a little shorter in front than it was in the back. The wide belt, which served to emphasize her narrow waist, was trimmed with tiny gold beads where it met the daringly plunging neckline.

Jennifer was adjusting the straps of the high-heeled red sandals she had bought to go with the dress when Alejandro came out of the bathroom. A towel wrapped around his slim hips was his only concession to modesty.

Involuntarily her mouth fell open a little. Her attention was completely captured by the ripple of muscles on his massive shoulders. His powerful chest was covered with a mat of curling dark hair that tapered to a narrow band as it continued down his belly. His thighs and legs were well shaped and sensuous, and although the rest of his body was tanned, the top edge of the towel, where it hung on his hips, revealed a strip of very fair skin that had never been exposed to the sun.

Jennifer forgot all about her sandals at the sight of him, this half-naked man who suddenly had the power to excite her more than she had ever dreamed possible. What's more, she didn't understand why she felt that way now and not before, when he had taken off his clothes to make love to her. She realized then that she had been so nervous at that moment that she hadn't even noticed.

"That's one sexy dress, lady," Alejandro's voice

broke into her thoughts. He came to her and her skin tingled as he put a possessive hand on her hip and with two fingers of his other hand delicately pushed aside the fabric to plant a kiss between her breasts. "Mmm, I'm not sure I want all the men at the party to see so much of you, though. You'd better pin it or something."

Jennifer looked down at the front of her dress, and her face reflected her disbelief when she looked up at him again. "Pin it?"

"Yes, pin it," he repeated. "You're showing too much cleavage."

She went to stand in front of the mirror and examined her image. The gap of the fabric was very slight. She wasn't revealing much at all. "I think it looks just fine."

She began to turn away from the mirror, but Alejandro was suddenly standing behind her, and his eyes caught hers in the glass. "I'm not taking you anywhere until you pin that dress together. Is that clear?"

Jennifer was too independent—and too stubborn— to accept an order so bluntly given. The expression on her face was mutinous as she retorted with justified indignation, "I'm not a child, Alex. I don't need your permission to wear this dress, and I'll go wherever I damn please! Now is *that* clear?"

Angrily she turned on her heel and walked away. She was almost at the bedroom door when he caught up with her. Unceremoniously he spun her around, and one look at his face was enough to make Jennifer realize that he wasn't going to give in.

"Don't provoke me, Alba." His voice was barely above a whisper and his squarish jaw was set.

Jennifer's eyes widened. She was independent but not stupid, and she realized that getting into an argument with Alejandro at this moment would serve no useful purpose. Taking the most prudent course of action she could think of, she composed her features, and in the coolest tone she could muster, said, "All right, Alex, I'll pin the dress."

She saw the flicker of surprise that flashed through his eyes before he nodded curtly. She went back to stand in front of the dresser and proceeded to pin the folds of material together—a mere three inches above the waistband. The exercise exposed a good deal more of her flesh than the neckline had originally, and the result wasn't a great improvement on her modesty. Turning to face him again, she leaned seductively against the dresser, knowing instinctively that he couldn't help responding to the sight of her.

"If you want me to...alter it you'll have to do it yourself," she murmured huskily, straightening her shoulders so that the red material pulled against her breasts.

His eyes darkened, but when he didn't move, she laughed softly. "Life is full of compromise, Alejandro. Particularly between two people as different as we are."

THE PARTY WAS BEING GIVEN at a large modern apartment in a building much like the one they had just left. It was in full swing by the time Jennifer and Alejandro arrived.

After their disagreement at the apartment, she had been cool and distant toward him—and he'd pretended to take no notice. But since it wasn't in her nature to hold a grudge, a few minutes after they arrived at the party she had reverted to her usual friendly self.

Alejandro introduced her to the host and hostess almost immediately. Raul Soler was a contemporary of Alejandro's, and from their conversation Jennifer was able to learn that the relationship between them dated back to their school days. In addition, the nature of their respective businesses kept them in touch, since Soler owned a mill, the textile products of which found their way to foreign markets. His beautiful wife, Amanda, who was somewhere in her late twenties, was a little taller than Jennifer and blue eyed. Her light ash brown hair was beautifully coiffed in a simple style that enhanced the perfect classic features of her face. The ice-blue satin gown she was wearing did nothing to hide the fact that two pregnancies had failed to spoil her figure—which years earlier had won her the title of Miss Colombia, Jennifer found out.

Alejandro was acquainted with most of the people present, and he saw to it that Jennifer met them. Even though she had no trouble communicating, sometimes in Spanish, sometimes in English, he remained at her side.

They were engaged in animated conversation with a few other people when Amanda Soler joined them again.

"You must bring Alba to our *finca* for some weekend, before she goes back to the States, Alex," the woman invited. Jennifer had just mentioned that she enjoyed hiking and horseback riding.

Alejandro nodded. "I'll give you a call to set the time."

"Please do." Amanda's attention then turned to the maids who were setting out the buffet supper. "Excuse me a moment, will you?" she asked as she slipped away.

"What's a *finca*?" Jennifer inquired when the hostess had left them.

"A country house," he replied. "Somewhere between a ranch and a farm. For most people it's a place to spend weekends and holidays, only sometimes it really is a working farm or ranch. Would you like to go?"

"Perhaps," Jennifer said with a shrug of her shoulders. This had been the longest exchange between them since their quarrel, and she knew that he was trying to get back into her good graces.

Just then Amanda returned. "I'm sorry, but that girl was setting the plates all wrong," she apologized. With a sigh, she added, "It's not easy to find good servants any more. Most of the country girls nowadays prefer to work at the flower plantations or in the factories. In a way, who can blame them, but it certainly doesn't make it easier for us to run a household properly." She paused, then smiled charmingly. "But, please, forgive me! I'm sure that for a career woman like yourself, these little calamities must sound very trivial."

"Not really," Jennifer smiled wryly. "I spend too much time away from home in the course of my work, and I assure you that when my cleaning lady doesn't show, it's panic time for me. I don't mind cooking, but I hate housework.''

Amanda laughed, and putting a hand on Alejandro's sleeve, smiled up at him. "Alex, darling, would you mind getting me a champagne cocktail?" she asked.

"Alba?"

Jennifer saw that her glass was still full. "Nothing, thank you.''

Amanda looked after Alejandro and gave a little sigh. "Charming man, isn't he?"

Charming was not an adjective she would have applied to Alejandro before today, Jennifer thought. Still, she had to admit he could indeed be charming when he wanted to. "Yes, I suppose he is,'' she replied, hoping she sounded noncommittal.

"Suppose?" There was a note of amusement in the hostess's voice. "My dear Alba,'' she replied, "there's no need to pretend. I'm on your side.''

Taken aback, Jennifer remained silent. Was her love for Alejandro so obvious?

"Raul and I are his best friends,'' Amanda went on. "We want him to be happy. God knows there's been enough misfortune in his life.''

Imagining she was referring to the loss of Alejandro's wife, Jennifer bit her lower lip. "There are... obstacles to anything serious developing between Alex and me,'' she pointed out.

"Ofelia?" Amanda made a small gesture with her hand and added with a conspiratorial smile, "With the kind of electricity that exists between you,

I don't think you have anything to worry about."

Jennifer chose to let Amanda believe as she did, and not wishing to pursue the subject observed, "Alex said you're originally from Cali. Isn't that the city where his sister lives?"

Amanda wasn't expecting the sudden change of subject. "Nancy?" she repeated. "Oh, yes. She went to live there after she married Carlos Verdugo."

Something in her tone of voice told Jennifer that her hostess wasn't very fond of the man. She was tempted to ask why, but even as she was telling herself she shouldn't, Amanda added, "Perhaps I shouldn't speak of this, but I wouldn't be too surprised if Nancy suddenly decided to return to Bogotá."

Jennifer looked at her in surprise, and Amanda shook her head and said, "Whatever you may hear, you shouldn't judge all our men by the actions of a few, Miss Maitland."

Jennifer was a little mystified by such a cryptic statement, but she saw that Alejandro was returning with Amanda's drink. A movement directly behind him caught her eye as well.

A young woman was advancing toward her, a grin of recognition on her face. With a jolt of dismay, Jennifer placed her immediately. It was Becky Simms, a former neighbor of hers from California. With a single word she was going to ruin everything!

CHAPTER EIGHT

IN THE FEW SECONDS that passed as Jennifer watched the American woman advanced toward her, several courses of action to avoid the impending disaster flashed through her mind. Her most immediate worry was that Becky would call her name out loud. She had to stop her from doing so. But how?

Although the hostess was still at her side, Jennifer was quick to notice that her attention had again been diverted by the maids setting up the buffet table. Then Jennifer's prayers were answered when someone called to Alejandro and he paused for a moment to talk. Taking advantage of that momentary diversion, she signalled her old friend with a brief shake of her head accompanied by a discreet wave.

The gesture effectively stopped Becky in her tracks. Her face became a study in surprise, but she didn't approach any closer.

As Alejandro rejoined them and handed Amanda her drink, Jennifer noticed that a tall, lanky, blond-haired man apparently in his early thirties came up to Becky. From the puzzled glances both of them were casting in her direction as they conversed, Jennifer knew her secret was out.

"I see an American couple that I'm sure you would

like to meet, Alba,'' Amanda said smiling and waving at Becky and the blond man. ''He's an engineer in charge of a big project in La Guajira—a coal mine, I think—and you might have something in common with his wife, Becky.''

So this man was Becky's husband, Jennifer realized in relief.

''Larry and Becky Mathews, I'd like you to meet a compatriot of yours who's been in Colombia only since last week,'' Amanda said. ''Miss Dawn Maitland.''

''How do you do.'' Jennifer tried to convey a message in the pressure of her handshake. Becky accepted it with a bemused expression on her face when she heard the strange name being used by her old friend. But she didn't give her away.

Jennifer tried to remember the last time she and Becky had met. Their interests had been different, and they had been friends mostly because Becky had dated Tommy until her father, a marketing executive for a large corporation, had been transferred to another state. They had lost touch after that. And why, after all these years, did they have to meet again now?

Alejandro was introduced to the American couple in turn, and the five of them stood in a group making desultory conversation. Then the buffet was served, and they all went to fill their plates with the tempting array of food displayed on the long tables. The tables, like the apartment itself, held an abundance of flowers. Predominant in magnificent floral arrangements were a variety of orchids, the national flower of Colombia.

In the confusion Jennifer extricated herself from Alejandro's company and looked for an opportunity to approach her friend.

"What's going on?" was Becky's greeting. "Why are you going under an assumed name?"

"Oh, Becky, it's such a long story that there's no time to tell you now," Jennifer said in a low voice. "Please bear with me for just a little longer, only don't let on that we've known each other before tonight. If you do, my life could be in danger. Do you understand?"

"Your life?" Becky was clearly taken aback. "But . . . why, Jennifer? What *are* you doing here in Colombia?"

Jennifer looked around her to make sure no one was listening before she replied, "All I can tell you right now is that my presence here involves Tommy. He's in prison, Becky, and he's innocent."

"Tommy?" Becky repeated in disbelief. "In prison? But how? Why?"

Jennifer smiled, as if they were talking about perfectly natural things. "Let's get together for lunch on Monday, and I'll tell you everything then. Do you know of a place where we could talk in private?"

Becky nodded. "Come to my house. Larry will be going back to the project in the morning and the maid speaks hardly any English, so there'll be no one to disturb us there."

"By the way, did you tell Larry about me?"

"I'm afraid so," her friend nodded. "But don't worry about him, he won't say a word. He's a good guy."

Jennifer had to laugh. "He seems to be. How long have you been married?"

"Three years. And you, Jennifer? Last time I had a letter from Tommy, he mentioned you were preparing for your own wedding. What happened?"

"Jim was killed a few days before the date."

Instinctively Becky reached for her hand. "Oh, gosh, Jenny, I'm sorry."

Jennifer waited for the sharp pain, the gnawing guilt that invariably followed any reminder of that tragic event. She was surprised when all she felt was a kind of bittersweet sadness and regret. It was then she realized that her time of mourning and penance was over. She had loved Jim and he would always be a part of her life, but he belonged in the past. The years ahead were hers to live.

"It's all right, Becky." Her smile was wistful. "I'm all right now."

THE DREAM WAS SO REAL that Jennifer found herself responding to it. She was being kissed—gently but thoroughly, and she parted her lips to grant access to the tongue that caressed and curled around her own after it had explored the moist warmth of her mouth. She sighed as long and teasing fingers gently stroked her face and her throat, then moved down to her shoulders and breasts. Her mouth was claimed again, this time more urgently, and she lifted her arms. When they entwined around a firm strong neck, she woke up.

She blinked rapidly, startled. "Alex!"

"Good morning," he smiled.

"What are you doing here?"

"Waking you up."

"You shouldn't have come."

"I know." His fingers were warm and gentle on her face when he added, "I succumbed to the temptation when I couldn't stay away any longer."

Relishing his touch, Jennifer closed her eyes. The lassitude of sleep was compounded by the languorous response she felt to his caresses. She was unable to resist his touch; she was perhaps more vulnerable, her body more receptive to his lovemaking in this first waking moment than she would be at any other time of the day. As his mouth sought hers again, she pressed against him, and his hands explored and caressed her until she was trembling with desire for him.

It was Alejandro who drew back at last. His breathing was shallow, uneven. "You're right, I shouldn't have come. I don't seem to be able to keep my hands off you when we're together." His voice grew huskier as he gazed into her eyes, limpid pools, which passion had darkened to a brilliant green. "Especially when you look at me like you're doing now."

He got up from the edge of the bed where he was sitting and shook his head as if to dispel her hold on him. "At any rate, I have polo practice at eleven. I thought you might like to come and watch. We could have lunch at the club afterward and go for a drive in the afternoon."

"What time is it now?" Jennifer yawned. Stretching out luxuriously, much like a contented kitten, she was unaware of the provocative effect her arching body had on Alejandro.

"About 9:30."

"Nine-thirty!" She sat up abruptly. "Why did you let me sleep so late?"

The corner of his mouth tilted in amusement at her panic. "We got home very late last night. I thought I'd let you sleep in."

"I'll be ready in half an hour."

Alejandro turned and walked away. When he was at the door he paused and looked at her again. "Anita was fixing breakfast when I left. I'll wait for you there; just come right in."

As soon as he had gone out the door, Jennifer threw the covers aside, jumped lithely out of bed and rushed to the bathroom. After quickly performing her morning ablutions, she went through her closet, trying to decide what to wear to a polo match at the exclusive Jockey Club. After some deliberation she decided she couldn't go wrong with a white silk dress printed with tiny lavender flowers. She buttoned the standing collar at the throat and adjusted the narrow lavender leather belt around her waist. The semicircular skirt moved sensuously around her knees, while the breezy cap sleeves left her slender arms bare.

Quickly she brushed her hair and pinned it in a knot on top of her head and, before rushing out the door, grabbed a floppy wide-brimmed hat of Italian raffia.

She knew her way to the dining room, where they had eaten dinner on her first night at the *quinta*, and since there was no one around when she arrived at the house, she did as Alejandro had told her and simply walked right in. The table had been set for two, but Alejandro was not there.

"Dónde está—where is Señor Adler?" she asked the maid who entered the dining room.

The young woman grinned and pointed in the direction of the salon where Jennifer had met Alejandro's relatives. Then she launched into a complicated sentence in Spanish, spoken so rapidly and in such an unfamiliar accent that it left Jennifer as much in the dark as before. It was funny how much more easily she could understand Alejandro, Sara, and the people she had met at the party, she thought.

But the girl's gestures were clear enough, so she nodded and smiled, *"Gracias."* Not wanting to sit alone at the table, she went to the parlor to look for Alejandro. It was empty, and when he hadn't arrived after a few minutes, she sat down on the divan and picked up a copy of a *Cromos* magazine from the cocktail table.

Lack of practice had affected her spoken Spanish more than the written language. Within minutes, she was engrossed in an article about the political candidates running for president in the next election. She noticed, however, that more space had been given to the candidates of the approaching Miss Colombia beauty contest. Page after page of the magazine was crammed with brief bios, interviews, and photographs of the shapely contestants, who represented each of the many regions of the country.

At last Jennifer's concentration was interrupted by the murmur of voices suddenly rising in anger. Jennifer recognized one of the voices, which were coming from an adjacent room, as belonging to Señora de Adler. A second voice, a feminine one, was unfamiliar to her. Even though they were speaking Spanish she could understand them without much difficulty.

"I said I'm not going back!" the new voice said. "It wasn't an easy decision to make, and I'm not going to change my mind!"

"Marriage is not something to be discarded when things don't go your way. There's never been a divorce in our family." It was Mariana who had spoken.

"Well, if you ask me, there should have been," the first woman retorted.

"For heaven's sakes, Alex, talk to your sister," Señora de Adler said. "Make her see reason!"

Jennifer could hear Alejandro's voice, but it wasn't as loud as the others and she couldn't make out the words. She felt uneasy about eavesdropping on what was obviously a family argument. She started to get up, but the next words she heard froze her in her seat.

"Sure, that's easy for you to say," Nancy snapped. "You're a man. When you and Roxana weren't sleeping together, it was all right for you to go out and find someone else. But what am I going to do? Do you expect me to sit at home like a nun in a convent and suffer in silence while Carlos continues to humiliate me? Well, I'm not going to do it! I'm getting a divorce!"

"I'm not going to sit by and let you ruin your life,

Nancy,'' Señora de Adler insisted. ''If I can't make you see the error of your ways, then we'll have to call your uncle.''

''The error of my ways!'' Nancy gave a derisive laugh. ''Oh, mother! Carlos is the one who's been in bed with half the women in Cali under the age of fifty!''

''I warned you he was a wild one before you married him,'' the older woman replied dryly, ''and you still chose to go ahead with it. It's too late now for recriminations. Your duty is to stay with your husband.''

''I knew you would say something like that.'' There was no mistaking the bitterness in Nancy's voice. ''That's why I came here instead of going to your house. If I had known you were staying with Alex, I wouldn't have come. You don't care for any of us, mother. All you care about is your precious Navarro name! Well, I'm not a Navarro. My name is Adler! Daddy wouldn't have sent me back to Carlos like you're trying to do!''

Jennifer had heard enough. Before she could leave the room the door suddenly flew open and a tall beautiful woman burst in. Two red spots tinging her cheeks betrayed her anger. She stopped abruptly, startled to find Jennifer there.

From her seat on the edge of the divan, Jennifer stared back, unable to think of anything to say. She was spared having to make an apology when Nancy turned on her heel and stalked out of the room.

Jennifer jumped to her feet, wanting to get as far away as possible from the place, she was so embarrassed. She was at the door leading to the dining room when Alejandro emerged from the other room. "Alba, wait!"

Totally mortified, she turned to look at him, but instead of waiting she hurried out into the courtyard. She had gone only a few steps through the front door when she was stopped by a strong paid of hands, which prevented her flight.

"Let me go!" She tried to twist out of his grasp, but instead of releasing her, Alejandro held her tighter.

He kept his hold on her until she stopped struggling, then he led her to a room she had never seen before, a combination study-library, the walls of which were covered with floor-to-ceiling shelves of books.

Alejandro offered her a seat on the brown leather sofa, then sat down next to her. "So you overheard our little discussion back there, and you've more or less met my sister," he said with a sigh. "I...I suppose you heard what she said about me and my own marriage?"

Jennifer refused to meet his gaze when she replied, "I didn't mean to eavesdrop, and I'm so embarrassed!"

He was silent for a moment, then went on, "I thought so. And I suppose you assume I was sleeping all over town while I was still married. You might even infer that I'm some kind of Don Juan who gets his kicks by chasing after every skirt in sight."

"You owe me no explanations," she said dryly.

"No, I don't, do I?"

Jennifer pursed her lips.

"Look at me, Alba."

When she still refused to obey, he gently but firmly turned her face until she was forced to meet his eyes. "I want you to look at me while I tell you this, because I want you to believe me. What you heard—that Roxana and I were not sleeping together while we were married—was true." He paused briefly, as if wondering what to say next. "Roxana and I were married very young," he said at last. "She was high strung, very mercurial. I don't know what she expected from marriage, but whatever it was, she didn't find it with me. Perhaps it was my fault, I don't know. After Heidi was born, she refused to accept any responsibility for her." Again he paused, apparently choosing his words with care. "She traveled for a while and became interested in art. She said she wanted to pursue her artistic career and asked for a divorce. When I refused, she moved all her things to the cottage."

"Why didn't you let her go?"

"I couldn't." He shrugged his shoulders slightly. "She was self-destructive when things didn't go her way. Painting was only an excuse to run away from reality. She had no talent and she knew it, but she could always blame me for not giving her the chance to become a successful artist."

"Oh, Alex, I'm sorry. It must have been horrible for you."

He took the hand she had laid against his cheek and held it there. "What I was trying to say is that she was my wife and my responsibility, Alba. Nancy and Carlos have two children to consider, and I sincerely hope they can patch things up. But it's her life, and she's my sister. She'll have my support in whatever she decides to do.''

"Señora de Adler is very upset."

"Mother lives her own life the way she chooses. Nancy and I are entitled to do the same."

The message he was conveying was clear to Jennifer.

BY THE TIME THE FLURRY created by Nancy's sudden arrival and her announcement of her intentions to divorce her husband had subsided a little, it was too late for Alejandro to take part in his polo practice. Consequently, he and Jennifer decided to spend what was left of the day at the *quinta*. After a light lunch, Jennifer returned to the cottage to change into her new swimming suit for an afternoon by the pool. It was a rather modest suit—one piece and of white knit—and it suggested more than revealed the willowy lines of her body.

When she arrived at the pool, Heidi and her cousins were playing with a huge beach ball under the watchful eyes of their respective parents. Señora de Adler was nowhere to be seen.

Alejandro, looking lean and athletic in his brief black swimsuit, made the introductions between his houseguest and his sister.

A beautiful woman, Nancy was tall and her figure lithe. She had lustrous brown hair and eyes that were dark and thickly lashed. They were of the same color as her mother's Jennifer noticed, but more attractive because they were more expressive. And her reception was so warm and friendly that Jennifer wondered if Alejandro had told her the nature of their relationship went beyond business.

"I'm glad you overheard our argument this morning," Nancy admitted frankly. "Now I won't have to pretend about what I'm doing here. I'm tired of pretense. From now on I'll do and say exactly what I feel."

Jennifer was also tired of pretense. It was foreign to her nature and she despised what she was doing, but the stakes were very high. She couldn't afford the luxury of telling the truth.

She had told herself over and over that if only she could talk to Alejandro and explain, he would probably be the first to help her find the man who had framed her brother. Only two words prevented her from baring her soul to him—what if. What if she was wrong? What if Alejandro was working with the smugglers? What if it had been he who had planted the evidence against Tommy?

How much longer could she maintain the pretense? One entire week had already gone by, and she had been unable to find the slightest trace of evidence that was incriminating against Alejandro. Perhaps with Mateo's help she could speed up her investigation, before she ran out of excuses and Alejandro began to suspect she had deceived him.

In her heart she knew he had to be innocent of Tommy's accusations. With each passing moment, with each discovery of another facet of his personality, her love for him continued to grow. But what future could there be for their love? Even if he were innocent, how could he ever forgive her deceit? If she really loved him why couldn't she trust him?

There was no doubt in Jennifer's mind that she loved Alejandro. Had she been the only person involved, she wouldn't have hesitated for an instant in confiding in him. But it wasn't her fate alone she'd be placing in his hands....

JENNIFER WAS ALREADY DRESSED when Alejandro and Heidi knocked on the cottage door early the next morning. The three of them had made plans for an overnight pleasure-and-business trip to Lake Guatavitá and Villa de Leyva. She would have preferred to have Nancy and her children join them, but Señora de Adler had summoned her brother for a family consultation, and the monsignor was expected later in the day. Jennifer didn't think Alejandro would take advantage of the trip to change their relationship to a more intimate one if Heidi was along. Still, reluctant to go, she had mentioned her plans to meet her "new" acquaintance, Becky, on Monday. But Alejandro had insisted, and she had phoned her friend to postpone their meeting for a day.

After Alejandro had helped her in to the front seat and Heidi into the back, he went around the car and slid behind the wheel. He had obviously decided to dispense with the services of his chauffeur and was driving the car himself. More and more their trip was taking the semblance of a family outing.

"Since you seemed so interested in El Dorado, I figured you might as well get to see the lake where the legend was born," he told Jennifer. He slowed down the car as the guard opened the gates to the estate, then waved at them as they drove though.

"When Nancy and I were growing up, visiting the lake was not quite as easy as it is today," he continued conversationally, turning onto the highway that led back to the city. "The road didn't go as far as the lake, and the last leg of the trip had to be done on horseback. In some parts the trail got very muddy and narrow."

At Heidi's prompting, he described more of his experiences on previous visits to Lake Guatavitá.

"I think you'll enjoy the village," he went on. "There's an interesting story about it. Since water was frequently in short supply in Bogotá, a few years ago the city decided to increase the size of the reservoir at Sesquilé. The problem was that to do so would inundate the village. So they built an entirely new village on higher ground and moved all the people. The best architects and community planners were called in to do the job. Wait 'til you see it. It's become quite a tourist attraction."

Traffic grew heavier as they left Avenida El Libertador and took a modern *autopista* that climbed into the mountains. It was signposted Tunja. As they began passing many of the lakes in the area, Jennifer saw a good number of people preparing to picnic.

The scenery was breathtaking. The sharp green peaks of the Andes were clearly defined against a cloudless, cerulean sky, and profusions of wild flowers dotted the sides of the road with their whites, yellows, pinks and purples. The air was crisp and clear.

"Daddy, I'm thirsty," Heidi said after a while. "Can I have a drink?"

"Sure, *mi hijita*, but wait until we get to the village, okay? It won't be long now. The road to the lake is just ahead."

Jennifer saw a narrow road coming up on their left. Alejandro turned onto it, and after driving a little while longer they arrived at the village of New Guatavitá.

Traffic was not allowed in the town, so they parked in the square designated just outside of it. "Well, this is as far as we drive," Alejandro announced. "From here on we walk."

They got out of the car and headed toward the community. At the entrance to the town they were silently greeted by the large statue of a Chibcha Indian chief.

Everywhere she turned, Jennifer was enchanted by what she saw. Following the traditional Spanish style, the focus of the town was its main square, which was full of children playing. Some obviously from the city mingled with those from the village—little boys in short pants and girls in pastel dresses and crisp starched pinafores. The girls' glossy black tresses were carefully braided, their cheeks made rosy by the crisp mountain air. The women wore full colorful skirts and beautiful fringed black shawls that looked as if they were made of silk.

"I thought you said the inhabitants were Indians," Jennifer observed.

"They are," Alejandro replied.

"But they don't look it," she argued. "They're just as fair as you and me."

"I suppose they might have some Spanish blood," he said. "Only one percent of our population is pure Indian. But the Chibchas always had fine features. They're a very handsome people."

The buildings themselves were beautiful, made of subtly shaded stone, exquisitely carved wood, and richly colored mosaics. Each one, whether a house, a shop or a church, was individually striking and still harmonious with the whole. And as background to it all were the lake and the mountains.

"Oh, look!" Jennifer cried, pointing at the bull-ring, which, from this distance, looked toy-sized. "Is it real?"

"Of course it is!" Heidi laughed.

Alejandro took Jennifer's arm. "Let's get Heidi that drink before we go exploring."

They went into a small cafe where Heidi ordered a *jugo de granadilla*."

"Would you like one?" Alejandro asked Jennifer.

"What is it?"

"Passion-fruit juice," he replied. "It's very good and refreshing. Try it."

"All right."

After finishing their refreshments, they went back outside. Jennifer was a little surprised—and she felt a little awkward—when Heidi took her by the hand as they started down the street. She gave Alejandro a sheepish smile when he noticed his daughter's gesture.

Their first stop was at a church, decorated with bright mosaics. A group of children were being baptized.

"Would you like to ride the boats, Miss Maitland?" Heidi asked as they came out of the church.

Jennifer couldn't help laughing. The little girl's voice was so hopeful it was obvious she was dying to go out on the lake. "Don't you want to visit the markets first?" she asked teasingly.

"But if we buy anything now, we'll have to carry it on the boat," Heidi replied, wrinkling her nose.

"Good point!" Jennifer conceded with another laugh. She was certainly her father's daughter—she knew how to get what she wanted.

With a group of other tourists they boarded the outboard motor launch that would take them on a cruise around the lake, where other weekend visitors were already engaged in water sports, Jennifer noted. She almost jumped when Alejandro slung his arm around her shoulder as he sat down beside her on a bench.

Heidi, on her other side, was obviously delighted to have her wish. "Isn't this fun, Miss Maitland?" she grinned as they waited for the launch to fill up.

Jennifer blinked rapidly behind her sunglasses, glad for the cover they afforded. As the little girl spoke she had again taken Jennifer's hand in hers, and the contact of those small fingers, so warm and trusting, had caused a lump to suddenly develop in her throat.

She had always been fond of children, but her relationship with Heidi was a great source of concern.

She had tried very hard to keep her distance from the little girl, but to no avail. Heidi was bound and determined to be her friend, and short of outright rudeness, which was beyond her capability, Jennifer didn't know how else to stop her.

At last the motor launch was full, and the craft began its journey of that isolated world so high up in the Andes. To please Alejandro, Jennifer had left her hair loose, and only when they had boarded the launch had she tied it back with a beige scarf matching her khaki safari jump suit. As the craft got underway, tendrils of her hair flew around her face, stirred by the wind.

Alejandro purposely let the tip of his finger touch her lips as he removed one strand of hair that had caught in her mouth. "You're lovely, you know that?" he whispered in her ear as Heidi was busy waving at people on other launches that went by.

With a sigh, Jennifer leaned her head against his shoulder and moved closer to him. Comfortably, naturally his arm went around her waist. Under different circumstances she couldn't have asked for more—spending a day like this with the man she loved, and with his delightful child. But these were not ordinary circumstances, she told herself regretfully. The mirror surface of the lake, the sunny day, the cloudless sky, the mountains rising all around them were nothing more than the setting for a drama that waited to unfold.

She had never dreamed anything like this could happen. If someone had told her she would fall in love with the man who had sent her brother to prison, Jennifer would have laughed, it was such a ridiculous notion. But the Alejandro Adler she had expected to find when she came to Colombia was nothing like this Alejandro she had come to know— know and love. The former was capable of framing an innocent man; the latter was a generous friend; a loyal sensitive man; a gentle passionate lover. It didn't seem possible the two could be one and the same....

After taking them around the lake, the motor launch returned its passengers to the original point of embarcation.

"Where to next?" Alejandro inquired of both his companions.

Jennifer looked about her undecided, but Heidi knew immediately what she wanted to do next. "The priest's house!"

"All right," the two adults replied in unison.

"Is anything wrong?" Alejandro asked Jennifer when his daughter skipped happily ahead.

"Wrong?" Jennifer, who had tried to keep a happy countenance despite her musings, was taken a little aback that Alejandro wasn't duped by her pretense. "What makes you say that?"

"You don't seem to be enjoying the visit."

Jennifer gave thanks that his probing glance could not penetrate the shield of her sunglasses as he added, "Would you like to go on to Villa de Leyva?"

"Don't be silly! Of course I'm enjoying it!" she protested, perhaps a little too brightly. "This is a lovely place, and I'm so glad you and Heidi brought me here."

The look Alejandro gave her made Jennifer realize she had overcompensated with her little speech. They had arrived at their next stop, however—a little house surrounded by a beautiful garden, where the wild flowers of the area bloomed profusely around the fountain that rose in their midst. They had caught up with Heidi, and there was no chance to talk further.

It was time for lunch by the time they finished admiring the collection of antique paintings and drawings at the priest's house. The works of art depicted many Chibcha Indians and Fray José de las Casas, the Jesuit priest who had converted them to Christianity. Unanimously they decided to head for one of the local restaurants.

"I was beginning to wonder if Colombians ever ate their native food," Jennifer commented as she examined the menu.

"I'll admit we do tend to favor Continental cuisine," Alejandro said. "You must remember that the best restaurants in Bogotá were established by Europeans, so most of them have followed that tradition. But we do enjoy our own *cocina criolla*."

"I don't see any fish on the menu," Jennifer observed after scanning the list. She'd been looking forward to a delicious trout fresh from the lake, or something similar.

Alejandro shook his head, reading her mind. "There're no fish in the lake, if that's what you're wondering about. I'm not sure if the altitude is too high for fish or if the lake's simply been fished out."

She was a little disappointed by the news. "What would you recommend?"

"Try the *sobrebarriga bogotana*," he suggested. "It's a flank steak that I think you'll enjoy. I'm going to have the same."

He ordered an *aguardiente* cocktail for Jennifer and himself—the same thing they once had at the *quinta*—and a soda for Heidi. The drinks came accompanied by something similar to potato chips, which Heidi said were made of cassava. The crisp mountain air had stimulated their appetites, and the chips disappeared quite rapidly.

The generous portions of steak had a golden breading and were served on a platter with a savory sauce on the side. While Heidi ate her *ajiaco*, a kind of creamy potato soup with diced chicken, Jennifer and Alejandro shared a dish of *papas chorreadas*, the small highland potatoes covered with a delicate cheese sauce. They also had an avocado salad with a simple dressing of vinegar and olive oil.

"I couldn't eat another bite," Jennifer exclaimed, shaking her head when Alejandro asked her if she wanted dessert. Finally Heidi persuaded her to taste her *flan de piña*, a creamy pineapple custard in caramel sauce.

They spent the afternoon at the open air markets, which in addition to a rich variety of vegetables and fruit offered articles made by the inhabitants of the village.

Jennifer was interested in hearing Alejandro talk about the products found in the market. Apparently the district of Boyaca was one of the few areas of the country where sheep were reared in sufficient quantities to make fine woolen articles of clothing. He pointed out the quality of the blankets, the exciting patterns of stripes and checks, and the fantastic combinations of colors—orange, pink and red, or green and red offset with gray.

In the cold Andean mountains, the favorite native garb, understandably, was the *ruana*. The native ponchos were being sold in solid colors or checks, in hues ranging from subtle oatmeal through varying shades of bright red and blue to black. The fringed shawls worn by the Indian women were on display as well. Feeling their texture, Jennifer could not distinguish their material from silk. Sandals and straw hats like the ones worn by the village men were also on sale.

Jennifer examined several clay pots, which Alejandro said were Indian crockery, and Heidi fell in love with a collection of tiny animals beautifully carved from shiny polished stones. The same type of stones had been used to make interesting ashtrays.

Their bundle of purchases—of these articles and then of fruit at fresh produce stalls—grew as the afternoon went on, and it was with armloads of merchandise that they returned to the car at dusk. Heidi, who hadn't stopped going all day, fell asleep in the back seat as soon as they left the village.

"Must you keep so far away?" Alejandro asked after they had been driving for a while. Jennifer was sitting at the opposite end of the front seat, almost leaning against the door.

"I didn't want to crowd you." The excuse sounded lame even to her own ears, but it was the only one she could think of at the moment.

She heard his low chuckle in the dark, then he said, "Come over here and crowd me."

Half reluctantly, Jennifer inched her way across the wide seat until she was next to him. He cast a brief sidelong glance in her direction but then continued to keep his attention on the road.

The traffic was heavy. It seemed as if all the people from Bogotá had stayed until the very last minute to make the most of their Sunday outing, then had decided to go home at precisely the same time. When Alejandro reached the main highway, however, he turned in the opposite direction, toward Villa de Leyva, leaving most of the traffic behind.

Jennifer would have preferred to make the drive in the daylight. Then the beautiful view of lakes, mountains and wild flowers, very much like a Swiss postcard, would have served to distract her. Now darkness hid all that beauty, and she was left with nothing but her own thoughts—and Alejandro's perturbing nearness. There was little conversation between them, but a great deal of awareness, and she almost gave a sigh of relief when they finally arrived at the colonial-style town Monsignor Navarro had praised so highly.

It had been founded back in 1572, and named after the colonial governor, Don Andres Diaz Venero de Leyva, perhaps the most progressive ruler the Spanish colony had ever had. The period of his administration had been referred to as the Golden Age, and the town, situated in an area with perfect climate and a picturesque location overlooking a rich plain, had attracted many settlers. Numerous Spanish noblemen had lived there in splendor, as attested to by the mansions that remained. The tranquil beauty of the place had made it a favorite resort in modern times.

The hotel they went to was a charming converted sixteenth-century mill. The patio, full of vivid blooms in pinks, purples and yellows, had a little stream winding among the landscaped bushes.

"Will you help me put Heidi to bed?" Alejandro asked as he carried his sleeping daughter up to the room she and Jennifer were to share.

Jennifer hesitated briefly before saying, "All right." When they reached the door, she followed him inside. A plain wooden crucifix and a religious painting were the only decorations adorning the stark whitewashed walls. Animal skins were strewn on the wooden floors.

Heidi mumbled something unintelligible when her father laid her down on the rough four-poster bed covered with a brightly colored blanket. He smiled wryly at Jennifer, who stood there awkwardly, uncertain as to what to do next. She felt uncomfortable with the domesticity of the situation, with sharing a room with the little girl who would be a victim if she was successful in her mission.

"Get a pair of pajamas from her overnight case, will you, my love?" Alejandro asked as he sat down to remove Heidi's shoes.

Jennifer's hands were shaking while she did as she was told. They were still shaking as she helped Alejandro changed Heidi's clothes.

After Alejandro tucked the covers around his daughter he turned to Jennifer and took her tense body in his arms. She wanted to pull away, but her need to be held in his arms was greater than her conscience.

"Oh, Alex!" she whispered, slipping her arms around him. When she lay her head on his broad chest, she could hear the tattoo of his heartbeat.

"This is what I've been promising myself all day." His mouth sought hers and drank thirstily of her sweetness in a kiss that was full of tenderness and controlled passion.

His desire inflamed her, and even if she had wanted to, Jennifer would have been unable to resist the weakness that stole through her body when he touched her.

CHAPTER NINE

THROUGH HER DROWSINESS Jennifer became aware of the warmth of a body pressing against her under the covers. It was a small body, light and slender, and it felt vaguely comfortable snuggling against her side. She opened her eyes, and felt momentarily disoriented when she didn't recognize any of the austere furniture she could see in the pearly gray light of dawn, only beginning to invade the room. Then she heard the even sound of a child breathing....

It all came back to her now—the joys and sorrows of the day she'd spent with Alejandro and his daughter. A day that had ended on a promising, yet at the same time disturbing note.

Looking up at the rustic beams running across the ceiling, Jennifer remembered those blissful moments she'd spent in Alejandro's arms. As, little by little, the sun continued its ascent toward the mountain peaks and the grayness in the room slowly became lighter, she recalled detail after detail of the evening before.

Even now her heart beat faster, her body tingled with the remembrance of the intimacies they had shared. How could she have so little willpower when it came to his kisses, his caresses? They had become an addiction she was powerless to refuse. Regardless of how her mind dictated caution, her body, her emotions responded to his touch with a will of their own. No man had ever held such power over her before.

It was an experience, this loving beyond reason, that filled her with a wonder such as she had never dreamed possible. But it also frightened her that she had become so vulnerable...to a man she couldn't even trust with her real identity.

After they had put Heidi to bed last night, she had been just as reluctant as he was to part, even though their separation would be brief.

He had gone to his room, giving her time to freshen up before they met again. She had showered quickly and changed her jump suit in favor of an off-the-shoulder dress of a gauzy material that enhanced her femininity. Jennifer knew she was playing with fire, but the joy she felt surging inside her when he had looked at her had made her reckless to the danger.

Avoiding the bar, a cave permeated with the musky smell of sherry drawn straight from the barrel, they had gone into the small dining room lighted by lanterns. It, too, had wooden beams across its high ceiling, and ancient helmets and other pieces of armor decorated the walls. There they had shared a simple meal, accompanied with wine that had proved far less heady than the sound of Alejandro's voice, the touch of his hand.

Later, when they'd gone out for a walk, the town had been quiet, with moonlight spilling like silver on the deserted cobblestones in the main square. The strong arm that went around her, the kisses stolen in the dark, had protected her more effectively against the chill than the *ruana* she had thrown over her dress.

They had both been reluctant to return to the hotel. Their longings could have been so easily satisfied there, yet they had understood without words that they wouldn't make love. Dreading the moment of separation, however, they had kept walking, both of them loathe to say good-night.

They had been crossing a white bridge spanning a rushing mountain stream when Alejandro pulled her pliant body into his arms and once more sought her lips, which parted eagerly. As she surrendered to the demands of his enticing kiss, she could feel the rapid beating of his heart under her hand, which was splayed on his chest. She could sense the strain of passion in him as he pressed against her.

"Te quiero," he had whispered against her mouth in a voice husky with passion.

A sudden weakness had filled her, and Jennifer had been glad he was holding her so tightly. Literally translated, the words he had whispered meant, *I want you*. But by now she was familiar enough with the language of Cervantes to know that they were used more commonly to say, *I love you*.

Could it be true, she asked herself, still unable to accept the knowledge. Could it be true that Alejandro returned her love, that it was not simply desire that bound him to her?

"You're trembling, my dove," he said then, letting his lips tenderly touch her hair.

It was true. Even in the warm circle of his embrace, she couldn't stop shaking. All of a sudden she was terrified.

Alejandro adjusted her *ruana* around her shoulders. "I should not have kept you out so long, darling." Wistfully he touched the tip of his fingers to her pale cheek moistened by the fine mist that had started to fall moments earlier. "Come, I'll take you back to the hotel, where you will be warm."

Jennifer had been incapable of speech on the way back to the hotel, and from the veiled glances he gave her every now and then, she'd been aware that Alejandro was a little puzzled by her reaction.

"Are you all right?" he asked when after winding through the long corridors dotted with antique chairs and carved benches, they paused in front of her door.

Only wishing to escape his presence, Jennifer nodded. When he took the key from her nerveless fingers and unlocked the door, she entered the room and was dismayed when he followed her in.

Jennifer could tell that he was still reluctant to leave her. He took a few steps toward the bed and checked on his daughter, who was all tangled up in the covers and sprawled across the double bed.

"Are you sure you don't mind sharing your room with her?" he asked without taking his eyes off Heidi.

"No, of course not," Jennifer managed to say. Her throat was tight and even to her own ears her voice sounded strained.

She turned away and busied herself searching in her suitcase for her nightgown while Alejandro moved his daughter to one side of the bed and restored some order to the covers. Her back stiffened involuntarily when she heard his soft footfall behind her.

"Alba." When she felt his hands on her shoulders, Jennifer willed herself to relax. Still, she was tense when he drew her against him. "Heidi's very fond of you," he said softly as his arms encirlced her waist. "I've never seen her take to anyone so quickly."

"That's because she thinks I know Mickey Mouse." Jennifer tried to keep her tone light. "That's the secret of my attraction."

"Perhaps, but it's a start." He leaned forward until his chin was pressed against her temple. "She wants very much for you to like her."

Jennifer had to bite her lower lip to keep herself from weeping at this point. She closed her eyes when he whispered against her ear, "She was all I had until you came along." He paused. "I realize I may be asking a lot from you, *mi amor*—my love—but won't you try and give her a chance?"

That plea from Alejandro dispelled all her doubts about his feelings for her. How she had managed to keep herself from throwing her arms around him and confessing the truth? She didn't know even now, in the pale light of morning. . . .

Heidi snuggled even closer against her, seeking her warmth, and Jennifer turned to look at her. She was tempted to remove the thumb the little girl sucked in her sleep, to caress the soft cheek. Without the sparkle of her mischievous eyes, she looked so innocent in repose. Suddenly it all became too much for

Jennifer. Her fleecy robe protected her from the chill as she slipped from bed and tiptoed toward the window.

Although the front of the hotel faced the village, the window at the back offered a magnificent view of the mountains on one side and of a sweeping meadow on the other. The whole scene was just coming alive with the first rays of the rising sun.

Hoping to find solace for her conscience, Jennifer decided to go for a walk. Surely the open spaces would relax her as they always did. She quickly discarded her gown and put on her safari jump suit. After braiding her long hair in one thick plait that she let fall down her back, she donned the espadrilles she had worn the previous day and left the room.

As she wandered through the hotel, looking for the way out through the back, she encountered only one old woman sweeping the courtyard. The woman looked up with a smile and said, *"Buenos días, su mercecita.* Good morning."

Jennifer forced herself to smile back. *"Buenos días."*

Even though her sleep pattern had changed since coming to Colombia, Jennifer had always been an early riser. She didn't care for jogging, but she loved to walk, and many a sunrise over the California mountains had found her strolling along the beach. Her route out of the hotel took her by the stables, however, and as a groom was already on duty, she discovered that the hotel not only offered horses for rent, but that she immediately selected a chestnut filly.

She waited almost impatiently while the horse was saddled, and as soon as it was ready took off at a brisk canter.

There was something very special about the first hour of sunlight, Jennifer felt. The world had just awakened and there was a fresh softness in the air, in the colors, in the fragrance of the earth still damp with dew. Each day was a new beginning, a chance for the cycle of life to begin again. She had always known that to be true, but never more than when she'd gone camping high up in the mountain. No-where else did she feel so insignificant and yet so much in tune with all the living things of the earth.

But this morning the wonders of nature failed to bring Jennifer the peace of mind she so desperately sought. She rode through an extensive olive grove, then tried to concentrate her attention on the strange ridges, the crevasses and weather-sculptured forms decorating the strangely beautiful, desolate land-scape. She waved as she passed an old couple who were on their way into town. Their burro, heaped with huge parcels of pottery, told her they were tak-ing the fruits of their labor to market.

After a while Jennifer got off her horse and al-lowed it to rest and feed on the scrubby grass. She herself sat down on a boulder, letting the sun caress her face.

She gazed at the architectural beauty of an ancient monastery visible in the distance, but she wasn't real-ly seeing it. What was she going to do now? How could she still go on, trying to entrap a man who had placed his heart in her keeping and whom she so desperately loved in return? There was little doubt now in her mind that Alejandro wanted to marry her, and she was in a quandary. She also had to seek justice for her brother—how could she do both?

There was only one answer. She would have to find the man in the organization who was involved with the smugglers, the real culprit. She refused to believe any longer that Alejandro himself was guilty, yet those two words, what if, still bound her to silence.

She was praying he would one day forgive her deception when she saw her horse look up abruptly and expectantly turn its ears in the direction they had come from. This alerted her to the rider silhouetted in the distance against the cloudless sky.

Momentarily frightened by the sudden apparition, she expelled an audible sigh of relief and stayed where she was.

Her relief lasted only until she saw the expression on Alejandro's face. It was thunderous.

He dismounted and stalked toward her. "Don't ever disappear like this again, all right?" he breathed. Then she was being enfolded in his arms and held tightly against his tense body.

Jennifer was momentarily stunned into silence, until she realized that he was angry only because he'd been worried about her safety. Moments after she slipped her own arms around him and held him tightly in return, she felt the tension ebb away from him.

"I'm sorry, Alex," she said contritely. "I didn't mean to frighten you like this." When he didn't answer, she asked, "How did you find me?"

He finally loosened his hold on her. "I've been

looking for you for ages," he replied, looking down at her. "I finally ran into an old man and his wife who said they had seen you riding in this direction."

She reached up to touch his face. "Darling, there was no reason for you to worry. I was never in danger."

"You don't know the area," he argued, still concerned. "You might have gotten lost."

Jennifer's laughter was soft when she said, "I wasn't lost at any moment, Alex. Believe me, I could have found my way back to town."

"Okay, you weren't lost. But I still don't like your venturing so far from town on your own."

She was going to argue the point, but remembering her own initial fright when she had discovered someone coming, she remained silent. "Where's Heidi?" she asked instead, to distract him from their discussion.

"Back at the hotel. She begged to come along, but I didn't want her to hold me back while I was looking for you." He put one large hand on the base of her throat. "Besides, I had promised myself I would wring your pretty neck when I found you safe and sound, and I certainly didn't need any witnesses for that."

Jennifer wasn't frightened. His caressing touch belied the threat. Provocatively, she looked up at him. "Is that how you intended to punish me?"

She saw the laughter in his eyes when he shook his head. "You richly deserve it, but I can think of better ways," he said before his mouth descended on hers.

Jennifer's lips parted eagerly, yielding to the exploration of his kiss. With their arms still entwined they sank to the ground, where she lay beneath him, allowing him to trace the contours of her lips with the tip of his tongue.

"Do you know the first thing I noticed about you?" he asked. When she shook her head, he said, "I thought you had the most kissable mouth I had ever seen."

"Well, you certainly took your time to find out if it was true," she chided him.

He caught her lower lip between his teeth in an playful love nip. "Mmm, you're so delicious. I was wise to take my time. I had a feeling that once I kissed you, I'd never want to stop, you see, and I was right."

His fingers found the zipper at the front of her jump suit and pulled it down. In her rush to get out of the room, Jennifer had not bothered to put on a bra, and his hand cupped and stroked her naked breasts.

"You're not only delicious, you're beautiful," he said seriously, watching her nipple blossom at the touch of his fingers. She sighed as he kissed each satiny globe, now crested by rosy peaks of desire, until the glow that had begun inside her belly had become flame and she could think of nothing else but the touch of his lips and his hands.

Urgently she undid the buttons of his shirt and pressed her lips to the pulse of his throat, tasting the salty flavor of his skin as her hands caressed his chest. His own nipples hardened under the caress of her fingers just as hers had done. She tugged his shirt out of the waistband of his jeans so that she could caress the taut muscles of his flat belly. But with a sharp intake of breath he caught her hand when she began pulling at the buckle of his belt.

"My God, Alba, let's stop this before it's too late."

"It's not fair!" she cried in frustration, "Oh, Alex!"

He took her in his arms, holding her body, which trembled with the need he had aroused in her, close to his. "Hush, my love," he crooned, rocking her back and forth. "You're right, it's unfair. It's just that you're so responsive when I touch you that I forget you are still innocent."

Jennifer suddenly tensed. So distracted had she been by her inner turmoil that it took her a few moments to assimilate the impact of his words. Slowly she pulled back, to look quizzically up at him.

"Forgive me, my love." He touched a finger to her lips before she could speak. "I won't let it happen again."

It was then she realized why he was treating her that way. He believed her to be a virgin! She opened her mouth to deny it but closed it again before the words could come out.

It was only his belief in her innocence that had kept him from making love to her. She was in love with him and he with her, but the possibility of a happy future for them was so very remote. Jennifer knew herself well enough to realize that the physical consummation of their love would serve only to make her secret more painful, the moment of parting even more difficult than it was already bound to be. And so she clung to her silence, weeping inside for yet one more deceit, and for the unhappiness in store for both of them.

The smile she gave him was bleak, but she assured him, "I'm all right."

He kissed her then, a chaste kiss so full of tenderness that it made her eyes well up with tears of regret for the sweetness of a love she would never know to the fullest.

They got to their feet and self-consciously adjusted their clothing before remounting their horses.

As they rode back to town, Jennifer was surprised to discover how far she had come that morning. The height of the sun told her she must have been gone for at least two hours.

It was already after ten o'clock when they arrived back at the hotel, where Heidi was waiting impatiently for them. She glanced worriedly from one to the other and seemed relieved to see that there were no ill feelings visible between them.

Even though she had skipped breakfast, Jennifer found that she had little appetite for lunch. Neither she nor Alejandro were really in the mood for shopping, and after half an hour of walking through the displays of merchandise in the markets he proposed that they head back home. She accepted immediately.

A STEADY DRIZZLE WAS FALLING on the streets of Bogotá as the chauffeur-driven sedan advanced slowly through the heavy traffic. With the sky so overcast it seemed as if the city had decided to share in Jennifer's gloom.

From the back seat of the sedan she gazed out the window at the other cars heading toward the suburbs on the Autopista del Libertador. But she wasn't really seeing them; instead she was wondering at Alejandro's uncanny ability to read her moods. Sensing her need to be alone, he had stayed away from the cottage after she had declined his invitation to dinner at the main house the previous evening. She had gone to bed early, expecting another troubled night, but so physically and emotionally weary had she been that shortly afterward she had fallen into a deep sleep, undisturbed by dreams.

Even under the best of circumstances, pretense was difficult for Jennifer to maintain. In spite of her earlier determination to keep a wary distance from Alejandro, the recent intimacy in their relationship now made her duplicity, her inability to confide in him, such agonizing torture that she could think of very little else.

She tried to take some comfort in the thought that in a few more minutes she would be able to speak her mind freely to someone, if not to Alejandro himself. Perhaps in voicing all the facts to friendly ears she would be able to get her bearings.

Pulling her attention back to the present, Jennifer saw that they were now cruising through an affluent residential district, where the streets were wide, the houses modern and surrounded by well-kept gardens. A few minutes later the chauffeur stopped in front of a two-storey house, which was built in the traditional Spanish style of architecture.

Becky had obviously been waiting expectantly, for

the front door opened while Jennifer was still instructing the chauffeur to come back for her in two hours.

"Thank heavens you're here!" Becky exclaimed as Jennifer came up the walk. "After what you told me last Friday, I've been climbing the walls. I didn't know whether to believe that excuse you gave on the phone, or if it had been extracted from you under duress!"

"Oh, Becky, I'm sorry you were so worried," Jennifer replied, taking her friend's hand. "I wish I had been able to tell you more the other night, but I couldn't run the risk of being overheard. What I said on the phone was true. I just couldn't get out of that overnight trip to Villa de Leyva with Alex and his daughter."

"Well, you're here now," Becky said in obvious relief. "You can fill me in over lunch."

Jennifer followed her friend through rooms elegantly furnished in a mixture of styles—Spanish and American—that blended harmoniously with each other.

"Can I get you a drink?" Becky inquired once they had reached what even in Bogotá Becky called the family room. "We still have a few bottles left of an excellent amontillado we brought from Spain."

"Fine," Jennifer agreed.

Becky filled two glasses and sat down on the sofa next to her. "Skol," she offered.

"Skol," Jennifer replied in kind.

They sipped their drinks for a while, then started lunch. Still not ready to tackle the subject of Tommy's imprisonment, they reminisced about old times and old friendships. Becky told Jennifer that through the years she and Tommy had continued to keep in touch occasionally by letter. That explained how she had known of Jennifer's engagement.

The life of a mining engineer was obviously a varied one. During her marriage Becky had followed Larry through three different countries in as many years.

"I was a little afraid of coming to Colombia," she confessed. "So many people said it was such a dangerous country. Perhaps it was, during the time of *la violencia*, when there were bandits in the hills. But right now I don't think Bogotá's more dangerous than any other large city in the world. And we've been lucky in finding good friends, among the Colombians as well as in foreign circles."

"How well do you know Amanda and Raul Soler?" Jennifer inquired.

"As a couple, not very well," Becky admitted. "We've met them at a few parties. She's a volunteer at the planned parenthood clinic where I work three times a week, however. She's gorgeous, isn't she?"

"A former Miss Colombia, from what I understand."

"And that contest is only one of many," Becky chuckled. "I've never seen such preoccupation with beauty anywhere else, have you? I suppose it's all to keep the men at home—and faithful."

Jennifer was reminded of Nancy's accusations about her husband.

"I guess it's a question of machismo," Becky continued. "That was one of the problems the clinic had to fight. It seems that getting their wives pregnant increases some men's pride in their manhood. The planned parenthood program was an uphill battle, but we've made so much progress that now the birth rate is one of the lowest in South America."

They had finished eating, and after a brief silence Becky said, "It's been a long time, Jenny."

"Yes, it has, hasn't it?" Jennifer repeated pensively. "Who would have thought ten years ago that we'd be meeting again half a world away and under such strange circumstances?"

Becky listened quietly as the story unfolded, almost of its own accord.

"And you came to Colombia with a false passport?" She shook her head in amazement when Jennifer reached that point in her narrative.

Jennifer nodded. "I took the name from a tombstone—of a woman who had been born approximately the same year as I. All I had to do was obtain a copy of her birth certificate, take out a driver's license in her name and apply for a passport. It was as simple as that." She paused briefly before she added, "When the passport was stolen, I was afraid to request a duplicate, naturally. I didn't know what kind of investigation they might start, and I didn't want to run the risk of being deported."

"You know, I was always a little jealous of you," Becky said, shaking her head.

"Jealous!" Jennifer looked up sharply in surprise, taken aback by her friend's admission. "But why?"

Becky shrugged her shoulders slightly. "You al-

ways were so free, so...well...unafraid,'' she said
at last. ''And what you're doing right now proves my
point.''

''Unafraid?'' she repeated dumbly.

''I suppose daring is a more appropriate word,''
Becky replied with a wry smile. ''You could keep up
with Tommy no matter what he did. It wasn't easy to
live up to the image of girls you had created for him.''

''Is that what I did?'' Shaking her head, Jennifer
confessed, ''If the truth be known, I was terrified at
some of the stunts we pulled.''

''But that didn't stop you.''

Jennifer looked at her friend and smiled sheepishly.

''Although I didn't understand it, as I grew older I
learned to accept that very special affinity that existed
between you and Tommy,'' Becky said. ''It was a little
disconcerting to me how two people could be so much
alike, especially when they looked so different.''

Jennifer thought immediately of Alejandro, of
that uncanny ability he had to sense her feelings and
needs. She wondered if once freed from the burden
of deceit, she would be able to gauge his feelings as
well as he did hers. But Becky was right; it had never
happened with anyone but Tommy before.

''So what are you going to do now?'' Becky broke
into her thoughts.

''Now?'' Jennifer frowned.

''You're in love with Alex, aren't you?''

Jennifer cast her a quick nervous glance. ''Is it that
obvious?''

Her friend shrugged. ''Only to anyone who's ever
seen the two of you together.''

That was funny, Jennifer thought, unable to stop the flush in her cheeks. Amanda Soler had given a very similar reply to the same question.

Becky leaned forward and took Jennifer's clenched hand in her own. "Be careful, Jenny," she said gently. "You must look at things objectively. You know as well as I do that Tommy would never become involved with drug smugglers."

Jennifer nodded in silence.

"And from what you just told me, Alejandro Adler's testimony contributed to the verdict against him," Becky reminded her. "Doesn't it stand to reason that he did so to clear himself of suspicion?"

CHAPTER TEN

WHY, WHY, WHY? The word kept running through Jennifer's mind for the rest of the afternoon. Could it be that loving Alejandro had made her lose her ability to see things objectively? Was she trying to clear him of guilt simply by wishing it away?

There was only one thing to do if she was going to find out the truth: she had to put aside her love for Alejandro. And the only way she was going to manage that to some degree would be by keeping her distance. By misjudging her reasons for avoiding Heidi, Alejandro had given her the perfect excuse for rejecting any further expression of love between them.

On impulse she picked up the phone and dialed Mateo's number. He was delighted to hear from her and immediately agreed to meet her after work at the usual place in the lobby.

She hadn't seen much of Sara since her boss's return. Ricardo Tejeda was obviously keeping her busy. Too busy, perhaps, to exchange confidences with her new friend? He hadn't taken Jennifer to see the warehouses, either.... The more she thought about him, in fact, the less Jennifer liked the man.

But wait, she thought, catching herself. She was doing it again, letting her impulses cloud her judgment.

The phone on her desk rang, interrupting her efforts to draft a memo—efforts that were meeting with little success due to her lack of concentration. Even after all her resolutions, she found her pulse quickening with excitement at the sound of Alejandro's voice, the special intimate inflection with which he said *mi amor*.

"I'm sorry, Alex, but I already made plans to meet a friend after work," she replied when he invited her to dine with him that evening. She was glad she had followed her impulse to make a date with Mateo, thereby eliminating the temptation of Alex's company.

"I thought your date with Mrs. Mathews was for lunch."

"Yes, it was."

There was a pause at the other end, as if he was waiting for an explanation that she purposely withheld. "Very well." The tone of his voice had lost its delicious intimacy and had become dry. "I'll see you later, Alba."

"Bye, Alex."

Her hand was shaking when she hung up the phone. Even though the skirmish had been minor, it had left her drained.

Fearful of being detained by Alejandro, Jennifer left the office early and, consequently, was the first to arrive at the lobby.

As she waited she took the opportunity to study the painting of Manuela Sáenz, the woman who had earned the title of La Liberatora. The picture was of a beautiful young woman, perhaps in her mid-twenties, in a low-cut white gown. She was wearing her midnight-colored hair in a tiara of plaits adorned with tiny flowers. Jennifer's eyes were drawn directly to her oval face. Her nose was delicate, slightly aquiline; her eyes dark, challenging, mischievous. And her lips spoke of sensitivity and passion. . . .

"Beautiful, wasn't she?"

Jennifer had been so absorbed in her examination of the painting that she hadn't heard Mateo approach until he spoke.

She smiled at him. "Yes, she was." Pointing at the golden medal the Liberatress wore pinned to a white-and-purple sash, she asked, "What's that for?"

"That was the Order of the Sun," Mateo replied.

"Is that what she earned for saving Simón Bolívar's life?"

"No." Mateo shook his head. "She earned it in Peru, before she and Bolívar met, for her participation in the conspiracy against the Spanish Crown. It was the highest decoration revolutionary Peru could bestow at the time."

They turned away from the painting, and as they went through the exit, Mateo took her by the elbow to help her down the steps, which were still wet from the earlier rain. As he did, Jennifer's gaze was drawn to a tall man standing at the curb, about to get into a waiting car. Even though his face showed no emotion, Jennifer had to fight to keep from showing her dismay. Instead, she forced herself to pause beside him and perform the introductions.

Imagining Alejandro's thoughts behind the shuttered expression he wore, Jennifer tried to control her jitters while the men shook hands briefly, per-functorily. She would have preferred anger to the cold hauteur he showed both Mateo and her before he got into the car and drove away. He was so proud. Perhaps too proud, she reflected, grieving for the pain she had inflicted on the man who only last night had told her he loved her.

Jennifer was so upset after this chance encounter that she scarcely heard Mateo's conversation as they sat down at a table in a tea salon. Her mind—and her heart—were with Alejandro.

"You haven't heard a word I've said, have you?" Mateo said at last.

"What?" At Mateo's pained expression, she said, "I'm sorry, Mat. I guess I'm not very good company this evening."

He reached across the table for her hand. "What's wrong, Jennifer? You've been a million miles away all evening. Have you discovered anything about Alex Adler?"

She was tempted to say yes; that in the last three days she had discovered not only that she was in love with him but that he loved her back. Instead she shook her head. "Nothing new," she replied in a small voice.

To break the heavy silence that fell between them, she went on to tell Mateo about her meeting with Becky Mathews at the Soler party on Friday, and about their conversation at lunch earlier that day.

"Becky was a good friend of Tommy's while we were in high school," she added. "Actually he had a big crush on her all through junior year, and vice versa. One disadvantage of being so close to Alex is that it's been impossible for me to have any communication with Tommy. Becky promised to contact him for me. She'll call me as soon as she gets a letter back from him. Oh, Mat, if only I could see him again! It drives me out of my mind just to think how close we are and that I can't see him, talk to him, make sure he's all right!''

"Hey!" Again Mateo reached for her hand and gave it an affectionate squeeze. "You're really down tonight, aren't you?"

Jennifer began searching through her purse for a tissue to blot the tears that were running down her pale cheeks. "I'm sorry, really I am. I guess I'd better go home before I make a spectacle of myself."

Mateo shook his head. "That would be a dreadful mistake," he said, handing her his handkerchief. "As a matter of fact, I know the best remedy for a case of the blues like you have tonight. Disco dancing."

About to blow her nose, she stared at him open mouthed. "You've got to be kidding!"

"I've never been more serious in my life." He bobbed his head and stated, "Trust me. There's absolutely no way you can dance to the music of the Bee Gees and weep."

"You're out of your mind, you know that?" She had to laugh.

"Perhaps," he grinned. "But you must admit Dr. López's cure is already working."

THE UNICORN WAS VERY MUCH like its American counterpart with colored lights reflecting on a crowded floor where couples gyrated to the loud music.

However, there was not a single pair of jeans to be seen in the place, not even designer jeans. The disco reflected the affluence of Chapinero, the area where it was located, and the jewelry and clothes worn by the exclusive clientele made Jennifer wish she had taken time to change into something a little more appropriate than her yellow blouson dress.

"You look absolutely terrific," Mateo retorted when she expressed doubts as to the propriety of her attire.

And not giving her a chance to lose her nerve, he immediately drew her onto the dance floor.

He was as good a dancer at disco as he had proved to be at the more sedate dances of the tea salon they usually frequented. Dr. López's prescription for the dispersion of the blues began to take effect during their very first dance.

It had been a long time since Jennifer had been to a disco. She had never been too fond of crowded places or loud music, but tonight the confusion, the noise and the extravagance were a welcome change for her. At the moment she was glad she had allowed Mateo to talk her into what at first she had thought to be a mad escapade.

After several vigorous dances in a row, she was a little breathless and begged to be allowed to rest for a few minutes.

Back at the table she sipped her drink and watched the dancers spinning, twisting, and pirouetting under the colored lights. Then she looked casually toward the tables at the other end of the dance floor. The certain amount of composure she had managed to recover by then suddenly deserted her when she spotted a familiar face among the occupants of a crowded table. By an incredible coincidence, it was Alejandro.

He was listening to the beautiful woman sitting next to him and appeared too wrapped up with her to pay attention to anyone else, Jennifer noticed with a pang of jealousy. As they got up from the table and went out on the dance floor, Jennifer had a chance to get a better look at his companion.

The woman was tall and moved with seductive feline grace. When touched by a beam of light, her dark hair, which fell straight to her shoulders, shone with a bluish cast. Jennifer couldn't begin to guess her age, perhaps somewhere in her thirties; no younger woman could have achieved such magnificent poise, such self-assurance. The emerald-and-diamond necklace at her throat was probably worth a small fortune.

Jennifer felt herself choking with envy as the woman turned to Alejandro and he took her slender body, sheathed in an expensive bare-shouldered creation, in his arms. The way their bodies melted together proclaimed a familiarity that only lovers could have.

Even though she had never seen the woman before, Jennifer didn't have to be told her name. She knew intuitively that this was Leticia Roman. She could almost hear Mrs. Vargas's voice advising Alejandro of her earlier call.

Her heart ached at the sight, yet she still couldn't make herself look away from the two figures so languidly intertwined as they moved on the parquet floor. What a fool she was to have believed Alejandro's words of love! They had been only a ploy, a ploy to...what? Seduction? No, not that. He could have made love to her once, even twice, and he had refused.... And she had been naive enough to believe his excuse about her virginity.

But now the truth was staring her in the face. Why should he bother with her when he had a woman like Leticia Roman to warm his bed? Never in her life had Jennifer felt so terribly humiliated.

Abruptly, she jumped to her feet. "Let's dance, Mat."

He needed no further encouragement, and immediately they joined the other dancers. Mateo must have been surprised by the way Jennifer clung to him, but he wasn't one to protest. They danced together for several minutes before a familiar voice asked, "May I?" Her body grew tense immediately.

Mateo released her, and she found herself looking into Alejandro's cold gray eyes as they exchanged partners. Jennifer hated herself for the way her body, almost of its own accord, molded itself to the contours of his.

"Why are you doing this, Alba?" he rasped in her ear.

"Why not? Is it considered a crime in Colombia to date more than one man?" The airy tone of her own voice surprised Jennifer. "Or is it a male prerogative to play in more than one game at a time? Tsk, tsk." She shook her head in mock disapproval. "Not fair, Mr. Adler."

"Is that all this is to you? A game?"

She heard the bitterness in his voice, and aware of the tension of his body, she was glad she didn't have to look into his eyes when she said, "Isn't that, after all, what life is? A game?" She tried to say more, but her voice failed her.

It had been enough. The music ended at that moment, and after returning her to Mateo, Alejandro walked away with Leticia Roman on his arm.

Now that her pride had been saved, Jennifer was unable to maintain the facade of composure a moment longer. "I want to leave now, Mat. Please, let's get out of here."

The urgency in her voice brooked no argument, and a few minutes later they were crossing the parking lot on their way to Mateo's car. By the time they reached it, however, the dam of Jennifer's tears had already broken. After looking at her helplessly for a second or two, Mateo drew her into his arms and tried to comfort her by patting her on the back.

"Now, now, Jenny, what's the matter?"

She was weeping so hard she couldn't speak, and he had to wait until her tears began to subside. At last she took a deep breath to steady herself. "Oh, God, I feel like such a fool!" Voices and laughter were approaching. "Let's go, okay?"

He unlocked the door and settled her inside before going around the car and sliding behind the wheel. Jennifer's sniffles accompanied the sounds of the key turning in the ignition and the engine starting.

"Where would you like to go?" Mateo inquired after he had pulled out of the parking lot.

Jennifer sighed. The idea of going back to the *quinta* was totally abhorrent to her at this moment. She didn't want to be alone. "What time is it?"

"Close to eleven."

She wondered if Becky was still up. Perhaps she could spend the night with her. "I have to make a phone call," she replied.

They drove around until they found a public phone, and Mateo stayed in the car while Jennifer made the call. Becky was still up and encouraged her to come to her house and spend the night, so when Jennifer returned to the car she gave Mateo Becky's address.

As the car pulled away from the curve, Jennifer sent up a mental prayer of thanks for having found such wonderful friends. Mateo had asked no questions, but she knew he must be wondering about what had prompted such emotional display on her part.

"Thank you, Mat," she said. "I don't know what I would have done without you."

He nodded, not taking his eyes off the road.

She knew she owed him an explanation. Trying to keep from crying again, she told him everything—how she had fallen in love with Alejandro in spite of her efforts not to, of her difficulties in avoiding Heidi, even of Alex's veiled reference to a future together.

"It was all a lie, Mat, and I was foolish enough to believe him. I even felt guilty about deceiving him! But you saw Leticia Roman. What would Alejandro want with me when he can have her?" she finished dejectedly.

She was unaware that they had reached their destination. Mateo pulled over to the curb and switched off the engine before he turned to her. She heard his soft chuckle in the dark. "If you don't know the answer to that, I suggest you take a good look in the mirror, Jennifer. A man would have to be insane or blind not to be attracted to you. Don't you know how beautiful you are?"

"There are things far more important than outward beauty, Mat."

"Granted. But let's face it—that's the first thing a man notices."

"I suppose you're right," she sighed.

"Of course I am. Dr. López is never wrong."

She turned to look at him. "Does Dr. López have another of his famous prescriptions?"

"That's the one thing he never runs out of," Mateo replied, taking her hand. "He's a firm believer in that the best cure for an unlucky love is to find another."

He had kept his tone light, yet she could hear the emotion underlining his words.

"Mat, I do care for you very much, but—"

"Ssh." He touched a finger to her lips. "Don't argue with the doctor."

He leaned forward to kiss her, and Jennifer accepted the tentative gentle caress. It was pleasant, nothing more.

"Good night, Mat," she said with a tremulous sigh, starting to get out.

"I'll walk you to the door."

She waited for him to go around the car, then he escorted her up the front walk. The door opened immediately, a sign that Becky had been aware of their arrival and had waited discreetly until they had said their farewells.

Jennifer introduced the two of them. Insisting it was too late, Mateo declined the nightcap Becky offered.

"Thank you for letting me stay with you," Jennifer told Becky after he had gone. "I hate to impose, but I didn't know where else to go."

"Nonsense," Becky shrugged. "As a matter of fact, I'm glad you came. With Larry at the project, I'm delighted to have some company besides Felicia. Would you like a cup of coffee? American, for a change?"

"Only if you're having one." Jennifer followed her friend into the spacious modern kitchen. "Can I help?"

"Just make yourself at home. It'll only take a minute." Becky gestured toward the round dinette table and two chairs and turned her own attention to filling the drip coffee maker with water. Then she measured coffee grounds into the filter and flipped the switch. "Felicia has a fit every time she sees me drinking this stuff," she went on conversationally. "If it were up to her I'd drink nothing but *tinto*, which is fine, but not all the time. I still like my American brew."

"You miss home, don't you?"

"In the beginning it was all I thought about," Becky admitted as she sat across the table. "I don't know how many times I packed and unpacked my suitcases. Then one day I ran into another woman who kept moaning about how bored she was and complaining about the inconveniences of living abroad. Frankly, I found her quite irritating. It was a sobering experience because I realized I was doing the same thing myself." She shook her head. "Poor Larry! I must have driven him crazy. At any rate, I took inventory and reached the conclusion that regardless of where he worked, I love my husband and want to be with him. That was the last time I ever complained. Instead I started looking for the positive rather than the negative, as well as for ways to do something meaningful. My life has been richer, and I've been much happier ever since. I'm sure Larry has, too. Ah, here's the coffee!" She filled two mugs and carried them to the table. "Cream and sugar?"

Jennifer shook her head. "Black's fine."

They sipped their coffee in silence until Becky said, "You sounded very upset over the phone."

Taking a deep breath, Jennifer began narrating the events of the afternoon and evening. "I don't know what came over me," she reflected ruefully when she'd finished. "All of a sudden I just broke down and couldn't stop crying."

"You've been under a terrible strain, Jenny," Becky observed. "I don't know how you've been able to maintain such a dangerous charade, but it was bound to take its toll sooner or later."

"I don't know what I would have done without you and Mat, Becky."

"Speaking of Mateo," her friend said with a half smile, "he didn't seem too adverse to offering a little consolation. Why don't you let him? He's cute, too."

"He's just a friend," Jennifer replied.

"A kissing friend?"

The heat Jennifer felt on her cheeks made her aware that she was blushing.

Becky laughed. "Jennifer Blake, I don't believe you're for real!"

Her friend's teasing remarks helped Jennifer forget her troubles for a while, and she found herself liking Becky more and more. She felt a little regret that they had not been closer friends in high school.

Their conversation was interrupted by the shrill ring of the phone. They looked at each other quizzically. Who would be calling at that hour?

Becky answered, "Hello?" After she had listened for a few seconds, she beckoned to Jennifer. "It's for you."

"For me?" Jennifer's brows rose in surprise. "Who is it?"

Becky simply handed her the receiver.

"Hello?"

"Are you planning to return to the *quinta* tonight?" Alejandro asked without a preamble.

"I don't see how that's any of your business," Jennifer replied, instantly resentful of his interference in her comings and goings.

"It becomes my business when you so thoughtlessly neglect to release one of my employees," he returned dryly. "Your chauffeur has been charged with your safety, and the man has been frantic, not knowing what happened to you. Let me remind you that privilege also entails responsibility. Before you wander off again without giving them a second thought, I suggest you consider the fact that those who serve you are people, Miss Maitland, not machines.''

By this time Jennifer's resentment had dissolved totally. She felt nothing but chagrin when she realized she had totally forgotten her chauffeur.

Before she could reply, Alejandro said, ''I have instructed Roberto to call for you at nine. Good night, Miss Maitland.''

There was a click and then silence.

''Oh, damn!'' she muttered putting down the phone none too gently.

''What was that all about?'' Becky inquired.

''I forgot about the chauffeur,'' Jennifer replied. ''Apparently he called Alex when he didn't hear from me. I should have told him to go home.'' She shook her head wryly. ''But how did Alex know where to find me?''

''It couldn't have been too difficult. You don't know many people in Bogotá,'' Becky replied. She looked up at the wall clock, which indicated it was almost two in the morning. ''Oh, my gosh, look at the time! I'd better show you to your room or you're going to be dead on your feet in the morning!''

They carried their mugs to the sink and turned off the kitchen lights. As she was showing Jennifer to a large comfortable guest room on the second floor, Becky paused and listened intently. ''What was that?''

The two women looked at each other expectantly. The sound was becoming clearer. It was the music of guitars.

Jennifer couldn't understand the source of her friend's amusement when Becky started laughing. "What—?"

"This, my dear Jenny," Becky gasped between gales of laughter, "means that you're being sere-naded."

"Serenaded?" Jennifer's mouth opened in disbelief as she stared at the other woman. "Are you serious?"

Becky gave her a mocking bow. "Just look out the window and see for yourself."

By this time the music was quite loud. Jennifer finally became convinced that, indeed, a serenade was going on outside her window. She and Becky threw the windows open and stepped onto the little balcony overlooking the garden, and the lyrics of a romantic song immediately surrounded them.

After a moment Becky said, "Don't you love it? Larry serenaded me on our last anniversary. It was very romantic."

Mateo was standing below with a trio of profes-sional musicians. They played well—and enthusias-tically. As soon as they finished one song another started, and the music went on for at least half an hour. Everyone—musicians, Mateo, the two women on the balcony—were obviously having great fun. Finally the trio packed their instruments and left. Mateo threw a kiss at the ladies and followed.

It had been an incredible evening!

"Mr. Adler would like to see you in his office, Miss Maitland." Mrs. Vargas's voice was cool and precise over the telephone.

"Thank you. I'll be right there."

Her nerves still jarring from the shrill of the telephone, Jennifer gingerly returned the receiver to its cradle. Becky had been right in predicting she'd be dead on her feet in the morning. She hadn't warned her about the possibility of a king-size headache, which was now pounding at Jennifer's temples with a vengeance. Little wonder, after such a tumultuous night. When she'd finally got into bed she hadn't been able to sleep. Her emotions had run the gamut of rage, indignation, and plain undisguised jealousy as she tormented herself with thoughts of Alejandro and Leticia Roman making love. And now he wanted to see her....

Jennifer rose to her feet and nervously smoothed the circular skirt of the same yellow blouson dress she had worn the day before. Even in her weariness, the belligerence she felt knowing that only hours before Alejandro had left Leticia's bed, sent a shot of adrenaline through her system. It gave energy to her step as she went down the hallway to his office.

With a nod of her beautifully coiffed head Mrs. Vargas indicated that she go straight in, which Jennifer did without breaking stride. In spite of her dislike for Tejeda, for once she felt a certain amount of relief to find him there with Alejandro. Both men stood up at her entrance.

With a minimum of civilities, Alejandro went immediately to the object of the meeting. "I assume that by now you are prepared to present us with a list of the manufacturers you wish to visit in Medellín, Miss Maitland?"

Jennifer's mouth went dry suddenly. "I'll have it ready for the typist later this morning, Mr. Adler," she bluffed. To her relief, he simply nodded his assent.

"Very well. Please have it delivered to Mrs. Vargas as soon as it's ready so that we can go over it and make the necessary arrangements. By the way, the samples you requested at the leather show have arrived. I'd like to see your suggestions before we leave for Medellín next Thursday."

Jennifer tried to conceal the panic that she felt growing inside her. Mistakes could easily unmask her and put an end to her investigation, which so far had proven fruitless. "It would be very helpful if I could visit the warehouses and make arrangements for proper storage, Mr. Adler," she hedged.

Alejandro glanced at his general manager. "When will Miss Maitland be able to visit the warehouses, Ricardo?"

Tejeda cleared his throat before replying. "I'll contact the foreman this afternoon and schedule the visit for tomorrow." He looked at Jennifer when he added, "I'll have my secretary confirm the time, Miss Maitland."

Jennifer nodded. "Will there be anything else?"

"That'll be all," Alejandro replied. He waited until she had got up from her chair to add, "Except please be ready to leave by six o'clock this evening, Miss Maitland. Your chauffeur has the day off, and you'll be driving to the *quinta* with me tonight."

Jennifer bit her lip before saying, "Yes, sir."

Blast him, she thought mutinously as she walked

out of the office. How easy it was for him to control her movements! She wished she had never accepted his hospitality, which at first had seemed such a magnanimous act on his part. All she had accomplished was to put herself at his mercy.

After she returned to her office she closed the door and sat at her desk, hiding her face in her hands. Regardless of her resentment, in her heart she still couldn't believe that Alejandro had anything to do with the traffic of narcotics. Who did, then? Ricardo Tejeda? Someone at the warehouses?

She glanced at her watch, and suddenly inspired, picked up the phone and dialed Sara López's extention. It was answered on the second ring.

"Hello, Sara?"

"Hi!"

"Are you too busy to have coffee with me this morning? It seems as if I haven't seen you in ages."

"I'm swamped," Sara replied, "but I guess the company will survive if I take ten minutes away from my desk."

"Good. I'll see you in a few minutes then."

Jennifer was smiling a bit grimly to herself as she hung up. Something had suddenly clicked in her mind—something Sara had once mentioned, which had seemed unimportant at the time. It was a shot in the dark, but she felt a little digging wouldn't hurt....

While she waited for Sara to appear, Jennifer turned her attention to the list she had to deliver to Alejandro later that morning. She hadn't been totally idle, thank heaven, and the notes she had taken previously aided her in its preparation.

A few minutes later Ramón came in and served the coffee, and Sara came almost immediately and with a weary sigh flopped down on the chair across from Jennifer's desk.

"I'll tell you one thing," she said in greeting. "I like this job, but I like it even better when Mr. Tejeda is away. The man can drive me absolutely crazy at times, and today is one of those days. He's on the warpath."

"Perhaps he had a quarrel with his girl friend," Jennifer suggested casually. "That may account for his bad temper."

"Amen," Sara sighed.

When she picked up an *empanada* without elaborating further, Jennifer inquired, "Did you ever find out who she was?"

"No, he's too mysterious about it," Sara replied. "But there is someone for sure. He got very upset the other day when I opened a bill from a jewelry store that came in the mail. I got mad at him in return and told him that if I could read minds, I wouldn't be working here. I told him he should have his mail marked personal if he doesn't want me to open it, and that otherwise, he has nothing to complain about. He didn't like it, but he simmered down after that."

"Good for you," Jennifer chuckled. "Did you say it was from a jewelry store."

"Um-hmm," Sara nodded. "And I'll bet you anything he didn't buy that emerald bracelet for his wife."

"An emerald bracelet?" Jennifer repeated. "He

must have quite a bit of money to be able to afford such expensive trinkets. Is he rich?''

Sara shook her head. ''As far as I know he's very well paid here, but *nobody* makes that kind of money working at a job. Have you heard of anyone getting rich by working nine to five?''

Jennifer stirred her coffee slowly. ''You know, I've thought about what you said, and I have a theory about who his girl friend might be.''

Sara was immediately interested. ''Who?''

''Correct me if I'm wrong,'' Jennifer began, ''but didn't you tell me the former receptionist—what was her name?''

''Regina Quintana,'' Sara supplied immediately.

''Yes, that's right, Regina,'' Jennifer nodded. ''I only saw her once, when I came for my interview. But from what I noticed, she seemed very fond of expensive jewelry. I remember an emerald ring she was wearing. I don't know much about emeralds, but they certainly looked real to me.''

''Regina wouldn't be caught dead wearing a fake,'' Sara confirmed. ''I remember when she got that ring. She made sure everyone in the office saw it. So you think Regina and Mr. Tejeda...hmm.'' The Colombian woman was pensive as she chewed her *empanada*. ''You might have something there, Alba. I don't know why I never thought about it before—probably because I can't picture Mr. Tejeda with *anyone*. Ugh!'' She made a face. ''But, yes, it could be.''

''By the way, don't forget you promised to lend me that book on the life of Manuela Sáenz,'' Jennifer said, deliberately changing the subject. ''Last night

Mateo told me how she earned the medal she's wearing in the painting. The more I hear about her, the more I want to know.''

"Oh, sure, I'm sorry, I forgot all about the book. I've just been so busy lately....''

"Are you still seeing Flavio?"

Sara shrugged. "On and off."

"Do you still like him as much?"

"Not really," Sara admitted after a small hesitation. "I don't know what's wrong with me, Alba. Every time I fall in love it's the same story. While the man doesn't even know I'm alive, I'm mooning over him constantly. But right after he starts to notice me, I lose interest. Why do you think that happens?"

"Could it be that you fall in love with the image you create rather than with the man himself?"

Sara considered the suggestion for a moment before she nodded, "You could be right." She glanced at her wristwatch and jumped to her feet. "I've got to run!" Mischievously she added, "Believe me, I haven't imagined Mr. Tejeda. *Ciao!*"

Jennifer returned to her work, but in the middle of compiling her list, she paused thoughtfully. Had she, like Sara, fallen in love with an image she had created of Alejandro, or with the man himself?

CHAPTER ELEVEN

A FEW MINUTES BEFORE NOON Jennifer received another phone call, this time from Mateo. He sounded excited.

"Have you seen the papers this morning?"

"No, I haven't," she replied carefully. Her suspicions about being watched made her wary of saying too much on the phone. She tried to warn Mat by adding, "Perhaps we could meet for lunch, if you're free."

He immediately got the message. "Lady, you've got a date. Our rendezvous point in ten minutes?"

That brought a reluctant smile to Jennifer's lips as she acknowledged, "Check. Oh, by the way," she added as an afterthought, "thanks for the serenade. I enjoyed it."

Mateo used his Dr. López voice when he replied, "It was my pleasure, beautiful *señorita*."

What a lovable nut, Jennifer thought as she put the receiver down. She had become so fond of him! Yet she wasn't really worried about hurting his feelings. In a way, she suspected he was very much like his sister when it came to romance. There was no question in her mind that Mat would love to wine, dine and romance her, but there would never be any real spark, any real fire to their relationship. A pseudo-romantic friendship was more his style, at least at this stage of his life, and that suited her perfectly.

With only minutes left she put the finishing touches on the list she had prepared for Alejandro's perusal, and handed it to a typist on her way out.

As she approached the rendezvous point, she noticed that Mateo was carrying a copy of *El Tiempo*, the oldest newspaper in Latin America and Bogotá's major daily, folded under his arm.

He glanced at his wristwatch when he saw her. "Ten minutes on the dot," he grinned. "Such wonderful American punctuality!"

"You were here before me," she laughed, accepting his arm.

They took a taxi to an *hostería*, and found a table in the dining room of the quaint hostel. In the enchanting setting, a verdant indoor garden, they could talk without fear of being overheard, for their voices were muffled by distant guitar music and by the murmur of a fountain that stood amidst a profusion of crimson geraniums.

The soup Jennifer ordered, called *puchero*, was very much like one she had already sampled, combining several different meats with plantains and other vegetables. Accompanying it was a cool avocado salad as well as *arepas*, a native bread filled with cheese and made of a special kind of flour derived from the white corn grown exclusively in the Andes. But her attention wasn't on her meal. Barely containing her impatience, she pored through the newspaper while her soup grew cold, for the news that had prompted such excitement in Mateo had a similar effect on her. *El Tiempo*'s front page carried the photographs of a number of people, both men and women, trying to hide their faces from the cameras. These couriers, known in narcotics circles as mules, had each been apprehended recently before boarding international flights at the El Dorado Airport. All in all, several kilos of cocaine had been found concealed on their persons and in their luggage.

"You know what that means, don't you?" Mateo asked expectantly.

"There's so many of them!" Jennifer exclaimed.

"It's big business," Mateo nodded. "As I told you before, we're not playing with amateurs. There's too much money involved."

"I guess I've been living in a different world!" She shook her head wryly. "Oh, I've always heard about the drug problem, but you know how the media tend to exaggerate. I knew the stuff was easy to obtain if you wanted to, but since I was never interested, it seemed totally remote from reality."

"Unfortunately the problem is very real," Mateo reflected, "and it's one that touches every strata of society. But go on reading. The patrol boats got lucky, too. And with all those heavy losses, it won't be long before the dealers are really going to start hurting for new supplies."

"You think they're going to try using Adler Exports again, don't you?" The thought of discovery— at last—made Jennifer a little breathless.

"Stands to reason, don't you think?"

Jennifer nodded in silence and took a bite of her

salad. Her next words, however, were proof that her concentration had not been on the food. "I was talking to Sara this morning, and from what she said I think we might have a good suspect."

Mateo was immediately alert. "Oh?"

"Ricardo Tejeda, her boss, is apparently keeping a mistress."

"My dear Jenny, have you any idea how many men such a clue would incriminate?" He tired to keep a straight face, but even his mustache could not hide the way his mouth twisted at the corners in amusement.

"I can imagine," Jennifer said dryly. "But all that aside," she went on, "his mistress has quite a penchant for expensive jewelry. It only follows that she requires many other luxuries—and our man is far from being rich. So where does he get the money?"

Mateo's eyes narrowed. "Keep talking," he said when she paused.

"I think I have an idea who the girl might be," she continued. "The former receptionist, Regina Quintana, recently resigned. Apparently she had found a very generous protector. She never said who it was and there's been a lot of speculation on the subject at the office. I met her only briefly, but even on the job she was wearing a fortune in jewels." She looked at him expectantly. "Interesting?"

"Very," he nodded.

When he offered no suggestions, she asked, "So how do we go about confirming all this?"

"Leave that to me. In some of the divorce cases my firm has handled, we've used a fellow who's an ex-

pert at this kind of investigation. It wouldn't raise
any suspicions if I asked him to look into our friend's
activities."

"Thanks, Mat."

"And speaking of divorces," he went on, "we
have a new client you might know." At her quizzical
look, he added, "Adler's sister, Nancy."

"So she's going ahead with it."

"I understand she had the papers served to her
husband yesterday."

"It's always sad to see a marriage fall apart," Jennifer reflected. "Even more so when there are children involved."

"Sometimes divorce is the best solution, however."

Jennifer heaved a rueful sigh. "I guess you're
right." But it hadn't been the solution for Alejandro
during his marriage because his wife had been self-
destructive, he'd said. She wondered what he had
meant by that. She wasn't able to dwell on the subject, though, for at that moment the group of musicians strolling through the restaurant approached
their table and Mateo asked them to play a song she
remembered from his serenade.

When they finished, it was time to go back to
work.

Jennifer's meeting with Alejandro that afternoon
was brief, and even though she was somewhat relieved by the fact, she felt curiously sad in the face of
his cool businesslike behavior. Telling herself it was
for the best didn't help much. Her mind kept wan-
dering off to those moments when his gray eyes had

gazed at her with tenderness, softening the angular planes of his face that now appeared so somber, so forbidding. It was with considerable effort that she answered his probing questions about some of her suggestions, but she managed to muddle through without making any blatant mistakes.

Then it was over. As she reached the door to his office, however, she paused, finding herself reluctant to leave him. "Alex."

He looked up from the papers in his hand. "Yes?"

Her eyes searched his face for some sign of encouragement. She found only indifference. "I'm sorry about the chauffeur last night. It totally slipped my mind."

He simply nodded and returned his attention to his work. She had been dismissed.

Biting her lip with chagrin, she turned and went out.

He ignored her, too, during their drive to the *quinta* that evening, and spent the whole journey working out of his briefcase. She took some comfort in the thought that even if he was indifferent toward her, at least he would not be spending the night with Leticia Roman.

The traffic was heavy, the drive long, and as a result of her weariness she dozed off without even realizing it.

"Alba."

"Hmm."

Her head was comfortably pillowed, and there were warm fingers on her cheek as she heard Alejandro's voice saying, "We're home."

Abruptly, she sat up. "What?"

"We're home," he repeated.

"Oh." Her disoriented gaze moved from him to the window, and she realized that the car was parked near her cottage. Before getting out of the door, which the chauffeur held open for her, she said, "Good night, Alex. Thank you."

"Good night, Alba."

She kept herself from looking back as she heard the car drive away. Had she seen a flash of tenderness in his eyes? Heard a hint of sadness in his voice? Or had it been only her confused imagination?

Inside the cottage Jennifer went straight to the bedroom, where she hurriedly undressed before continuing on to the bathroom. Before turning on the taps of the shower, she stood naked in front of the mirror and removed the pins that through the day had confined her luxuriant hair in a tight French twist. With some alarm she saw a red flush on her cheek. It must have been caused by Alejandro's shoulder, which she apparently had used as a pillow during her nap. The blush that hurried to her face when she thought about it didn't even conceal it.

She finished unpinning her hair and gave it a brisk brushing before getting into the shower. Later she donned a short terry-cloth robe and used a blow dryer on her hair, still fragrant with the faint herbal scent of her shampoo.

Without bothering to dress she stepped into the studio portion of the cottage, to find that a tray of food had been delivered from the main house. Having dinner sent over was a convenient arrangement for her, since she rebelled at the idea of having to dress up for a meal with Alejandro and Señora de Adler. Except this evening it served as another reminder of Alejandro's thoughtfulness. It was he who had instituted the practice when, during one of his visits, he had found her munching on cheese and crackers and a piece of fruit, preferring to skip dinner rather than go to the trouble of fixing a proper meal just for herself.

How could he be so gentle, so tender and thoughtful one moment, and just as easily turn into the cold forbidding stranger he'd been for the past two days? She clenched her fists in exasperation and kicked at one of the sofa pillows, which was on the floor. She had just bent down to pick it up and toss it onto the couch when she became aware of someone standing in the doorway.

It was Heidi. And the girl's eyes were wide and round as she asked, "Are you all right, Miss Maitland?"

Hearing the slight quaver in her voice, Jennifer felt suddenly awkward. She wouldn't be surprised if Alejandro's daughter believed she had completely lost her mind. "Hello, Heidi," she said with an attempt at a smile.

Her welcome seemed to encourage the child to take a few tentative steps into the cottage, even though she continued to regard Jennifer a little warily.

"Would you like some milk and cookies?" Jennifer offered, not knowing what else to say.

"Yes, please," Heidi nodded. "Thank you."

What a polite little girl she could be when she

wanted, Jennifer thought fondly as she went to the pantry with Heidi at her heels.

"Sit down," she invited, pouring a glass of milk and setting it on the table. Then she turned away to arrange a handful of cookies on a plate, which she also put on the table.

For a second or two Heidi sat there, touching neither the milk nor the cookies. Then she burst out, "I'm sorry if I kicked you, Miss Maitland. I didn't mean to. I'm sorry!"

Jennifer stared at her in surprise. She had no idea what the girl was talking about, but it was plain to see that Heidi was very distressed. Sitting down next to her, she took one small hand in her own. "Just calm down, Heidi," she said soothingly, "and tell me why you're so upset. I have no idea what you're talking about. What do you mean, you're sorry you kicked me?"

"Edna says that I always kick her when I sleep in her bed," Heidi said haltingly. With the back of her free hand she wiped at the tears that were starting to run down her face.

"Who's Edna?" Jennifer inquired, still a little confused even though the explanation of sorts was beginning to shed some light on the problem.

"My cousin."

"But, Heidi, what makes you think you kicked me? I never said you did, did I?"

Heidi's eyes were puzzled. "No, you never said so, Miss Maitland, even when daddy got mad at you because you ran away."

The whole picture came together at last in Jennifer's mind. So involved had she been in her own tribulations that she hadn't considered the tendency in children to feel responsible for trouble among adults. Poor Heidi must have decided her own disappearance that morning in Villa de Leyva was due to some fault of hers—and that kicking in her sleep was the only thing she could think of. The fact that Jennifer had failed to return to the *quinta* the previous evening may have increased the child's anxiety.

Spontaneously she put her arms around the girl and held her close. The frailness of her small body moved Jennifer incredibly. "Oh, honey, you didn't kick me," she said sincerely. "And I didn't run away. I just went out for a ride and forgot about the time, that's all. Besides, your daddy wasn't really angry, he was just worried about me. You had nothing to do with it, I promise."

"But you didn't come home last night," Heidi wept, in confirmation of Jennifer's earlier assessment. "I thought you didn't want to live with us anymore."

"I only went to spend the night with a friend, Heidi. You do that sometimes, don't you?"

Heidi drew back to look at her face when she asked, "Then you're not mad at me, Miss Maitland?"

"Of course not, honey. You've never done anything to make me angry. On the contrary, you've always been so nice to me." She paused for a moment, then gave the girl another squeeze. "Say, why don't you call me Alba, like my friends do? I'd like that very much."

"Please don't ever go away, Alba!" Heidi cried, throwing her small arms around Jennifer's neck. "I love you!"

Jennifer found herself almost choking in response, so quickly did her own eyes fill with tears. Finally she gave up fighting her natural impulses and returned Heidi's embrace. God forgive her! She had tried so hard to avoid getting close to Alejandro's daughter, but it wasn't meant to be. She couldn't withhold her affection for the girl, just as she couldn't stop loving her father.

To stop herself from dissolving into sobs she affectionately rubbed Heidi's back. "Your milk is getting warm."

Once Heidi had settled down to enjoy her milk and cookies, Jennifer said, "You know, Heidi, sooner or later I'll have to be going back home."

"Why can't you stay and live with us? I want you to stay, and daddy does, too. I know he does."

"Because you see, Heidi, my home is back in the United States. I only came here to work for a little while."

Heidi was silent for a few moments, then she asked, "Could daddy and I come visit you sometime?"

"If you want," Jennifer replied carefully, avoiding a promise she couldn't keep. "Of course, you must know that most of the time people forget about each other after a while."

"Oh, Alba, I'll *never* forget *you*."

"Well, we'll see," Jennifer sighed. "Finish your milk now. I think it's past your bedtime."

"I don't have to go to bed so early," Heidi grinned. "I'm on vacation."

"Oh." Jennifer tried to hide her dismay.

"Besides, Uncle Carlos came over and grandma is very upset because Aunt Nancy won't go home with him. Aunt Nancy said she's getting a divorce. They're all having an argument."

"Yes, well, maybe we can play cards or something. What do you say?"

"Oh, yes!"

Jennifer went to get the deck of cards she had discovered in one of the drawers. "Do you know any games?"

"No." Heidi shook her head.

Jennifer took a moment to consider what to do next. "I think you're old enough to learn gin rummy," she said at last, and spent the next two hours teaching Heidi the game until Alejandro came and took his daughter home.

JENNIFER WASN'T SURE what she had expected to uncover during her visit to the warehouses, but she was disappointed to find nothing that could be considered out of the ordinary. At least it was a blessing the visit had been scheduled for the early-morning hours, and she had the rest of the day free.

She sorely needed to be alone. Working at her regular job, as a soil scientist, she spent many hours out in the fields on her own. Here in Colombia, however, in addition to the tensions caused by her investigations, her conscience, and her relationship with Alejandro, she was always surrounded by other people. She recognized the loss of control she had experienced the night she'd seen him in the discotheque as a warning—to pull back for a while in order to regain her balance. Although far more outgoing than she, Tommy had always understood her need for solitude. He had jokingly referred to this retreat into herself as her time to "recharge her batteries."

She had completed the work expected of her before the trip to Medellín, therefore, Jennifer returned to the *quinta* in search of solitude after she'd toured the Adler Exports warehouse.

When she arrived back at the cottage she made herself a peanut butter and sliced banana sandwich and poured herself a glass of milk. Alejandro had laughed at what he had considered an outrageous combination when she had mentioned it as one of her favorite foods. But a few days after that conversation a jar of peanut butter had miraculously appeared in her pantry. Since it was not an item popular to the Latin taste, Jennifer knew it must not have been easy to find, and she had been deeply touched by Alejandro's solicitude. How could she stop loving a man like that, she wondered with a sigh as she ate her lunch.

The swimming pool was deserted when she went for a swim in the early afternoon. Jennifer was tired but felt much better after an invigorating dip. Refreshed as well by a brief nap, she pulled on a dark pink divided skirt and a knit shirt of the same color and went out for a walk. Jealous of her solitude, she decided to head in the opposite direction to the main house, toward the mountains.

It was the first time she had had the opportunity to explore the area, and inevitably she was drawn to feel the soil with her hands. She needed no lab equipment to tell her that this was fertile land. It had been precisely that, plus the availability of water and the healthy climate, which had prompted the European conquerors to select the beautiful plateau inhabited by Muisca Indians as the site for their city.

Jennifer continued climbing up the mountain trail. A bit later she found a rock to sit on, and from that vantage point she looked down at the house. Diminished by the distance, it seemed like a plaything with its white walls and sienna-colored roof, as appropriate for a doll as was everything around it, the emerald lawns, the willow trees, even the centuries-old cedars.

A sound behind her made her turn around, and her solitude was broken by the appearance of a rider.

"Are you all right?" It was Nancy, Alejandro's sister. The woman dismounted rapidly and hurried toward her. Before Jennifer could reply, she asked, "Were you thrown? Where's your horse?"

"I'm all right," Jennifer said, trying to quell her alarm. "I'm just out for a walk."

Nancy looked at her in surprise. "All the way up here?" Apparently she had trouble believing that Jennifer could get so far from the house on foot.

"I'm used to walking," Jennifer smiled.

Nancy shook her head in disbelief. "You must be stronger than you look." She sat down on the rock next to Jennifer and took a pack of cigarettes out of her pocket, offered her one. "I ought to give them up," Nancy said when Jennifer declined. "Perhaps I will, after all this mess is over." She lit a cigarette, which she smoked pensively. "I don't know if you heard that Carlos was here last night," she said at last.

Even though she was reluctant to become involved, Jennifer forced herself to remain and listen. It was obvious that Nancy needed to talk about her problem.

"He was shocked when he was served with the divorce papers. He apparently thought I was bluffing, that after a few days I'd be back and everything would continue as it used to be. He even acted outraged—the nerve of the man! When I wouldn't budge, he promised with tears in his eyes he would change his ways. I've heard that tune before, however—too many times. I'm so angry with mother for siding with him!"

Jennifer refrained from comment, knowing none was expected. All Nancy needed was a friendly ear.

"I don't know what's going to happen," Nancy said unhappily, and looking up a little shamefacedly added, "I'm scared, Alba. Really scared."

Jennifer reached for her hand in a comforting gesture. "I understand that's normal under the circumstances."

"I suppose." Nancy flashed her a quick nervous smile. "Only sometimes I think mother is right and that I should go home and forget the whole thing. But then I remember how miserable I've been all these years with Carlos's womanizing, and I tell myself that whatever happens can't be worse than that.

He even had me believing it was all my fault! I've completely lost my confidence as a woman, Alba.'' She paused thoughtfully before she shook her head and said, "No, I'm not going back to that! I don't care how long it takes me, but I'm going to pull myself together until I feel like a human being again.''

It was painful for Jennifer to witness the other woman's distress. "I'm sure you can do it, Nancy. Ending a marriage can be devastating, but people manage to build their lives again. You will, too. You're young, you're beautiful, and even though it may seem like it now, your life is far from being over. The best part of it is yet to come, I'm sure.''

Nancy's smile was tremulous when she said, "I hope so!''

For the next few minutes they sat in silence, until Nancy said, "We haven't seen much of you at the house lately.''

Jennifer shrugged. "I pretty much keep to the cottage.''

"It's Alex's house. Don't let mother intimidate you,'' Nancy urged. She paused briefly then added, "She's very good at that, you know.''

"She doesn't really intimidate me, however, I do know how she feels about me,'' Jennifer replied. "But I'll be gone soon enough. I don't see any point in creating a difficult situation.''

Nancy gave her a puzzled look. "But I thought.... Alex is going to be very disappointed,'' she finished at last.

"I only work for him, Nancy,'' Jennifer said unhappily. "Señora de Adler has nothing to fear, not from me."

"Are you in love with him?"

Caught entirely by surprise at the direct question, Jennifer felt the warmth of her embarrassment surface to her cheeks. Evading Nancy's gaze, she looked away, stammering, "I—I—"

"You're a fool if you let mother chase you away, Alba," the woman reproved mildly. "She likes to rule over us as if we were still in kindergarten. Your going away won't make any difference with her plans, anyway, because Alex is not going to marry Ofelia."

Jennifer shrugged, not wishing to discuss the subject. Ofelia was not her rival, that much she knew.

"I don't know how much you know about his first marriage," Nancy said when Jennifer remained silent, "but I can tell you this—it was miserable. He's not going to make the same mistake again. Please don't misunderstand me. I'm only saying that Ofelia is still too young, not that she's anything like Roxana. That woman—my God! I don't know how he could put up with her. Anyone else would have had her committed, and good riddance. But not Alex, oh, no! My brother—"

"Committed?" Jennifer interrupted. "Why? Was she insane?"

"Insane?" Nancy repeated. "That would have been preferable, believe me. No, Roxana wasn't insane, at least not in the regular sense. She was a drug addict."

"She what?"

Looking at Jennifer's pale face, Nancy repeated, "She was a drug addict." Several seconds went by before she added, "I don't know what her problem really was. She was one of those people who is never satisfied. She said she wanted a child, but when Heidi was born she wouldn't have anything to do with her. She hated Alex, but she wouldn't let go of him. At any rate, to make a long story short, when she came back from a trip to Europe she said she had decided to be an artist."

After pausing to light another cigarette, Nancy continued, "Shortly after that Alex found out she was using drugs. He tried every treatment in the world to help her, but she would have none of it. I was visiting once when he found her sniffing coke and took it away from her. She started screaming at him, and when he wouldn't give it back she told him Heidi wasn't his child. I'm almost sure she did it because she knew that was the worst way she could get back at him. For a while I was afraid he might have believed her. The main reason he moved out here was to make it harder for her to obtain drugs, but she still managed to get them through her nurses. In the end she died of an overdose."

CHAPTER TWELVE

NANCY'S REVELATIONS LEFT JENNIFER SHAKEN and at a loss as to what to do next. Of one thing she was now sure: Alejandro was innocent of the crime Tommy accused him of. He had to be. Nothing would convince her of his involvement in the traffic of narcotics after finding out he'd had firsthand experience of the suffering and destruction caused by drug addiction.

What she really wanted to do was go to him and confess the truth, tell him of her suspicions about Ricardo Tejeda and ask for his help in exonerating her brother. But what proof did she have to offer? How could she expect him to believe anything she said after she told him everything he knew about her was a lie, that even the name she was using was not her own? How could she take her word against that of a man whom he had known for most of his life, whom he trusted? Jennifer was too much of a realist to believe a confession at this point would solve all her problems. And she now understood how strongly he must loathe anyone involved with narcotics. Two days ago she might have counted on the love he had professed for her to make him consider her side of the story. But after their encounter at the discotheque, after seeing him with Leticia Roman, Jennifer knew that whatever it was he felt for her, it wouldn't be enough to make him believe her.

The only way she would be able to convince him would be by presenting irrefutable proof of Tommy's innocence. And this could only be accomplished by finding the real culprit and making him confess.

She wondered how long it would take for the investigator hired by Mateo to uncover anything that could be used against Tejeda. Now more than ever she was convinced she had the right man. It had to be him. She knew it in her heart just as she had known all along it couldn't have been Alejandro.

If only she could get out of the trip to Medellín! It meant four days—the two-day trip plus the weekend—during which she would be unable to do anything to further her cause.

But wait! Now that their relationship had become so strained, Alejandro probably wouldn't expect her to spend the weekend with his family or even stay at the *quinta*. Perhaps he wouldn't mind if she said she wanted to stay on and tour Medellín, the second largest city in the country. Once he returned to the capital on Friday, she could go on to La Gorgona and visit Tommy.

Not only was she impatient to see her brother; perhaps he could also give her some information that would help her find the proof she needed. Even if he couldn't, at least he would know she was doing everything in her power to free him. That might give him the courage to survive a little longer in his living hell. Each passing day increased her concern over the possibility that he'd try to escape, and she couldn't erase the memory of those crosses she had seen marking the graves of the inmates who had tried it.

It was with all this in mind that Jennifer prepared herself for the ordeal awaiting her—that of spending the next forty-eight hours in close contact with a man she loved with all her heart and to whom she had to lie with every breath. She tried not to dwell on this dilemma because she was more than a little frightened. So much depended on her being able to carry through with her role.

But even so, her courage faltered as she came face to face with Alejandro when he called for her in the morning. The only thing that saved her was that he seemed as cold and as distant as he had been toward her during the last several days.

This time it was she who came prepared with busy work to keep conversation at a minimum. It was scarcely needed. On the way to the airport Alex looked out the car window in silence while she pretended to study the material she had collected on the firms they were about to visit.

She had expected to take a commercial flight and was surprised when the car deposited them at an air terminal used by private crafts. A gleaming white twin-engine Cessna had been readied. Alejandro helped her aboard before taking over the controls.

"I didn't know you were a pilot," she said as he prepared to go through the preflight check.

"In my business it's a necessity," he replied without pausing in his preparations. "We need the flexibility of flying our own plane."

Something had clicked in her mind the moment she saw the plane. Something Tommy had said. If only she could remember!

Alejandro called the tower for instructions and taxied to the runway. Clearance for takeoff was given, and she waited until they were airborne to ask, "Why is it a necessity? Do you have to travel so much?"

"Not anymore," he replied. "Ricardo does most of the traveling now. Even with our fine road system, flying is the best method of transportation in a country with such varied geography. I don't know how familiar you are with Colombia, but it's divided by three mountain ranges. But there are benefits, too. The mountains provide us with many different climates, from cold to tropical."

"Does Mr. Tejeda fly himself, or does he need a pilot?"

"He flies himself. I think it's his favorite part of the job."

"You've known him for a very long time, haven't you, Alex?"

"All my life, I guess," he shrugged. "He came to work for my father as a young man. Started at the bottom and worked his way up, so he knows the business inside out. He's a good man."

"Then he must be pretty old, even if he doesn't look it," she observed. "Isn't it dangerous for him to fly by himself?"

Jennifer heard a note of amusement in his voice when he said, "You may think he's very old, but he's only in his late fifties. Besides, his license was recently renewed, so it must be all right."

"Is he married?"

Alejandro gave her a puzzled glance. "Why the sudden interest?"

"I was just making conversation," Jennifer said with apparent indifference, "and Mr. Tejeda seemed like a safe enough topic. Do you mind?"

Alejandro shook his head before he finally answered, "Yes, he's married. I haven't seen much of his wife in all the years I've known him, however. From what I remember, she's a mousy little thing. They have no children." He glanced at her sideways. "Is there anything else you'd like to know?"

Plenty, if only she had the nerve. But she'd better not go on. She had a feeling Alejandro was becoming a little suspicious of her curiosity about Tejeda. "Tell me about Medellín," she said instead. "Is it a large city?"

"Over two million. It's the capital of Antioquia and one of the richest, if not the most wealthy, areas of the country. There are many industries—food processing and textiles, mainly. You remember Raul Soler, don't you?" At her nod, he added, "He owns a mill there."

"Don't they also grow coffee?"

"Yes," he nodded, "on the mountain slopes. It's also grown in Caldas and Risaralda. The best *café suave* in the world, as you probably know."

"Café suave?"

"Mild coffee. It derives its quality not only from the soil and the climate but also because it's grown in the shade, not in full sunlight. Of course, the processing is also very important."

"Processing?" she echoed. "Does that mean the way it's toasted?"

"It involves more than that. To begin with, only the ripe grains are picked, by hand. Then the red husk of the berries is removed by machines, and the moist grain is allowed to ferment. This is when the sugars of the mucilage—that's a kind of gelatinous casing—decompose. After that the mucilage is removed and the grain washed. This process is what mainly accounts for the mildness of Colombian coffee, but there's more.

"After the grain is washed it's set to dry in sun, although nowadays some drying is also done artificially. This step, too, is a very important one, because excessive drying spoils the quality. Only then is it ready to be toasted."

"No wonder coffee is expensive," Jennifer exclaimed.

"A lot of people make their living from it," Alejandro replied. "There are some large plantations, but much of the coffee is grown by families on small parcels of land. Everybody takes part in the cultivation, the picking and the treatment. You could say it's a labor of love. Perhaps that's what makes it the best in the world."

"Didn't I hear someone mention that your family owns a coffee plantation?"

"There's some coffee on my mother's *finca*," he replied. "However, much of the land could be put to other uses. We've been considering other crops, but so far nothing has been done."

Knowing this was the reason her brother had been

hired, Jennifer was curious as to how Alejandro would react to her probing into the matter. "Why not?" she queried.

"There've been some complications," he shrugged.

"What kind of complications?"

"Personnel," was all he would admit.

Jennifer was alert to his reactions. The tightening of his jaw when he fell silent was an indication that it would be better to desist from this line of questioning. On the other hand, this was the first mention of the Navarro land he had made in her presence.

"What a shame," she commented politely. "Could you use it for recreation purposes then?"

"That would not create jobs, Alba, and that's what we need. Too many people are leaving the country for the city, hoping to improve their lot. Unfortunately, what they find is more poverty. You've seen how they live, the number of children running loose in the city, living by their wits and increasing the crime rate. Social programs may help, but the real solution is to provide jobs. Jobs and decent wages both in the country and in the city."

"Are there many people living on your mother's land?"

"A few families have been there for generations. As a matter of fact," he added, "we're supposed to be going there for a wedding next week."

Barely able to conceal her excitement, Jennifer waited, hoping he would ask her to attend the wedding. She simply had to get to that planation. It was the place where Tommy had worked, and where perhaps she could find a clue to prove his innocence.

"A country wedding, I suppose. That ought to be interesting," she said eventually, when Alejandro remained silent. "Who's getting married?"

"The manager's daughter."

He certainly wasn't making it easy for her. Wondering how to obtain an invitation without making her interest too obvious, Jennifer turned to look out the plane window.

Lofty ranges, misty peaks, crags, ragged slopes—that was the view that met her eyes. She remained entranced until they landed at the Olaya Herrera Airport, with time to spare for their first visit, to a leather-goods manufacturer.

LOCATED ON THE BEAUTIFUL HILL of Las Palmas overlooking the Aburra Valley, the Intercontinental Hotel offered a magnificent view of the city. From the window of her room, Jennifer gazed down at Medellín with interest. In the seventeenth century it had been a small colonial village nestled in the mountains, and the modern metropolis clearly combined the old with the new.

Jennifer liked Medellín's lovely climate, its wide tree-lined boulevards, its welcoming, generous people. Señor Ramos, the charming owner of the pottery factory they'd toured, had actually presented her with an armful of lovely flowers when she had admired the wares of some flower vendors. He had taken them out to lunch, and the glances he had directed at her during the meal had told her that only Alejandro's presence prevented him from expressing his admiration in a more emphatic way. He flirted with such finesse that Jennifer wasn't sure if Alejandro had noticed anything.

It had been a busy day. All the activity had made the day pass much more easily than she had expected, but the evening was still ahead. Jennifer was glad they had a dinner engagement with another couple, a prospective supplier and his wife. She felt more confident of being able to play her part in a business atmosphere than under more personal circumstances.

The gold trim on the double ruffle of Jennifer's wraparound-style georgette dress made it elegant enough for evening wear. On a white background, the soft watercolors of its hand-painted print combined with the fluidity of the full skirt and long full sleeves to make her appear more feminine, more delicate than ever. She had brushed her hair back, away from her face, exposing her ears to show the tiny gold earrings that were her only adornment.

Before dressing she had spent precious minutes on the telephone trying to find out the best air connection to Cali, only to find out that there were no direct flights between the two cities. The best way for her to travel would be to return to Bogotá with Alejandro Friday evening. She could use the pretext of spending the weekend with Becky to catch an early-morning flight Saturday. That way she would waste some time, but at least she wouldn't have to come up with an excuse to remain behind in Medellin. There shouldn't be any problem—unless Alejandro became suspicious of her friendship with Becky after what was supposed to be such a short acquaintance.

She was filling her small clutch purse with the

necessities for the evening when she heard the knock on her door. Where were her shoes? Oh, well, she sighed. She'd better answer it.

She padded across the room in her stocking feet and opened the door. "I'll be ready in a minute," she told Alejandro, who stood there looking at her. Without her high heels, she had to really tilt her head back to look up at him, and since she just couldn't leave him standing in the hallway, she invited, "Won't you come in?"

He followed her in and stood by the door. She was aware of his eyes on her while she found her shoes.

"Oh, darn!" she exclaimed when in her nervousness she dropped her lipstick. The tube rolled under the bed before she could catch it.

She was tempted to forget it. She was not going to be undignified and go down on all fours in front of Alejandro. On the other hand, it was her one and only lipstick.

"What's the matter?" he inquired while she debated with herself.

"Oh, nothing." She tried to shrug it off. "I just dropped my lipstick."

He came toward her. "I'll get it for you."

"Don't worry about it. It rolled under the bed."

Ignoring her protest, Alejandro knelt down on the floor and lifted the edge of the coverlet. "I don't see it. What color is it?"

"It has a tortoiseshell case." Realizing it wouldn't be easy to spot on the dark carpet, Jennifer got down on her knees as well. Knowing better than he what they were looking for and the direction it had gone, she immediately spied the small cylinder shape. It was completely out of her reach. "Over there, toward the middle," she pointed. "Can you see it?"

Even though Alejandro's arm was much longer than hers, he had to stretch to the maximum under the king-size bed. "I've got it." He straightened up. "Here you are."

"Thanks."

The contact of his fingers when he put the lipstick into her outstretched hand made her tremble a little. She looked up at him and found that his gaze had fastened on her mouth. Her stomach muscles tensed as her lips parted slightly to draw in breath.

Even though she had dreaded falling again into the trap of intimacy, Jennifer was unable to quell the dangerous excitement that surged through her when she sensed his desire. When he made no move to kiss her she willed him to do so. At that moment she wanted his arms around her more than anything she had ever wanted in her life. Her lips quivered for the warmth and taste of his.

The sense of loss, the wave of desolation that washed over her when he tore his eyes away threatened to engulf her. She couldn't look at him as she accepted the hand he offered to help her to her feet again.

Aware of the wild pounding of her heart, Jennifer turned away and busied herself checking the contents of her purse. She heard the faint click of his lighter and didn't dare look in the mirror. From the burning she felt on her cheeks, she knew her color had heightened. She kept her back to him in order to give herself time to recover her composure.

When she finally managed to pull herself together, she turned to find Alejandro looking out of the window. One hand held a cigarette; the other was jammed in the pocket of his trousers.

"I'm sorry I kept you waiting."

He turned to face her and shrugged his shoulders in reply, crushing the cigarette in an ashtray before heading for the door.

"Don't forget your key." He had picked it up from the top of a commode and carefully avoided touching her hand when he gave it to her."

"Thanks."

Together they walked through the corridors to the elevator, where the presence of a young couple made the silence between them less awkward. Jennifer felt their presence was a blessing until their glances, their whispers and hand holding betrayed them as newlyweds. On the way down she found herself envying their happiness. Alejandro, however, seemed to ignore them.

La Playa Avenue, filled with movement, noise and lights, was to Medellín what the Champs Elysees was to Paris. The two faces of Medellín, old and new, were never more prominent than in Plazuela Nutibara. The life of the city seemed to gravitate around the busy square, where modern skyscrapers towered over traditional government buildings.

The Hotel Nutibara, perhaps the most popular spot in Medellín, was where they had agreed to meet David Perik and his wife, Irene. The Periks were a nice couple, Jennifer decided immediately. Of Dutch extraction, David was a partner in one of Medellín's leading textile companies. Irene owned a small art gallery, which Alejandro told her was beginning to establish an excellent reputation in the city. Beautiful, elegant and poised, she presented Jennifer with a good example of the modern woman of Colombia, just as competent in the business world as she was at home.

Under different circumstances Jennifer would have enjoyed their company. But it didn't take long for her to understand that Alejandro's main purpose in arranging the evening had been to avoid being alone with her. It was the prudent thing to do, she realized, but it didn't help the hurt she felt at this discovery.

When the same Señor Ramos who had been their host earlier in the day stopped by their table to say hello, Jennifer's conversation became breezier, her laughter gayer. Forcing herself to appear in a cheerful mood, in fact, and purposefully ignoring Alejandro's frown, she accepted the Colombian's suggestion that they all end the evening at the nightclub of the Nutibara.

The floor show's main attraction was a female singer who sang Spanish torch songs in a sultry voice. As soon as the orchestra began playing again afterward, Señor Ramos invited Jennifer to dance.

"It is indeed a pity you will be leaving so soon, Miss Maitland," he said as they started moving to the music. Although generous with his gallantries, Señor Ramos held her at a respectful distance while they danced. "I would have loved to show you some of our fair city."

"I'll always have good memories of Medellín because of your kindness, Señor Ramos."

His gaze was intense when he said, "Perhaps I may hope you will come back?"

Jennifer was well aware that one word from her would encourage her admirer. Although he was a reasonably attractive man, her state of mind was such that she could derive no satisfaction from his obvious interest. "I'm afraid that my work will be taking me to many cities," she said with an apologetic smile.

The song ended, and before the band started again Alejandro cut in. Señor Ramos gave a wistful sigh and walked away.

"I don't know what the hell you've been trying to prove all evening, but whatever it is, I want you to stop."

"Prove?" She looked up at him. "I'm not trying to prove anything, Alex."

"Oh, no?" She could feel his controlled anger in the hand he had at her waist, in the fingers holding her own. "Then tell me what it is. Must you seduce every male who comes within your reach?"

"You have no right—"

Her words were cut off by the force with which he drew her against him. "I have no right?" Even though he still held her tightly, she became aware of the change in his embrace as he murmured, "Oh, Alba."

He could alter her world with one word.

Was she being a fool in reading a need to love in the way he had spoken her name? Jennifer closed her eyes to better savor the pervading warmth as her body molded itself to his. They moved in silence as if

in a dream, two willing captives of the sinuous glittering web that love was weaving all around them as
they danced to the music and to the rhythm of their
heartbeats.

Jennifer wished she could make the moment last
forever. For her there would be no one else who
could make her feel the way this man did. So strong,
so tender and giving, he could awaken her senses,
could stir her heart. This was a brand-new love, like
she had never known before. A love of passion and
infinite tenderness.

Soon, much too soon, the dance ended. The orchestra began a livelier tune, and hand in hand they
reluctantly returned to the table.

A few minutes later Señor Ramos said good-night
and left. No one seemed sorry to see him go, least of
all Jennifer, who was hardly aware of anyone but
Alejandro. It took all of her concentration to par-
ticipate in polite conversation with their table companions until at last it was time to say goodbye.

Their return to the Intercontinental was far different from their earlier taxi ride. Sitting close
together and gazing into each other's eyes, they were
oblivious to the interested glances the taxi driver
occasionally stole in the rearview mirror. The world
was theirs alone.

Jennifer was walking on a cloud as they entered the
hotel and crossed the lobby. The nervous fluttering
within her didn't start until they were in the elevator
going up to their floor.

Was Alejandro planning to stay with her, make
love to her? As much as she wanted to be with him,

she was suddenly assaulted by self-doubt. How could a man who had known women like Leticia Roman be content with someone who had so little expertise in the art of making love? As much as she felt for him, would she be able to please him? How could she ever hope to win him from the seductive clutches of that glamorous woman?

Her hand was trembling a little when she handed him the key to her room. He unlocked the door and followed her in.

"Alex," she began as soon as the door closed behind them, but he wouldn't let her speak. She was drawn into his arms as soon as they were inside the room, and her mouth was captured hungrily by his.

Her lips parted to welcome his warmth, the heady caress of his tongue as it savored her responses. She had waited for what had seemed a lifetime for this kiss; all he had to do now was touch her and her heart and flesh took over from her reason.

Her limbs had weakened so much that she welcomed the softness of the bed beneath her when he eased her down on it. Then he parted the delicate fabric of her dress to expose and explore her throat with his lips. Trailing down the slender column of her neck, the curve of her jaw, he finally traced the contours of her lips with his tongue, teasing them to part and yield the sweetness within as his hand sought the curve of her breast.

He pulled his mouth away only to groan, "My God, Alba, what do you do to me! Have you any idea what you've put me through?"

She drew in her breath. If it was anything like what

he did to her, she did know—but she couldn't tell him. All she could do was look up at him. "Were you jealous of Señor Ramos?"

"As jealous as hell," he nodded. "You have no idea how close I came to beating the living daylights out of him before I dragged you out of that restaurant this afternoon."

She reached out to caress his cheek. "It was just a harmless flirtation, darling. I didn't think you noticed."

"I noticed." He held her hand to his face. "Haven't you discovered yet that very little escapes me where you are concerned?" He moved her hand to his mouth and kissed the open palm. "I've never felt this way about another woman before."

"Not even Leticia?" Too late she bit her lip. The words were out before she could stop them. She saw one dark brow arch.

"She has nothing to do with us."

Abruptly, she pulled away from him. "You have the nerve to get upset over some harmless flirtation, and you say Leticia Roman has nothing to do with us!" she exploded. "Anyone can see a mile away that you two are lovers!"

She started to get off the bed, but he spun her around to face him. "I won't deny that we were lovers once, but not anymore."

"You certainly didn't lose any time in running back to her when—" She stopped in mid-sentence, realizing her blunder.

"After I saw you with Mateo López?" he finished for her. "And what were you doing with him?"

The tables had turned, and now it was she who was on the defensive.

"He...he's just a friend." Her hesitation was only momentary. Knowing intuitively that she had to keep the offensive, she challenged, "Is that what I can expect from you? That you'll run to your former girl friends the minute you don't get things your way?"

"For your information, I didn't run to her. I asked you to have dinner with me, remember? I simply joined her party after you had turned me down." He heaved a sigh of exasperation. "Damn it, Alba, why are you trying so hard to pick a fight?"

In self-protection; Jennifer had to admit the fact to herself. She desperately wanted to believe his affair with Leticia was over. The thought of them together was much too painful to bear.

Alejandro took advantage of her hesitation to pull her gently into his arms. "I've lived long enough to know that what we can have is a rare thing, *amor mío*," he said huskily. "I'm not going to risk losing it over some meaningless affair. You're far too precious to me."

Sorrow was not the cause for the tears that stung her eyes. When he dipped his head to touch his lips to hers again, Jennifer had no time to think before she totally lost herself in the caress.

"WHERE ARE WE?" Jennifer cried, alarmed by the sight of the sparkling blue sea that suddenly appeared below them.

"Cartagena de Indias," Alejandro replied.

She tried to hide her dismay. "But... I thought we were going back to Bogotá."

He glanced at her briefly before saying, "I thought we needed time by ourselves. I was planning to tell you this week but...the occasion never arose."

Jennifer leaned back in her seat and closed her eyes, trying to organize her jumbled thoughts. When Alejandro had left her the previous evening, she had been disappointed, yet somehow relieved, that he had not stayed and made love to her. Now she understood why....

"Why didn't you tell me last night?" She heard the quaver in her own voice.

He glanced at her and saw her sudden pallor. "Darling, I thought you wanted this as much as I do." When she remained silent, he added, "The arrangements can be changed."

The tightness she saw at the corner of his mouth told Jennifer of his inner tension, as did the grip he had on the controls of the plane. Now she understood why he had refrained from taking advantage of all the other occasions when they could have made love. She was deeply moved by his thoughtfulness.

She reached for his hand. "That won't be necessary, Alex."

When he lifted her hand to his lips and kissed her fingers, Jennifer had to blink rapidly. Still, her tears made everything hazy when she looked down at the jewel of a city gleaming under the torrid Caribbean sun.

Cartagena de Indias, like Medellín, was a city that felt comfortable with both its antiquity and its modern architecture. In the newer part of the city modern apartment buildings and hotels lined the wide beach. If asked to describe the city in one word, she would have chosen colorful, Jennifer thought as their taxi took them to a modern hotel in Boca Grande, the most recently built section of the city.

The brightest notes of color in the sumptuous lobby were the red cushions of the wicker sofas arranged here and there on the brown-and-white tiled floor. They followed a uniformed bellboy along a corridor carpeted in lush green and yellow. The room they were shown was not very large, but it contained all the comforts anyone could ask for. Excellent taste and style were reflected in the furnishings and decor, which were definitely Colombian in flavor.

After the bellboy finished showing them around and had left them alone, Jennifer stood uncertainly in the middle of the room.

"Come over here and look at the view," Alejandro called from the window.

Slowly she did as he suggested. As much as she loved him, as much as she longed for him, she needed time to come to terms with the situation. When she finally stood next to him, Alejandro simply put his arm around her waist. She leaned against him, and they stood looking in silence at the waters of the blue Caribbean glittering like a jewel in the tropical sun.

Alejandro lifted her chin to look into her eyes. "Would you like to go to the beach or should we explore the city?"

She gave him a grateful smile. "Explore the city."

His fingers gently touched her face as he reassured

her, "We have all the time in the world, my love."

"Oh, Alex!" She put her arms around his waist and nestled her head on his chest. He held her tenderly until she drew back and said, "I didn't bring my swimming suit."

"I'll buy you a dozen," he laughed, giving her a hearty squeeze.

"You're spoiling me, you know."

"Mmm, I can think of only one thing I'd like to do more."

Again she felt the telltale warmth on her cheeks. "I'm serious."

"So am I."

Any further protest was silenced with a kiss—a long lingering kiss that made Jennifer a little dizzy. Finally he drew back and fingered the lace collar of her blouse. "You'd better change into something a little cooler."

"I'm afraid I came prepared for a business trip in Medellín, not a seaside holiday."

"Touché," he laughed, amused by her chiding tone. "Then I guess I can only make amends by taking you shopping before lunch."

At the fashionable boutiques of El Laguito, a modern shopping center in the tourist section of town, Jennifer bought a saucy red peasant blouse to wear with a triple-tiered skirt of white cotton trimmed with rickrack in red, yellow and green. A wide white leather belt emphasized her slim waist. Since her summery outfit called for white sandals and bare legs, she complied by sending her stockings and high-heeled shoes back to the hotel with the rest of their purchases. There were numerous packages, since Alejandro seemed determined to buy her everything that even remotely struck her fancy. Even though she tried to stop him, she ended up with far more than she needed for the weekend.

The old fort of San Sebastian de Pastelito on the island of Manga housed the Club de Pesca, a yacht club and restaurant where they went for a late lunch. Located inside the bay, the island had become a residential district when the old families had moved out of the old walled sector of Cartagena.

From their table, which was set in a tiled courtyard under the shade of an enormous banyan tree, they watched the fishing and pleasure boats gliding across the blue waters of the bay.

"Mmm, *paella con mariscos*," Jennifer read on the menu.

"Do you know what it is?" Alejandro inquired.

"Sure," she nodded. "Seafood cooked in saffron rice. A friend of mine in Los Angeles made it for me once, and I loved it."

"It says here it'll take an hour and a half to prepare," Alejandro pointed out.

Jennifer's mouth opened. "An hour and a half!"

"It's cooked to order. Do you want to wait that long?"

"I don't think I could," she shook her head. "I'm starved right now."

"That's one thing I like about you," Alejandro chuckled.

"And what is that?"

"You're never bashful when it comes to food."

She gave him a sour look. "Are you implying that I eat too much?"

"My darling, you eat like a drill sergeant, but I have no idea where you put it all."

"I happen to have a very active metabolism," she told him dryly.

He laughed when she stuck out her chin in mock vexation and looked pointedly back at the menu. Actually, she was remembering with a certain amount of amusement that their first argument had been over food—the enormous dinner she had ordered at the Tequendama Hotel after her purse was stolen. A few seconds later she asked, "What's *pargo*?"

"Red snapper."

In the end they ordered the grilled red snapper and coconut rice: *patacóns*, which turned out to be fried slices of plantain; and a salad of tomatoes sprinkled with lime juice.

"Where should we go next?" she asked as she finished the last bite of her coconut and pineapple pie. With a golden lattice top it had proved to be as delicious as it looked.

Alejandro put down his demitasse and lit a cigarette. "By now it should be cool enough to visit the walled town."

Jennifer lifted her face to the sea breeze. The worst heat of the day was gone, but she still didn't want to move from the spot. "Tell me a little about it. It must be very old."

"It is," he nodded, and went on to tell her how Cartagena had been dubbed "of the Indies" back in 1533, in order to distinguish it from the port on the southeastern coast of Spain. Then, as now, the life of the city was dominated by the sea. From its capacious natural harbor not only had sailed the treasure ships of the New World when it became the main link between the Spanish Empire and its South American colonies, but years later it was the point of arrival for the slaves brought from Africa to work the extensive plantations.

When Jennifer mentioned the two forts she had seen from the air before landing, Alejandro spoke of the days of the Spanish Main, when those very walls had been the colonists' defense against pirate attacks. "The original walls were built in 1586," he continued, "but they had to be replaced several times after all the pounding they received from pirate cannonballs. Tropical storms battered them as well, of course."

"I never was very good at history," she said, "but I always loved reading about pirate adventures. Cartagena seemed to be one of their favorite targets for looting."

"It was a very rich city," Alejandro agreed.

"This place is so different from Bogotá and Medellín," she observed. "It's almost like the three cities are in different countries."

"That's why no one can speak about Colombia without saying in the same breath that it's a country of contrasts. Here, again, our geography is responsible. Each region has developed a personality of its own."

"Oh, I love it here," she sighed. "One of my favorite things is to get up early in the morning and walk along the beach, to see the sun come up."

Thoughtfully, he crushed his cigarette in the ashtray. "It can be beautiful in the mountains, too," he said.

Jennifer reached for his hand and smiled into his eyes. "Yes, darling. The mountains are beautiful, too."

The plain stone facades of houses, which, with their wooden balconies and heavy doors, rimmed the narrow streets of the older part of the city, gave no clue as to what they hid within their walls. Sitting on a park bench in the shade of some tall almond trees and palms, Jennifer and Alejandro watched the inhabitants come and go. They had already explored the town on foot; had walked down Street of the Ladies, Street of the Inquisition, and Street of the Lamps—all of which had transported them back two hundred years. The main square was particularly impressive. An equestrian statue of Simón Bolívar stood in the center and fountains marked the corners, while across the street was the cathedral. A magnificently carved door and a charming inner courtyard with a huge tamarind tree contributed to an atmosphere of peace and beauty at the Palace of the Inquisition, also on the square, but the instruments of torture on display were grim reminders of a violent age gone by.

A short taxi ride got them back to the hotel in time for a swim in a sea, which was colored flame by the rays of the setting sun.

No bride could have wished for a more delightful spot than this for her honeymoon, Jennifer thought as she dressed for dinner. Or for a bridegroom more conscious of her needs than Alejandro was. Listening to him singing a little off key in the shower, she smiled at her reflection while she touched perfume to the pulse of her throat and wrists. The fragrance had a flowery quality that soon developed into a spicy woody blend.

Once she could prove Ricardo Tejeda's involvement in the drug smuggling and her brother's innocence, she was sure Alejandro would understand why she had been forced to lie to him. All the fears of inadequacy she had experienced in Medellín had been swept aside, because now she was sure of his love. He had shown it not only with every glance and every word, but in the way he had waited for everything to be so right between them before they consummated their love....

She tied and retied the drawstring of the neck of the silk peasant dress Alejandro had bought her that morning, until the amount of shoulder it exposed was to her satisfaction. Gold loops and a gold necklace complemented the outfit perfectly. The rich mélange of colors of the print made wearing a bra unnecessary, and she felt deliciously wicked with nothing but a pair of brief bikini panties underneath it all.

Her hair was still slightly damp, and she was just arranging a pair of golden combs to hold it away from her face when Alejandro came out of the bathroom wearing a towel around his waist. He captured her in the circle of his arms as he stood behind her and looked at their reflection in the mirror.

"Mmm, what a temptation," he said, fingering the ends of the drawstring that held her dress. When he kissed the side of her neck and the curve of her shoulder, the silk could not disguise the tautening of her nipples. He became aware of her nakedness beneath the dress when his gaze was drawn to the peaks pushing against the thin material. When he looked back at her face he found twin spots of color staining her cheeks.

"You're exquisite," he smiled at her reflection, cupping her breast with his hand.

The warmth that began spreading through her body as he caressed her made her limbs grow weak. Abruptly she turned in his arms, needing suddenly to run her hands over his shoulders, over the broad expanse of his naked chest. She lifted her face to receive the kisses that he rained on her cheeks, on her nose, but when she parted her lips he drew away, just a little.

"If I kiss you now, I won't be able to let you go," he murmured huskily.

"Must you?" She was a little breathless.

"For just a little while." A wistful half smile played on his lips as he traced a finger down her cheek and looked into her green eyes. "We've waited this long. I won't rob us now of the exquisite pleasure of the last hours of painful anticipation."

Even though she didn't understand him then, the next few hours revealed to her the truth behind his words. The yearning to belong to him, to possess him at last became an exquisite torture as they sat across the table from each other in a romantic courtyard. She had no idea what she ate that evening; she was conscious only of his loving whispers, of the touch of his hand when it closed over hers and he gazed into her eyes. And later, on the dance floor, when their bodies melded together to the soft romantic music, their dance was simply a prelude to what the night held in store for them.

A velvet sky strewn with diamond stars witnessed their return to the hotel, and there was no longer doubt or fear within Jennifer when she came into his arms at last. All she needed to fulfill his dreams was to give him her love.

A gentle tug loosened the drawstring of her dress, and the silken garment fell unheeded around her feet.

"My love," he murmured, drawing her into his embrace.

Jennifer's fingers were trembling a little as they undid the buttons of his shirt, as they touched his naked skin. "Oh, Alex, I love you so!"

She helped him out of the rest of his clothes, and as they embraced, their naked bodies were pulsatingly aware of their need to become one.

"Mi amor, mi tesoro," he whispered as he lowered her to the bed.

She closed her eyes, listening to his loving murmurs as his fingers caressed the satin curve of her shoulders. His lips trailed down her cheek until they found her own, parted and yielding, but it was much too soon to satisfy her need. He teased her mouth with his until she quivered with the longing to kiss him.

Her breath was ragged as desire built up within her, as his hands and his mouth captured and possessed the rosy peaks of her breasts and ventured further. He led and she followed along a path of pleasures never explored by her before, and still thirsty for his kiss, she relished the feel, the scent, the taste of his skin, the sensuality of his muscles rippling under her fingers. And when his mouth was hers at last, she drank his taste as heady wine.

He aroused her flesh until the need to be a part of him was overwhelming and her heightened senses clamored for the fulfillment only he could give. And when at last their flesh was one, she knew it was the moment she had waited for all her life, when her body and her heart responded to the call of his and she was whole at last.

Her yearnings eased, the overflowing tenderness filling her heart could only be expressed by tears of joy, of wonder as she came down from the heights of passion to drift into a peaceful dream of love.

How long the dream lasted she didn't know, but when she reached out to seek the warmth of Alejandro's body, she found only emptiness beside her.

She sat up in bed and looked around the room. It was still dark, and only the glowing tip of a cigarette betrayed the silhouette by the window.

"Alex?"

He didn't answer, and when her vision adjusted to the dim light in the room, she could see that he hadn't moved even though she was sure he had heard her.

"Darling, what's the matter? Is anything wrong?"

She had started to get up and go to him when she heard his voice. "How many others have there been?"

The deadly tone paralyzed her. "Others?" she echoed with a shiver of dread.

He turned to face her at last. Even in the dark she could feel his eyes boring into her. "How many?"

Like a supplicant, she held out her arms. "Alex—"

"How many?" he cut her off.

She let her arms drop. "Would it matter?" she asked bitterly.

"No. It wouldn't."

She sat down on the edge of the bed because her legs refused to support her. The loss she felt inside was so great she couldn't even find tears to express her misery.

He crossed the distance separating them and loomed over her. "Why did you lie? Did you think I'd be stupid enough not to know the difference?"

She turned her face as if she had been slapped. "I didn't lie!"

His laugh was bitter, totally without humor. "No, you never actually said you were a virgin. You only let me believe it. Very clever."

"Stop it!" she cried, covering her ears with her hands. "I don't have to listen! I won't! I have nothing to be ashamed of!"

He turned and walked away, back to the window. "You told me you'd never been married," he said. "Was that another lie? Or, pardon me, another half truth?"

"Alex, please, don't do this to us."

"There is no us," he said quietly. "Not now."

"My God, Alex, is that the extent of the love you professed for me? What kind of emotion is it, that you can turn it on and off so easily?"

He spun around to face her. "The woman I loved doesn't exist!"

"How can you say that? I'm the same person I was yesterday and the day before, Alex; the same woman you said you loved. I had a life of my own before I met you. You have no more right to demand an account of everything I did during those years than I have of you."

"That's different. I'm a man."

"And *that* makes a difference?" Her tone had lost some of its bitterness when she added, "We're both human beings, Alex. We both need to love and be loved. Well, I'm not going to ask for forgiveness. There's no shame in having loved someone else before you came along."

The silence between them lasted so long that she had almost despaired when he asked, "Did you love him?"

"Yes. We were going to be married."

"What happened?"

"A car accident a few days before the wedding. Jim. . .he was killed instantly.".

She waited, and when the silence became too much for her to bear, she tried to reach out again. "I love you, Alex."

He didn't answer, and she knew it was all over.

CHAPTER THIRTEEN

"OH, DEAR!" Becky said when Jennifer had finished unburdening her grief. They were sitting at the dinette table in the Mathewses' kitchen.

"It was horrible, Becky. He looked at me as if he hated me."

"You should have told him, Jenny. Latin men are a jealous lot. Being the first with a woman still means a lot to them."

As jealous as hell, Alejandro had said once. *Oh, why did I let it go so far without telling him he was wrong?* Jennifer wondered to herself. She heaved a wistful sigh. "It's too late now, Becky."

The American woman paused a few seconds, then asked, "So what happens now?"

"I don't know," Jennifer shrugged. "As soon as I can prove Tommy's innocence, I suppose I'll be going back to the States. I'll just have to try to put all this behind me." It wouldn't be easy, but there was nothing else she could do.

"Have you heard from Mateo yet?"

"No," she shook her head. "He was with a client when I phoned this morning, so I left word for him to call me back at your number."

Becky was pensive for a moment, then said, "Perhaps it would be better if you came to stay with me for the next few days, Jenny. Until things cool off a bit between you and Alex.''

''Thanks. I was hoping you'd ask me,'' Jennifer admitted. ''Although things couldn't be any colder between us than they are right now. He's hardly spoken to me since Sunday morning. Oh, Becky, I never dreamed he would take it so hard! My gosh, we're not in Victorian England anymore!''

Becky made a comforting clucking sound as she patted Jennifer's hand. ''He might come around once he's had a chance to think things over.''

Jennifer shook her head. ''I don't think so. Besides, even if he did, what's going to happen when he finds out that I've been lying all along? That Tom Blake, the man he sent to prison, is my brother? No, he'll never forgive that.''

''But you had good reason to lie!'' Becky argued. ''Tommy is innocent!''

''You don't know Alex, Becky. He can be quite. . . implacable.''

''Then if he's such an unforgiving man, you might be better off without him.''

''Perhaps,'' Jennifer replied, absently stirring her coffee. But he had so many other qualities that had made her fall so deeply in love with him, even when she'd still had every reason to doubt his integrity. If she could discount how easily he aroused her to passion—which she couldn't—there was still that marvelous tenderness, that gentleness he had displayed toward her on so many occasions; his teasing sense of humor; his ability to read and respond to her emotional needs.... *I love him,* she thought. *With all my heart, I love him.*

A ringing telephone interrupted her thoughts. Becky got up to answer.

"It's for you," she extended the receiver to her. "A Dr. López."

Jennifer smiled and took the phone. "Hello, Mat?"

"How's my favorite patient this morning?"

Nursing a broken heart. "I'm fine. I wanted to reach you this weekend, but I couldn't. Have you heard anything from the investigator yet?"

"He started checking last Friday and promised a report by this evening."

"Oh." Jennifer couldn't disguise the disappointment in her voice.

"Patience, lass," Mateo said. "These things take time. However," he added when she sighed, "something might break quite soon. I...." He let his voice trail off, then added, "I think I'd better wait and tell you in person."

"I'm flying to Cali first thing in the morning, Mat."

"On business?"

"My own. I'm going to see Tommy. He said something once about a plane, but I didn't pay much attention at the time. However, I just learned that Tejeda is a pilot, and that he often flies the company plane."

"Mmm, interesting."

"I thought so. Perhaps Tommy could give me some other information we could use."

"Should we meet after work, then?"

"I won't be going back to the office this afternoon, Mat. I'm staying at Becky's." Jennifer covered the mouthpiece when she noticed her friend mouthing a message to her, then added, "She says why don't you come over for dinner this evening."

"What time?"

"Sevenish?"

"I'll be there."

"Talk to you later, Mat."

"Well?" Becky inquired as Jennifer hung up.

"He's got something, but he won't say what it is over the phone."

Becky clasped her hands. "The suspense is killing me."

"Me, too," Jennifer admitted.

The afternoon was long, even though the two women reminisced over old times and made every effort to make the time go faster. When Mateo arrived promptly at seven, he was taken into the family room, handed a drink, and immediately assaulted with questions by both of them.

"Wait, ladies, please!" he protested laughingly.

"We've been dying to hear what you have to say." Jennifer's smile was sheepish. "You sounded so mysterious."

"In confidential matters I prefer face-to-face conversations," Mateo replied. "You never know who might be listening." He saw that he had their attention and said to Jennifer, "Do you remember I mentioned I had already done some investigating? When Sara told me about the cocaine found in the coffee shipment?'' At her nod, he continued, ''Well, I did get to know a fellow in the DEA and—''

''What's the DEA?'' the women interrupted in unison.

''The Drug Enforcement Agency,'' Mateo replied. ''It's linked with the American Embassy, although their offices are located elsewhere.''

''Is it a secret organization?'' Becky wanted to know.

''Not really. Everybody knows where it is. They're the ones who investigate the narcotic traffic into the United States from Colombia. But since they're not empowered to make arrests in this country, they pass any information they get on to the Colombian police.''

''Go on,'' Jennifer encouraged when he'd finished. ''You made a contact with the DEA. Who is he?''

''His name wouldn't mean anything to you,'' Mat replied. ''But I told him about your case.''

''Everything?'' Jennifer was immediately alarmed.

''Hey, relax,'' Mateo said soothingly. ''The fellow is on our side. He's as interested in getting the right man as we are. Well, almost,'' he had to admit at the look of disbelief on Jennifer's face.

''Did you tell him about my being here illegally?''

''Yes, and he'll see what he can do with the embassy about getting you a passport and a visa. I'll let you know when he gets back to me.''

The sigh Jennifer gave was one of relief. At least that would be one less thing to worry about. ''Thanks, Mat.''

"So what did this DEA man have to say?" Becky interposed impatiently.

"They've been successful in locating a number of labs around the city. The police should be raiding them at any moment."

"Labs?" Jennifer questioned.

"Where they process the cocaine. You see, it comes in paste form from Peru and Ecuador. It's processed here into powder, and then it's smuggled out of the country."

"Oh, I see," she said.

"What that means to us is that supplies are getting more scarce all the time. Very soon now some people are going to be very desperate not only to get some raw material in but also to ship the finished product out. They're going to start tapping all their sources of transportation, especially those that aren't under suspicion."

"Namely, our Mr. Tejeda," Jennifer offered.

"Exactly," Mateo nodded.

Jennifer told him then of her plans to question Tommy more thoroughly about the plane he had once mentioned, and of the wedding the Adlers were planning to attend at the Navarro *finca*.

"Wait a minute!" Mateo exclaimed when he heard the date of the marriage ceremony. "There are rumors on the street about a delivery being made somewhere around that time. Is Tejeda attending the wedding?"

"He might be," replied Jennifer. "Do you think he might be receiving the cocaine paste there?"

"Perhaps," Mateo replied thoughtfully. "I only wish I could go with you."

"I don't know what even my own chances of being invited are. My relationship with the Adlers is not at its best at the moment. But I'm going to be around for that party one way or another, because after what you've told me, I'm sure Ricardo Tejeda is going to be there."

Mateo's voice grew serious. "Remember we're dealing with very dangerous people, Jennifer. Don't try anything on your own, or you may never live to tell about it."

At his warning, a cold shiver of fear went through her. "I'll be careful, Mat," she said soberly.

IN THE VISITING AREA of the Gorgona Correction Facility, Jennifer waited expectantly for her brother to appear. She turned swiftly from the window when she heard the door open. Tommy came in, escorted by a guard.

"Tommy!" She ran to him and threw her arms around him. "Oh, Tommy!" was all she could say as she held him tightly.

"Hi, sis."

The lack of warmth in his voice made her draw back a little to look at him, and her face creased in a puzzled frown. "Are you all right?"

The gauntness of his face filled her with sorrow. He looked harder now. The look in his dark eyes made her shudder with an apprehension she couldn't describe.

She stepped back and stared at him for a moment, at a loss as to what to say to him. He was like a stranger. "You've lost weight," she said lamely at last and suddenly realized that the guard had left them alone.

"With the food they serve here, I'm in no danger of ruining my waistline," he said with a smile that was grim and bitter.

That reminded her of the gifts she had brought for him, and turning away, she walked self-consciously toward the table in the center of the room. "I brought some of your favorite treats," she said, offering him one of the boxes that had been opened and inspected by the guards.

"Did you bring any cigarettes?"

Jennifer regarded him with dismay. "I—I didn't know you smoked now," she replied in a small voice.

Tommy shrugged indifferently. "It doesn't matter." He sat down at the table, and after selecting a cookie from the open box, looked up at her and asked, "What are you doing here, Jenny?"

Jennifer sat down across the table from her brother and asked eagerly. "Did you get my letter?"

He held up his hand in deprecation. "Don't tell me you're seriously planning to go through with that insane scheme," he replied tersely. "Come on, Jenny, be serious! This is not a game you're playing."

"But I *am* serious!" she protested, bewildered by his manner. "I already got a job with Alejandro Adler and—"

"You what?" For one disbelieving moment he stared at her in silence. Then he heaved himself out of his chair and began pacing the floor in a manner that reminded her of a caged tiger. Suddenly he swung around and faced her angrily. "Look, I can take care of myself in here," he said in a voice that was harsh and irritable. "I want you to forget the whole thing and go home, do you understand me?"

She frowned in annoyance. "But, Tommy, very soon now I'll be able to prove that someone else and not you was smuggling those drugs. There's going to be a wedding at the Navarro's *finca*, and we believe there's going to be a delivery—"

"My God, Jenny!" Gripping her by the shoulders with urgent hands, he pulled her to her feet. "Don't you know what you're getting into? You could get killed!" Roughly, he pulled her into his arms and held her against him. "Oh, Jenny, don't you see that I can't bear the thought of you getting hurt on my account?" His embrace tightened and his voice was a hoarse whisper when he said, "I love you, sis. God, it's so good to see you again!"

"Oh, Tommy!" Jennifer clung to him in a paroxysm of sobbing.

He held her for a moment and then, drawing back a little, said, "Hey!" She stopped weeping and looked up at him, and he grinned disarmingly at her. For a moment she had a glimpse of the Tommy she knew and loved. "Your nose is getting all red and runny, did you know that?"

Smiling through her tears, Jennifer bobbed her head as she left his embrace to search through her purse for a tissue.

"You always were the emotional half of the pair of us," he mocked her mildly as she dried her tears and noisily blew her nose.

When she had composed herself, they sat down at

the table again. She bent forward eagerly and said, "I think I know now who it was that framed you, Tommy." She went on to tell him all she had done since her arrival in Colombia. Tommy listened intently to her narrative interrupting with a question every now and then. He also told her what he had learned from other inmates about the drug traffic in Colombia.

During their hurried conversation Jennifer discovered that, after nursing a grudge for months against Alejandro Adler, Tommy couldn't easily accept the man's innocence, no matter how much she insisted he wasn't to blame. He listened to her arguments anyway; Jennifer felt he was at least keeping an open mind. When it was almost time for the guard to return, he got up, went to the window and stood there looking out in silence.

When he turned to her again, he said, "My cell mate, a man named Patricio Martínez, is being released today. He owes me one, Jenny, because I saved his life once during a fight. And he has connections... you know what I mean. If you get into deep trouble and need help, get a message to him. It won't be difficult."

JENNIFER WAS ONE of the few passengers aboard the rickety bus bouncing up and down the dark mountain road that linked the thriving city of Cali to Buenaventuara. The squalid seaside town that she'd just left was the most important port on the Colombian Pacific coast. It also had the dubious distinction of being the point of embarcation to the island prison of La Gorgona.

But Jennifer wasn't thinking of the town, or of the uncomfortable ride. She was thinking of Tommy. Even though she understood that at first he had been putting on a performance in order to protect her from her own impetuosity, she was still shaken by the transformation the months in jail had caused in her brother. Looking back, she realized that what had frightened her most were his eyes. They were the eyes of a man who had learned to hate.

And the object of his hate was Alejandro.

She actually felt frightened at the thought of these two men, the two men she loved most in the world, ever coming face to face. Only one of them would walk away from the confrontation, she knew. No, she could never allow that to happen. As soon as Tommy was released, she would have to get him out of Colombia by any means at her disposal.

But what was the point in worrying about something that was still in the future? Too many other things demanded her attention before that could ever happen, and finding the evidence that would free her brother was first on her list.

Even though Mateo had warned her about the widespread—and deadly—organization they were up against, Jennifer had not really grasped the enormity of the danger she faced until after her conversation with Tommy. Sharing that island with the worst criminals in Colombia had given him a tremendous insight into a world that, to her, still existed only in shadows.

The information Tommy had given her coincided with Mateo's—of how the paste extracted from coca leaves was brought over the border from Peru and Ecuador to be processed in laboratories hastily set up in different points of Bogotá. After Jennifer told Tommy about the recent losses suffered by the smugglers, he had agreed with Mateo's prediction that it wouldn't be long before the services of Ricardo Tejeda—or of Alejandro Adler—would be called upon.

When she'd questioned Tommy about the plane he had mentioned earlier, he had told her about a certain field where he had found tire tracks belonging to a small plane—of the very type the smugglers might use. Since his Spanish hadn't been good at the time, he wasn't sure what had been said about it during his trial. The interpreter appointed by the court had been evasive, and afterward Tommy had been under the impression the man had been bribed by Alejandro.

From these facts Tommy had become convinced he'd been framed by his boss. Jennifer knew it couldn't be true, however. If anyone had paid a bribe, it had been Ricardo Tejeda or one of his accomplices....

She turned her attention to the passenger sitting on the bus two rows ahead of her. It was the same man who had been aboard the boat she had taken back to Buenaventura from the island prison. The man Tommy had told her was named Patricio Martínez. Trying not to seem too obvious about it, she recorded every detail of his features in her memory. At a glance, there was nothing sinister about him that she could see, yet Tommy had said he belonged to one of the families operating in La Guajira. The peninsula bordered on Venezuela and was suitably remote. These facts, plus the lack of attention that the Colombian government paid to the area made it a smuggler's paradise.

Jennifer knew somehow that whether she succeeded or failed, the island prison would not keep her brother captive much longer. Although he hadn't said anything to her, she had seen the signs of restlessness and knew he was about to explode. He was going to get out one way or another. She had to prove him innocent before he attempted escape, and she was frightened. Her quest for the truth would become a race against the clock.

She was so deep in thought, wondering how to finagle an invitation to the Navarro *finca*, that she was almost surprised to see the outskirts of Cali outside the bus window. She consulted her watch. It was purely a reflex action, since she had known before leaving for Buenaventura that she would never get back in time to catch the last flight to Bogotá.

The room she had reserved at the Hotel Aristi was a welcome haven after the day she had gone through. Jennifer's first action was to place a call to Mateo. The connection was made immediately, but he wasn't at home. The maid didn't know when he would be back, but took the number Jennifer left and assured her Señor López would return the call as soon as he came home, regardless of the hour.

Jennifer hung up the phone, and anxious to wash after being in the sordid prison, the feeling of which still seemed to cling tenaciously to her body and clothes, she left a trail of discarded garments on her way to the shower. After shampooing her hair she stood under the spray, letting the jet of lukewarm water ease the fatigue of her muscles. She felt almost like a new person when she finally came out.

She was in the process of drying herself when she heard a knock at the door. Donning a short robe, she wrapped a towel around her head in turban style and went to answer it.

She paused with her hand on the knob before opening the door, however. Who could it possibly be? She couldn't think of anyone who would be visiting her at such an hour in this strange city. "Who is it?" she called through the closed door.

"Alejandro. Open the door."

Her heart made a somersault and instinctively she recoiled, drawing her breath in sharply. Wildly she looked around her, as if to find some place to hide.

"Open up, I said," came the curt order again.

There was nothing she could do but obey, and admitting defeat, she finally did open the door. Her hands were shaking.

They looked at each other in silence for what seemed a lifetime. She was pale and trembling; he looked somber and forbiding.

"How...how did you find me?" she managed to say at last. Her throat was so dry the words came out almost painfully.

He entered the room and closed the door behind him. "What difference does it make, *Mrs.* Blake?"

Since Jennifer had used her real name in registering at the hotel, the fact that he was standing there before her meant that he knew everything. The way he had stressed the word "Mrs." took her unawares.

"That story you invented was touching," he said before she could speak, "but the truth was even better."

She regarded him quizzically. "What are you talking about? What are you saying?"

"The tragic death of a fiancé shortly before the wedding. What I still can't figure out is how going to bed with me was going to help you free your husband."

"My husband?" Jennifer echoed. In her fright and confusion she was still unable to comprehend the meaning of his accusations.

"Don't bother to deny it, Mrs. Blake. I've known what your game was all along."

The import of his words hit her with the force of a physical blow. "You knew?"

"Come now, sweetheart," Alejandro said dryly. "Did you really think I'd be so taken by those green eyes of yours that I wouldn't bother to check on the credentials you presented? Why do you think I hired you, if not to keep an eye on you?"

Suddenly a bitter taste was in her mouth. He had never loved her! He had simply used her.

It was pride that came to her aid and gave her the strength to face him squarely. "Then if you know the truth, you must be aware that Tommy is my brother, not my husband."

"Your brother!"

The surprise she read on his face couldn't have been feigned. Jennifer understood then that although Alejandro didn't have all the facts, he knew enough to endanger her plans. There was no other choice but to lay her cards on the table and hope for the best. "Yes, he's my brother. You sent an innocent man to prison, Mr. Adler, and I came here to prove it."

"Your brother wasn't railroaded into prison," he retorted, although she could see he had been shaken by her accusation. "He had a fair trial and was convicted based on the evidence presented against him."

"Evidence?" she scoffed. "Planted by whom?"

"Are you accusing—"

"No." She shook her head. "Perhaps in the beginning I believed it was you who had framed him, but not anymore."

For a moment he looked at her as if trying to read her thoughts. "I suppose that means you have another suspect."

"I do." She braced herself for his reaction before she finally said, "Ricardo Tejeda."

"Ricardo—" He stared at her in disbelief and then exclaimed, "Impossible!"

"I'm sorry, Alex, I know how you feel about Mr. Tejeda, but—"

He turned on her angrily. "Has it ever occurred to you that in spite of all his protestations your brother may really be guilty?"

It was only natural that he would still try to resist believing her. She could understand what he must be going through—having to consider the fact that someone he trusted implicitly might have betrayed him. And she knew intuitively that he wasn't a man who would take lightly the fact that he'd sent an innocent man to prison. "No, Alex," she said gently.

"You see, Tommy is not only my brother; he's my twin. There's a very special relationship between us. We know each other better than most people ever do. He'd never get involved in anything like the trafficking of narcotics. I know."

He regarded her for a long moment. "I suppose you have some proof?" he said at last.

"Not exactly," she admitted reluctantly.

"What is that supposed to mean?"

How could she hope to make him believe her when she had nothing concrete to offer against Ricardo Tejeda? As if in answer of her unspoken prayer, the shrill of the telephone broke the tense silence that hung between them. She ran to answer it; it could only be one person. "Hello, Mat?"

"Jennifer? Is anything wrong?"

"No, everything's fine. I'm sorry to call you so late, but I was impatient to know if you heard from your . . . friend."

"Your hunch was right," Mateo replied. From the sound of his voice, she could tell he was in excellent spirits. "Our Mr. Tejeda is paying the rent of a lovely young lady by the name of Regina Quintana—and a very high rent it is indeed."

Jennifer's eyes didn't leave Alejandro's face as she listened, and she saw his scowl when he heard Mateo's name.

"There's something else," Mateo continued. "It may be nothing, but then again—"

"What is it?"

"Something in the report about Tejeda meeting very briefly with someone. Our man said the fellow looked somewhat familiar, but he couldn't remember who it was. He was under the impression he had to look for women only, so he didn't think it was too important.''

"Oh, no!" Jennifer exclaimed.

"Luckily, he's a very methodical man, and he put it down on the report nonetheless.'' Mateo paused briefly. ''You know it was a little unfair to have him working in the dark, so I decided to take him into our confidence. I thought he'd be able to make more progress if he knows exactly what we're looking for.''

"I suppose you're right.'' She hesitated briefly. "Oh, Mat—Alex is here.''

"What?'' The volume of his voice made Jennifer move the receiver away momentarily. When she held it to her ear again, Mateo was asking, ''Does that mean he knows about you?''

She nodded, even though Mateo couldn't see her. "He knows, but there's no reason to be alarmed. Please don't worry. Look, I'll see you tomorrow, okay?''

"Wait, Jennifer. Let me talk to him.''

"All right.'' She held the receiver toward Alejandro. ''Mat wants to talk to you.''

When he took it he listened so intently that Jennifer wished she could hear what Mateo was saying. "Well?'' she inquired when he finally hung up, after a brief reply that didn't make much sense to her.

"He just wanted to make sure you were safe.''

"Mateo's been a very good friend,'' she said. ''I don't know what I would have done without him.''

After a brief hesitation, she asked, "Was that all he wanted?"

"He's coming to the *quinta* tomorrow morning." He started for the door.

"Alex?" she called after him. When he turned to face her, she said, "If we can prove to you that my brother is innocent—"

"If he's innocent, I'll be the first one to demand his release, Miss Blake."

In spite of her knowledge of how he had used her, Jennifer couldn't help the deep sense of desolation that washed over her when she saw him go out the door. With a sigh she turned away and made her way back to the bathroom, where she removed the towel from her head. Her hair had partially dried, and she had to spend some time working out the tangles. As she did so her thoughts stayed persistently with Alejandro.

Had he told the truth when he said he had suspected her all along? Could she have been so misled? Her heart would not accept the possibility that all the love, all the tenderness she had seen reflected in his eyes had been false.

Jennifer finished drying and brushing her hair, then turned off all the lights and she finally went to bed. Lying awake in the dark, she thought of the things Alejandro had said to her during their visit to Villa de Leyva with Heidi. Would he have involved his own daughter in his efforts to trap her? She didn't think so. And no lover could have been more gentle, more loving than he had been in Medellín and Cartagena. How could she forget their night together, that glorious night when she had been so much a part of him?

Perhaps it had been his jealousy, his pride that had prompted him to say the things he had that night. Had he not believed Tommy to be her husband? But it was much easier to lie with words than with actions, and his actions that night had proved to her he loved her....

She thought again of his cruel rejection. Unable to hold back her tears at the memory, she called herself a fool because even now she could not stop loving him.

JENNIFER FELT A STRANGE SENSATION when she walked into the cottage the next day. Even though everything in it was familiar, it seemed as if she had never been there before. And in a way it was true, now that she had resumed her own identity. Alejandro coldly addressed her as Miss Blake. The name Alba had entirely disappeared from his vocabulary. For some crazy reason, she wanted to hear him say it again.

But those were things best forgotten. What she had to concentrate on now was convincing Alejandro of Ricardo Tejeda's involvement with the smugglers. Mateo's presence was a blessing. The testimony of one of Alejandro's own countrymen, a man of good reputation, would carry more weight than her own. And Mateo had no emotional ties to Tommy, other than his friendship with her. She noticed there was almost no color in her cheeks when she looked in the mirror, and the hand that held the sable brush to apply a stroke of blusher was trembling a little.

Even the long sleeves of her teal crepe blouse didn't protect her from the chill when she stepped outside of the cottage on her way to the main house. She was tempted to go back for a cardigan, until she realized the day was sunny and pleasantly warm. The cause of her shivers had to be nerves. Jennifer berated herself for her nervousness. Her worse fears had not materialized. She should be relieved that even now when Alejandro knew the truth about her, he was willing to listen to her arguments on behalf of her brother.

A servant showed her in to the library when she arrived. Alejandro was not there, but Mateo rose to his feet when she entered the room. "Hello, Mat," she said warmly, advancing toward him. "Thank you for coming."

He held the hand she offered in both of his as he smiled encouragingly at her. "You didn't really expect Dr. López to leave his favorite patient to take her medicine alone, did you?" He abandoned his teasing tone to say more soberly, "We're in this together, Jennifer."

Since the sudden constriction in her throat wouldn't let her speak, she showed her gratitude by hugging him quickly and kissing him on the cheek.

"If we're all finished with our little display," a voice said dryly, "perhaps we can get this show on the road."

Caught by surprise, Jennifer and Mateo separated abruptly and turned to find Alejandro scowling at them. He was standing in the doorway with his hands jammed into the pockets of his brown slacks. From his manner of dress, Jennifer knew he was not planning on going to the office. She was inadvertently aware of how the epaulets of his casual long-sleeved blue shirt made his shoulders appear broader than ever. Confusion and vexation warred within her, and her cheeks burned. She shouldn't let Alejandro make her feel so guilty over something as innocent as kissing a good friend.

CHAPTER FOURTEEN

THEY ARRIVED at the Navarro *finca* the day before
the wedding. For Jennifer the past week had been
one of constant tension and suspense. She had seen
little of Alejandro after their meeting with Mateo,
during which the young attorney had presented certain facts about Ricardo Tejeda that until then Alejandro hadn't known.

The additional information uncovered by the investigator in the course of the following days served to
tighten the noose around Tejeda's neck. Apparently
he was more than willing to satisfy the insatiable appetite for luxuries his young mistress had. He had installed her in one of the most expensive apartment
buildings in the city, and he was a favored patron at
more than one jewelry store. The numerous credit accounts established in her name at the most exclusive
shops indicated a pattern of indiscriminate spending.

In spite of Alejandro's reluctance to accept Tejeda's duplicity, he'd had to face the fact that there
was no way the man could meet such financial obligations, even on the generous executive salary he
earned at Adler Exports. He must have another
source of income, therefore—one which—to all ap-
pearances—had to be illegal. And there were only

two products being smuggled out of the country that could involve such staggering amounts of money: emeralds and drugs.

On Wednesday the front pages of *El Tiempo* had carried extensive coverage of the raids on a number of illegal cocaine labs around the city. Tejeda's activities during that time had been almost definitely incriminating, for the investigator was able to identify some of his companions as active members of the narcotics trade. Tension continued to mount when the police announced the capture of an aircraft that had been carrying cocaine paste from a neighboring country. The dragnet was closing fast. More and more it seemed possible that the smugglers would use Tejeda's visit to the Navarro *finca* to effect another delivery—probably of the paste.

At long last, fate was smiling on Jennifer. There had been one close call—when she had taken advantage of Sara's absence during lunch hour to search her boss's office. Tejeda had returned unexpectedly just as she was leaving, and Jennifer wasn't sure he had believed her explanation that she had been looking for Sara.

But if all went well and Tejeda could be caught with the evidence, Tommy would soon be released and they could go home....

Their arrival at the *finca* caused a flurry of excitement among the peasants, who saw little of their landlords during the year and very seldom saw anyone else from the city. Ricardo Tejeda was a known entity, of course, but Jennifer, with her glowing American looks, drew a lot of admiring attention. Mateo López received his own share of glances from the house maids. He was presented as Jennifer's friend without any other explanation given. She was not at all surprised that Alejandro's mother, after meeting the young attorney, became friendlier toward her than she had ever been.

But perhaps her good mood was also due to the marriage about to take place, Jennifer decided. Señora de Adler was the godmother of the bride-to-be, who had been named Mariana after her. The older woman was already taking part in the wedding preparations.

Anxious to go out and look for the airfield Tommy had described, Jennifer changed into riding clothes as soon as she unpacked. She was just stepping out of her room when she ran into Heidi, who was obviously looking for her.

"Don't you want to go swimming, Alba?" the little girl asked, eyeing with dismay the plaid shirt and brushed-cotton pants Jennifer was wearing.

To make things easier for everybody, Alejandro had omitted informing his family about Jennifer's real identity.

"Perhaps later, Heidi," she replied. "Right now I promised your father and Mateo I'd go riding with them."

"Could I come, too?"

"Mmm, you're all ready to go swimming," Jennifer pointed out. When Heidi's face started to fall, she added, "I've got an idea. Why don't you go swimming with your cousins now, and we'll play cards later this afternoon, all right?"

"All right!" Heidi grinned, accepting the offer for what had become one of her favorite games. In a very short time she had learned to play gin rummy so well that she could give Jennifer a run for her money. "I'll see you later, Alba."

Jennifer waved, and her smile hid the stab of sorrow she suddenly felt. This little girl, who had become so dear to her, could have become her daughter if only she and Alejandro. . . .

She shook her head, refusing to follow that train of thought once again. How many times had she done the same during the past week?

Did Alejandro ever think about her, or had he been able to put her out of his mind and his heart as he appeared to have done? Jennifer found herself wondering about this on her way to the stables, where she found the object of her thoughts saddling two horses with the help of a stable hand.

"Isn't Mat coming with us?" Jennifer inquired.

He shook his head. "Your lawyer friend has an aversion to horses. He preferred to go swimming with Nancy and the children. Do you mind?"

Jennifer's reply was a shrug, and she watched while he turned his attention to finishing his task. Only someone who had known that face when it was gentled by love would notice the tightness around his mouth and the other little telltale signs that betrayed his tension.

"You'd better take this horse." He held the reins of a chestnut mare while she mounted, and once she was on the saddle he adjusted the stirrups for her. "Is it comfortable there?"

"Yes, thank you."

He turned away, got on his horse, and she followed him as they walked their mounts in the direction of the field Tommy had told her about.

Since he was well acquainted with the terrain, Alejandro had known immediately which one it was. He rode ahead, and Jennifer noticed as he did so that his back was stiff and straight, not relaxed as it had been that day in Villa de Leyva when they had returned to the hotel after her early-morning escapade. And not once did he look back to see if she was behind him.

Jennifer looked around her in an effort to put the unbidden thoughts out of her mind. By now, if Tommy had been able to finish the work he had been hired to do, this fallow land could have been cleared of the existing brush and planted with crops. She tried to think about what would grow well in the area. Soybeans, perhaps. There were many uses for the crop that would create the jobs Alejandro wanted for his people. Or sugarcane. Or cotton.

They didn't have far to go. Beyond a small rise in the terrain was a field that made a perfect landing strip. She looked around for a good place to hide and witness the arrival of a plane. There were only a few trees growing on the edge of the clearing. The bright flowers of a huge jacaranda tree made it look as if its spreading branches had burst into flames. Would its massive trunk afford enough coverage?

They walked their horses down the hillock onto the flat field beyond. Would they find traces that a plane had landed there before? Jennifer decided it would depend on how long it had been since a plane had been there and how many times it had rained since then.

There were no clear signs on the grass itself, which wasn't very tall. But after a while she saw Alejandro dismount and squat down to look closely at the ground.

"Come and look at this," he called to her.

Her heartbeat accelerated. Had he found something? Please, let it be so, she breathed. The ground was hard under her booted feet as she dismounted near him.

"What is it?" she asked.

The grass had died on a small patch of ground, leaving it bare. The hardened soil had a clear imprint of tire tracks. "Do you think it could have been made by the plane Tommy saw?" she asked excitedly.

Instead of answering, Alejandro got up and took a few steps away, still looking at the ground. "Here's another one," he said, squatting down again to touch the ground. "Yes, it was a plane all right, although it's been some time since it was here."

"Could it be the same one you flew to Medellín?" she inquired, fervently praying for a negative answer.

"I don't think so. The Cessna is a twin engine, too heavy to land safely on this field. No, this one must have been a bush plane, a single-engine craft."

Jennifer lifted her gaze to look at him and saw how grim his expression was. She couldn't help reaching out to touch him. "Alex."

The look he gave her was one of agony. "What do you say to a man you helped send to prison for something he didn't do?" The bitter question was obviously addressed to himself.

"Darling, don't," she pleaded, putting her arms around him. "Don't torment yourself."

He didn't seem to have heard her. "My God, how can anyone make amends for robbing an innocent man of part of his life?" His arms closed tightly around her as if to find comfort—or forgiveness—in the act of holding her.

"Don't do this to yourself, darling, please!" Jennifer drew back a little to look at him and was frightened by what she saw in his eyes. "Listen to me, Alex," she urged him. "Mat says that finding these tracks won't be enough proof to get Tommy out of prison. We must get enough hard evidence against Tejeda. Promise me you'll wait just a little longer before you confront him, darling, please!"

"Don't worry. We're going to get that evidence if I have to beat it out of him." Jennifer was terrified by the deadly tone of his voice.

"No, Alex, no!" She grasped him by the arms. "Don't you see that wouldn't do any good? We must wait for the plane to come, catch them in the act. I'm sure it won't be too long now."

Her urgency seemed to finally penetrate the anger that had kept him in its vise. Before her eyes he seemed to pull himself together again. "It's all right, Jennifer. As much as I'd like to get my hands on Ricardo Tejeda, I'm not going to jeopardize your brother's freedom now. I owe it to him." He looked down at her hands, which still gripped his arms. She dropped them quickly.

For a moment she had instinctively responded, had thought only of easing his torment by offering the comfort of her love. But she was quickly reminded that love existed in her heart, not in his. Flushing with embarrassment, she turned away.

"What are we going to do about the plane?" she asked to break the awkward silence that hung between them. "How will we know when it comes?"

"I suppose Mateo and I will have to take turns watching."

She spun around to face him. "What about me? I can take a turn as well."

He raised a quizzical brow. "You?" He shook his head. "No, it's too dangerous."

"Oh, stop being so chauvinistic, Alex!" she exploded. "Women have come out of the kitchen and the nurseries, you know!"

"So I've heard."

"I can take care of myself as well as any man!"

It was he who grasped her by the shoulders and made her look up at him. "Listen to me, you little fool." He gave her a gentle but firm shake, as if trying to instill some sense into her. "This is no game we're playing. A man could get killed, and so could a woman. . .eventually. Do I have to draw a picture of what they'd do to her before that happened?"

Jennifer swallowed hard. But even after she had shaken her head, he still held her. She saw his steel eyes grow gentle, and an incredible joy surged within her as she felt his long fingers touch her face. "Jennifer," he said tenderly, deeply.

How long had she yearned to hear him speak her name like this! Trembling with joy she lifted her face to offer him her lips, then quivered at the kiss she read in his eyes. But instead he released her and abruptly turned away. "Alex!" she cried in dismay.

"Leave me alone!" he said, pulling away when she tried to touch him.

"Why? Don't tell me you don't love me, because I know you do." Her tone became more persuasive. "You're only torturing both of us, Alex. I love you. The past isn't important anymore, don't you see? It's the future that counts. A future that can belong to us if only you let it."

"Damn it, Jennifer! I can't!"

"Oh, Alex!" was all she could say before a sob rose in her throat. No, she wouldn't cry or beg for his love. It wouldn't do any good anyway. He loved her, she knew it, but his love wasn't strong enough to put aside a lifetime of prejudice. If they were to have a future together, he would have to accept her as she was—or not at all.

THE TROPICAL HEAT made the swimming pool the favorite place for children and adults alike. They spent much of the day there, and even had lunch served at the poolside tables.

Perhaps for the first time in her life, Jennifer had no appetite at all. She contented herself with a few bites, but mostly toyed with the delicious-looking fruit salad on her plate, oblivious to the conversation between Ricardo Tejeda and Señora de Adler. The general manager was devoting his attention to his employer's mother, while Mateo and Nancy, who seemed to have hit it off from the start, shared a nearby table by themselves. Watching the animation on Nancy's face, listening to her carefree laughter, Jennifer decided that "Dr. López" held the right prescription for what it was that ailed Alejandro's sister.

Alejandro himself, afraid of venting his anger on Ricardo Tejeda, was keeping his distance from the man. Instead of eating with the others he was in the pool playing water polo with his daughter and with Nancy's children.

"Come in the water, Alba!" Heidi called to her. "Come and play with us!"

Jennifer's first inclination was to make an excuse and go inside the house. But before she declined the invitation, a thought crossed her mind. Why should she? It was Alejandro who had a problem, not her, and damned it if she was going to make it easy for him to continue rejecting her.

"I'm coming!" Lithely she rose to her feet and advanced to the edge of the pool. There she paused to unwrap the matching ruffled skirt she had been modestly wearing over her swimsuit. Her smile was provocative as she stood for a moment under the pretense of trying her hair in a ponytail. In reality she was giving Alejandro a chance to have a good look. Physical attraction was too powerful a weapon to be discarded in the war of love. She wanted it all: his love, his tenderness, his passion, and she was not going to lay down her arms and declare defeat without staging one last battle.

She was aware that the daring V-neck of her black maillot allowed a tantalizing glimpse of her breasts; that its high cut made her legs look longer; and that the stretch material that fitted her like a second skin would serve to remind Alejandro of the curves and hollows he had explored and caressed. But when she finally gathered enough nerve to glance at him again, she was a little crestfallen to find that he had returned his attention to the children.

At first when she joined the water-polo game, she had to make an effort to show some enthusiasm. But because she was fond of children and not the type of person to dwell too much on unhappy thoughts, not long afterward she was having as much fun as the mischievous Heidi. The two of them engaged in what became an uproarious water fight against Alejandro.

Some order was restored when the *señora* insisted on a more sedate game, showing her disapproval in the glance she sent to her American guest. Meanwhile, Jennifer was amazed at the tremendous amount of good humor and patience Alejandro showed while the children used him as a human springboard.

I'm not going to lose him, she thought. *Not without a fight. He's all the things I want: lover, husband, friend.*

He could have been hers already if it wasn't for that pride of his. Yet she couldn't resent his pride; it was as much a part of him as all those other qualities that had made her love him.

After a while she got out of the pool and sat down with Nancy and Mateo.

"You have more energy than anyone I've ever seen," Nancy told her, offering her a glass of cold lemonade.

"Thanks." Jennifer took a long swallow. It tasted

good. "I like to keep active. Exercise is good for you."

"You should have seen how far up the mountain she climbed," Nancy told Mateo. "I thought her horse had thrown her. I couldn't believe she had gone up on foot."

Mateo regarded Jennifer with affection. "Yes, our little friend here is a lot tougher than she looks."

"I think I'll take that as a compliment," Jennifer retorted wryly.

"Oh, Alba, Mateo was telling me of a new program he's involved with," Nancy told her excitedly. "It sounds terrific!"

"What is it?" Jennifer asked.

"Tell her, Mateo," Nancy urged him.

"It involves gathering all the gamines—the wild children—roaming about the city and providing them with decent housing and education."

"They need volunteers," Nancy interposed. "I already told him I want to take part in the program."

"And I told her she's hired." Mateo smiled at Nancy.

"Congratulations," Jennifer said. She was sincerely glad for Nancy. Working in such a worthwhile project would be of tremendous benefit not only for the gamines, but for her as well. It would help her rediscover her own worth as a person. Obviously Mateo had already done marvels to restore her confidence as a woman.

Later that evening Jennifer had her earlier belief confirmed when Nancy confided she had accepted a date with Mateo.

"Mother will be livid when she finds out." Nancy's giggle had a lot of shyness behind it. "But I feel wonderful, Alba."

"I'm so glad for you, Nancy." Jennifer smiled at her friend. "Mat is a lot of fun. As a matter of fact, I could have easily fallen in love with him if it hadn't been for Alex."

"I don't think Mateo is ready for anything serious, Alba, but neither am I," Nancy replied. "It'll be a while before I'm ready to fall in love again. I was too young when I married Carlos. I've never had a chance to find out about the person I am, what I really want to do with my life."

"You're not scared anymore," Jennifer stated.

"Oh, I'm still scared," Nancy laughed, "make no mistake about that. But at least now I know that things will turn out all right, in time, if I work at it. There are no magic formulas."

No, there weren't, Jennifer reflected. But she still wished she had one to offer Alejandro....

The two men had agreed to take turns watching the airfield through the night, since the smugglers would probably find a daytime rendezvous far too risky with all the people now at the *finca* for the celebration.

That night it was Alejandro who took the first watch. Only Jennifer, who had been watching for him, saw him slip out of the house and make his way toward the airfield. She was tempted to follow but decided against it, knowing he would only send her back. Still she tried to stay awake and listen for the sound of an engine. When she woke with a start it was morning. She had slept the night away.

Perhaps Alejandro was right in not letting her stand guard. The plane could have come and gone, and she would have slept through the whole thing!

Anxious for news, she rushed through her morning ablutions. Still tucking the tail of her shirt into the waistband of her jeans, she went looking for Alejandro and Mateo.

"Morning!" she said at the sight of Alex at the breakfast table. It was still early, and he was alone. "Anything?"

He shook his head. "We'll try again tonight."

If he was going to add to that, the arrival of Ricardo Tejeda prevented it. Jennifer immediately noticed the tightening of Alejandro's jaw, although he tried not to reveal his tension. In spite of her concern, she couldn't help a smile. He was such a poor actor! If she was not already convinced it had been his pride talking that night at the hotel in Cali, his present performance would have done away with her doubts.

"Alex, you promised to take me horseback riding early this morning, remember?" she said to him. "Come on. Stop being such a grump, and let's go!"

Without bothering to finish his breakfast, he got up and followed her out of the house. "What's the idea?" he demanded gruffly when they were far enough away not to be overheard.

"Darling, I love you with all my heart," she replied airily, "but I must tell you this—you'd never make it as an actor. I had to get you away from Tejeda before he noticed your attitude toward him. As a matter of fact, you and I are going to be so busy with each other that he won't have a chance to get near you. Isn't that clever?"

He gave her a sour look. "It's not going to work, Jennifer. I already told you."

She chose to ignore his meaning. "Of course it will, Alex. Especially with all this excitement about the wedding, Ricardo won't have much of a chance to corner you with business talk."

"That's not what I meant and you know it."

"Look, I'm really trying to help you," Jennifer insisted. "I know how hard it must be for you to realize that a man you trusted so completely could betray you like this. Especially when your wife—"

"Damn it, Jennifer!" he cut her off. "Is there anything you don't know about me? You've certainly done your homework, haven't you?"

Oh, damn, she thought as he turned and stalked away. *When am I going to learn to keep my mouth shut?*

When she turned toward the house, she spotted Ricardo Tejeda in the shade of the crimson bougainvillea sprawling across the front porch. How long had he been standing there watching them? Had he heard anything of their argument, she wondered as she walked slowly back to the house.

"What's the matter with Alex this morning?" Tejeda asked her.

Jennifer shrugged. "We...we had an argument last night over...over a personal matter," she admitted, pretending reluctance. "He's not over it yet."

"I see." Ricardo nodded with an understanding smile that to Jennifer looked more like a grimace.

How she hated this man! It took a supreme effort on her part to even be civil with him. She made that effort and, excusing herself, went back into the house.

Heidi and her cousin Carlitos came running toward her.

"Have you seen the *lechona* they're roasting for the party, Alba?" Heidi was breathless from her run.

"Lechona?" Jennifer repeated. Distracted as she was, it took her a moment to understand Heidi was talking about the pig being roasted for the party. "No, I haven't," she said at last. "Is it big?"

"It's huge!" Heidi exclaimed, opening her arms wide. "Like this."

"Mmm, that really *is* big," Jennifer nodded thoughtfully. "I've got to see that for myself."

"Then come on!" Heidi urged, taking her by the hand. "I'll show you."

Carlitos took her other hand. "Me, too," he said.

Aware those were the only two words Nancy's son could say in English, Jennifer allowed herself to be taken to see that marvel of a pig.

The children were right. The *lechona* was a big one. As it slowly turned on a spit built over an open fire, drops of juice and fat fell on the burning wood and sizzled, adding a smoky scent to the delicious aroma of roasting meat in the air. The skin was already turning a very appealing toasted color.

Jennifer and the children stayed to watch. It took a while for the two men in charge of brushing the pig with a prepared marinade and working the spit to lose a little of their bashfulness. The children helped Jennifer communicate with them, however, and they found out more about the coming festivities. In addition to a mountain of food and rivers of drink, there would be plenty of music, singing and dancing. Since the wedding wasn't supposed to start until later that afternoon, Jennifer imagined the party would continue well into the night.

What a perfect opportunity for the smugglers to make the delivery, she reflected. An opportunity too good to be missed. But perhaps they would wait until the party was over. After all that merrymaking, very few people would be left in any condition to notice the arrival of a plane. Yes, they would come tonight, of that she was sure. All she and the men had to do now was keep a close watch on Ricardo Tejeda.

She wanted to talk to Alejandro or Mateo, but the former was nowhere to be found and the latter was still sleeping after his turn at the watch. Now that they were so close to catching the smugglers, Jennifer felt quite useless at not being allowed to do anything but wait while the men did all the work. Fortunately for her, keeping Heidi and her cousins entertained helped her pass the day, and she was surprised when the children were called in to get ready for the wedding.

Even as she dressed in her room, Jennifer could hear the voices and laughter, the music of guitars. All this told her people had already begun to gather outside in large numbers. In Colombia, as all over the world, festive occasions such as weddings presented country people who ordinarily had little in the way of entertainment with a great opportunity for celebration. And because Marianita, the *mayordomo*'s eldest daughter, was Señora de Adler's godchild, this one promised to be an occasion more special than most.

There were flowers everywhere. The bride was very young, a pretty girl with rosy cheeks, whose dark brown eyes shone with the joy only love can bring. She wore her white wedding dress with pride, and Jennifer found herself wondering with sadness if the symbol of purity reminded Alejandro of her own deceit.

Hugs, kisses, tears and laughter followed the marriage ceremony, and then the celebration began in earnest. Rivers of beer and rum flowed, complementing the abundance of food: tamales, boiled potatoes, cassava, plantains. The roasted pig now had olives for eyes. Señora de Adler's special contribution was a magnificent wedding cake from one of Bogotá's leading pastry shops. Jennifer discovered that Colombian wedding cakes were different from American ones as soon as she sampled her portion of it. Under its white meringue frosting, the cake was dark. At first she thought it was chocolate cake, but it turned out to be more like an English plum pudding filled with rum-soaked raisins and bits of candied fruit.

Feeling totally alien to the merrymaking going on all around her, Jennifer ate little and drank even less. Alejandro had managed to avoid her since their argument that morning. Since she didn't want to intrude in the friendship that was rapidly developing between Nancy and Mateo, she was left very much on her own. She kept her eye on Ricardo Tejeda, who seemed to have no other care in the world except to enjoy himself with the rest of them. After a while few of the men gathered together to play tejo, a favorite game

something like bowling, while the women visited
vivaciously among themselves.

By the time the dancing began, night had fallen
and the newlyweds had long since departed on their
wedding trip amidst a shower of rice and cheers. Jennifer had never seen anything like the dance they
began with, and she was reluctantly fascinated.
Señora de Adler herself explained to her that this was
the Colombian *cumbia*.

Carrying bunches of burning candles that they
handed to the women, the men formed a circle
around a small group of musicians. The instruments
they played were an Indian bagpipe, two different
kinds of drums, a flute and another instrument that
Jennifer, who had no idea what it was, imagined was
of Indian origin as well.

The women, now holding the blazing candles,
formed a separate circle enclosing the men. One circle moving clockwise, the other counterclockwise until each dancer had found a partner. Then both
circles moved together.

The woman's movements were shy yet flirtatious
as they waved their long white skirts and moved their
hips to the contagious rhythm of the *cumbia*. At the
same time they held up their candles as if to fend off
the assiduous advances of the males, who twisted and
pirouetted around them with sensual abandon.

Then the circles broke into lines, and the dancers
interchanged partners, moving back and forth, not
so much with footwork as with sensual body movements, repeating the dance figures until at the end
they returned to their initial places. Then, couple by

couple they abandoned the dance, which came to its own conclusion when there was no one left on the floor.

More dancing followed—hours of it—until the evening finally began to wind down. The babies had long since fallen asleep, but now even the older children, weary from all the excitement and the late hour, could barely manage to keep their eyes open.

"Why don't you go to bed, Heidi?" Jennifer asked gently when she noticed the little girl stifling a yawn. "It's getting very late."

"Will you tuck me in, Alba?"

"Of course." Two weeks ago, Jennifer would have tried to get out of the invitation. Now, all her qualms about letting Heidi into her heart had been quelled. Her father was not Jennifer's enemy.

Nancy's children had already been put to bed in the room Heidi was sharing with her cousins. Very quietly Jennifer helped Heidi change into her nightgown and get into bed.

"Will you tell me a story, Alba?" Heidi whispered, making an effort to keep her eyes open after Jennifer finished tucking her in.

"All right." Jennifer sat on the bed's edge. "What would you like to hear?"

" 'Goldilocks and the Three Bears.' "

Jennifer began the story in a low voice, but long before Goldilocks even came across the little house in the forest, Heidi was fast asleep. Smiling to herself, Jennifer adjusted the covers and kissed the little girl's brow before she turned away. "Oh!" she gasped, startled by the tall figure looming in the darkness of the doorway. "How...how long have you been there?"

"Long enough," Alejandro replied dryly, closing the door behind her after she'd stepped into the hallway. "Don't tell me you've developed maternal instincts all of a sudden."

"That was below the belt, Alex."

"Was it?" He took one step toward her. "You couldn't wait to get rid of Heidi while she was bending over backward to make you like her. Do you think for a moment I'm going to be fooled by the bedtime-story act?"

"Alex, don't," Jennifer pleaded, still in a low voice for the sake of the sleeping children. "How do you think I felt each time she came near me and I thought I was trying to send her father to prison? You know why I couldn't let myself become attached to her."

"And what did you feel when I came near to you, Jennifer?" He moved even closer. "Did you have to pretend when I touched you?"

"No," she shook her head. "I never pretended with you."

He lifted his hand and let it trace the side of her neck. "You responded the first time I touched you, and yet you must have hated me," he said in a voice barely above a whisper. "Tell me, Jennifer. Would you have let me make love to you even then?"

It was a question she had asked herself before. She wanted to deny it, but couldn't stop the truth from shining in her eyes.

You idiot, a little voice screamed at her when she

felt his tension and he drew away. *Why couldn't you have lied?*

No, she wouldn't. Not anymore. There had already been too many lies between them. Love based on lies wasn't love, but illusion. And illusions didn't last. If he couldn't accept the truth, then his love for her wasn't strong enough.

She was thankful the darkness in the hallway didn't allow him to see the tears welling up in her eyes. She would be making a fool of herself very soon if she didn't get back to the party.

Suddenly she was aware of the reigning silence. "Has everyone left?"

"The party is over."

"Then I think I'll go to bed. Good night Alex."

He didn't reply or stop her when she went past him.

Deeply hurt by his accusations, Jennifer gave rein to her tears once she had reached the safety of her room. All along she had been telling herself he was only trying to hurt her because he himself was hurting, but she could no longer believe he was simply striking back. Perhaps he still felt desire, but any love he had ever felt for her had turned to hate.

She had lost him.

Desolate at the thought, Jennifer went through the motions of preparing for bed almost by reflex. So deep in her misery was she that the tiny noise almost went unnoticed by her. The noise of an airplane. The moment she had waited for had come at last!

Immediately, all her worries took second place. She had already undressed, and now she rushed to pull on a pair of jeans, her boots, and a red-and-white plaid cotton shirt. The fact she had not yet unbraided the thick long plait of her hair saved her a few seconds of time.

How long would she have to wait until Ricardo Tejeda was unmasked and captured, she wondered as she impatiently paced the floor. But perhaps she shouldn't remain here going quietly out of her mind. Perhaps she could be doing something to help out. Besides, she didn't like the idea of Alejandro watching for the smugglers on his own.

It took her all of two seconds to make up her mind to go fetch Mateo. After tiptoeing down the hallway she knocked quietly on his door, but even though she repeated the knock, there was no answer. What a fool she had been! Of course Mateo would have heard the airplane. He must have already gone to join Alejandro.

At that moment Jennifer was too excited to remember any of Alejandro's warnings. All she could think of was capturing Ricardo Tejeda—and freeing her brother. Unable to remain behind a second longer, she left the house and started for the field where they had found the tire tracks.

It was a little farther on foot than she had realized, and she began to run, fearful that the smugglers would disappear before she could get there. A thin sliver of moon lighted the way, although at times Jennifer was startled by a sudden shadow that turned out to be a bush or a rock. At the top of the rise she looked down and gasped. Someone had used torches to mark the landing field for the aircraft.

Alejandro had been right. It *was* a single-engine craft, and three men were standing next to it.

Suddenly Jennifer dropped to the ground, realizing that if she could see them, they could probably see her as well. Craning her neck and scarcely daring to breathe, she looked around for Alejandro and Mateo, but couldn't find either one. But surely they must be there!

She had to get closer. Keeping close to the ground, she began her descent of the hillock. She stepped cautiously, trying to avoid any dry twigs that would snap and betray her presence. Finally she reached the safety of the line of trees bordering the field. The trunk of the jacaranda was just wide enough to conceal her from the clearing.

There was only one man talking to Ricardo Tejeda now; the other one was nowhere in sight. Jennifer decided he must have got into the plane, although she couldn't see into the cockpit. She could hear their voices, but she couldn't make out the words very well, only a phrase here and there. More than a conversation, the exchange looked much like an argument.

It was then that she heard a faint rustling behind her, and before she could turn to see what caused it, a hand clamped over her mouth to keep her from crying out.

CHAPTER FIFTEEN

"DON'T MAKE A SOUND."

The whispered command had a calming effect on her tumultuous heartbeat. Jennifer relaxed in her captor's grip, and the hand was immediately withdrawn. She turned around, to see Alejandro's signal to be quiet and follow him.

Keeping close to the ground, she followed him away from the clearing. They had advanced some thirty feet and sought cover behind a bush before he stopped to listen.

"What is it?" Jennifer whispered after a few minutes passed.

In response, Alejandro touched his index finger to his lips to silence her.

Jennifer strained her ears but could hear nothing.

"Where's Mat?" she asked at last.

"Back at the house, I guess. Now be quiet."

More interminable minutes of silence, which was broken by the noise of the plane engine being started.

"They're leaving!" Jennifer started to get up.

"Stay down!" Alejandro pulled her down none too gently. "You might as well be waving a flag at them!"

"But, Alex—" Her words were abruptly cut off as

he grabbed her tightly against him with one arm while he again covered her mouth with his hand. The tension of his body communicated immediate danger and discouraged her from struggling.

A dry twig snapped only a few feet away from their hiding place. Then nothing. Tension built up inside her. She was even afraid to breathe.

"I want you to stay right here," Alejandro whispered in her ear. "Wait a few minutes and then get out. Stay close to the ground, and once you're over the rise, run as fast as you can. Understood?"

Realizing what he was trying to do, Jennifer shook her head.

"Damn it, woman, this is no time to argue!"

It was too late for self-recriminations. She had been wrong in disregarding his orders, but she was not going to compound her foolishness by deserting him now. "I'm not leaving without you."

He cursed under his breath. "All right," he relented at last. "Stay down."

Alex took the lead as they started to move. Keeping close to the ground, Jennifer followed, and it was she who saw the shadow that moved as Alejandro went by.

"Alex!" she tried to warn him.

He started to turn, but it was too late. The butt of a rifle caught him on the side of his head as it came crashing down. It sent him sprawling on the ground.

Disregarding the barked command of the man holding the rifle, Jennifer rushed over to him and fell on her knees at his side. "Alex!" Her fingers touched his hair, already warm and sticky with blood, before she was roughly pulled to her feet. Her struggles were cut short as she found herself staring at the mouth of the rifle.

She heard rushed footsteps coming near, and a few seconds later Ricardo Tejeda and the other smuggler became a part of the tableau. Tejeda directed the beam of the flashlight he carried in his hand to their faces, then cursed in Spanish. The flashlight had also revealed the face of the man who had hit Alejandro with the rifle. Jennifer gasped as she recognized him.

"Do you know these people?" the first smuggler was asking.

"Yes," Ricardo Tejeda nodded. "That one on the ground is Alejandro Adler, my employer, and she's the American bitch who's been snooping around."

Jennifer understood every word even though they were spoken in Spanish.

"We'll have to get rid of them," the second smuggler said. He gestured toward the smuggler holding the rifle, but the man hesitated.

"Wait!" Ricardo Tejeda intervened. "They have to be killed, but not here. I don't want to attract any attention by having their bodies found in this place."

"So what do you suggest? That we take them with us?"

"Yes," Ricardo said, nodding emphatically. "Drop them over the jungle or some other place where they won't be found."

The second smuggler, who seemed to be the one giving the orders, scratched his head while he considered the situation. "All right, we'll take them with us, but it's going to cost you," he said at last.

Ricardo Tejeda looked relieved. "How much?"

"Five thousand U.S.—each."

"Ten thousand!" Ricardo exclaimed.

"Take it or leave it," the smuggler shrugged. "We're not in this business just for the exercise, my friend. And we can always find another courier."

Ricardo Tejeda seemed defeated. "I suppose I haven't much of a choice, have I?"

The smuggler grinned. "You take the woman, and I'll help Patricio with the man. He's a big one."

Jennifer's brain, which had been numbed by fear, began to function again the moment Ricardo Tejeda grabbed her by the arm and pulled her with him toward the clearing. A quick death by a bullet wound if she ran now would be more merciful than what would happen to her at the hands of her captors. Perhaps it was a mistake trying to stay alive under the circumstances, but Alejandro was still living—and probably injured. Jennifer's survival instincts were much too strong to ignore. As long as there was life, there was hope. And the beam of light from Tejeda's flashlight had revealed a face she had seen before. She was sure the man had also recognized her. It was a long shot at best, but she had to try.

Jennifer winced when the rope Tejeda used to tie her hands behind her back cut mercilessly into her flesh. Even though still unconscious, Alejandro was bound in the same manner. Then they were both dumped unceremoniously in the small cargo space behind the pilot's seat. She was greatly relieved when they didn't gag her. That would have taken away the last weapon left to her—her voice.

She tried not to think of how badly Alejandro was hurt and concentrated on keeping a tight grip on her panic while the small plane picked up speed and lifted off the ground. Bound as she was, she could barely move inside the tiny space. Alejandro's inert body weighed heavily against her, and by the time she managed to get herself up on her knees, they had been airborne for what seemed to be a long time.

One of the smugglers was talking almost nonstop, apparently exhilarated by the unexpected windfall of five thousand dollars for getting rid of two witnesses.

It was his mention of money that inspired Jennifer with a story that might save their lives. Based on the principle of divide and conquer, the tale had to make the smugglers believe that keeping their two captives alive was far more profitable than killing them. Hoping the story she quickly concocted was convincing enough, she waited for the opportune moment in the conversation, then forged ahead with her arguments.

"What you don't know is that you got the short end of the bargain," Jennifer put in, managing to keep her voice from trembling. "While you're doing the dirty work, Tejeda's the one getting the big money."

As she had expected, she immediately caught their attention. "What big money?" It was the one called Patricio who asked.

"Why, the ransom money, of course. Or did you really believe that story about why Tejeda didn't want our bodies found?" She laughed, a short ironic laugh. "He's been planning to kill Alejandro all along, only he's too much of a coward. He hasn't got the nerve to do it himself, so he had to find someone to do it for him. Obviously, his plan worked; he got you.

"Why do you think Alex and I were there?" she went on. "Because he told Alex he had found tire tracks on the airfield. You see, Alejandro is Señora de Adler's only son. With him gone, she's going to depend heavily on Tejeda. He could name his own price as long as he can make Mariana believe Alejandro is alive. Do you want proof of what I'm saying?" she scoffed. "He neglected to tell you who I really am."

"And who are you, *señorita*?"

Jennifer could feel their interest even though they tried to appear unimpressed by her arguments. "That's precisely it," she replied. If Patricio had failed to recognize her, this was the time to send her message, to remind him of his debt to her bother. "It's not Señorita Jennifer Blake anymore, but Señora de Adler. Alejandro and I were married last week."

She let the piece of information sink in before she went on. "Can't you see that we're more valuable to you alive than dead? If you kill us now, you'll each earn your five thousand dollars and that will be the end of it for you. Tejeda can ask for all he wants, however. He knows Alex well; he could make it appear as if he's still alive when his mother asks for proof. On the other hand, if you let us live, Alex will write a letter to his mother—anything you say—in his own hand. She'll pay the ransom." She waited for a few tense seconds before adding, "It's up to you now who gets the *real* money. Are you going to let Tejeda cheat you?''

The ensuing silence was not very encouraging, so she decided to appeal to their pride in addition to their greed. ''Think of how he must be laughing at the two of you by now,'' she said. ''Not only will he have the ransom money, but after Alex's death becomes public, he'll be in charge of all the Adler Exports business affairs. He won't need you then. How long do you think five thousand dollars will last you? Señora de Adler is an old woman, and she trusts Tejeda. He could bleed her dry and spend her fortune on his mistresses, while you two continue running the risk of being caught by the police.''

It was Patricio who nodded to his partner, ''She has a point, Manolo.''

Jennifer's heart did a somersault. Was that an indication the man was going to help them, or was he simply thinking of the money? Whatever it was, perhaps she had bought a few more hours for Alejandro and herself.

She tried to listen to the whispered conversation of the two smugglers, but couldn't hear what they were saying. The fact that she and Alex had not been shoved out of the plane in midair was enough for her to know that her arguments had given the smugglers pause.

Now that she had given them food for thought, she began to worry about Alejandro's condition. Perhaps it was her own fear, but it seemed to her they had been flying for a long time, and he was still unconscious. She couldn't hear him breathing. Oh,

God, don't let him be dead, she breathed silently.

She twisted her body until she managed to catch a glimpse of his face. A shiver went through her at the blood she saw trickling from the wound on his head. How bad was it? She twisted again and was reassured by the strong heartbeat she could feel when her body was pressed against his.

Until that moment her own fear had kept her from paying too much attention to the pain the ropes were causing as they cut through the tender flesh of her wrists. Now that all she could do was wait and see if her gambit had paid off, she began to feel it. It was excruciating to move her arms, yet she had to keep doing so to keep them from going totally numb.

It was such a little thing when compared to what could happen, she told herself over and over, trying to keep her head and not give way to panic. But no matter how hard she tried to fight it, pain made her eyes fill with tears, which in turn streaked the dust on her cheeks as they flowed. And it was in that condition that Alejandro found her when he opened his eyes at last.

"Jennifer," he whispered. "Are you all right?"

"Oh, Alex!" She tried not to sniffle and failed. She leaned against him, seeking the comfort of his warmth, and would have given anything to have his arms around her.

She felt the tension building up inside him when he asked, "Did they hurt you?"

She shook her head and smiled through her tears, "I'm all right." She lowered her voice even more to say in his ear, "Tejeda wanted us killed, Alex, but I think they're going to hold us for ransom." A little lamely she added, "I told them I was your wife."

He winced when he tried to nod, and closed his eyes. It took her a few seconds to realize he was unconscious again. He had got a nasty crack on the head, and it would probably take some time before he recovered completely. If only she could do something to help him!

Fearful that he'd got a concussion, Jennifer tried to keep him awake by talking to him and pushing herself against him. He kept slipping in and out of consciousness for the balance of the flight.

Finally, with a bumpy painful landing, they reached their destination. She and Alejandro were taken into a shack that looked as if it would fall apart at any moment. Almost immediately she asked for water and bandages.

"No water," the smuggler shook his head. "Water is scarce around here. This is the desert, lady."

So they had taken them to La Guajira after all! "Fine," she bluffed. "Then you can kiss your money goodbye, because unless we bring Alex around, he's not going to be able to write that letter to his mother."

The smuggler's grin was truculent. "We still have you."

"I'm just a daughter-in-law," Jennifer shrugged, refusing to appear intimidated. To show fear would only serve to undermine her already tenuous position. "He's her son. If she gets a letter from me, she'll know something has happened to Alex. You look like an intelligent man. Tell me, which one of us do you think will be more effective?"

The man heaved a sigh. "I'll get the water."

"And some bandages," Jennifer threw at him as he was leaving.

It was stifling hot inside the cabin. After the man had gone, Jennifer fell down on her knees and bent over Alejandro, who had been left lying on the dirt floor of the shack. "Alex," she called. "Wake up, Alex."

He didn't respond, but she kept at it, trying to get his attention. Her arms were numb, but her wrists felt as if they were on fire. She could not allow herself to dwell on her pain or her terror, however—not now. She could go to pieces later—as she probably would—if they survived this ordeal.

"Alex, it's me, Jennifer," she kept repeating over and over, and finally she was rewarded by a slight flutter of his long thick lashes. In a less virile face, they could have been considered feminine. She found herself thinking how amazing it was that she had never noticed them before. "Answer me, darling."

He was only half-conscious, and not knowing what else to do to awaken him, she bent down and covered his mouth with her own. She didn't wait very long for a response from him.

Thank God his body responded to her as her own did to him, she thought as she drew back to look at him, smiling when she saw he was awake.

"Oh, darling!" she breathed, her eyes filling with tears.

"Where are we?"

"Somewhere in La Guajira. Do you remember what happened?"

"Yes."

"I'll have some water soon to cleanse and bandage your head, darling. Just lie still, but please don't fall asleep. You must stay awake for the next twenty-four hours. You might have a concussion." She couldn't help the tear that slid down her cheek and fell on him.

"Since when are you a doctor?" he tried to quip.

She sniffled. "I got my degree watching 'General Hospital.'" When she saw his bemusement, she added, "That's a TV soap opera we have back home."

They heard footsteps outside and Jennifer was dismayed to see him close his eyes again. "Wake up, Alex!" she was crying as the smuggler came into the shack carrying a pan of water and a box of bandages. "Oh, he lost consciousness again! Untie me, please! He might go into a coma!"

"Just keep him awake long enough to write that letter, lady." The smuggler put the pan and the other things he was carrying on the floor. Then he cut Jennifer's bindings.

She cried in pain as her arms fell lifelessly to her sides. Seconds later, as blood began to flow through her veins again, she felt as if an army of warlike ants was marching up and down her arms. It was pure agony but she rubbed her arms, trying to restore the circulation. When she tried to cleanse the blood from Alejandro's face, she found her hands couldn't even hold the cloth. The presence of the smuggler was the only thing that kept her from weeping. "Will you untie him?" she asked, choking back her tears.

"Oh, no!" The smuggler shook his head.

"But he's unconscious," she argued. "Besides, where would we go without food or water? Didn't you say we're in the middle of the desert?"

"I only untied you so that you could take care of him," the smuggler replied.

Biting her lip in frustration, Jennifer picked up the cloth again and began cleaning Alejandro's wound. The smuggler came closer to look over her shoulder.

"Oh, leave us alone!" she exploded. A show of anger was always an effective way to hide fear. "The only thing you're accomplishing by breathing down my neck is to make me nervous!"

The smuggler was first surprised by her explosion, then he smiled grimly. "I'll be back in a few minutes with paper and pen for your husband to write that letter," he said. "He'd better be awake by then."

She was shaking visibly as he turned and walked out of the shack.

"Jennifer."

She looked at Alejandro and found him gazing up at her. "Oh, darling, thank heaven you're awake!"

"Don't push him too hard, Jennifer," he warned her. "Right now he's amused by your bravado, but sooner or later he's going to get tired of it."

"You heard! Then you were conscious."

"I do feel a little stronger now," he admitted. "But for the moment, let's play my injury for all it's worth, okay?"

"Do you think we might be able to escape if they let down their guard?"

"It's our only chance. There isn't going to be any ransom, if that's what you're counting on."

"No ransom?"

"No." At her dismay, he continued, "It's a matter of common sense. If ransoms were paid, kidnapping would become the most lucrative of professions. No one would be safe, don't you see? That's the reason it's forbidden by Colombian law to pay ransom money. Oh, some people still manage to do it, but if I know mother, she'd never go for that. If she paid a ransom for us, Heidi or Nancy's children would be doomed."

"Oh, Alex!"

"Besides, do you really think they'd let us go?" He shook his head painfully. "They'll keep us alive only until they get the money. You were smart enough to buy us a few hours. And mother will keep her end by temporarily agreeing to their terms. They'll have to grant her some time to get the money together. If we're lucky, we'll be gone by then...."

Or we'll die trying, she ended silently. "Oh, Alex, I'm sorry I got you into all this trouble." She hugged him and began to weep again. "It's all my fault! You told me not to go to the airfield, but I didn't listen!"

"Hey, don't go to pieces on me now!" he teased her. "What happened to the little hellion that was here a moment ago?"

Sniffling still, she managed to stop crying. He was right. They both had to keep their heads. She remembered she had not told him about Patricio yet. "Do you think he'll help us?" he asked when she had finished doing so.

"We'll see, but don't count too much on him," Alejandro replied.

She sighed. "How's your head?"

"If you're worrying about my being able to cross the desert, then don't. I'll just play dead for as long as I can."

"Just make sure you stay conscious."

He winked at her. "If I fall asleep, you can wake me up the same way you did before."

Jennifer felt her color rise as she wiped at her tears with her hands. "I love you, Alex," she said before she could stop herself.

He gave her a wistful smile but didn't reply. She realized then that all the tenderness he had shown her so far was his way of giving her comfort during the danger they faced. He might still desire her, but he no longer loved her.

She had just finished cleaning and dressing his wound when the smugglers returned. Alejandro played the invalid convincingly enough as they untied him, and even offered a weak protest when the smugglers-turned-kidnappers mentioned the sum of money they were demanding.

After the letter was written and signed, both of them were bound again, this time hand and foot, putting an end to Jennifer's hopes of escape.

Her discovery that Alejandro no longer felt anything for her had left her in an emotional state that even fear had not managed to create. Until that very moment she had been convinced that only Alejandro's pride kept him from her. To discover that he felt absolutely nothing for her left her desolate and empty inside. In despair she lay on the floor of the hut, staring blindly at the ceiling as the day slowly grew darker.

She hadn't realized that she had fallen asleep until she woke with a start. Whether or not Alejandro loved her, she still had to prevent him from falling asleep. "Alex, are you awake?"

"Yes."

She heard the sound of him dragging himself on the ground. "What are you doing?" she asked, twisting her body.

"Trying to get to you. Why don't you meet me halfway?"

"What for?"

"I've been trying to loosen these ropes, but so far I haven't accomplished anything," he replied. "That blow on my head must have been harder than I thought. It's taken me this long to figure out how much easier it would be to untie you first, so that you can untie me."

Jennifer immediately shook herself out of her apathy and began pushing with her feet until she and Alejandro met somewhere in the middle of the floor. Once they were together, Alejandro instructed her to turn until he managed to reached her bindings. The chafing of the rope had left her flesh raw, and she had to bite her lip to keep from crying out as he worked the rope loose. It look a long time, for they had to pause every now and then to listen for the smugglers, but at last he managed to release her hands.

As soon as she was free, Alejandro turned his back to her so that she could untie him. The knot was tight and she broke a couple of fingernails in the process, but at last she succeeded in her task. Both of them immediately started on the ropes binding their feet. Alejandro finished before she did and helped her with the last knot. He aided her in getting to her feet as well. Although the temperature had grown considerably cooler, her efforts had left Jennifer drenched in perspiration. He gave her a brisk rubdown to restore the circulation before he went to the door to check on their surroundings. She came to stand behind him. It was already dusk. She must have slept longer than she'd realized.

Beside the shack they were in, there was only one other building visible. It was larger and in better shape than theirs, but only slightly. Although there was a battered vehicle parked by the other shack, they saw no trace of their captors. The airplane was gone. Still, they couldn't believe the smugglers had left them alone without a guard.

Alejandro pointed at the scrub on the far side of the clearing. "We're going to try for those bushes over there. Stay as close to the ground as you possibly can. Once we're there, I'll see if I can get into that other shack. It's the most likely place for them to keep their gear. We'll have to take some water and food with us if we're to survive in that desert."

Jennifer nodded, promising herself that this time she would follow his instructions to the letter. Alejandro opened the door and quietly slid outside. Jennifer waited until he motioned her to follow.

They had started to cross the clearing between the two buildings when the door of the other shack opened suddenly, and they were caught in the beam of light coming from it. The man silhouetted in the doorway didn't move, although he must have seen them. In one hand he carried a rifle, in the other two canteens.

"Alex, wait," she whispered. She had recognized Patricio, the man whose life her brother had saved in prison.

Patricio advanced slowly toward them and stopped a short distance away. "*Señorita*, you can tell your brother when you see him again that Patricio Martínez has paid his debt." With that he offered them the two canteens and a small package of food.

"Where's your partner?" Alejandro inquired, accepting the offerings.

"Manolo has gone to deliver the letter to your mother, *señor*. He won't be back until much later tonight. You have about five hours before he starts searching for you. The keys are in the jeep and the tank is full. I don't know how far it will take you, but it's better than walking all the way to the sea." He gave them a compass and directions on how to get to Riohacha, a village on the coast. "Good luck," he finished.

The men shook hands.

"Before you go, *señor*, I must ask you to hit me. When Manolo comes back and finds you gone, I'd better have a lump on my head to show him." When Alejandro hesitated, he added, "If it makes you feel better, I was the one who hit you over the head with the rifle."

Alejandro grinned and drew back his fist. From the sound of the impact, Jennifer had no doubt that Patricia's bruises would be more than convincing.

While Patricio lay unconscious on the floor, Alejandro recovered the wristwatch and wallet the smuggler had taken from him earlier. He then picked up the rifle, slinging it over his shoulder before he went into the shack. When Jennifer followed him inside he was stuffing more food into a knapsack.

Then he took her by the hand. "Let's go. We have only a few hours of advantage."

Before getting into the ancient Land Rover, he walked around it to look at the tires.

Then he whistled. "No wonder your friend said this wouldn't take us far," he said.

"What's wrong?" Jennifer came to stand by his side.

"Look at this." He pointed at one of the back tires. "There are only three nuts holding that tire. It won't last very long, but like the man said, 'it's better than walking.' Get in. We have a long way to go."

Jennifer climbed into the passenger seat and waited until he had started the jeep to inquire, "How far are we from Cerrejón?"

"The Cerrejón coal mine? Mmm, it's hard to say. If I remember correctly, that's in the vicinity of Barrancas, near the Santa Marta mountain range."

"Is it closer than Riohacha?"

"I'm not sure. Why?"

"Because Becky Mathews told me her husband is working in that vicinity. I believe they're developing a very large project there at the coal mine. They've got an airport and private planes that fly into Barranquilla, where the main offices are located."

"Yes, I remember now. The newspapers all carried

the story when the project was awarded to an American company. The coal deposits are one of the largest in the world." He drove pensively for a few minutes. "You may have something there," he said at last. "You can bet that when Manolo gets back to the camp, he's not going to sit back and forget about us."

"Wouldn't it be safer to head toward Cerrejón then, instead of Riohacha?"

"Not only that," Alejandro observed. "Even after we reach the coast, we'd still have to find transportation to Santa Marta, and this whole area is smuggler's territory. It won't be easy for us to find someone who's not associated with them, someone we could trust not to turn us in."

"I'm sure Larry could arrange to fly us to Barranquilla."

"Then the Cerrejón it is," he said, turning the jeep around.

CHAPTER SIXTEEN

DESPITE THE DARKNESS, they drove at a furious pace through the desert. Jennifer had the curious feeling that they were on another planet. The faint illumination of the headlights revealed deep-channeled ruts in the track that ran across the sand dunes, while the vague shapes she could see looming in the shadows became clumps of cacti as they flashed by, always farther into the desert.

Every now and then they saw flickers of light in the distance, but they tried to avoid these settlements. The local people had been long exploited and largely ignored by outsiders. They would have no hesitation in handing them over to the smugglers, who had given them the opportunity to earn a welcome income by participating in their illicit trade.

For generations, smuggling had been the main trade of La Guajira Peninsula. Because of strict controls on imports maintained by the Colombian government, many goods were unattainable not only because of legal restriction, but also because of prohibitive prices. The Guajiro Indians were allowed to cross the border into Venezuela, a country made rich by petroleum dollars, where anything could be bought. Official neglect of the Guajira area had made the peninsula a smuggler's heaven, and Riohacha a contraband capital.

All this and more Jennifer learned from Alejandro as they drove through the desert that night. She was bone weary after two consecutive nights without sleep, but the bumpy ride kept her awake. Even her teeth were rattled by the terrain through which they were traveling.

"We must drive through the night to take advantage of the cooler temperature," he had told her earlier when, after driving for hours, she had asked if he was planning to stop and get some rest.

"Would you like me to drive for a while?" she offered. "You must be exhausted."

He shook his head. "I'm all right. Right now all I want is to put as much distance between us and our friends back there as I possibly can. I'll let you know when you can take over."

Jennifer was silent for a while. "How long do you think it will be until Tommy can be released?"

"I've already discussed it with Mateo, and we agreed he would start the proceedings as soon as we had gathered enough evidence against Ricardo."

"But Mateo wasn't there the night the smugglers took us away, was he?"

"No, he was to take over the second watch as usual."

"Then he never witnessed the meeting between Tejeda and the smugglers," Jennifer observed. "What can he do against Ricardo with us gone? Will he have enough evidence against him without our testimony?"

"Probably not, unless he found the cocaine paste in his possession," Alejandro replied.

"Based on his past record, he must have hidden it where it can't be traced to him," Jennifer reflected. After a few silent moments, she added, "We must get back as soon as possible, Alex. When I last saw Tommy, I got the impression he was reaching a point where nothing could keep him there much longer. I was really frightened."

"Do you think he'll try to escape?" She heard the alarm in his voice.

"I don't know when," Jennifer replied. "I asked him, begged him to wait just a little longer. But I know my brother, and I really don't think we have much time."

"Damn!"

Since her vision had adjusted to the dimness, Jennifer was able to see the grim expression on Alejandro's face and immediately regretted having added to the load he already carried on his conscience. Although she wanted to offer some words of comfort, she knew nothing she could say would be of any use to him. Like his country, he was a man of contrasts: capable of immense tenderness and gentleness, yet so hard and unforgiving. And she knew that as implacable as he was to others, he was even harder on himself.

"He'll be out of that prison as soon as we get back," he said, looking straight ahead. "You have my word on it."

Jennifer noticed the grip he had on the steering wheel; it was so tight that his knuckles looked almost white in the gloom. She tried to think of something she could say to change the subject and came up empty-handed.

Darkness became total when the sliver of moon finally hid behind a cloud. Suddenly Jennifer sat up, alert. "Listen!"

He braked the jeep to a halt and turned off the headlights. Jennifer's ears had not been mistaken; the faint sound they had picked up soon became the roar from the engine of an airplane flying somewhere overhead. They sat tense and silent, scanning the blackness above.

"Where is it?" she asked at last.

"Over there, a little to the right," Alejandro replied after a tense pause.

Jennifer looked in the direction he had indicated and spotted the tiny lights, easily confused with the few stars blinking in the sky.

With a shudder of apprehension, she asked, "Do you think it's Manolo?"

"Could be," Alex replied. "He's had plenty of time to return to the camp and start searching for us. He shouldn't be able to see us, especially while the moon is behind that cloud."

As they sat watching in silence, the moon slipped from behind the cloud and again spilled its pale light on the desert. The roar of the airplane came closer and closer. For what seemed an interminable stretch of time it circled overhead before moving away again. Then the sound began to fade, until it finally disappeared in the distance.

"Okay, here we go again." Alejandro started the

engine and turned on the headlights. To lighten her mood he turned to her and winked. "Keep an eye peeled in case the plane returns."

They had advanced only a few meters when they heard a snap.

"There goes the tire," Alejandro said, heaving a sigh of exasperation. He stopped the jeep, got out, and went around the back. He was using the flame from his cigarette lighter to examine the damage when she joined him. "That was only one nut, so we're down to two," he told her.

"Will it hold?"

He made a gesture of helplessness. "With some luck, we might be able to get a kilometer or two more out of this contraption."

"How much longer do you think we have to go?"

"I'd only be guessing," he shrugged evasively.

"Then guess."

"About forty, maybe thirty kilometers."

She stared at him in silence.

"Don't worry," he patted her gently on the back as he led her around the vehicle. "We have water and food, and sooner or later we're bound to run into some Guajiro settlement. Once we get to the Rancheria River, we'll find a boat or canoe to get the rest of the way. We're going to make it out of this desert, don't worry."

She waited until he had slid back behind the wheel to point out, "I thought you said the locals would turn us in to the smugglers."

"If they see us. It's not my intention to knock on anyone's door and ask for help." He paused briefly.

"These Indians are nomads for the most part. We may find an abandoned shack or some other type of shelter where we could rest during the day."

He was only trying to give her courage, Jennifer realized. Their situation was desperate, and she was the one responsible for it. Never before had she felt so weary and depressed. They had to get back to civilization. Not only their lives were at stake; Tommy's was also.

A snap and a jerk put an end to her self-recriminations. Alejandro stopped the engine. "Well, looks like this is as far as the jeep is going to take us."

He got out and without even taking the trouble to look at the tire, slung the rifle on his back and started collecting the canteens and the knapsack containing their food.

Jennifer took the canteen he handed to her and started after him, putting one foot in front of the other by simple reflex. So exhausted was she that she didn't even notice when the darkness began to dissipate and the sky grew pale. Little by little she kept falling behind.

"Couldn't we stop and rest for a few minutes?" she called to Alejandro.

"Later," he replied curtly. "We have to keep going until it gets too hot to travel. Then we'll sleep for the rest of the day."

On they went. For the first time in her life, Jennifer found no pleasure in watching the sun come up. This day, it had become her enemy. Her mouth was so dry that the measured sips of water she took from her canteen couldn't begin to satisfy her thirst as the heat continued to increase. There was no shelter in sight, only miles and miles of sand stretching before them.

"If you're going to waste precious moisture, don't expect me to carry you the rest of the way," Alejandro said. His tone was dry, unsympathetic, and it wasn't until then that Jennifer realized that she had been crying. "You asked for adventure and now you've got it, lady. This will teach you not to bite off more than you can chew."

"Oh, why don't you go to hell!" she exploded.

"Thanks, but this desert's hot enough for me. Now, stop dragging your feet and get going, or I'll have to leave you behind."

Feeling her temper rise, she said defiantly, "You would, wouldn't you?"

"Why not?" he shrugged indifferently. "Aren't you the one who's been telling me all along that women can do everything as well as men? Of course, if you admit to being wrong, I'll be glad to give you a hand." He paused. "Well?"

"Oh, you—"

He looked at her, amused by her defiant stance. "Should I take that to mean you don't need my help?"

Angrily clenching her fists, she scoffed, "You bet I don't!"

"Fine." He turned around and walked away.

Oh, he was unmerciful, unforgiving! His sense of humor was awful, and at this point Jennifer was so angry that she asked herself what in the world had ever made her fall in love with him. Well, she'd show him! If he could walk across the desert, so could she! With a sudden burst of energy she picked up the canteen she had been dragging for the last hour and started in the direction he had taken.

They walked for at least another hour before he called a halt. Jennifer, whose adrenaline had stopped flowing a long time ago and had lasted only on sheer force of will, slumped to the ground with a sigh, too tired to take another step. Peering over the edge of a sand dune, Alejandro tapped her on the shoulder and said quietly, "Look."

Jennifer turned on her stomach to look in the direction he had pointed, and her heartbeat picked up speed at the sight of a group of Guajiro Indians going by. At the head were two men, wearing patched vests and loin clothes tied at the waist, with belts of dangling colored pom-poms and tassels. Two women followed behind them, their colorful dresses flowing like Arab robes as they swept over the sand. A third woman rode a little burro, whose head had been covered with some type of knitted headgear that reminded Jennifer of a ski mask. In protection against the fierce sun, the women had blackened their faces up to their eyes, making their teeth gleam whiter as they joked and talked among themselves.

Jennifer and Alejandro maintained their silence until the group was out of earshot, and even then they kept their voices low.

"We're in luck," he whispered. "Their settlement should be somewhere nearby. Why don't you stay here and I'll take a look."

Tired as she was, Jennifer had no desire to be left behind. "I'd rather go with you."

He got up and held his hand toward her. "Come on."

They didn't have far to go. Two little huts—wooden framed and mud plastered—were only about two hundred meters away. They approached with caution, although the area seemed quite deserted.

Inside they found a modern portable radio, a hurricane lamp, and some hammocks that seemed like a gift from heaven to Jennifer, who couldn't wait to lie down in one of them.

Meanwhile Alejandro was searching for food and water. "Look at this." He was pointing at a modern refrigerator hidden in a corner. Since there was no electricity for miles around, Jennifer wondered what the Guajiros could possibly be doing with it. She got her answer when Alejandro opened the door. There *was* food inside after all, and none of it immediately perishable. "Are you hungry?"

Jennifer shook her head. "Just thirsty. All I want is to drink some water and go to sleep."

"Why don't you?" Alejandro asked, handing her a cup of water. "I'll take over the first watch."

"Thanks." Jennifer climbed on one of the hammocks and was immediately asleep.

"JENNIFER."

She woke with a start. "What?" Alejandro was behind over her, and she remembered where they were. "Is it my turn to watch?"

"Yes," he nodded. "There's some food over there if you're hungry."

She was ravenous. "What time is it?"

"Close to four."

"Oh, Alex, why did you let me sleep for so long?" she protested. That left him with barely three hours of sleep if they were to leave by dusk.

When she started to get up he came to help her, and she found herself being held in his arms. All the love she had for him came rushing back in full force, and she longed to touch the lines of weariness that she saw etched in his face, grown haggard by exhaustion. The dark bristles of his growing beard gave him a fierce appearance. Before she could succumb to the temptation, however, he released her and turned away.

Jennifer's cheeks burned with embarrassment. How many times did he have to reject her before she understood once and for all that he wanted nothing to do with her? How could she have so little pride as to keep throwing herself at him? Because she loved him with all her heart, she knew. Because she would give anything to be held in his arms again and spend the rest of her life with him. . . .

Her stomach growled, reminding her that it had been a long time since she had put any food into it. She drank more water, and absently munching on a piece of candied fruit, she let her mind wander while she sat at the door of the hut to keep her watch. The heat was only beginning to abate.

Looking at the desolation that surrounded her, Jennifer decided it was very much like the desolation she felt inside her at the thought of leaving Colombia and never seeing Alejandro again. She needed him. His strength, his tenderness, his touch, all of those things were as necessary to her as the air she breathed. And yet she would have to learn to exist without them. It frightened her, and she realized that the fear she had experienced while in the hands of the smugglers had vanished ever since Alex regained consciousness. He could make her feel secure just by being with her.

She smiled when she thought of their argument that morning. She had been too exhausted to think clearly, and like a perfect fool had fallen for his needling. But it had accomplished his purpose, which had been to keep her from giving in to her exhaustion.

She thought of other times, too. Of Villa de Leyva, when he had told her that he loved her. Of Cartagena, where hand in hand they had walked through city streets, seeing nothing but each other because nothing else had existed for them. Of their one magic night of love....

Out of the corner of her eye she saw a movement that immediately brought her out of her reverie. The Indians were coming home.

"Alex!" she cried, jumping to her feet and rushing to shake him awake. "Alex, wake up! The Indians are coming back!"

He was alert the instant he opened his eyes. "Get our things!" he told her briskly, jumping from the hammock.

She obeyed while he went to the door to check on

the Guajiros's progress. They were only a short distance away.

"Did you get everything?" he asked, taking the canteens from her. At her nod he said, "Let's go through the back."

They ran toward the brush growing in back of the huts and hid there, not knowing whether they had been seen. Jennifer was out of breath. Her heart was hammering in her chest.

"It's okay," he told her, "I don't think they spotted us. Even if they did, I doubt they'd come after us. But we'd better get going."

They had covered some distance when Jennifer stopped in her tracks and said, "Oh, Alex, we left the rifle in the hut!"

He turned to look at her. "It's too late to go back for it now."

"But they'll know we were there!" she argued.

"It doesn't matter. They would have found out anyway when they saw someone had been eating their food."

Shaking her head as they resumed their journey, Jennifer said, "I really feel bad about that. Those poor people have so very little!"

"Don't worry about it," he consoled her. "I left some money for what we took, and they'll probably sell the rifle."

She accepted his statement, and it wasn't until they had advanced a few more paces that her curiosity got the best of her. "Where do you think they got that refrigerator, Alex?"

"From the smugglers, where else?" he replied.

"You'd be surprised at the things you could find behind the modest facades of the houses of Riohacha, for example. People there don't flaunt what they have because they don't want to have to explain where they got the stuff."

The landscape began to change. They were still following a trail of sorts, but instead of barren, endless sand dunes the ground was hardened clay, firm under their feet. Clumps of cacti and scrub near dried-up waterholes still subsisted on the little moisture that was left. As she forced herself to move, Jennifer would have given her soul for the cool feel of water on her heated skin.

She thought they'd been walking for hours when Alejandro finally called another stop to eat and rest. Abandoning the trail, they settled down in the shelter of some rocks and brush.

Jennifer was aware of how far he was pushing himself. Not once had he complained about the blow to his head but she imagined that, especially in the heat, he was probably still feeling the effects. He had gone into a deep sleep during his nap, which had given him less than two hours of sleep during the last twenty-four hours.

"There's more vegetation around here than we've seen so far," Jennifer observed, chewing on a piece of dried beef from their meager food store. "I suppose that means we're getting closer to the river."

"If we walk all night, we might get there sometime tomorrow."

"But you must get some sleep, Alex. At least for half an hour. You're ready to drop."

"All right," he had to admit, "but don't let me oversleep." He handed her the watch he had recovered from the smuggler. "Wake me in exactly half an hour."

She watched him stretch out on the ground and was surprised when he cushioned his head in her lap. All it meant, she told herself, was that he wanted to make the most of this brief spell of relaxation. He was out like a light.

Fearful of disturbing him, Jennifer leaned back against a rock. Her hands balled into fists just to keep themselves from touching his face, stroking his hair. She ached to touch him but didn't dare. It was the longest half hour of her life.

Then it was time to waken him.

"Alex," she called softly. When he didn't stir, she allowed herself to touch his face. "Alex, it's time to go."

His eyelids fluttered only slightly but failed to open, as if his consciousness were staging a battle against the power of sleep. Jennifer knew he would awaken if she shook him by the shoulder or called his name out loud, but she couldn't bring herself to do either. Instead, she let the tip of her finger trace the contours of his lips. "Alex, darling, wake up."

She didn't know whether he was entirely awake when he opened his eyes, but she didn't resist him when he lifted his hand to the back of her neck and forced her head down so that her mouth descended on his. Her heart was hammering inside her chest as their lips met at last. Hers parted instantly, yielding to the caresses of his tongue.

His kisses made her feel liquid, almost boneless. They were a drugging habit she couldn't, wouldn't want to break. They revived her and made her spirit soar—nothing could hurt her as long as he kissed her and held her in his arms as he was doing now.

"Oh, Alex, I love you so!" she breathed raggedly. She wanted to hear him say that he loved her, too, but even when he didn't she welcomed his heady nearness, the maddening response that made her forget the danger they were in.

She wanted to be a part of him again, as they had that wondrous night of love, the night that would live etched in her brain and in her heart for all eternity. After the night they had shared, how could he not know, as she did, that they belonged together? He had tried to push her out of his heart. But now his kisses told her differently....

Their positions had shifted and she was now lying beneath him, her flesh quivering under the kisses that had become more demanding, more heated. Closing her eyes to the sky above, Jennifer gave herself entirely to the feeling of belonging to the man she loved. Passion made her heedless to the scratchy wiry bristles of his beard on the sensitive skin of her neck as she arched against him.

Reaching, searching for the feel of his naked skin, her hands pulled the tail of his shirt out of the waistband of his jeans and slid beneath it to caress his back, his chest, his shoulders. Drunk with desire, she became a tigress, a seductress, wantonly returning each kiss, each maddening caress with one in kind.

Then, suddenly, he drew away and she whimpered, "Alex!"

He covered her mouth with his hand and whispered, "Shh!"

It was then that she became aware of another sound, one that seemed to be getting closer and closer to their hiding place. It took her only a few seconds to identify it: the familiar noise of a Land Rover bouncing on the rutted ground and rapidly approaching.

Alejandro released her and sprang to his feet.

Jennifer's eyes were wide and frightened when he looked at her. "Manolo?" she whispered in dismay.

"Could be," he answered.

Half rising from the ground, Jennifer watched him as, concealing himself behind the rocks surrounding them, he watched the approaching vehicle. Unable to contain her anxiety, she finally pulled herself up and went to join him.

Silently they watched as the jeep went by only meters away from their haven. It passed so close she could see that the man in the passenger seat carried a rifle across his lap, ready for action. Another rifle was at ready by the driver. And the faces were too familiar.

Jennifer cast a quick nervous glance at Alex. "They're going toward the river," she whispered once their pursuers had gone by. "They'll be waiting for us there."

Hearing the quaver in her voice, Alex tried to calm her fear by putting his arms around her. "It's a long river, Jennifer."

"They must have seen us from the plane," she sighed, relishing the comfort of his embrace. "Oh, Alex, I'm scared."

"So am I," he admitted.

Surprised he would admit to fear, she drew back a little to look at him. "Are you?"

"Only a fool wouldn't be afraid in a situation like this, don't you think?" With a disarming smile he bent toward her, and gently drawing the tips of his fingers over her cheek, he said, "And even though I may be a fool in certain ways, I'm not a complete idiot."

The expression on Jennifer's face was a study in puzzlement as she looked up at him. What was he trying to tell her? Could it be that—

"We better get going." He released her and took a step back, buttoning up his shirt and tucking it in. It was at that moment Jennifer realized that her own shirt was open, too. Her cheeks were burning as she turned around and tried to establish some order to her clothing.

As she helped gather their belongings, she thought about the scene the smugglers had interrupted. She had been shameless, acting like such a wild creature. Only a few seconds before she'd been hoping Alejandro had changed his mind about letting her go from his life. But now—what must he be thinking of her now? After the heady wine of passion, the memory of her loss of control left her with a bitter taste.

A curious glow stretched over the sand as the sun began to go down, a gleaming orange that darkened and thickened to a burnt-ocher color. Then it slowly turned brown, a color that in turn became a shadow and, at last, nothing at all.

They paused only for short intervals during the night. In spite of her exhaustion, Jennifer welcomed the forced march. Alejandro was acting as if nothing had happened between them, but she couldn't put the earlier scene out of her mind.

Trees, birds, thicker vegetation told her they had reached the river long before she could even smell the water or hear its welcome murmur. She wanted to run to it and abandon her overheated body to its cool embrace. Her need for a respite was so overwhelming that she had to forcefully remind herself of the danger lurking in the green coolness ahead.

But it was quiet as they advanced warily through the trees. Either Manolo and Patricio had already gone, or else she and Alejandro had reached the river at a point beyond where their hunters waited. Because that was precisely what it had come down to—a hunt. And to survive the human prey would have to depend on their wits and their instincts.

Jennifer entertained no illusions about expecting further help from Patricio Martínez. The man had already paid his debt to her brother; he wouldn't spare them again.

Only after Alejandro had made sure no one was around did he allow her to go to the river and splash water on herself. What she really wanted was to take off her clothes and have a good refreshing swim, but he wouldn't let her.

"Where are we going to find a boat?" Jennifer asked, feeling considerably better.

"We'll follow the river upstream," he replied. "Sooner or later we're bound to find one."

She was pensive for a moment. "What about Manolo and Patricio?" she inquired at last. "Won't we offer a perfect target once we're on the river?"

"That's a risk we'll have to take—unless you want to walk for another fifty kilometers or so."

She looked at him, stunned. "Another.... No, thanks. I'll take my chances with the boat."

They had taken a few more paces before she asked, "Why didn't you tell me the truth, Alex?" At his confused look she clarified her question. "About how far we really were from Cerrejón, I mean."

"Because I didn't want to discourage you," he admitted. "Even though Cerrejón was farther than Riohacha, it's our best bet in the long run. It's heavily patrolled by the army to avoid having smugglers get involved with the people working on the project. We'll be safe once we get there."

"You could have told me that in the first place. You don't have to treat me as if I were a child."

"You're right," he smiled at her. "I—" He didn't finished. Instead, his attention was wrenched away. He looked past her and suddenly threw himself on the ground, carrying her with him. Before Jennifer could ask what was going on, she heard the distinctive roar of an outboard motor coming upriver. Peeking through the dense bush, she saw Patricio at the stern, steering the boat, while Manolo scanned the shores, rifle in hand.

"They're still looking for us," Jennifer whispered. She flicked a wary glance at Alejandro who seemed to be trying to figure something out. Immediately she knew what he was thinking. Surprise lifted the inflection in her voice when she said, "Not *their* boat, Alex!"

He made a small deprecating gesture. "I don't see any other around, do you? Besides, it has an outboard motor. We could get to Barrancas in less than ten hours."

"But it's too dangerous! Don't forget they have two rifles."

His brow creased in concentration, he didn't react to her warnings. At last he said, "Okay, this is what we'll do."

And with growing uneasiness, Jennifer listened to his plan.

THE EERIE SOUNDS of the river made Jennifer shiver with apprehension as they watched the smugglers preparing their meal. Even though she'd had little to eat in the last two days, the smell of cooking food drifting toward her had no effect on her appetite. She was much too frightened by what lay ahead to think of food.

The smugglers must have abandoned their jeep at some point downstream. Stealing their boat was the only hope of escape. But wanting to get the whole thing over with once and for all, Jennifer was barely able to contain her fidgeting as the first hour ticked slowly by and the smugglers sat around their campfire eating and drinking. When they started smoking and talking at leisure, she was ready to scream out of sheer frustration.

At long last, when she decided the smugglers were finally settling down for the night, Manolo stood up and started walking toward them. She had to bite her lower lip to stifle a cry or even a whimper of alarm as he came closer, and so loud were her heartbeats that she marveled their hunters could not hear them. Once he had reached the edge of the circle of light cast by the campfire the man stopped, and with a sigh of relief Jennifer looked away as he unzipped his fly and relieved himself. When he finished and returned to the campfire, Patricio was already stretched out on the ground. Manolo sat down again, obviously prepared to take the first watch.

After that they didn't have much longer to wait, for Manolo's head slumped forward on his chest. He was asleep.

It was time to act.

Alejandro turned to Jennifer and signaled with his hand for her to stay where she was. Then he began to move stealthily toward the dozing Manolo. He was less than two meters away when the smuggler stirred. Alex froze, and Jennifer's pulse drummed in her ears in a crescendo of terror while the man moved his body into a more comfortable position before he dozed off again.

He didn't hear Alex come up behind him, and his eyes flashed open in surprise for one second as the hunter became the prey. Alejandro's hand covered the groan Manolo emitted as he slumped unconscious to the ground.

The attack had been so swift, so silent, that Patricio slept undisturbed through the whole thing.

When he was abruptly shaken awake, he opened his eyes to see the barrel of a rifle pointed at his head.

"Sorry friend," Alejandro grinned at him, "but I'm afraid we need your boat. Jennifer!" he called, but she was already running toward him. When she came up to him, he handed her the rifle and said, "Watch him while I tie them up."

She did as she was told and then, voicing the question she read in Patricio's eyes, asked, "What are we going to do with them?"

"We'll leave them here," Alejandro replied. He finished tying Patricio and turned his attention to the still unconscious Manolo. "Eventually they'll work themselves free, but by that time we'll be long gone."

Once their pursuers no longer posed a threat, Jennifer and Alejandro helped themselves to their provisions. Suddenly she was ravenous.

After they had eaten and gathered some food to carry with them, they turned and waved at Patricio, who silently watched them as they untied the boat and climbed in. When Alex started the motor and turned the boat upriver, Jennifer thought it was the sweetest sound she had heard in a very long time.

In a few more hours they would be safe.

CHAPTER SEVENTEEN

JENNIFER'S EYES WERE FILLED with tears as she hung up the phone. The connection to La Gorgona had been full of static, but it didn't matter. The main thing was that Tommy was all right, and that he was aware he'd be out of prison before the end of the week.

"How is he?" Alejandro asked. Since their arrival at Cerrejón that morning he had been on the phone to Mateo, who had informed them both not only that Ricardo Tejeda had been found in possession of the cocaine paste and arrested, but that he had also named one other warehouse employee as his accomplice. The confession had allowed Mateo to start proceedings to set Jennifer's brother free.

"He's fine," Jennifer sniffled, wiping her eyes with the handkerchief Larry Mathews had given her. "Can't wait to get out."

"Well, folks," Larry interrupted, "the plane will be ready to fly you to Bogotá at two this afternoon. In the meantime, Jenny can use my trailer if she wants to rest. Dr. Rogers wants to see you, Alex. He hasn't had a chance to look at you yet."

"I'm all right," Alejandro replied with a dismissing wave of his hand.

"Humor me," the American said. "You know how companies are, always afraid of lawsuits."

Put that way, Alex had no choice but to comply with the request.

"I talked to Becky a few minutes ago. She was beside herself when I gave her the good news," Larry told Jennifer as he escorted her to his trailer. "That brother of yours must be quite a guy."

"I think he is," she replied, smiling at him.

"So does Becky."

With a worried frown, Jennifer looked up at him. "You're not jealous, are you, Larry?"

"Of a high-school boyfriend?" Larry chuckled, "No, of course not."

"Becky loves you very much," she said with a sigh of relief.

"She must, to have followed me through all my foreign assignments and still have to content herself with seeing me only on weekends." They had arrived at the trailer. "Here we are. It's reasonably comfortable, and it's air-conditioned."

"The ultimate luxury!" Jennifer sighed.

"You know where to find me if you need anything," Larry told her before going away.

She was greeted by a blast of marvelously cool air as she stepped into the trailer. She had already taken a bath, shampooed her hair, changed into a borrowed outfit Larry had found for her and eaten a good meal. All she needed now to restore her was some sleep. She undressed at once and got into bed.

Her Colombian adventure was over, she thought. Just as she was falling asleep she remembered that over, too, was any chance of a future with Alejandro. The thought left her with an empty feeling.

In spite of her weariness, her sleep was fitful and full of dreams. Faces, voices, laughter, noises all came and went so quickly she couldn't recognize them.

"Jennifer," someone called softly. "Jennifer, you're having a nightmare."

Even in her sleep she recognized the voice. "Alex?" She woke up.

He was sitting on the edge of the bed. The bandage she had put on his head was gone, and he had shaved. She could smell the fresh scent of soap, and even his hair was still a little damp from a recent shower.

She blinked rapidly, as if unable to believe that he was really there. "What are you doing here?" she asked at last.

The corners of his mouth curled in a slow smile when he said, "I came to wake you up."

"Is it time to go?" She was unhappy that the time to part had arrived so swiftly.

He shook his head briefly. "No, not yet."

She gave him a searching look before asking, "Then why did you want to wake me?"

"Because," he said, bending toward her, "you do have the most marvelous awakenings."

"Please, don't," she breathed, splaying the palms of her hands on his chest to keep the distance between them.

But her resistance was only token. He gathered her in his arms, and his mouth precluded further protests as it covered hers. With a will of their own her lips parted and yielded to him, and she savored the taste of his kisses. Over and over he kissed her, until her mind was spinning and her entire body melting, yet she never wanted this moment of tender passion between them to end.

"Oh, Jennifer," he sighed against her mouth, "will you marry me?"

She drew back abruptly and looked at him in surprise. "Marry you?"

Brushing the tips of his long fingers over her silken cheek, he nodded. "Will you?" he prompted her gently.

More than anything in the world she wanted to say yes, but a faint uneasy fear pricked at her heart like a knife. What had prompted such a proposal? Why was he asking her now, after he had rejected her love so many times before? Was it because of some misguided sense of guilt for having sent her brother to prison?

There was a little quaver of fear in her voice when she asked, "Why, Alex? Why do you want to marry me?"

He gave her a crooked smile. "Because I love you."

But she was unable to forget the things he had said to her in Cartagena. She had to be sure. "Do you?"

Unhurriedly he took her hand in both of his and fervently pressed his lips to the open palm before he replied, "More than anything in the world."

With her heart in her voice she asked, "And are you sure it's me you really want?"

A faint smile touched the corners of his mouth. "I

suppose I deserve that, after the things I said to you," he admitted. "But yes, Jennifer Blake, it's you I want, just the way you are, the way you always were. Warm and passionate, impetuous and shy, stubborn and brave." His voice was as caressing as his touch as he added, "And so very lovely."

She felt her eyes mist with emotion. "Oh, Alex, I love you so!"

Gently, he lowered her back on the pillow and bent over her. "I love you, Jennifer," he said, stroking her silken hair and regarding her lovingly. "From the first moment I saw you I could think of no one else but you."

"But you suspected me," she chided him. "Why?"

"You felt somehow familiar to me, but I knew I had never seen you before." A wry smile played on his lips as he added, "I would have remembered you."

After a brief pause, she asked, "What did I do to make you suspicious?"

"Mmm—you were trying too hard to get the job. You were very. . . suggestive. And frankly, my darling—" he gave her a disarming grin "—you didn't seem the type to use such methods."

She smiled at him a little shamefaced, and said, "Ah, but you still hired me."

"That's right," he nodded. "I had always suspected your brother might have been working with someone within my own organization, but I didn't know who it was."

Her delicate eyebrows arched in surprise. "And you thought I would lead you to him?"

It was his turn to become a little shamefaced when

he replied, "I have to admit I didn't know exactly
what I suspected you of, but after what had happened with your brother, I had to be very careful. I
hired you because I wanted to keep an eye on you until I could figure out what you were up to. However,
after I got to know you a little better...well, I
couldn't believe you would have anything to do with
smuggling drugs. You might call it an act of faith on
my part."

"My darling," she said, deeply moved by his admission. She reached out to caress his cheek. "It was
so easy to hate you before I came to Colombia," she
told him then. "But somehow, after I met you, I
couldn't believe you were capable of the things I had
thought you guilty of. Even when I wasn't sure, I
loved you."

He covered the hand she had pressed to his cheek
with his own. "Did you still doubt me when we went
to Cartagena?"

"No." She shook her head and smiled up at him.
"By that time I was sure not only that I loved you
with all my heart but that it wasn't you who had
framed Tommy. Little by little I had begun to suspect
Ricardo Tejeda."

"What made you think it was him?" he inquired
with a frown.

"I supposed it was impossible for you to suspect
him because of how you felt about him," she began
tentatively. "But since I wasn't encumbered by such
emotional ties, I was able to see him more objectively. First of all, by being responsible for the warehouses, he was in a perfect position to carry on with

his secret trade. And I had another advantage over you in having Sara López as my friend. Working day in and day out with someone, a secretary learns things about him that it's practically impossible for other people to know. And what Sara told me about Tejeda only confirmed my suspicions.''

Her voice became urgent as she continued, ''Oh, Alex, I wanted so much to tell you the truth! But I realized I couldn't expect you to believe me, once you found out I had been lying to you all along. It would have been my word against that of a man you had known all your life, whom you trusted. I had no other choice but to find proof against him in order to make you listen to me. That's why it was so important for me to go to your mother's *finca*, especially after Mateo told me of the rumors he had heard about a delivery of cocaine paste. Perhaps it was a shot in the dark, but we had to find out. As it was....'' Leaving the sentence unfinished, she paused briefly, gathering enough courage to bring up another painful and delicate subject. ''I never meant to lie to you about—''

''I know,'' he said, touching his fingers to her lips to silence her. ''It doesn't matter.''

''Oh, Alex, are you sure?'' She looked at him searchingly, as if trying to read the truth in his eyes.

''I am now.'' He drew back a little and rubbed his forehead, as if searching for the right words to explain his feelings. ''I've waited this long to tell you because I wanted to be sure about it myself,'' he said at last. ''It wasn't only that I was jealous of your having loved another man that made me say those things, Jennifer.''

He paused briefly, then said, ''When I discovered that you had lied to me about your innocence, I thought I must have been mistaken about you completely. I began suspecting you again, fearing that I had fallen in love with an image you had created for your own purposes.

''The day after we came back from Cartagena, I called you at Becky's. The maid told me that you had flown to Cali, so I went there looking for you. The hotel clerk told me your name from the description I gave him, and when I found out your real name was the same as Tom's, I thought he was your husband. I was so jealous all I could think of was that you had played me for a fool by lying to me.'' He took a deep breathe before adding, ''I hate lies, Jennifer. Some of them can hurt very deeply.''

Now that she knew the details, Jennifer could understand his reasons. She looked at him, first with surprise, then with concern as she asked in a small voice, ''Roxana?''

Heavily, he nodded, ''Yes.''

She took his hand in hers. ''Then you really believed her when she told you Heidi wasn't yours.''

He shrugged. ''For a while I didn't know what to believe.'' There was a small bleak silence while she waited for him to continue. His eyes were brooding when he looked at her. ''Have you any idea of what it means to a man to be told that his child isn't really his?''

Vividly feeling his anguish, she gave his hand a

reassuring squeeze. "Darling," she said gently, "Heidi *is* yours. She loves you very much, and you love her; that's all that really matters."

"Yes," he nodded sagely. "It's all that matters."

She felt her heart burst with love for this man—her man—who knew so deeply and so truly how to love. Not trusting herself to speak, she reached out to smooth the crease that had begun furrowing his brow. In a throbbing wave of tenderness, she gazed at him with eyes that felt suspiciously bright.

His expression softened as he stroked her cheek with loving fingers. "Jennifer," he whispered huskily, and as his face drew near she closed her eyes with a long soft indrawn breath.

At first his lips moved softly over hers. When at last the kiss deepened, and his tongue thoroughly explored her yielding mouth, she felt as if her eager body were melting.

Again and again he kissed her, until she was mindless of everything but this wondrous moment. A wild exquisite rapture took possession of her senses, and as if in a dream she heard her own voice whisper, "I love you," over and over. Passion mounted hot and reckless in her blood as his lips traced her arching neck and pressed sweet gentle kisses on her swelling breasts. His tongue teased the throbbing buds of her nipples and his hands caressed her fevered skin until she was swept by the dizzying current of desire he had awakened.

Her entire body was quivering with the intensity of her feelings when, suddenly, he moved away. Raggedly, she called to him, and when, undressed, he came back to her, she clung to him as if she'd never let him go.

Every nerve in her body tingled with a growing need for him as they touched and caressed each other. At last it came, and with a cry of joy she welcomed the deep communication of their flesh and spirit, the wild rapture of their moment of love.

The ecstasy still lingered when later, in perfect attunement, they lay in each other's arms. In wonderment, Jennifer realized they belonged to each other, now and for always.

Her quiet voice held a note of breathlessness when she looked up at him. In a wave of tenderness she said, "You'll never have reason to doubt my love, Alex."

His arms closed warmly around her, and brushing his lips against her temple, he replied, "Nor you mine, my darling."

And she believed him.

Enter a uniquely exciting world of romance with the new

Harlequin American Romances.™

Harlequin American Romances are the first romances to explore today's new love relationships. These compelling romance novels reach into the hearts and minds of women across North America...probing the most intimate moments of romance, love and desire.

You'll follow romantic heroines and irresistible men as they boldly face confusing choices. Career first, love later? Love without marriage? Long-distance relationships? All the experiences that make love real are captured in the tender, loving pages of the new **Harlequin American Romances.**

What makes North American women so different when it comes to love? Find out in the new **Harlequin American Romances!**

Send for your introductory FREE book now!

AR-SUB-2

Get this book FREE!

Mail to:

Harlequin Reader Service

In the U.S.
1440 South Priest Drive
Tempe, AZ 85281

In Canada
649 Ontario Street
Stratford, Ontario N5A 6W2

YES! I want to be one of the first to discover the new **Harlequin American Romances.** Send me FREE and without obligation *Twice in a Lifetime.* If you do not hear from me after I have examined my FREE book, please send me the 4 new **Harlequin American Romances** each month as soon as they come off the presses. I understand that I will be billed only $2.25 for each book (total $9.00). There are no shipping or handling charges. There is no minimum number of books that I have to purchase. In fact, I may cancel this arrangement at any time. *Twice in a Lifetime* is mine to keep as a FREE gift, even if I do not buy any additional books.

_____

Name   (please print)

_____

Address   Apt. no.

_____

                        State/Prov.   Zip/Postal Code

(If under 18, parent or guardian must sign.)

...ed to one order per household and not valid to current American
...ers. We reserve the right to exercise discretion in granting
...e changes are necessary, you will be notified.

...s January 31, 1984   **154-BPA-NADK**